*To Elizabeth, Tommy, and Ellie, who make my
joy complete.*

DEATH IN THE SHADOWS

A
FATHER GILBERT
MYSTERY

PAUL McCUSKER

LION FICTION

Text copyright © 2016 Paul McCusker
This edition copyright © 2016 Lion Hudson

Published by Lion Fiction
an imprint of
Lion Hudson plc
Wilkinson House, Jordan Hill Road
Oxford OX2 8DR, England
www.lionhudson.com/fiction

ISBN 978 1 78264 122 3
e-ISBN 978 1 78264 123 0

First edition 2016

A catalogue record for this book is available from the British Library

Printed and bound in the UK, July 2016, LH26

DEATH
IN THE
SHADOWS

OTHER WORKS BY THE AUTHOR

A Father Gilbert Mystery: The Body Under the Bridge

The Mill House

A Season of Shadows

Time Scene Investigators: The Gabon Virus
(with Dr. Walt Larimore)

Time Scene Investigators: The Influenza Bomb
(with Dr Walt Larimore)

Time Thriller Trilogy:
Ripple Effect
Out of Time
Memory's Gate

Adventures in Odyssey *(12 novels)*

Passages *(6 novels)*

The Imagination Station Series *(18 novels)*

The Colossal Book of Quick Skits

ORIGINAL AUDIO DRAMAS

The Father Gilbert Mysteries: Investigations of Another Kind

C.S. Lewis at War: The Dramatic Story Behind Mere Christianity

The Life of Jesus: Eyewitness Accounts from The Luke Reports

Bonhoeffer: The Cost of Freedom

Amazing Grace: The Inspiration Stories of John Newton,
Olaudah Equiano and William Wilberforce *(with Dave Arnold)*

NON-FICTION

C.S. Lewis & Mere Christianity: The Crisis That Created a Classic

Screwtape Letters: The Annotated Edition

ACKNOWLEDGMENTS

With gratitude to the many organizations working to help women, men, and children caught in the horror of "inhuman trafficking" – without whose help and information this novel couldn't have been written. Thanks to Jessica Tinker, Sheila Jacobs, Drew Stanley, and the rest of the diligent staff at Lion, who always push for the very best, and to the ever-watchful eyes of Elizabeth McCusker, my insightful proofreader and critic. Appreciation goes to Adrian Plass, Dave Arnold, and Philip Glassborow, who are always influencing a project like this, whether they know it or not.

The body of the young woman was found in a skip full of rubbish behind a seaside restaurant on the south side of Englesea. According to the newspaper article, the woman was probably Chinese, in her late twenties, and had no identification in her possession. The police were treating the death as suspicious, but were withholding any further details. The reporter had learned from an inside source that the woman was dressed in only a T-shirt and cut-off jeans.

"Rough night."

Father Louis Gilbert pulled his attention away from the newspaper article and looked up.

Reverend Brad Planer sat directly across from him at a small table pressed against the wall of the hotel's modest dining room.

"The *storm*," Planer said, tapping the opposite page of the newspaper. "Last night."

Father Gilbert nodded. He had arrived by train for the church conference just as the first lashings of rain hit. The taxis had disappeared, as they often seemed to do in the rain, so he walked from the station, up the hilly streets to the Masthead Inn. He was soaked to the skin by the time he reached the lobby. The faux-maritime look of the place only added to his rather damp feeling of entering a sinking ship.

Father Gilbert returned to the newspaper article. Detective Inspector Morris Gwynn was in charge of the case. *Morris Gwynn.* It had to be the same Morris Gwynn he'd known at Scotland Yard. He wondered how Gwynn had gone from the Metropolitan Police to a midsized resort town.

"What is this?" Planer asked as he used his fork to chase a shiny tinned mushroom between the eggs, tomato, and baked beans on his plate. He was a man in his forties, with shaggy brown hair, done in a style to suggest a hip connectedness with the youth of his non-denominational church near High Wycombe. The hairstyle and deep lines on his face made him look more like a has-been rock star. He lanced a mushroom and popped it into his mouth. "It's like eating an eraser."

"You don't have to eat it."

"It's part of the price," Planer said, as if that explained everything.

Father Gilbert had avoided the hotel's "full English breakfast", choosing instead the "Continental breakfast", which consisted of bread with gum-destroying hard crusts, old cheese, and pastry with a mash of unidentifiable fruit in the middle. He wondered what continent the breakfast had come from and why it would feed its citizens such things.

"Any expectations about the conference?" Planer asked.

Father Gilbert shook his head. "Not really." The three-day conference was called *Issues Facing the Church* and had the usual denominational representatives from around the country talking about relevancy, sexuality, social justice, climate change, global economics, immigration, and the other hot topics. His own Bishop was speaking about "The Compassionate Church", after which Father Gilbert would participate in a panel discussion. He dreaded the event. His Bishop had insisted he do it.

"You're not hopeful?" Planer asked, with a wry look.

"Of what?" Father Gilbert asked.

"That we'll come up with policies to substantially change the state of our world?"

"'Policies' and 'substantially change' rarely go hand in hand." Father Gilbert knew they'd hear the usual sentimental twaddle with a lot of handholding and emotional back rubs. One year they had ended a conference by singing John Lennon's *Imagine*. Why the organizers thought a song that dismantled the Christian faith was a good idea was more than he could imagine.

"I take it you're not a team player when it comes to these things," Planer said.

"Not the way *they* talk about it."

He took a drink of his tea. It tasted of metal.

Planer stabbed at a tomato and eyed it for a moment as if

something might crawl out from between the seeds. He shoved it into his mouth. "What do you think about the timing of *that*?" Planer asked, pointing to the newspaper.

Father Gilbert looked down. The small headline announced "Vandalism at St Sebastian's".

Saint Sebastian's was an ancient church on the top of the hill overlooking Englesea. It had a small abbey attached to it, housing fewer than a dozen monks. Father Gilbert had considered paying the church a visit, if only to say hello to Brother Gregory, the abbot. They'd met several months before at a weekend retreat about spiritual direction and had stayed in touch through emails.

Planer chewed and swallowed. "Somebody defaced the altar last night. Spray paint, offensive graffiti, symbols. Mostly sex stuff." He pushed his plate aside.

The paragraph reported only as much as Planer had said. Father Gilbert didn't know much about Englesea as a town, so he had no way to gauge if defacing a church, or finding a murdered girl in a skip, were normal or aberrations.

"I hope it's not related to the conference."

"Why would it be related to the conference?"

Planer shrugged. "There are a few Christians I know who wouldn't be beneath that sort of behaviour when it comes to Catholic churches." He leaned forward and spoke in a stage whisper. "Catholics are in league with the Antichrist – or haven't you heard?"

"I've heard the rumour," Father Gilbert said. From his peripheral vision, he became aware that someone had stepped up to the table. The waiter with a refill of tea, he hoped. He put the newspaper aside and moved his empty teacup towards the edge of the table. But the person lingered without doing anything at all.

He was aware of a feeling of nausea and a sensation on the back of his neck like the feet of a dozen spiders scrambling to invade his hairline. He heard a dripping sound, as if large drops of water slapped against a mould-covered mattress.

He turned and recoiled at the sight of a young Chinese woman only a few feet away from him, hanging in the air – not from a defiance of gravity, but as if she were floating in water. Her jet-black hair snaked around the sides of her face, neck, and shoulders. Her eyes were almond-shaped black holes; the pupils, if she had any, recessed in a deep darkness. Her pale lips were shaped into an "O", as if she might be trying to whistle or preparing for a kiss. A rag that had once been a black T-shirt, with a faded logo, clung to her shoulders and chest. Her arms, pale with large smudges of blue and purple bruises, hung at her sides. A large rusted chain dangled loosely from iron clasps on her wrists. She wore fashionably torn denim shorts. Her legs were streaked with lines of mud, or they might've been scars. Her bare feet floated several inches above the carpet, water dripping from her toes. A glint of light took Father Gilbert's eyes back to her throat where he saw a necklace with a charm shaped like something that might have been a horse in a circle. The necklace lifted up as if a current of water had caught it.

Father Gilbert pushed back in his chair, his elbow banging the table and rattling everything on it. Flies, fat and green, came from nowhere and everywhere, landing on the faded red velvet wallpaper and then the table and food.

"What's wrong?" Planer asked, his voice coming from a great distance away.

Father Gilbert kept his eyes on the apparition. He had experienced these sorts of things before. How and why they appeared to him was rarely clear. All he knew was that they usually meant he was about to be pulled into trouble.

He was aware of Planer speaking to him, unaware of what was happening. He kept his eyes on the girl.

Would she speak to him? *Could* she? What if he reached out to her? Would his fingers touch water just as his ears heard the dripping? He lifted his hand, extending his forefinger to test his theory.

Suddenly there was a loud crash. Father Gilbert snapped in the direction of the sound. A young woman, dark-skinned, possibly Middle Eastern, had dropped a tray full of dishes and cutlery. The woman was looking his way. Her eyes were wide with fright and fixed on the floating Chinese girl.

She sees it, Father Gilbert thought, surprised. *She sees what I'm seeing.* That was a first.

The girl put a hand to her mouth.

A manager appeared at the kitchen door and growled, "What's going on here?"

The young woman lowered and angled her face away from the spectre, dropping to her knees to clean up the mess from the tray.

Father Gilbert turned back to the apparition. She had disappeared. In her place, the flies swarmed, then flew as one mass to the large front window, escaping through an open pane at the top. Beyond the window, out on the street, a man in a dark coat faced him. A black hat obscured the man's facial features, but there was no doubt the man was looking straight at him. A passing truck cut off his line of sight and then he was gone.

The other diners seemed oblivious to the flies. They stared at the commotion by the kitchen door.

"I'm so sorry," the manager announced to the room. He bent to help the girl pick up the broken glass, quickly throwing the pieces onto the tray. The girl's eyes came back to Father Gilbert.

Planer asked, "What was that all about?"

Father Gilbert stood up. "Excuse me."

He took a step towards the girl but stopped as his feet squished into the sodden carpet. He looked down, half expecting to sink into a marsh of carpet fibres.

"Where are you going? Come back here!" the manager shouted.

The girl had pushed past the manager and through the swinging door to the kitchen. He stood with the tray of broken dishes just as Father Gilbert approached. They danced to the left and right as Father Gilbert tried to move around him, his eye on the girl through the small panel of glass in the swinging door. She disappeared into whatever area lay beyond the kitchen.

"That girl," Father Gilbert said.

The manager blocked him. "What about her?"

"I'd like to have a word with her."

"I'm afraid you'll have to wait your turn," the manager said and backed through the door into the kitchen with the tray. "Employees only. Safety rules and all that. Come see me at the front desk."

Frustrated, Father Gilbert turned to the dining room. All heads at the various tables were turned towards him. Planer watched him.

Father Gilbert gave them an apologetic look and strode out.

* * *

"She's gone," the manager said from behind the teak reception desk. He fidgeted with a pen and slid papers around.

"To where?" Father Gilbert asked.

"I don't know. She dashed out the back door. Which is just as well, since I would have sacked her anyway."

"Why? Has this happened before?"

"The breaking dishes or the running off? Both," he said, scowling. "She's been unreliable from day one. As jittery as an alley cat."

"I'd like to speak with her."

"Good luck with that."

"Can you give me her name and address?"

"Her name is Cari – but I can't give out any of her personal details."

"Because you're not permitted or because you don't have them?" Father Gilbert asked. It wasn't uncommon for employees in these seaside towns to work under the radar, especially the foreign ones.

"What do you want with her?" the manager asked, gesturing to his priest's collar. "I doubt she's a member of the C of E. More of the burka or towel-head type, I would think."

Father Gilbert frowned at him, restraining the varied unkind responses that rushed to be voiced. "Is she likely to come back – for unpaid wages or anything like that?"

"She might."

He reached into his jacket pocket for a piece of scrap paper and remembered that Mrs Mayhew, his secretary at the church, had printed up business cards for the conference. He grabbed one and handed it over. "Please give her my card. Tell her to contact me – on my mobile phone, or here at the hotel. I'll be back later."

"I wouldn't get my hopes up," the manager said.

"Just give her my card," Father Gilbert said and quickly added, "Please."

* * *

In 1884 an aging pontiff, Leo XIII, had just celebrated Mass at his private chapel in the Vatican when he suddenly stopped in his tracks. A few others were with him and watched with concern as the Pope stood for ten minutes as if in a trance, his face ashen white. Then he snapped out of it and went back to his office where he wrote something quickly.

He later explained that he'd heard two voices near the altar. One voice was gentle and kind; the other was harsh and guttural. In a Job-like exchange, the harsh voice claimed it could destroy the church with enough time and power. The gentle voice enquired as to how much time and how much power would be needed. The first voice asked for 100 years. The gentle voice, accepting the challenge, granted the time and power to be used however the harsh voice decided.

Pope Leo XIII handed over a prayer to his subordinates, stating that it should be prayed after all low Masses everywhere. And so it was until the changes brought about by Vatican II ended the practice.

Pacing in his room, hands clasped behind him, Father Gilbert now prayed the prayer, whispering, "Saint Michael the Archangel, defend us in battle; be our protection against the wickedness and snares of the devil. May God rebuke him, we humbly pray, and do thou, O Prince of the Heavenly Host, by the power of God, thrust into Hell Satan and all the other evil spirits who prowl throughout the world seeking the ruin of souls. Amen."

If the apparition was a signal for trouble to come, he needed to be prepared.

CHAPTER 2

Father Gilbert shifted his messenger-style briefcase onto his shoulder and stepped from the front door of the hotel onto the pavement. The pedestrians passed by with shoulders hunched against the drizzle. The wheels of the cars and cabs hissed against the tarmac, with the occasional horn or squeaky brake penetrating the normal noises of a wet morning.

He glanced to the left and right for the man in the dark coat but didn't really expect to see him. When the man appeared, if he appeared at all, it was often at a distance. There was no sign of him now.

Going to a nearby Boots, he bought a spring-loaded-put-your-eye-out-if-not-careful umbrella for five pounds. He had the presence of mind to buy a tourist map and stopped inside the front door of the shop to get his bearings. Built on a hill, Englesea's streets were mostly cobblestone and laid out according to centuries of horse-paths that served to take the traveller further up towards the mainland or down to the docks servicing the boats on the sea. The larger roads stretched east and west, parallel to the sea, while the smaller streets ran north and south to connect the roads. Many of them were pedestrian-only areas to accommodate the nationally owned franchises and smaller boutique shops. The conference centre was two streets downhill from where he now stood.

"It must be worrying for you," the woman at the till said.

Father Gilbert turned. A young Chinese woman, similar in age and look to the spectre he'd seen, was paying for cosmetics. "Yes. It is… sad. We are watching. But don't worry, we can protect ourselves," the girl said with an accent.

"Be extra careful," replied the shop assistant. "You never know what kind of sick people are out there."

"Thank you," the Chinese woman said. She grabbed her bag of merchandise and rushed out, glancing at Father Gilbert as she went.

He strolled towards the conference site under his newly purchased umbrella, trying to avoid bumping into the other pedestrians while sidestepping puddles on the pavement. The rain washed out all variance of light, blending the buildings, road, and people into one continual grey blur.

The image of the apparition of the dead Chinese girl stayed with him. There was no question in his mind that she was the victim he'd read about in the newspaper. Had she appeared because he'd been reading about her – or was there some other purpose to her arrival? Either way, he wasn't entirely surprised. He'd often had unexplainable encounters where the dead or dying suddenly showed up. At times, as with the Chinese girl, they came as spectres without any specific interaction. Other times he found himself playing out a scene with cryptic conversations and bewildering actions that connected to unfolding events. Usually, they were unrelated to him personally, making him feel as if he'd been dropped into some other time or place, a character in someone else's story. If there were specific rules of engagement to this supernatural reality, he hadn't figured them out. He had no explanation for why he, of all people, had these experiences. All he could do was wait to see what would happen next.

The biggest surprise was that the waitress at the hotel had also seen the apparition. That had never happened before.

He reached the conference centre: a large brick building with leaded windows and iron doors. According to a display just inside the lobby, the hall had originally been a market when the town had thrived beyond shipping and fishing. Pirates frequented here, according to a historic plaque. And the French invaded once, back in 1448, setting fire to the town and burning down the original building. It was rebuilt and repurposed as a meeting hall. Later, in the economic fallout of the First World War, the maritime industries moved elsewhere and the hall fell into disrepair. An initiative in the Thatcher era led to its being refurbished to cater to the tourist trade.

Father Gilbert greeted a few acquaintances, mostly met at other conferences he'd attended, and signed in to get his name badge and packet of information. He headed to the exhibition area to kill time before the official start of events. Pausing at the double doors, he had a strong feeling that someone was watching him. He turned to the lobby again. It was half-filled with men and women in clerical garb or suits and dresses. They chatted amiably, greeting one another with cordial handshakes or the occasional embrace. He mused that, though they were there to discuss church issues, most had come to get away from their routines of meeting the same parishioners to talk about the same things, going about the same parish duties, often with a seasonal rhythm that some might find comforting while others would find it mind-numbingly tedious.

Conferences, he knew, were an escape, if not to relax then to do something different. Or perhaps they came to *be* someone different – to be someone holier or funnier or more thoughtful or more reckless or someone downright wild. On the outside they were clergy, bound up by self-imposed or external expectations while, inside, they were impaired humans with deep secrets they dared not admit to anyone, ever.

He pushed open the doors to the exhibition area, a wide-open space now filled with a labyrinth of booths and kiosks. Some were set up to sell books, Bibles, and instructional media; others sold crosses, jewellery, paintings, and other gift ideas; most were dedicated to promoting various charitable organizations created to help church leaders, missions efforts, the inner-city poor, children, the elderly, or just people who needed a new start in life.

While getting a coffee at a small stand, his eye fell on a table of the latest Christian fashion accessories. Among the necklaces and rings, he saw a collection of gold, silver, and leather bracelets. He walked over to look more closely and picked one up.

"Those are new," the woman behind the display said as she busied herself unpacking boxes.

"JDFU" was inscribed on a small plate that joined the bracelet together. "What does JDFU mean?" he asked.

"'Jesus Died For You.' You wear the bracelet as a reminder. Or as a conversation starter."

"My collar does that often enough," he said as he put the bracelet down again.

Chains on wrists, he thought. He suddenly remembered reading about a series of homicides around the country where young women were sexually assaulted and then murdered. The press called the perpetrator "The BackList Killer" – so-called because the police believed he chose his victims from an online "classified ads" website called "BackList". The victims had either advertised as prostitutes or for easy, no-commitment hook-ups. They had always been bound somehow: handcuffs, leather straps, rope, even a chain. Their bodies were disposed of in dumpsites, bins, or skips, as if the murderer were making a statement about the worth of the women's lives.

He wondered if Detective Inspector Gwynn would make that connection. Glancing at his watch, he moved for the door. It was just shy of nine o'clock. Apart from the opening speeches for the conference, there was nothing he had to attend.

He asked the woman behind the table, "Where is the nearest police station?"

"These aren't *stolen*," she said sharply.

* * *

Englesea's main police station was only three streets east of the hall and sat on a circle with a war memorial at the centre. The building was made of cement, painted white to alleviate the look of a bunker. Unfortunately the white made a good canvas for graffiti, thinly hidden behind new coats of paint.

Father Gilbert pushed through two sets of scarred wooden doors into a small waiting area with walls lined with metal chairs. One woman sat alone, kneading her fingers, with a worried expression on her face. Directly ahead was a wall with a reception counter cut into the centre. Framed by the square window, a police constable sat with his head slightly turned, his eyes squinting at a computer screen.

A buzzer sounded and a door to Father Gilbert's right unlocked with a loud click. As the door opened a man backed out into the reception area, talking in a language that sounded to Father Gilbert's ear like Russian. He had a large, black Stalinesque moustache and gestured wildly with his hands. Behind him, a uniformed constable nodded impatiently, encouraging him with quick nudges to keep walking.

"I'm sorry. I can't help you," the constable said slowly as if it would help the man understand him better.

The moustachioed man, realizing he was being guided to the front door, stopped and protested. "No, no, no. Daugh-ter. Help."

The constable looked around helplessly.

Just then, a large man in a light brown suit stepped in from outside. He nearly collided with the man with the moustache, who shouted and gestured all the more.

"What's all this?" the suited man asked, trying to shake the rain from his arms and hands. He brushed a hand through his thinning grey hair.

Father Gilbert recognized him immediately as Detective Inspector Morris Gwynn.

"He doesn't speak English," the constable said. "He's Russian or something."

The man turned his attention to Gwynn and spoke quickly.

"It's Romanian," Gwynn said to the constable. "He's from Moldova, but they speak Romanian there."

"What does he want?" the constable asked.

Gwynn spoke to the man in what must have been broken Romanian.

The man's face lit up, unleashing a greater deluge of words.

"Slow down," Gwynn said. "I'm not that good with it."

The man took a deep breath and spoke more slowly, punctuating his words with an occasional English equivalent.

"Well?" the constable asked when the long explanation ended.

"He says he is the father of a girl who went missing from London – Shepherd's Bush," Gwynn explained. "He heard about an unidentified young woman found dead and raced down to find out if it is his daughter. He would like to see the body."

"Unless his daughter is Chinese, I don't know how it could be her."

Gwynn put the statement to the man.

The man shook his head emphatically. "No. Not Chinese."

"Then she's not your daughter," Gwynn said in English.

The man suddenly slumped with a painful expression of

despondency. He lowered his head and said softly, in a thick accent, "But... my daughter?"

Gwynn put a hand on his shoulder. "Give your name and details to the constable here—"

The constable looked stricken at the suggestion. "It's a London case. He needs to file a report there."

"Take his details anyway," Gwynn said.

The man turned to the constable. "I am Vadim Dalca. I am—" He stopped himself and finished the sentence in Romanian.

The constable glared at Gwynn.

"You'll figure it out," Gwynn said and gently pushed both the constable and Vadim Dalca back through the door.

Father Gilbert stepped forward. "Morris? Morris Gwynn?"

Gwynn spun around. His eyes fell on Father Gilbert's face, then down to the clerical collar below it, then back to the face. "*Gilbert?*"

Father Gilbert smiled and extended a hand.

Gwynn swore loudly and wrapped him in a bear hug.

* * *

"Nice place," Father Gilbert said.

They were in Gwynn's office – a high-walled pale green cubicle with a gunmetal desk, a matching swivel chair behind it, and a metal chair sitting to one side, presumably for guests or suspects. A side table was overrun with precariously placed piles of files. The cloth lining of the cubicle walls was littered with bureaucratic announcements, mugshots, and newspaper articles held up with pins.

"Is it too early to celebrate with a drink?" Gwynn asked.

"It isn't even ten."

"I don't care." However time had changed him, Gwynn still had mischief in his eyes. It made him look jovial, though Father Gilbert knew how ruthless he could be. After a quick rummage in his desk drawer, he brought out what was left of a bottle of the Dalmore. He dug further, found two plastic cups that he blew into, used his finger to give them a quick wipe, and then poured a small amount into each one. He handed one to Father Gilbert and then lifted his own. "To better days."

The two men shot back their drinks.

Father Gilbert didn't often drink, especially in the morning. The warmth of the Scotch working through his body had an immediate effect. "That's good."

"More?"

"No, thank you."

Gwynn put the bottle back in the drawer. He set the two cups on an exposed surface of his desk, and then waved for Father Gilbert to sit down in the guest chair. It creaked as he did. Gwynn dropped into his office chair. It groaned.

"How is it that you speak Romanian?" Father Gilbert asked.

"You remember Katrina," he said.

"Your wife."

"*First* wife – of three." He leaned back in his chair and clasped his hands behind his head. "Her father was Romanian. We used to play cards and drink a lot. I picked up the language in the five years I was wedded to his daughter. That poor man in reception reminded me of her. It must've been the moustache."

Father Gilbert laughed, his mind racing back to the Horse and Groom pub near Scotland Yard where he and Gwynn had often tossed back a pint or two when their schedules allowed it. Gwynn had worked on cases of theft, larceny, and fraud. Father Gilbert had worked with more serious crime, usually involving kidnappings, assault, and homicides.

DI Gwynn eyed him. "Look at you," he said. "A *vicar*, of all things. Or are you a priest? Which is it? Anglican, Catholic, I get them all confused."

"I'm an Anglican priest, on the Catholic side of the Church of England sensibilities."

"Does that make you a 'Father' or a 'Reverend'?"

"I usually go by 'Father', but will answer to 'Reverend', too."

Gwynn shook his head. "I'd heard you never really recovered from that one case. The one with the runaway who died. Adams, wasn't it? Paula Adams?"

"Patricia Atkins," Father Gilbert corrected him, and then asked quickly, "How did you wind up here?"

"It's all so boring," Gwynn said. "I was ready to retire and came to Englesea for a little holiday. I liked the town, they needed help, and I reckoned it was time to get away from the violence and crime of London."

"How is that working out for you?" Father Gilbert asked, smiling.

"It's getting more like London all the time. Especially with so many foreigners. We're overrun with them."

"Isn't tourism good for the town's economy?"

"These foreigners work here."

"Isn't *that* good for the economy?"

He shook his head. "With the foreigners, you get more crime. It's not politically correct to say so, but it's true."

"I read about the murdered girl."

Gwynn sat up. "That's unusual. Crime is one thing; murder is another."

"Can you talk about it?"

"Not much to say right now." He picked up a file from his desk. "Chinese. Late twenties, maybe early thirties. The owner of the restaurant found her when he took out the rubbish around two this morning."

"Is the restaurant usually open that late?"

"They closed later than usual because of a large party – an entourage of you church-types, in for the conference." Gwynn opened the file and pushed the contents around.

"Time of death?"

"Old habits, Gilbert? As an immediate guess: sometime around or past midnight."

"Witnesses?"

"It was a rainy night. There wouldn't have been very many people walking the seafront."

"Security cameras?"

"None that work. We're checking others leading into the area."

Photos taken at the crime scene slid into Father Gilbert's view. The harsh light of the camera flash intensified the unnatural look of the scene. The skip and the rubbish under and surrounding the dead body; a close-up of the young woman's face, her mouth slightly open, a gash on her forehead, her dead staring eyes looking somewhere beyond the camera lens. Father Gilbert recognized without surprise that she was the same one he'd seen as an apparition earlier.

"A real beauty, eh?" Gwynn said. His eye caught Father Gilbert's expression. "What's wrong? Don't tell me she's a long-lost daughter."

Gwynn chuckled and Father Gilbert gave a quick smile. The Detective Inspector couldn't know how close to home his joke hit.

"Cause of death?" Father Gilbert asked. He pointed to the bruises around the woman's neck and shoulders. "Was she strangled?"

"Maybe, but that's not how she died. The Medical Examiner said she probably drowned."

Father Gilbert was surprised. "Drowned? In the sea or in the skip?"

"He's not saying until he does the full autopsy. It could be either."

He remembered how, as unlikely as it seemed, skips could fill up with enough water and sludge to drown a person, especially in this weather. It wouldn't take much. He knew of homeless men and women, drunk and seeking shelter in a skip, who had drowned in less than an inch of water.

Father Gilbert leaned forward to look more closely at the photos. "What about the gash on her forehead?"

"Post-mortem. The ME found a fragment of metal in it. We're having it checked. Maybe the murderer banged her head while throwing her in the skip. Or while transporting her in a car, probably the boot."

Father Gilbert's mind went back to the logistics of transporting a dead girl from a hotel room to a car to a skip.

"She also had traces of sand and seawater in her hair and what was left of her clothes. But the skip had the same, so she likely picked them up from there."

Father Gilbert thought about the chains he'd seen on the apparition. "Was she bound?"

"She has bruising around her wrists that might've been caused by something metallic, maybe handcuffs. The ME isn't sure yet. And there's a harsh scrape on her neck that's different from the scratches on other parts of her body, as if she wore a necklace that had been pulled off violently." He held up his hands as if inspecting his fingers. "And there was something found under her fingernails, as yet to be identified."

He hadn't asked the obvious question – and did now. "Was she raped?"

"No forced trauma," he said. "Probably consensual, considering her profession."

"Her profession?"

"I'm sure she was on the game," Gwynn said.

"How do you know that?"

"Around here, most of the girls from the Far East are."

"But you can't assume—"

"I'm not assuming anything," Gwynn said quickly. "I'll go where the facts of the case lead me. But my educated guess is that she was hired for some kind of sadomasochistic activity, what with the bindings on her wrists."

Gwynn shuffled the photos back into the file.

"I assume you haven't identified her," Father Gilbert said, feeling as if closing the file might somehow erase the girl's life from reality.

"Not yet. Her fingerprints aren't in our database." He folded his arms and gave Father Gilbert a scrutinizing look. "Why are you interested? Why did you come to see me? It's not for old times' sake."

"I assume you're familiar with the BackList Killer," Father Gilbert said.

"Some guy has been targeting women who advertise their services on BackList. Six or seven girls have been raped and murdered."

"You may want to check the details of those cases. The MO may be similar with this case."

"Good idea." Gwynn nodded, impressed. Then he smiled. "You can't get rid of it, can you? Being a cop. Once it's in your blood…"

Father Gilbert offered a small shrug. He couldn't count the number of times someone had said to him *you're more like a detective than a priest*.

An idea seemed to strike Gwynn and he turned to the computer, tucked away on the other side of the desk. With his back to Father Gilbert, he pushed the mouse around and the monitor came to life.

He typed in his access information and found a search engine. A few more taps on the keyboard and the BackList website appeared on the screen. "Have you ever seen this site?"

"No." Father Gilbert pushed closer to get a better look. "I thought it's like an online boot-sale."

"It's more than women selling baby-clothes and men selling unused tools." Gwynn navigated the mouse pointer to different categories. "You want escorts? Men's clubs? Body rubs? Massages?"

"Don't forget – I'm a priest."

"Are you?" he teased. "Are you sure you're not working undercover?"

"I'm sure."

"Then look away while I check this out."

Father Gilbert turned away from the screen. He looked down at his shoes; they were black and scuffed, in need of a polish. "What are you looking for?" he asked.

"The dead girl. If she was local, then she might be on here." Father Gilbert could hear Gwynn clicking the mouse and the occasional "hm". "The escorts generally use real photos, even if they're dated ones from younger and less-worn days. The massage places post pictures of generic models. Unless they have girls that really are pretty, in which case…" Another click and he said, "Ah. I think this is her. Take a look."

Father Gilbert turned to look at the screen, bracing himself for an image that would be less than pure. He was half-right. The girl on the screen had taken a "selfie" in a bathroom somewhere. She was dressed in a bikini top and cut-off shorts. Though her face was slightly blurred and in a half-shadow, her smile came through as a seductive appeal. It was the same girl found in the skip; the one who had appeared to Father Gilbert.

"She calls herself 'Anna'," Gwynn said. "But that won't be her real name."

Father Gilbert pointed to the screen. "She's wearing a necklace."

Gwynn tried to zoom in on the necklace. It pixelated the image, but Father Gilbert could make out the circle and horse design he'd seen earlier in the apparition. Gywnn restored the original page where the photo appeared with other photos of young women from the Far East. At the top, it said "Lily Rose Day Spa" and "You Won't Be Disappointed." The hours of operation were from 9 in the morning until midnight. There was a phone number and a small box with a map. A red dot identified the location.

"Is it near here?" Father Gilbert asked.

"It's within walking distance." Gwynn punched a button. Somewhere in the cubicle – off to Gwynn's right – a printer came to life and spat out the image from the screen. He collected the printout, pushed back in his chair, and stood up. "Come on. Let's find out who this girl is."

Father Gilbert also stood up. The effect of the Scotch slightly tilted the floor. "Won't it be distracting to have a priest with you?"

"Yes. It's the last thing they'll expect."

27

CHAPTER 3

The rain had stopped. Between the buildings across the street, Father Gilbert could see crested waves of grey on a choppy sea. They turned left at the closest street and ascended up into the town. After six or seven streets, they turned right on Tanner Lane. Further along, the shops and restaurants became noticeably dingy. To the left was a place called "Magic Fingers Massage", advertising Thai and Swedish massages. The Lily Rose was a few doors down on the right. The windows were covered with a thick curtain, leaving room for only an "open" sign that flashed in bright colours.

Gwynn pushed the door open and stepped in. The small entryway had the look of a chemist's shop. There was a counter, behind which an older bald-headed Chinese man stood wearing a white physician's coat. Behind him was shelving lined with dozens of glass containers, each one labelled with Chinese characters and typed English translations. Father Gilbert saw names like Honeysuckle Leaf, Wolfberry, Reishi Mushroom, and Morinda Root.

"Herbal medicine?" Father Gilbert asked.

"They think it makes them look legitimate," Gwynn said. He leaned on the counter.

The Chinese man forced a smile. "Hello, Detective Inspector."

"I want to see *Mamasan*."

"She no want to be disturbed," the man said.

"Disturb her anyway," Gwynn said. "Unless you want me to send my men in to check your licences, immigrant documentation, and what's in those jars."

The man scowled at him and rushed off down a long hall to the back of the shop. The two men exchanged glances as sharp words, presumably in Chinese, echoed back to them. A sudden silence and then a short woman wearing an ornate robe appeared at the end of the hall. She strode towards them, adjusting and readjusting her long, dark hair as she did. She had a round matronly face with cunning eyes. Her eyelashes were thick with eyeliner and her mouth was a gash of red lipstick. Her cheeks looked tight and inflated, like small balloons, probably from Botox injections.

"How good to see you, Detective Inspector," she said. Her eyes darted to Father Gilbert, noted the collar, and then flashed back to Gwynn. "Why do you need a vicar to visit us?"

"To protect me from the unholiness of your establishment," Gwynn said.

"It never bothered you before," she replied.

Father Gilbert glanced at Gwynn, wondering if the woman was teasing or if Gwynn truly had been a customer there.

"Would you like a massage?" she asked Father Gilbert. She tried to sound sultry but years of smoking had given her voice the sound of dry leaves clawing at the face of a tombstone. "You wouldn't be the first vicar we've had in here. I give you first time for free."

Father Gilbert shook his head. "No, thanks."

"Why are you here?" Mamasan asked Gwynn. "You have come about murdered girl? You want to tell me you are doing everything you can to protect innocent Chinese girls in town?"

"You're half-right," Gwynn said. "She was one of yours."

Mamasan pressed a hand to her chest and gave an expression of shock. "One of mine?"

Gwynn brought out the printout from the Internet site. "This is the girl in an advertisement for your place."

Mamasan eyed the picture and looked as if she was formulating a denial. Instead, she pushed it away and said, "She worked here from time to time."

"What was her name?"

"Anna."

"Her *real* name."

"*Anong*," Mamasan said.

"Last name?" Gwynn asked, his impatience putting an edge to his tone.

Mamasan hesitated, clearly deciding between the truth or a lie. "*Chuan*. She did massages here occasionally. Mostly she worked the streets. I don't like those kinds of girls."

"In spite of the percentage you get from them."

Mamasan looked indignant. "I am a good citizen."

"I'm sure all the girls here are – and that they'll be very cooperative," Gwynn said, taking a few steps down the hall.

Mamasan tried to block his way but quickly realized she was no match for a man his size. "You need a warrant to search my shop."

"I'm not searching. I'm an enquiring customer. Come on, Gilbert," Gwynn said.

With no way to stop them, Mamasan walked backwards in front of Gwynn, jabbering about how clean and reputable her "spa" was.

The hall was lined with doors on both sides. All but one stood open, each revealing a massage table with white sheets, a side table with a Tiffany-style lamp, a portable music player, and bottles of oil and lotion. At the end of the hall was an office. Mamasan must have assumed they were going there, because she turned and walked in ahead of them. Gwynn had other plans. As Mamasan entered her office, Gwynn suddenly grabbed the handle of the one closed door and pulled it open. He quickly stepped through and descended a dimly lit staircase. Father Gilbert followed him. Mamasan, realizing too late what had happened, screeched and raced after them.

At the bottom of a dozen stairs, they came into a large room, decorated with red and gold wallpaper, Asian-style art, and statues of Buddha, warriors, and geishas. A small fountain trickled water from the mouth of a large vase into a small pool. More doors faced them from all sides. As Gwynn strode past, he pushed the doors open, revealing rooms containing more massage tables – though they were more like beds than the tables upstairs. The rooms were windowless. Of course they were, being in a cellar. But clearly there was a more nefarious purpose here. Each room said to come in, relax, this is a place where the world outside can't see you or judge you. You're safe here. Live out your fantasy. There'll be no consequences because no one need ever know. It's just our secret. These walls will never talk.

Mamasan continued to screech, trying to get in front of Gwynn.

Father Gilbert was struck by a feeling of uneasiness, as if he'd walked into a dark cavern filled with traps. Behind the ostentatious oriental decor was a foul presence, like something had crawled into the woodwork and died there. Instinctively, his muscles tensed.

They reached the back of the room where Gwynn pushed open one of three doors there. Three Far Eastern women were inside, one standing at a sink wearing a thin robe, applying make-up, another in shorts and T-shirt, sitting on a small chair and lacing her shoes, and a third had just come out of a shower wrapped only in a towel. They seemed amused by the intrusion.

"Sorry, girls," Gwynn said and closed the door again.

The second door opened into a small room with a bed adorned with white twinkling Christmas lights and a table sitting opposite holding a lamp and a laptop.

Mamasan made a valiant effort to get between Gwynn and the last door. He blocked her with his immense body, shoving the door open to reveal a room with mattresses scattered on the floor. Half a dozen Far Eastern women of varying ages were spread out on the mattresses, dressed in tracksuits and pyjamas. Some were texting, one was doing her nails, another was sleeping, and one sat with a laptop. The women were startled, but didn't move, each looking up at them with puzzled expressions. The girl on the laptop suddenly closed the lid and pushed it aside. Father Gilbert noticed a single mattress propped up in the corner and wondered if it had belonged to the dead "Anna".

As a detective, Father Gilbert had seen this kind of set-up before. The women lived in this room when they weren't servicing customers. It was home for as long as they worked there. They had limited freedom to leave the premises, if they left at all. Food was brought in or meals were made in the small kitchenette in a curtained area at the back of the room.

Mamasan shouted at them and the women all stood up, like soldiers at an inspection. The sleeping girl was frightened awake and struggled to her feet. Father Gilbert scanned the faces. Most of the women were thirty years old or under. They were attractive, two or three even beautiful. One of the girls looked familiar to him, but he wasn't sure why. She had black hair cut stylishly short and wore heavy blue eyeliner. Her eyes were red-rimmed and he wondered if she'd been crying about Anong's death.

"You have gone too far," Mamasan said to Gwynn.

"One of your girls was murdered last night. Don't you care?"

"There is nothing I can do about it." Mamasan pointed an accusing finger at him. "You know the Mayor is a frequent customer here. He won't tolerate any bullying by you."

Gwynn spread his arms in innocence. "Bullying? Am I bullying anyone?"

"Yes," she said. "Look at the fear in these poor girls' eyes."

Father Gilbert was amused to see that the girls actually looked tired and bored rather than fearful.

Mamasan and Gwynn glared at one another.

Father Gilbert broke the showdown by clearing his throat and asking, "Did Anong keep her things here?"

"Why would she do that?" Mamasan whined. "I *told* you, she worked here only occasionally."

Gwynn asked, "Where did she live? If she was an employee of yours, then you must have that information."

Mamasan frowned at him. "If you want to see my files, come back with a court order." She folded her arms in defiance. As she did, her robe shifted and Father Gilbert saw a necklace at the base of her throat. It was a silver chain with a symbol of a horse in a circle – the same one he'd seen in "Anna's" apparition.

"Where did you get that?" Father Gilbert asked.

She reached up and enclosed it in her hand. "It is a personal heirloom. Now, unless you want a massage, please leave."

"I'll be back," Gwynn said.

As they were about to leave, something in the corner of the room, where the mattress was propped up, caught Father Gilbert's eye. A greenish light glowed from behind the mattress. Then a hand, grey and shrivelled, reached around, the fingers claw-like, and scratched at the mattress cover. The fingernails must have been razor-sharp as five tears ripped opened the fabric. Instead of the expected mattress stuffing or springs spilling forward, bright red blood oozed out of the five widening lacerations.

"Gilbert?" Gwynn said. "What's wrong?"

Father Gilbert turned. Gwynn looked at him, perplexed.

Mamasan, her brows pinched together, was looking at him, then back at the corner, then back at him. The girls in the room stared at him as if he'd just sprouted a third eye.

He looked at the mattress again. It appeared undisturbed and unmarred. "Nothing," Father Gilbert said.

* * *

Back on the street, Gwynn swore softly and pulled out his mobile phone. "Court order," he muttered. "I'll give her a court order." He called someone at the station and barked orders to get the warrant he'd need.

Father Gilbert waited, his eyes going back to the door. Through the glass, he could see the young woman with the blue eyeliner standing inside watching them. She dabbed at tears in her eyes. Thinking she wanted to say something, he reached for the door. Mamasan suddenly came into view, pushing the girl back and glowering at the priest. Father Gilbert turned away.

He often wondered how women in that line of work got where they were. Why would they choose that kind of life for themselves? Did they have a choice? Was this massage parlour part of the sex slave industry, or were the women there because circumstances had robbed them of a better way to make money? The choices, circumstances, and consequences of life were a great mystery.

"Let's get a coffee," Gwynn said and marched off. Father Gilbert followed him around the corner to a café. They went in, ordered at the counter, and sat down at a table by the front window.

"What kind of place is it?" Father Gilbert asked, thinking about the unnerving sight of the hand clawing at the mattress.

"Wasn't it obvious?"

"Unless things have changed since my days at the Yard, there are different kinds of massage parlours. Some do full erotic massages. Most limit themselves to nothing more than sensual touching. Others offer the full gamut. Which is this one?"

"I think it's strictly rubs and touch," he said. "Which may be why 'Anna' hit the streets. She could make a lot more money from johns than from massage tips."

"And you're sure Mamasan was getting a percentage?"

"No doubt," Gwynn said. "All of the girls are connected to a syndicate of pimps. The bosses around here won't put up with girls working independently."

"Why do you allow it to go on?"

Gwynn shrugged. "Technically, the massage places are legit. We've tried raiding them from time to time but we can never catch them doing anything blatantly illegal. Both the massager and the therapist can claim it was consensual. The only success we've had happened a couple of years ago. One of the parlours brought in underage girls – and I mean *underage*. We put a stop to that right away."

"What about the streetwalkers?"

"We bring them in if they're too obvious or aggressive," he said. "Other than that…"

Their coffees arrived, delivered by a black waitress who said "thank you" with a heavy accent that Father Gilbert thought might be from somewhere in Africa.

"This certainly is an international town," Father Gilbert said. He doctored his drink with copious amounts of cream and sugar.

"They come and go with the tourist season – and the conventions."

Father Gilbert drank his coffee and looked at the African waitress behind the counter. She had a name – a life – somewhere beyond the confines of this café. He thought about the anonymity of the girls at the massage parlour. They each had names, lives, even hopes and dreams at one time. Yet, who would know it to look at them? Did the men who entered that place give a thought to the human being behind the service she provided? Or was an impersonal encounter the whole point?

"Does Mamasan have a real name?" Father Gilbert asked.

"I never needed to know until now. I'll find out. If she's the owner, her name will be on all the official business information. I'll check when I get back to the station."

"At least you have a name for the victim."

"Anong Chuan," he said with a groan. "For all I know, it's the same as 'Jane Smith'. I'll be surprised if she's in the database."

"Everyone leaves a trail of some kind."

"Not these girls. They come and go like ghosts." He gazed at Father Gilbert. "What happened back there? You looked like you saw one. A ghost, I mean."

Father Gilbert frowned. He couldn't say anything to Gwynn about the apparitions he'd seen. Another thought came to him. "That mattress in the corner…"

"What about it?"

"If you get a court order to search the room, you'll want to check inside of the mattresses. The girls might hide belongings there – the kind they wouldn't want Mamasan to see."

"You think the mattress belonged to Anong?"

"Possibly."

"And the necklace?"

"Anong wore one like it in the picture. And hers is missing."

"You think Mamasan killed her to steal the necklace?" Gwynn asked.

It seemed absurd to hear it said out loud. Father Gilbert said, "I was curious about the symbol – the horse in the circle. Does it have a cultural meaning or is it something else?"

"It's probably something she picked up in Hong Kong on the way over. Years before she turned into the dragon queen. Or maybe she gives one to all her girls." Gwynn pushed his cup aside. "It's a waste of time. Mamasan will coach the girls about what to say. And I'm sure they'll clean the place out thoroughly for anything incriminating."

An awkward silence fell between them.

Gwynn had not aged well, Father Gilbert thought. His thinning light brown hair had blended with the grey to create a colour that defied categorization. The sweat matted it against his scalp, making it look greasy, as if he hadn't bathed in days. The suit didn't help, wrinkled and stained as if he'd taken it straight from a dirty laundry basket. The deep lines around his red-rimmed eyes and pronounced veins in his pitted nose suggested more than just casual drinking. Father Gilbert wondered if there had been more to his leaving London than just semi-retirement.

"What kinds of men go to massage parlours for full body massages? – or, worse, use streetwalkers?" Father Gilbert asked.

"You're a priest, you should know the answers to questions like that."

"I'm asking you."

"As a detective or a man?"

"Is there a difference?"

Gwynn used his thumbnail to scratch at a dried crumb on the side of his coffee cup. "It's men behaving like naughty boys."

"There has to be more to their motivation than that."

Gwynn smiled. "You know what the motivation is."

Father Gilbert shook his head. "That's too easy."

"Is it?" Gwynn asked. "Put a man in a bad marriage with a non-accommodating wife and you'll see how simplistic it is. A man wants to feel like a man."

"What does that mean? Is it about being a great lover? How can a man believe he's a great lover when he pays money for it?"

Gwynn shrugged. "Maybe it's a way to alleviate the boredom of life, to get a thrill without a personal commitment – just use the girls and leave."

"Maybe. Or it could be a sense of control or power over someone else – or his environment. It's a way to dominate, to regain a feeling of strength."

Gwynn drank his coffee, then put his cup down. He glanced at the girl behind the counter, then fixed his eyes on Father Gilbert. "Have you ever had an affair?"

Father Gilbert flinched at the unexpectedness of the question. "No."

"Then let me tell you how it happens. A man thinks he wants or needs something that he's not getting in his relationship at home or somewhere in his life. It may be sex, but it's usually deeper than that. Then an opportunity comes along. He meets her at work or at a bar. Or maybe he creates the opportunity – like some of these men do with the massage parlours. Either way, he rationalizes why it's all right and he's on his way."

"But that usually leads to guilt, some remorse…" Father Gilbert said.

"Sure. But he gets over that. You know how it works."

Father Gilbert nodded. "If the benefit is more powerful than the drawback, he'll do it again."

"It's like the pathology of a serial killer." Gwynn dropped his elbows on the table. "Different outcome, same behaviour."

"Then what?" Father Gilbert asked.

"The man fragments his life. He lives in multiple worlds. He compartmentalizes them. He's a solid family man at home, in his social circles. But he's created another world where he's someone special. Like Clark Kent and Superman." Gwynn eyed him. "Are you telling me you've *never* felt that way?"

"Not seriously," Father Gilbert admitted. "I suppose I was as tempted as any man to flirt, to fantasize, but I was never inclined to act on it."

"From a lack of opportunity or were things that good at home?"

Father Gilbert chuckled. "My wife and I did pretty well." They had loved each other. They had been good friends as well as lovers, he thought.

"A righteous man even then," Gwynn jabbed.

Father Gilbert smiled politely. "I thought of my marriage as a matter of commitment. I had committed to her with the same determination that I had committed to my job. I had no intention of messing up either."

"But you *did* leave. The job, at least. And now look at you," Gwynn teased.

"I left the job because of my wife's cancer – and the Atkins case made me rethink my priorities."

"Same difference," Gwynn said, spreading his arms as if he'd made his case. "A man gets into an affair for the same reason. Circumstances nudge him to think about it. Then a woman comes along with an aura of promise."

"What kind of promise?"

"She makes him feel good about himself."

"You're describing a full-fledged emotional affair," Father Gilbert said. "What about these massage parlours? Do the girls there affect a man that way?"

"The good ones do." Gwynn turned to the window, his eyes on

something far away. "They know how to make a man feel like he's the greatest thing in the world."

Father Gilbert watched him. "Are you speaking from experience?"

Gwynn slowly turned from the window and gazed at Father Gilbert. He smiled. "What does it matter if no one gets hurt?"

"Someone always gets hurt," Father Gilbert said.

Gwynn considered him a moment, then shoved away from the table. "Are we finished profiling our suspect?"

"I'm trying to think of who killed Anong – and why."

"Keep up the good work." Gwynn stood up. "I have to get back to the office. You're around for the next few days – for the conference – right?"

"Right."

"So, if I need another set of eyes on this case?"

"I'm out of practice."

"Once a copper, always a copper." Gwynn opened his wallet, took out a card, and put it on the table. "You know where to find me."

Father Gilbert reached into his pocket and pulled out one of his new cards. God bless Mrs Mayhew. "And this is me."

Gwynn took the card and looked it over. "Thanks, Detective Inspective *Father.*" He chuckled, and then the chuckle turned into a full-throated laugh as he walked out of the café.

* * *

Father Gilbert lifted his messenger bag onto the table and pulled out an electronic tablet. He didn't have a lot of tech-savvy. Some of his parishioners had conspired to buy him the device as a Christmas present. They thought it would help Mrs Mayhew keep him organized. Most of the time he forgot to use it, leaving it sitting on his desk, or shoved in a drawer. But Mrs Mayhew had insisted he bring it with him to the conference so he could check emails and be reminded of his commitments.

He turned it on and, once it had come alive, thumbed his way to a web browser. The café had Wi-Fi for its guests and he was able to connect quickly to a search engine. He clumsily typed in "BackList Killer" and hit the search button.

A results list with thousands of websites appeared. Some were singularly dedicated to the killer. Others were dedicated to serial killers in general, with specific articles about the details of the "BackList" killer. An online "encyclopedia" had a summary of the killer and his victims. Father Gilbert tapped on the link for that.

The murders began in the summer a year before, the article stated, with the killer striking one victim in June, another in July, and two in August. He was dormant until October, with another gap until February, and then he had struck again a month ago, almost a year after the first murder. The police were concerned that summer would see an increase in his activity. Father Gilbert wondered if Anong was the first of the summer victims.

There was no obvious pattern to the dates and times of the murders. But the murders themselves had a tell-tale consistency. Heather Grant, the first victim, regularly advertised on the BackList site in Blackpool as a "fun, passionate, redhead looking for a passionate experience" with a mobile number to call to set up a "great date". The phrasing allowed for the impression that she was merely a woman looking for a good time. Police confirmed, however, that she was a known prostitute with previous arrests. They believed she met the murderer somewhere for their encounter, he persuaded her to be handcuffed, and then he bludgeoned her with a blunt object, probably a leather truncheon. Her body was found in a large industrial rubbish bin in an alley behind a print shop, her clothes and handbag nearby. There was no sign of robbery. Even her money and credit cards were left in the purse.

The second victim, Bonnie Young, was the same as the first – a prostitute, this time working in Bournemouth, who advertised on the local BackList site. She'd also been bound with handcuffs and bludgeoned with a leather truncheon, though it appeared to be smaller than the one used on the previous victim. Her body had been dumped in a construction skip in an office building that was being renovated. Unlike the redheaded Heather, Bonnie was a natural blonde.

The third victim was not a prostitute. She was a single woman named Angie Drummond in Edinburgh who was described as a "swinger", often cruising the clubs for men who were interested only in one-night stands. An attractive brunette, she posted on BackList that she was simply "bored with conventional living" and wanted a man who would take her to "ecstatic heights". Police found no evidence that she had ever asked for money or engaged in her activities for business. Local pimps and prostitutes did not know her. In addition to being killed with a blunt instrument – yet another uniquely sized truncheon – she had been strangled. That was a change in the killer's behaviour. The police believed the killer was "graduating" – going from a method in which he didn't face the victim, to one in which he did. It took more courage that way, and made the killing more personal. She was found in a tip just outside the city.

Rose Kim, the next victim, was British-born but of South Korean descent. She was a prostitute advertising in the Reading area. Police learned that she was a student at a nearby university who had turned to prostitution as a source of income to pay her fees. Friends were surprised to learn of her extracurricular activities, stating that she was "beautiful, sweet and unassuming" and that they "never would have guessed she was capable of that kind of work". Bound by handcuffs, she had been bludgeoned with a truncheon the same size as the one used on the first victim. She was dumped in a skip in an industrial park on the opposite side of town from her home. Police noted that Rose was the first non-Caucasian victim and the first murder to take place away from a coastal town.

Janice Nelson of Grimsby and Alison Kendrick of Margate, both prostitutes, had the same MO as the earlier victims. Janice, a brunette, had been found in a skip next to a derelict building. Alison, with light brown hair, was dropped in a department store skip – nearly unseen because she was tossed in amidst mannequins the shop had thrown out earlier the same day.

The most recent victim was the killer's first black woman, calling herself Ebony Delight on BackList. Her real name was Chelsea Brooks. She had advertised body-to-body massages around South London. Her body was found in a skip behind a major hotel near Gatwick Airport. There was no evidence that she'd ever been in the hotel itself. Her wrists and ankles had been shackled rather than handcuffed or bound with leather straps. The shackles had been attached to heavy chains, the kind used for towing vehicles. The press speculated that the use of chains on a black woman was a racist slur to evoke slavery – as if being a racist was the worst thing that could be said of a killer.

Father Gilbert turned off the tablet. He'd seen enough. The remaining websites were unlikely to have the level of information the investigating detectives had assembled from the crime scenes. He imagined the kinds of connections they were trying to make between the girls, the methods, and the places. They questioned potential witnesses, pleaded with the public to come forward with any helpful information. No doubt they were checking into local workers, lorry drivers, tow truck drivers, salesmen, vendors, clients, or anyone else who might travel to those locations. Without fingerprints or DNA, it was like looking for a needle in a field full of haystacks.

Unlike the others, Anong had been strangled and drowned. She'd also been dumped without any personal belongings. All of the other victims had their clothes and handbags tossed near their bodies.

He thought of all the promises of life the girls may have known before their choices or circumstances led them into the pathway of their killer. He thought of their parents and siblings, who may not have known what kinds of lives their daughters were leading until it was too late. He thought of other women who had given themselves to similar vocations. Did the murders scare some of them away from selling their bodies? He thought of the men who had used those women before their murders. Surely the police had found some of them and put them through tough interrogations. Maybe the close call with the law, the exposure of their appetites to greater scrutiny, caused them to rethink their lives.

He wasn't sure how long he sat and thought about those things. He could only pray that the sadness and tragedy of the dead might be redeemed in the lives of the living. And that the police would catch the killer before he struck again.

Father Gilbert drained the last of his coffee, a tepid and bitter swallow. The apparition of Anong and the unfolding case – which wasn't his to solve – weighed on him. But he really should go to the conference.

A low rumble of an approaching truck caused him to turn to the window. Suddenly water splashed violently against the glass. It jolted him. He could only assume the truck had hit a large puddle.

For a few seconds, the world outside was a blur of distorted and impressionistic shapes and colours. In the midst of it all, he saw the dark figure in the coat and hat. The *Shadow Man* he had begun to call it. Faceless and menacing, it was there – until the water slid down the glass and took it away, perhaps onto the pavement and away into a drain.

* * *

Father Gilbert turned left out of the café. He walked without any motivation. He had to return to the conference. His Bishop would be looking for him, not because the Bishop liked or needed him, but because the Bishop thought he was out of control. Bishop William Spalding liked control over his flock. To the Bishop, Father Gilbert was a wayward sheep, prone to wander into the hills or into a pack of wolves.

Looking objectively, he couldn't blame the Bishop for feeling that way. When taking the job a year ago, the Bishop had inherited a priest who'd been forced to take a lengthy sabbatical because of family stress. His mother had passed away, which was difficult enough. Then he had learned that he'd fathered a daughter by his first girlfriend. He hadn't known she was pregnant and had left her to begin his training to join the Metropolitan Police in London. They'd lost touch. He'd got on with his life, later marrying another woman and eventually becoming a detective.

His life had changed dramatically with the tragic Atkins case and then his wife's diagnosis of pancreatic cancer. After her death, he'd left Scotland Yard and become an Anglican priest. He'd learned about his daughter only after Clare Gilbert, his mother, had died, allowing him a closer look at her papers and photos. His mother had kept it a secret all those years.

It turned out his mother had been good at keeping secrets. She had also hidden the fact that the man Father Gilbert thought was his father was not his father at all, but his father's brother – an uncle who had married his mother after his real father, a police constable, had been killed in the line of duty. It was an act of charity, not love, as Uncle George wanted to give Clare and his brother's baby a stable home. Unfortunately, George was an actor who was rarely home, travelling the world over for any stage, television, or film work he could get. As a child, Father Gilbert had felt abandoned. As a teenager, he had felt resentful towards the occasional and intrusive arrival of the man. As an adult, he felt alternately indifferent and annoyed at, if not resigned to, George's presence. If their relationship had been strained because George had hardly been a father to him, it was strained even further by the news that their relationship had been a lie from the start.

All of this was in the Bishop's files, Father Gilbert knew, including all the encounters with the supernatural. More recently, the suicide of the son of local crime boss Jack Doyle, followed by a series of bizarre murders, and accounts of demonic activity – all involving Father Gilbert – had made the Bishop more concerned. A political and pragmatic man, the Bishop didn't have any regard for apparitions, ghosts, or demons. He had less patience with his clergy getting involved in high-profile police cases. No doubt he felt it was his duty to keep Father Gilbert's "eye on the ball", to make sure "priorities were established and acted upon", to protect Father Gilbert from himself by staying focused on being a *priest*. And so the Bishop committed Father Gilbert to the conference – to watch over him.

What will he say when he finds out I've already met with a detective about a murder case? And the answer was: *Better he doesn't find out.*

Between a row of buildings directly ahead, Father Gilbert caught sight of St Sebastian's. He knew then where he needed to go next.

CHAPTER 4

St Sebastian's Church dated back to the twelfth century, though historians believed it was built on the site of an earlier church and its broken stones had been repurposed to build the walls of the newer building. It was Norman in its design – a large, thick rectangle with arched doorways and windows, a vaulted roof, and a squat tower. At the top of the hill, it was as imposing as any castle.

The path from the town to the church involved steep stairs and intermittent pathways of dirt and rock. It led Father Gilbert through a small park with a bench overlooking Englesea. His messenger bag dug into his shoulder, so he shrugged it off as he sat down, aware once again of his need to go to the gym more often. The town was covered in a dull grey, promising more rain to come.

Father Gilbert thought about his conversation with Gwynn and how it fitted the man to a tee: insightful about the workings of humanity without using any of that insight in his personal life. "I have no regrets," Gwynn had once said to him. "Regret is the result of a flawed perspective, believing we could have changed what we've done. Life is what it is. We do what we do, for better or worse. Regret is a waste of time."

He remembered now that Gwynn had introduced him to his first and only experience with cocaine. It was a "gift" from a lawyer who had been a suspect in a case but got off the hook because of Gwynn's investigative skills. It might have been a pay-off. At the time, Father Gilbert didn't want to know. They were in Gwynn's car behind the Horse and Groom pub and Gwynn had put some on one of his office keys. "Have a bump," he said.

Father Gilbert was curious enough to try it. Just the once. He inhaled the white powder. It burned his sinuses and something dripped into the back of his throat. He thought he smelled modelling clay – the kind kids played with – and then his nose went numb. He could feel his pupils dilate, giving the impression that everything around him was sharper, clearer. He and Gwynn went into the pub and, as he remembered later, he felt friendlier, more social and confident. He flirted with the waitresses with an ease he'd never had before. He didn't want anything to happen with them. He simply enjoyed the sense of power and control he had to do what he normally wouldn't do. Is that what men were feeling when they went to massage parlours or met up with streetwalkers?

The fear of addiction was why he knew then that he'd never touch cocaine again. Gwynn had obviously come to a different conclusion. He'd admitted using the white powder on occasion to help sharpen his senses while dealing with difficult cases. Maybe those occasions increased with time. And maybe Gwynn put it under his catch-all of "no regrets".

Father Gilbert continued up the path. Approaching the front of the church, he quickly saw that its true beauty was in the finer details. The main oak doors were richly carved with images of Christ and the disciples. The tympanum and arches featured symbols of a griffin, mermaids, a lion, and a figure of a sphinx. He had no idea why those symbols would have been significant to the architects or stonemasons.

He pushed open the door and stepped into a small entryway. Two more fat ironclad doors blocked him there. A sign announced that the church was closed due to an "incident". Inquirers with any urgent needs should use the door on the south side of the church.

Father Gilbert went out again and followed a pavement around to the south side, walking under large perpendicular and wheel windows, the images on the stained glass too dark to make out. He found another oak door under a smaller arched entrance and went through.

The dark vestibule just inside had racks of flyers and brochures and a bookcase with missals. A niche in the wall held a bowl with holy water. He touched it and did the sign of the cross as he walked in.

Entering the nave at this midpoint put him on an aisle with a view of thick pillars and dark Victorian pews. He moved past the pillars to get a clearer view of the chancel and altar. Men in black cassocks were silently cleaning up the vandalism from the night before.

Near the lectern, an older priest with white hair watched them, his right elbow cradled in his left arm, his hand pressed against his chin. Though the man was half-turned away, Father Gilbert knew it was Brother Gregory Stearns.

Father Gilbert drew close. "Brother Gregory?"

Brother Gregory turned. He had been frowning, but now his face brightened a little. "Father Gilbert?"

The two men shook hands.

"I'm so sorry about this," Father Gilbert said.

Brother Gregory lifted his hands, in a gesture of *what can you do?* "I only just saw your email about attending the conference." He led Father Gilbert to the front pew, where they sat down. "I planned to drop in on one or two of the speeches, but *this* happened."

Brother Gregory had milk-white wrinkle-free skin that belied his age. His eyes were an intense blue that looked as if they could penetrate any covering, be it skin or façade, to see what truly lay within. In another life, he could have been a matinee idol of the Paul Newman variety.

"What's the damage?" Father Gilbert asked.

Brother Gregory groaned, then pointed to a statue of Jesus in a central alcove behind the altar. "Well, for starters they scratched his eyes out."

Father Gilbert remembered profilers at Scotland Yard theorizing that some serial killers destroyed the eyes of their victims because they didn't like the sense of reproach they felt, or they didn't want their crime to be witnessed, out of a sense of guilt. In other cases, it suggested an angry message to whoever found the body not to look at what the killer didn't want people to see.

"They also clawed away at the Sacred Heart until there was nothing left of it," Brother Gregory added.

A monk with curly brown hair stood on a ladder with a small tin of paint and a paintbrush. He was studying the face of the statue, trying to decide what to do. Father Gilbert noticed that the monk used his sleeve to rub at his own eyes, thinking at first it was to wipe away sweat. He realized it was to clear away tears.

Brother Gregory saw the same thing. "That's Brother Sean," he said softly. "He's been particularly distressed about this."

Another monk wearing plastic gloves was on his knees in front of another alcove, this one empty. He swept at a pile of white plaster; some of it mixed with blue and light brown. "They smashed the statue of Mary. And not just smashed it. It's as if they tried to grind it into dust."

"With what?"

"Sledgehammers? Jackboots? Maybe a tyre lever. But they made a nasty work of it. They urinated on it."

Father Gilbert winced at the desecration.

Brother Gregory pointed to an alcove to the right of the statue of Jesus. "Our statue of St Peter was there. We found it in the woods on the north side. It looked as if they'd tried to hammer a tyre lever into it."

"Where, specifically?"

The monk looked away. "The backside."

"Another violation," Father Gilbert said. "Those aren't random choices."

"What do they mean?"

He hardly knew where to begin to explain. "The eyes and heart of Jesus seem obvious. The vandals didn't want him to see what they were doing; out of guilt or in defiance of any forgiveness he could offer. The heart – especially the *Sacred Heart* – could mean they were attacking his divine love, rejecting it. And the particular way in which the statue of Mary was defiled and destroyed suggests a specific aggression against her specifically, or women in general."

"And Peter?"

"Removing the statue of Peter is less obvious. Maybe they were running out of time to do the damage inside and had to finish the job in the woods. Maybe they thought the noise with the tyre lever would draw too much attention." Father Gilbert sighed. "Where they put the tire-iron suggests a particular kind of violation."

Brother Gregory folded his arms. "I thought this morning that *removing* Peter from the church points to the view held by some ex-Catholic sects that believe the 'Chair of Peter' is vacant – the Papacy is no longer valid."

"That's a symbolic level one wouldn't expect from vandals." Father Gilbert thought about the conference in town. Those kinds of events sometimes brought out the worst protesters – the Ian Paisley-types who had a grievance against any denomination that didn't line up with their interpretation of the Bible. But defiling the statues didn't line up at all.

"It could have been someone with a serious issue against the church, maybe someone who was abused by a priest," the monk said.

"Have you had any accusations?"

"No, thank God. But people take their aggression out on any Catholic church."

Brother Gregory waved a hand at tapestries hung in odd places on the walls. "Those are covering the graffiti. I'd show you, but I can't bear to look at them again."

"What did they use – spray paint?"

"I wish they had," he said. "They wrote with faeces and blood. Foul material to compose the foulest words and images. Profane. Blasphemous. I won't describe it. I can't." He shook his head. "We cleaned off what we could but want an expert in to do a thorough job. I want no trace of it in the stone. The tapestries will keep them covered until then."

"Was there anything unusual about how the graffiti was written?" Father Gilbert asked.

"Unusual?" A sardonic smile crept across the monk's lips. "As in the handwriting or penmanship?"

Father Gilbert smiled, too. It seemed absurd to ask.

"Come to think of it, the spelling was bad," Brother Gregory said. "Letters were missing. It was as if the vandals were writing phonetically."

"For example?"

Brother Gregory frowned. "How can I give an example without being offensive?"

"I'm not easily offended."

"Maybe you aren't, but *I* am," he said, then thought about it. "Instead of *ck*, they used just a *k*. That sort of thing."

Father Gilbert imagined that, in a town with so many foreigners, the vandals might not be literate in English. But that raised more questions than it answered. "You didn't hear anything?" Father Gilbert asked.

"Compline is at 8:15. Brother Max does a round through the buildings at 11:00 and saw nothing amiss. Our dormitory is on the far side of the abbey, so hearing anything from here would be difficult."

"Security alarms?"

"We have an old system that hasn't been working properly. Our insurance company wasn't happy to learn that we haven't had it checked in a couple of years. They may deny our claim."

"How did they get in?"

"We think they came through a door tucked away on the north side that we rarely use. They didn't close it when they left."

"They broke the lock to get in?"

"No. That's where we're puzzled. There was no damage to any of the doors or windows. We suspect they used a key to get in."

Father Gilbert shook his head. "Don't tell me you keep one hidden outside somewhere – under a mat or rock?"

"We're not that stupid," Brother Gregory said, then quickly added with a flicker of a smile, "Well, we aren't that stupid *now*. I found out that one of our brothers had hidden a key in a planter on that side of the church. But it was exactly where he'd left it and the planter was undisturbed. They got in by some other means."

"So they may have had a key and come in through an unused door," Father Gilbert said. "Wouldn't that suggest they have some knowledge of the church?"

"Possibly. We're trying to figure that out."

"When did you discover the break-in?"

"Brother Michael couldn't sleep, so he came to pray around 1:30. The damage was done by then. He came straight to me."

"He's lucky he didn't walk in on them," Father Gilbert observed. "What did the police say?"

Brother Gregory rolled his eyes. "The expected. They'll take the photos and evidence and fingerprinting back and see what turns up. They aren't hopeful about catching anyone. They said it was probably hooligans. Maybe members of a cult."

"Might they be right?"

"I can't believe this is the work of hooligans," he said. "Satanists? Maybe. But we've never had that kind of trouble around here – not even a hint of occultist activity, apart from a few fortune-tellers and the New Age shops. And if it was the work of a cult, they'd have attacked the tabernacle, to steal or destroy any semblance of the Body and Blood. The holy water would have been taken or stolen, too."

"Have you been vandalized before?"

"No. Certainly nothing like this."

"So, why now?" Father Gilbert asked, wondering if the incident was connected to the church conference.

Brother Gregory turned to the priest. "I have a theory. I've been outspoken lately about the corruption in the town."

"What kind of corruption?"

"You name it. It's in the town's DNA – from its history of smuggling and thievery, bootlegging and piracy, to the drugs and sex trade."

"Which have you been outspoken about?"

"Mostly the sex trade," he said. "I ask you: how is it possible for a town this size to have as many businesses dedicated to sex as some sections of London?"

Father Gilbert wondered if Brother Gregory really knew the vast number of sex shops in London.

Brother Gregory continued. "The timing seems undeniable. I made a rather forceful statement to the city council a week ago. And I gave an interview to the local paper only two days ago. You can be sure the people who run the sex industry in the area didn't like it. They sent their people to give me a message."

"Do you know who runs the operations here?"

"The rumour is that Jack Doyle is the puppetmaster."

"Jack Doyle does business here?" Father Gilbert asked. "I thought Southaven was his turf."

"I thought he ruled most of the South Coast," Brother Gregory said. "Didn't you have dealings with him when his son committed suicide?"

"We never met personally," Father Gilbert said, sidestepping the broader and bizarre events surrounding the Stonebridge Killings, as the press called them.

"Surely a man like that is capable of vandalism."

"Of this kind?" Father Gilbert wasn't so sure. "Unless Doyle had given marching orders to a few thugs who embellished his instructions, it's hard to imagine him sanctioning this kind of violence against a church. He'd come after you personally, maybe. But not this way."

"You think more highly of him than I do."

Father Gilbert laughed. "I doubt it. What did the police say?"

"They dismissed it out of hand."

"Why?"

Brother Gregory gave him a *you should know* look.

"You think the police are involved?" Father Gilbert asked.

"Without question." Brother Gregory turned away. The two men sat silently for a moment, watching the monks work to clean up the sins of others – as monks are often called to do.

CHAPTER 5

Venturing back to town, Father Gilbert had an uneasy feeling. He glanced around for the Shadow Man, half-expecting him to be lurking down an alley or in a doorway. He was tempted to shout out, "Stop playing games. If you're there, show yourself!" But he knew he'd only look and sound insane. It was unlikely it would show itself anyway.

He mused about the state of his life, that it had come to regular encounters with demons. That's what the Shadow Man was, without doubt. But he didn't know what *kind* of demon it was. In the hierarchy of the demonic realm, following prey around without actually attacking was an underling's work, something a "scout" would be tasked to do. Maybe they were trying to scare or intimidate him. Or maybe this particular scout, given the job of merely watching him, was being more overt than it should be. Demons, like humans, were seriously susceptible to acts of pride. It wouldn't be enough for it to hide in the shadows. It would feel compelled to say the occasional *boo*, just for the malicious fun of being known.

A theatre marquee caught his eye. "Much Ado About Earnest," it said. Underneath it proclaimed: "The West End Hit!" Father Gilbert had a vague recollection that the play was a comedic mash-up of the plays of William Shakespeare and Oscar Wilde. He had another vague recollection and walked towards the theatre to see if it was borne out.

The poster for the play had all the images one would expect for a farce – a man dressed as a Lady Bracknell-type character, actors with expressions of wide-eyed surprise, consternation, or alarm, characters hiding behind doors and in wardrobes, and a buxom woman looking as if she'd had an unexpected wardrobe malfunction. He couldn't imagine that either William Shakespeare or Oscar Wilde would look with pleasure upon what had been done to their works.

Father Gilbert looked down at the names of the cast. There it was: George Gilbert. *Uncle George.* The George whom Father Gilbert had thought was his father, only to discover late in life that George was an uncle who had taken on the role of father after Father Gilbert's real father had been killed. It was bad casting.

Father Gilbert subdued his automatic reaction to the name – which was to bristle and feel resentment and irritation. George Gilbert was something of a rascal, spending more money than he ever earned, usually on bets. Over the years, Father Gilbert's mother had dug into their savings to bail him out. When she could no longer afford to help, Father Gilbert had felt obligated to step up.

He lingered at the entrance to the theatre. A man in a parcel delivery uniform flung the door open. Father Gilbert took the opportunity to step through before it closed again.

The lobby was decorated in a vintage style of burgundies and golds, in the carpet and the wallpaper, the door handles and the frames. Father Gilbert went to the ticket window where an elderly woman busied herself applying a thick shade of red lipstick to her mouth. She looked up with mild interest when he cleared his throat.

"Box office isn't open yet."

"Is George Gilbert here?"

"George who?"

"He's one of the actors in the play."

"Oh, yes. He used to star in that police show. The one with the detective. Let me check." She picked up a phone and connected to someone in another part of the building. A muffled conversation and then she said to Father Gilbert, "He's not here right now. He'll be back before tonight's show."

"Might I get a message to him?"

She looked put out. "You could go around to the backstage door and leave one with the receptionist there. Or he's staying at the Angel Sea Hotel up the road. You might catch him there."

"Thank you."

"Do you want to buy a ticket?" she asked.

"Perhaps later."

* * *

Father Gilbert recalled seeing the hotel earlier, passing in front of it when he walked to St Sebastian's. Its lobby was modestly sized, done in an art deco style of an imprecise era by an ambitious designer at the international corporation that now owned the hotel. He scribbled a note and left it at the front desk with a young man whose posture and demeanour suggested he wouldn't go far in the world of hospitality services.

As he turned to go, Father Gilbert glanced down a hall leading to the hotel restaurant. The girl he had seen at his own hotel that morning – Cari was her name – now stood talking to another woman dressed in the uniform of the hotel. He lowered his head and walked calmly towards her, afraid that he would frighten her away if she saw him. He glanced up as the other employee walked off. Cari turned in his direction.

He was only a dozen feet away when she saw him. Her expression registered her recognition. She gasped and spun back to a door behind her.

Father Gilbert picked up his pace. "Wait. Please," he called out.

The door had a digital security box on the door handle and she fumbled to punch in a code. It made a loud clicking sound and she shouldered her way in. The door nearly closed on him, but he sandwiched his foot in and shoved it open. He entered a large room filled with baskets on wheels, overflowing with linens. The walls were lined shelves covered with stacks of sheets and towels. A woman dressed in a white uniform was folding napkins on a worktable. Her eyes were on an adjoining hallway, a puzzled look on her face. Then she turned to Father Gilbert and was startled to see him.

"What's all this?" she asked.

He didn't stop to answer, moving from a fast walk to a run as he saw Cari dashing down the corridor ahead of him. She reached another door and, again, fumbled with a security code. It didn't work. She looked up at him, her face a depiction of panic. She tried again. The box on the door gave an annoying beep to indicate that she'd failed a second time.

"I need to talk to you," he said, now within arm's reach. "Please."

She took a deep breath and resigned herself to her fate.

Just then, the woman from the laundry room came up behind him. "What are you doing here?" she demanded. "You're not allowed back here. Employees only."

"I need only a moment," he said to her and turned to Cari again. "You saw it this morning."

"I'll call the manager," the woman said from behind him.

"It is all right," Cari said to the woman in heavily accented English.

The woman looked at Cari, then at Father Gilbert. With a snort, she stomped away.

"You saw the woman – in the water," Father Gilbert said.

Cari nodded. "Dead," she said.

"Dead," he confirmed.

Cari put her face in her hands and began to cry.

* * *

Somewhere down the labyrinth of back rooms in the hotel was a break room with a few small tables and chairs, a compact refrigerator, and a counter with a coffee and tea maker. Cari hit various buttons on the machine to make tea. She grabbed a napkin and dabbed at her eyes and nose as they sat down at one of the tables.

"I'm Father Gilbert," he said. "Father Louis Gilbert. I'm a priest with the Church of England."

Cari gestured to herself. "Cari Erim."

"Where are you from, Cari?"

"Izmir. Turkey." She stood up again and went back to the tea maker. She found mugs in the cupboard and made them both tea. Father Gilbert watched her, afraid that she might still make a run for it. She had dark, wavy hair pulled back and tied into a ponytail. Her face was round and olive-skinned, with a distinctive long nose and large brown eyes with thick black eyelashes. She was of average height and build.

Back at the table, her hands shook as she drank her tea.

"I do not know how I see them," she said.

"Do you know what they are?"

"In my country, we call them *hayalet*."

"What is *haya-a-let*?" he asked, speaking the world carefully to imitate how she'd said it.

"Ghost," she said. "How do *you* see them?"

"I don't know either." He took a drink of his tea. It was hot and tasteless. "You said 'them'. Have you seen more than one?"

She nodded quickly with a look of anguish. He noticed that she had dark circles under her eyes as if she hadn't had a decent night's sleep in a long time. "I see them everywhere. This place" – she gestured as if to mean more than just that room or the hotel – "is filled with *hayalet*. Women, girls, men, boys. Most of the time women. They are sometimes dressed in rags and sometimes in very pretty clothes. But not always clothes from now."

"You mean they look as if they are ghosts from the past? Another time in history?"

"Yes."

Father Gilbert was intrigued. While, at times, he thought he had seen scenes from the past, he hadn't encountered a spectre that had come from the past.

"I think they are trapped," she said. "They are trapped between the living and the dead. Trapped and in pain."

The idea of purgatory came immediately to his mind, though not in a strict Catholic sense. Charles Dickens described something like it in *A Christmas Carol*. He knew of some Anglicans who speculated that purgatory was a kind of "terminal" where departed souls would make a final decision for the afterlife, as C. S. Lewis did in his story *The Great Divorce*.

"Why do you see them? Do they want something from you?"

She shook her head.

"Have you ever asked them?"

"In my anguish I have asked them," she said, her voice trembling.

"Do they answer?"

She shook her head again. "I see them but they do not see me. It is like I am the ghost to them." She brought her hands together, the fingers clawing at each other as if they had an old score to settle. "But the woman this morning saw *you*. Her eyes were on you. Was she speaking to you?"

"No," he said. *Not this time*, he almost added.

"Are we insane?" she asked. He felt the weight of her loneliness, of being apart from the rest of the world and unable to do anything about it.

"I hope not," he said.

"Some days I am afraid I will be. I will begin to scream and never stop."

A stiff man with stiff hair and a stiff, ill-fitting grey suit walked in. He looked at the two of them with an accusing glare. This was the boss the woman in the laundry room must have called.

"Are we conducting a church service in the middle of the workday?" he asked.

"No," Cari said, standing up.

"Good." He turned to Father Gilbert. "This area is for employees only and we already have a chaplain for the hotel, thank you."

Father Gilbert also stood up. He fumbled for his business card and handed it to her. "I would like to talk again."

She took the card, glanced at her boss, then scurried out.

The manager looked at Father Gilbert. "Well?"

"I had to speak with her about a personal matter."

"Then do so in a personal place, not where she works."

"Has she been here long?"

"A few months. Why? Is she in trouble?"

"That depends on how you define 'trouble'," he replied. "Can you show me the way out?"

* * *

A drizzling rain began. Father Gilbert didn't bother with the umbrella, choosing instead to let the rain hit his skin and hair, a cool spray to distract him from the conflicting thoughts ricocheting around his mind. It didn't work. As he looked at the pedestrians and traffic, the shopfronts and doors leading to offices and homes, he thought about the fragile reality most people cling to – and the thin veil separating that reality from the unwanted reality that waits on the other side. One reality is mostly happy, concerned only about paying bills, getting through school, being popular, dealing with family, protecting treasures, finding loved ones, and fulfilling whatever hopes and dreams it afforded. The other is unexpected and chaotic, invasive, brutal, destructive, unreasonable, violent, painful, and often leads to death. It is the sudden blow to the back of the head, the X-ray showing black spots on a lung, the knock at the door by a uniformed officer, the thrust of a knife in a dark alley, the brick through a sleeping child's bedroom window, the speeding lorry driver who didn't see the red light nor the family in the car in front of him. We work so hard to hold onto our reality while a darker reality waits to shatter it.

He thought, too, of an even greater reality; a reality containing hope and faith, grace and strength, love and light, perseverance and joy, redemption and freedom, that rarely invades, but quietly slips past the veil if one lifts it even slightly.

He walked through the doors into the conference and wondered what reality he would encounter. He paused in the front entryway to listen to the beehive hum of energy that came from people meeting and greeting each other and dashing from one event to another. A microphoned voice echoed from a meeting room down a hall. Sounds bounced out of the exhibit area like someone had left dozens of radios on, all playing different broadcasts.

"Out in the rain, eh?" Planer said as he stepped up.

"Have I missed anything?" Father Gilbert asked.

Planer smiled. "Let's see… the Charismatics did a seminar on healing in Room 3A and a woman had her damaged manicure miraculously restored. A group supporting alternative sexuality held a debate in 20C – complete with line drawings. And a youth club held a one-hour hunger strike in the cafeteria."

"Not much, then."

"No, not really." Planer wandered off.

Father Gilbert pulled the schedule out of a side pocket in his messenger bag. He was glad to see he hadn't missed the Bishop's talk on "the issues facing contemporary churches" – a keynote speech – which was later in the afternoon. The rest of the speeches and panel discussions didn't grab his attention, but he knew he had to attend *something*, if only to say he had. He saw one topic – "The Unique

Difficulties of Ancient Churches" – and thought it might hold his interest, since St Mark's was several hundred years old. He checked the location on a digital display on the wall. It was somewhere upstairs.

He took the stairs and, as he passed a makeshift café, a voice called out. "Father Gilbert!"

He turned to see Father Anthony Reagan, an Eastern Orthodox priest, sitting at a table with another man whose back was to him. Father Gilbert knew Father Anthony from various meetings and the occasional meal together whenever they had a chance. Like Father Gilbert, Father Anthony was a late convert to the faith, having become a priest after time as an ad executive in London.

As Father Gilbert approached the table, Father Anthony stood. He was a tall, thin man who looked as if he fasted more than he ever ate. The wild, wavy brown hair that he had unsuccessfully pulled back into a bun and the large beard that covered the upper part of his black robe framed his narrow eyes, prominent cheekbones, and hooked nose. He wore leather sandals, looking as if he was auditioning for a role as Saint Francis.

The two priests shook hands warmly. Father Anthony had a wonderful combination of holiness and energy that attracted Father Gilbert – and many others, too. His parish church was one of the fastest growing in the country.

Father Gilbert looked at the man seated at the table. It was the Moldovan man he'd seen earlier at the police station.

The man recognized him immediately and stood up to shake his hand. He muttered something in his native tongue, then corrected himself to say hello and add, "I am Vadim Dalca."

"Father Gilbert."

"I was hoping I'd run into you," Anthony said. "You see, this man is distraught over his daughter. She's gone missing and he believes she might be in the area."

"I saw him at the police station earlier," Father Gilbert said.

Father Anthony gave him a *why were you at the police station?* look. "Since you used to be a policeman, I had hoped you could give him some advice about what to do."

"He's done the right thing by going to the police."

"He doesn't believe they'll do anything. Is there anything else he might try?" Father Anthony waved to the chairs. "Sit down. Would you like a coffee or anything to drink?"

"I won't, thanks," said Father Gilbert. They sat down and Vadim Dalca looked at him anxiously. "How will we communicate if he doesn't speak English very well?"

"We both speak Russian," Anthony said. "I can help fill in the blanks."

"First, it'd be helpful to know his background and why he believes his daughter is here in Englesea."

Father Anthony translated what Father Gilbert had said. Vadim responded by speaking in a torrent of Russian.

"He's a cabbie in London," Anthony interpreted. "His wife is dead. His daughter, Veronyka, is eighteen. They came to Britain on a visa a year ago. He intends to stay, so three months ago he enrolled her in the Layton School of English in Shepherd's Bush. A man in front of the school talked about how beautiful his daughter was and said she could be a model if they would allow him to photograph her. The man made him nervous. He declined and took Veronyka inside to sign her up for classes. He did not see the man again. Later in the week, Veronyka went for her first evening class – and that's when she disappeared. The people in the school said she never came in for the class. Vadim suspects the man waited for her and took her. He told the police in London but they weren't helpful, apart from filling out a lot of forms. They said she was a runaway. One of thousands."

Vadim reached into his pocket and pulled out a photograph. In it was a beautiful young woman with light brown cat-like eyes, a thin nose, and lush pink lips that defied the need for lipstick and spread into dimples on both sides. She had thick, curly brown hair that spilled onto her shoulders. She wore a tight top and jeans that highlighted a figure more mature than he would have expected on an eighteen-year-old. She stood in front of a red door, the kind one might see in any London bedsit, as if the photo had been taken just before she went out for a night on the town.

"She's lovely," Father Gilbert said and handed the photo back.

"The police said the girl killed last night couldn't be her. So why are you still here? Why do you think your daughter is in Englesea?"

Vadim said through Father Anthony, "There is a School of English here that is the same as the school in London. I walked by today and saw the same man – the one who said he would take photographs – inside. He looked as if he worked with them. It is not a coincidence. I believe my daughter was taken by the man."

"Meaning, also, that you think her abduction has something to do with the school?"

Vadim nodded.

Father Anthony said, "I looked up the school online. They have locations in the major cities around the country." His expression reflected Father Gilbert's own feelings: it was a vain hope that Vadim was right.

Vadim grabbed Father Gilbert's hand, his eyes glistening from tears that threatened to come. "You must help," he said in English. "Bad people have my daughter."

"I don't know how to help," Father Gilbert said, his heart aching as he said it. The Atkins case came rushing back to him as he remembered Patricia Atkins' father pleading with him in the same way. "I'm not a policeman any more."

"But you know how the police operate," Father Anthony said. "You know how to get their attention."

Father Gilbert sighed. "I *did*. But those days are long gone."

"There's nothing you can do?" Father Anthony asked.

Before he could answer, his phone buzzed to indicate he'd received a text. He took the device out of his pocket and looked at the screen. The text was from Gwynn: "Come to the station if you have a few minutes."

He put the phone away and looked at the two men. "The Detective Inspector here is someone I knew at Scotland Yard. I'll speak to him about it." He wasn't sure what to say next. He didn't want to give any false assurances nor make any promises. "I don't want you to get your hopes up."

"Veronyka is in God's hands," Father Anthony reminded Vadim. "Any hope must rest with Him."

* * *

"The autopsy confirmed that she died by drowning," Gwynn said to Father Gilbert in his cubicle.

"In the sea?"

"No. The water in her lungs was straight from a tap, not seawater. And it contained nothing resembling the sewage you'd find at the bottom of the skip. However, her hair had sand and saltwater in it."

"Then she was drowned in a bath or a tank and relocated to the skip via the beach?" Father Gilbert tried to imagine how that would have worked.

Gwynn stood next to his desk, the photos of the dead Anong spread out in front of them. He tapped one with a pencil. "Those bruises you saw in the photo – the ones around her neck and shoulders – suggest she was held down underwater." He tapped another photo, a close-up of Anong's legs. "There are bruises on the outside of her knees, calves, and ankles to suggest she'd kicked against something hard, like the side of a bath, probably as she fought her assailant."

Death by drowning was one of Father Gilbert's personal fears. Though the common belief was that it was peaceful, like falling asleep, he knew better from other cases of drowning he'd investigated. An ME had explained that it was a torturous and excruciating way to die as the body fought against the violent invasion of water into the lungs and the brain rebelled against the loss of the oxygen it needed to function properly.

Father Gilbert looked closely at Anong's ankles. "The bruises actually circle the ankles. Were they bound or shackled?" He looked even closer, then shaped his fingers as if wrapping around a pair of ankles. "Were they gripped by hands?"

Gwynn looked, picked up the autopsy report, and scanned it. "Well-spotted, Gilbert. The ME noted that the ankles had been held tight as if by a pair of hands."

"Any fingerprints on the skin?" Father Gilbert asked.

"Nothing that survived the post-mortem experience."

Father Gilbert constructed the facts into a scenario. "One person holds her down by her neck and shoulders at one end of the bath. Another person pulls her ankles up out of the other end of the bath to leverage her head under the water. So we're talking about *two* killers."

Gwynn rubbed his neck as he thought about it. "*Or* he held her down under the water by her neck and shoulders long enough to subdue her. Then he finished the job by yanking her ankles up to keep her head submerged."

"So that eliminates the BackList Killer," Father Gilbert said.

"Actually, it doesn't. I've seen the reports on his victims, the details the investigators didn't release to the public. Three of the victims had similar bruising around the ankles. The detectives entertained the theory that there were two killers – one holding the ankles while the other did his business. The other theory is that it was one killer and he'd simply grabbed her ankles to move her from one place to another."

"The ME would have known if the ankles were held before or after death. Which was it?"

"Before."

"So the girls were still alive while he was dragging them around by their ankles?"

"Alive, but incapacitated," Gwynn said. "He would stun them with a blow to the head, then move them."

"So, how does that MO fit Anong's murder? Serial killers don't change their patterns of behaviour to that degree."

"The victim in Edinburgh was strangled," he said. "But the detectives don't doubt it was the same killer."

"Why the change? Why did he strangle her?"

"The current theory is that, unlike the other victims, the girl wasn't a prostitute. He may have asked her to do something the others did more willingly for money. When she refused, he strangled her to get control."

Father Gilbert closed his eyes, wanting to push from his imagination the scenes that appeared there. He looked again at the bruised ankles. "Have any of the MEs on the BackList case speculated about the size of his hands?" he asked.

Gwynn looked at the report again. "Average."

"And with Anong?"

"The same. Average, maybe slightly smaller than average."

"Possibly female?"

"Women are rarely serial killers. You know that," Gwynn said. "And don't forget the violations. Only a man could have done those."

"That's true for the BackList murders. But Anong may not have been the victim of that killer."

"So now you think it *wasn't* the BackList Killer?" Gwynn taunted him.

"I only suggested it."

Gwynn folded his arm and leaned back on his desk. "Anong had clearly been with a man around the same time she was killed. I don't see any scenario where a female accomplice makes sense."

"Do we have a conclusive time for the murder?"

"The ME initially guessed around midnight. Now he's expanded the time to 11:30 to 12:30."

"Why so large?"

"The rain and her time in the skip messed up a lot of the data that helps him determine the time of death. And he tends to be conservative about his conclusions." Gwynn glanced at the autopsy report again. "He found soap under her fingernails."

"Soap?"

"If she was drowned in a bath, it's possible she began to claw at the sides when she was pushed under. Her nails may have caught a bar of soap, or even a residue on the sides."

Again, Father Gilbert fought the scenes forming in his mind. He groaned, and then asked, "What kind of soap?"

Gwynn allowed a smile to form around his mouth. "The good news is that it wasn't common shop-bought soap. It's a brand used exclusively by upscale hotels. In this area that would be the Angel Sea Hotel. I had one of my men confirm it."

Father Gilbert thought through the many contingencies for killing her in a hotel room and transporting her all the way to the skip by the seafront.

"I'm going there to talk to the manager," Gwynn said. His look was an invitation. Gwynn's mobile phone beeped. He looked at the screen then wiggled a finger at Father Gilbert. "Come on."

"Where are we going?"

"My tech guy wants to talk to me."

*　*　*

The tech guy was a greasy-haired, spotty man in a closet-sized room on the other side of that floor. The room was jammed with a cluttered worktable and electronic and computer equipment thrown onto more metal shelves than a room that small should have had. Wires and cables hung like vines.

"Nigel Blum, this is Father Gilbert," Gwynn said as they walked in.

Nigel didn't look up from a laptop computer in front of him. "Nice to meet you," he said. "I've been looking over this laptop."

Gwynn said as an aside to Father Gilbert, "We picked this up from Mamasan's place."

"You got the warrant?"

"The magistrate was in an agreeable mood," Gwynn said. "As we expected, the girls had all their answers practised to confirm what Mamasan had said, so that part was useless. But you were right about the mattress. There was a mobile phone hidden in a small box sandwiched inside. She cut a slit in the side, like you thought."

"Is it Anong's phone?"

"We don't know yet. We lifted some fingerprints. I'm having them checked against the ones we got from her corpse."

"Cracking that phone will take some doing, what with passwords and encryption and all that," Nigel said. "But I'll figure it out. If there's data, numbers, or photos on it, I'll get to them."

"We nabbed this laptop from the room next to the girls' little dormitory," Gwynn said.

"Which room?"

"It had a bed with white Christmas lights and a small table."

Father Gilbert remembered it. He took a step closer to the worktable. The screen held a number of small icons with Asian labels. "Is the laptop Anong's?"

"Not specifically," Gwynn replied. "We think all the girls used it – to do emails or video calls or watch bad Asian soap operas."

"They used it for more than that," Nigel said. "I found a program connecting this laptop to one of those webcam sites."

"Webcam sites?" Father Gilbert asked.

"Girls get on a webcam and dance or strip or perform pornographic acts for a paying audience," Nigel answered. "I can show you."

"I'll take your word for it," Father Gilbert said quickly before Nigel could do it.

"Better yet, he can turn the camera on and *we* can do a show," Gwynn said.

"I wouldn't want to meet the kind of person who'd pay to see that," Father Gilbert said.

Nigel moved the mouse around. "The room is where they performed, using the camera on the laptop. I searched the site for Anong. She was listed as one of the 'models'. She logged in a week ago and did her little show for a couple of hours."

"Could you actually see her?" Gwynn asked.

"The site itself is live. I searched the Internet for any archival recordings – you know, made by the guys who watch them. They get their computers to record the girls and then post them on other porn sites later. I found a couple of videos of her."

"Was it bad?" Father Gilbert asked. Somehow, because of the ignobility of her death, he hoped Anong hadn't been all that bad in life. In spite of his experience, he yearned for the "whore with a heart of gold" to exist.

"She was fairly soft-core compared to some of the others," Nigel said. "A lot of tease, mostly, to get the clients to pay her to do more. There was one recorded in what the site calls a 'private room' – where the users pay more money for a special show. But she was fairly restrained there, too. Flirting, teasing, a bit of flash."

Father Gilbert knew that men in his parish dealt with addiction to porn. The problem was rampant. But he avoided looking, even as a matter of research. This was a world that had changed significantly since he was a detective. It was a world he didn't want to know any better than was necessary.

"The good news is that I have a clearer image of her face." Nigel tapped a couple of buttons on the keyboard and an image appeared. Anong was in the bedroom, the Christmas lights twinkling behind her. She looked at the camera with a furtive smile. It was meant to look seductive, but struck Father Gilbert as forced, even sad. Still, she was pretty in an exotic way; far more attractive than the version of her he'd seen in the apparition.

"This may help with finding any potential witnesses the night she was killed," Gwynn said. "At least I have something to show around."

"I've already sent it to you," Nigel said proudly.

"Anything else?" Gwynn asked.

"Nothing for now."

The two men crossed to the door. Gwynn turned back. "Oh, and how about lighting a fire under your pals about those fingerprints?"

"They're having problems."

"With the system?"

Nigel swivelled in his chair to face them. "With Anong's fingerprints."

"What's wrong with them?"

"According to the database, Anong couldn't have been killed last night," he said.

Gwynn frowned. "Why not?"

"Because she died nine years ago."

CHAPTER 6

"It has to be a glitch," Nigel explained.

They were back in Gwynn's cubicle. Gwynn was on the phone – on hold. He'd been trying to talk to someone in the Fingerprint database area in London.

"I've already talked to them," Nigel said, a hint of a teenage whine in his tone. "They're running the fingerprints again. I'll handle it."

"This is ridiculous," Gwynn said. He slammed down the phone.

Father Gilbert watched them with a nostalgic amusement. He knew the frustrations of dealing with bureaucracy while trying to solve a case.

Gwynn glared at Nigel. "Can't you do your tech magic and hack into their system or something?"

"I tried. I *did*," Nigel said. He pushed a nervous hand through his hair. "There's something about her information that keeps kicking me out. At first I thought it was because she was an immigrant. Our data on them is sketchy at best. Then I thought I was being stonewalled for some reason."

"Why?"

He shrugged.

Gwynn drummed his fingers on his desk. "I'll call an old friend." He picked up his mobile phone and began to search it for the phone number.

"Anyone I'd know?" Father Gilbert asked.

"Dan McCormick."

Father Gilbert shook his head. The name was familiar, but it wasn't someone he'd known personally.

"He's in the centre of things. If anyone can find out what's going on, he can."

Nigel gave Father Gilbert a quick, unhappy glance, then skulked out of the room.

Father Gilbert was aware of how long he'd been away from the conference. "I'll catch up with you later," he said to Gwynn.

Gwynn nodded.

Then Father Gilbert remembered his promise. "The man who was here earlier – searching for his daughter—"

"What about him?"

"I bumped into him again. He's understandably distressed. I said I'd mention it to you, to see if you could help."

Gwynn's expression reflected what Father Gilbert already knew: it wouldn't be a priority while he was investigating a murder case. "I'll get one of my men on it," Gwynn said diplomatically.

"Thanks." But Father Gilbert knew the reality. It was London's case, not Gwynn's.

Father Gilbert left the station with every intention of returning to the conference. But the feeling that he was being watched stayed with him. He looked around for the Shadow Man or anyone else who might be looking for him. Under the awning of a newsagent's, he saw a man pretending to look at a magazine. The long coat didn't quite cover the longer robe beneath. He also recognized the thick, curly hair on his head. It was one of the brothers Father Gilbert had seen at St Sebastian's. He knew it wasn't a coincidence and crossed the street.

The brother looked up from his magazine, startled to see him coming.

"Brother Sean?" Father Gilbert said as he approached.

Brother Sean was flustered. "Yes. Hello, Father." He shoved the magazine back onto the stand.

"Were you looking for me?"

"No," he said, then countered with a "Yes" and then a stammer of "Well, actually I—" and finally fell into a painful silence.

Father Gilbert held out a hand to test for rain. It had stopped. "I was thinking about walking to the pier. I'd like some company, if you have the time."

Brother Sean lowered his head, shoving his hands into his coat pockets. They walked on.

Father Gilbert didn't say anything until they'd crossed over to the seafront side of the road and a path that led to the pier. "How do you like life at St Sebastian's – apart from the vandalism?" he asked.

"To be honest, Father, I don't think I'm suited to it," Brother Sean said.

"St Sebastian's or a vocation as a priest?"

Brother Sean grimaced.

"Is that why you wanted to talk to me?"

"In part," Brother Sean said. "I know about you. About your reputation."

"My reputation for what?"

"You deal with... dark things."

"Don't we all?"

"Darker." He kept his eyes on the pavement ahead. "I've struggled with temptation my entire life. Abnormally so."

"What kinds of temptations?"

"Lust and everything that goes with it. I am... disordered."

"I don't think there's anything abnormal about that," Father Gilbert said.

The creases in the young man's forehead pressed together in an unspoken anguish. "Sometimes I think I'm possessed."

"What makes you think so?"

"Because..." his voice trailed off. "Father, if anyone lifted up the rock that is my mind and saw the disgusting filth underneath I'd be arrested."

"What are you talking about? Women, men, children, animals, small appliances? Just how bad is it?"

He looked indignant. "Women," he said, as if the answer was obvious. "I'm not interested in any of those other things."

"So far I'm not hearing anything that seems as extreme as you may be feeling."

"I have a vivid imagination," he said.

"Do you translate what you imagine into action?"

Brother Sean fell silent again.

"I'm sure you've investigated the criteria for possession," Father

Gilbert said. "And you must know that habit, addictions, even psychological breaks can look like possession."

"Maybe 'possession' is the wrong word."

"Give me another word."

He groaned. "I don't want to quibble about words. It's not about words."

"What is it about?"

Brother Sean slumped, looking as if he wanted to shrink into his coat. "Maybe this was a mistake."

They returned to silence. A man stood with his dog on a patch of grass to the left. Cars and buses moved past to the right. "Have you spoken to Brother Gregory about your struggles?"

"Yes."

"And?"

"He thinks I'm mentally unstable."

"He said that to you?"

"No. But I can tell it's what he thinks."

Father Gilbert smiled. "Mind-reading is one of your gifts?"

Brother Sean shot him a disapproving look.

"Unless he says so outright, you shouldn't presume to know what he thinks," Father Gilbert said.

They walked on. An ice cream vendor leaned on the counter of his hut, thumbing the screen of his mobile phone.

Father Gilbert asked, "Did you join the Order because you thought it would give you an escape from your temptations?"

He gave a shrug. "Sometimes I wonder. Though my heart's desire is to serve people."

"How?"

"I want to give them hope. To show them that there is a better way to live. I want to rescue them from all this *stuff*." He gestured to the lights on the pier, colourful smudges through a grey haze. "They're the invisible chains we shackle ourselves with. I want to help people break those chains."

"You don't have to put on a monk's robe to do that."

"I thought God called me," he said.

"To be a monk, specifically?"

A nod.

"You're not sure now?"

"I'm confused." Brother Sean sighed deeply.

"Why did you want to talk to me?"

"Because I thought you would listen," Brother Sean said, like an accusation. "Brother Gregory is so busy with his *causes* – fighting the townspeople about the *issues* – that he doesn't have time to listen. He doesn't understand."

"I haven't heard enough to understand anything," Father Gilbert said. "Something else is nagging at you. What aren't you telling me?"

Brother Sean's face screwed up. His eyes filled with tears. There was a hitch in his voice as he said, "The girl who was murdered."

"What about her?"

"It's terrible," he said. "I'm to blame."

"How?"

He shook his head. "I don't know how to say it."

Father Gilbert thought over his next words carefully, keeping his voice calm. "Did you kill her?"

Brother Sean stopped and looked at Father Gilbert. His eyes were red-rimmed. His face was pale. "Yes."

Father Gilbert heard the "yes" but didn't believe it. Confessions rarely worked this way. But it wasn't for him to second-guess the moment. "Sean, if that's true, we have to turn around and go to the police."

His eyes narrowed, a sneer came to the corner of his lips. "They won't believe what I have to say."

"They will if you killed her."

"The police are in on it," Brother Sean said, a fury replacing the tears in his eyes. "It's all corruption. Everything in this town is corrupt. We're all culpable. We're all victims. You, better than anyone, should see it."

"Should I?"

His face filled with disappointment. "I thought you would understand."

"I'm trying to."

"No. This was a mistake." With surprising swiftness, Brother

Sean pivoted himself at the road, leaping in front of a car that had to hit its brakes. The driver slammed on the horn. Brother Sean ran across another lane of traffic and up the street. Father Gilbert tried to follow but the light was against him and the traffic flow cut him off. He put up a hand to stop the cars. Some did; others ignored him and barrelled through. A bus stopped two lanes over, blocking his view. He moved to the left and the right, craning his neck to see where Sean had gone. By the time he'd made it to the other side of the road, there was no sight of the monk. He jogged up to one cross street and then another. The roads split off into alleyways. Brother Sean could be anywhere.

* * *

"I don't believe it," Brother Gregory said, his voice a thin representation of itself on Father Gilbert's phone.

"I'm only telling you what Sean said."

"It may be what he said, but it's not what he meant," Brother Gregory said firmly.

"So he said the same thing to you?"

"No, not about the murder," he said, his tone taut. "He told me this morning that the vandalism was his fault."

"Why would he say that?"

"For some reason, he wants to take the blame for things he can't possibly control."

"Is he mentally ill?"

Brother Gregory was silent for a moment. "He has trouble with depression. It's complicated."

Father Gilbert wondered if Brother Gregory would lie to protect his novice. "Where was he last night between 11:30 and 12:30?"

"Here. In his room."

"Are you sure?"

He hesitated. "Yes."

"Brother Gregory, are you *sure*?" Father Gilbert asked. He glanced around. He had stepped into the porch of a small medical office to avoid the new-falling rain and his voice boomed against the glass around him. "You're willing to be his alibi?"

"I'll talk to the other brothers to confirm it. But I'm sure he was here. He couldn't have left without one of us knowing."

"I have to tell the police."

"Please don't," he said quickly. "Not yet. Let me talk to Sean first."

"How? Will he contact you?"

"He'll come back here."

"He should be found, not waited for."

"Trust me," Brother Gregory said. "I've been dealing with Sean from the beginning. Whatever his problems, he isn't capable of murder. He's no threat to anyone. Let me handle it. I'll call you back."

Brother Gregory hung up.

Father Gilbert held the phone and stood for a moment to think. Brother Gregory was convinced about Brother Sean. Father Gilbert wasn't. Their conversation, Sean's agitation and admission of his sexual struggles, easily fit the profile of a killer who might succumb to temptation by meeting up with a prostitute. Then, after living out his fantasy, he'd feel shame and anger – directing those feelings against the woman who'd been party to his sin. Anong may have been the one to suffer.

He knew, too, that it was his duty – his responsibility – to tell Detective Inspector Gwynn about Brother Sean. In spite of Brother Gregory's plea, he had to make the call.

A man walked past him to the office doors, eyeing him suspiciously. Father Gilbert nodded and moved onto the pavement. Hunching over to shield the screen from the rain, he found Gwynn's number and dialled. It rang a few times.

Just as Father Gilbert thought it would go to voicemail, Gwynn himself barked, "Hello!"

"It's Gilbert. Where are you?"

"At the Angel Sea Hotel. I just got here. Where are you?"

The hotel was just around the corner. It would be better to talk to the Detective Inspector in person. "I'm coming your way. We need to talk."

Father Gilbert took only a few steps when his phone rang. He put it to his ear and said, "Hello?"

"Louis?" – pronounced *Lou-ee*. George Gilbert was the only person in the world who called him that.

"Uncle George."

"I got your note. Would you like to meet up for drinks at my hotel?"

"When?"

"Now. I have time before the evening show."

"I'll be there in a few minutes."

"I'll be at the bar."

* * *

Father Gilbert often thought in terms of contingencies. It was part of his wiring. If that happens, then this, this, or this might follow. It wasn't that he was particularly clever or analytical. He suspected it was born of the anxiety that comes from being the only child of a woman who was, for the most part, a single mother. He'd always considered how his actions would impact her – a side-trip to somewhere unexpected on the way home from school, staying later than expected at a friend's house, getting a bad grade, or getting roughed up by one of the neighbourhood bullies. How would she feel? Would it add to her stress? If I do this, then what will follow?

Thinking about contingencies was also a means of protection. Anticipating what might happen – what could go wrong – allowed him to avoid potential problems.

His spiritual director also suggested that it was a form of control. A contingency plan gave him a sense of being in control of his life, especially when he had no control.

Over time, thinking about contingencies spilled into all aspects of his life. He anticipated outcomes, based on the people or circumstances involved. This kind of thinking set him up to become a policeman and served him well as a detective.

A car sped past, nearly spraying him with puddle water. He stepped back and realized how his propensity to think about contingencies was one of the reasons he hated to drive a car. This route versus that route, this offensive driver versus that oblivious driver, entering the car park this way versus using the other entrance to avoid traffic, anticipating the pedestrians, the rain versus snow, roadworks versus capricious traffic lights, all required more brain cells than he wanted to give them.

He now thought of Brother Sean and the various contingencies that might be at play for the young monk. If Sean didn't return to St Sebastian's, where would he go? What would Detective Inspector Gwynn do with what Father Gilbert was about to tell him? Apart from a confession, was there proof that Sean had killed Anong?

Father Gilbert walked faster, his pace picking up as his thinking sped up. How could a monk without any financial means secure the services of a prostitute? Where would they meet so that he had the opportunity to kill her – and not just kill her, but kill her in a bath – and not just in any bath, but a bath where there would also be a particular brand of luxury soap? It didn't line up.

By the time he arrived at the door of the Angel Sea Hotel, he was less convinced that Sean had committed a crime or that he should tell Detective Inspector Gwynn about it. Not yet. He'd allow Brother Gregory time to find Sean and get to the truth of his confession.

As he entered the lobby, he hoped he wasn't making a mistake.

* * *

George wasn't in the bar, so Father Gilbert went on the hunt for DI Gwynn. The woman at the front desk said he was in the manager's office, behind the desk and down the hall on the right. He hoped it wasn't the same manager he'd met earlier.

He entered one door that led to a small cluster of glass-walled offices. The staff in each sat behind desks and talked on the telephones. He spied the manager's office – the only solid-walled room in the area – and tapped on the closed door.

"Come in," came the muffled response.

He opened the door and peered in. Gwynn sat in a visitor's chair with a box of soap in his hand. He was holding it up like he'd been given the Hope Diamond.

The man behind the desk sat in his chair as stiff and straight as a pencil. It was the boss Father Gilbert had met in the back room. His eyes narrowed when he saw who was at the door. "*You*. What is it now?"

"I'm with him," Father Gilbert said, hooking a thumb at Gwynn.

Gwynn looked at the two men. "You know each other?"

"He was here earlier," said the manager. The desk plate identified him as Mark Pinbrook. "Is Cari involved in this inquiry?"

"No. She has nothing to do with it," Father Gilbert said quickly.

Gwynn looked perplexed. "Who is Cari?"

"A personal matter." Father Gilbert was anxious to change the subject. "Is that the brand of soap?"

Gwynn handed him the box. "This is it. I'll take it back for analysis."

Pinbrook frowned as if that specific box of soap had committed the crime. "It's unlikely that a girl could have been murdered here without our knowing."

"That's what everyone thinks until it happens," Gwynn said.

"English Lavender," the box announced in swirling letters. "The luxurious way to caress your skin."

"What about the photo?" Gwynn asked.

Pinbrook held up a photo of Anong – a close-up from the computer image Father Gilbert had seen in the tech's workroom. "I've seen her here from time to time. I suspected she was on the game."

"What made you think so?" Father Gilbert asked, turning the box of soap over in his hands.

"The way she was dressed. Tight, provocative clothes, heavy make-up."

"That's how all the girls dress these days," Gwynn said.

Father Gilbert handed the box of soap back to Gwynn. "Did she wear a necklace?"

"That's not a detail I would have noticed," Pinbrook said. "Why?"

"One is missing that she may have worn." Father Gilbert asked, "Do you have a lost and found?"

"In my safe." Pinbrook crossed the office to a safe on the floor next to a credenza. He kneeled and punched a code into the electronic pad. Opening the door by a small handle, he pulled out a small box. "We keep clothes and larger items in a box behind the front desk. Anything the cleaning staff finds that looks valuable goes in here. What kind of necklace am I looking for?"

"Any kind," Gwynn said. He handed him a pen. "But don't touch it if you find one."

The manager rummaged around the box and said softly, "Oh. Margaret must have put this in here." He used the pen to hook something and lifted it up.

The necklace consisted of a silver chain and a prancing horse enclosed in a circle.

"Unless all the girls are wearing this necklace, it's hers." Gwynn reached into his jacket pocket and pulled out a small plastic evidence bag. He opened it wide for the manager to drop the necklace in. Then he sealed it up. "Who is Margaret?"

"My assistant. She's the only other employee who has the code to the safe. She works mornings."

"Where was it found?" Father Gilbert asked.

"I'll have to ask the cleaning staff," he replied. His expression had become more distressed as he picked up the phone. "It doesn't mean she was murdered here," he insisted. He punched three numbers. "Have the cleaning staff gone home?"

A voice responded, the words unintelligible.

"Do you know who turned in a necklace?"

The voice went quiet, and then came back with a burst of chatter.

"Find out," Pinbrook said. "I need the room number. And ring Margaret. Tell her I need to talk to her." He hung up.

"How many doors are there to get in and out of this place?" Gwynn asked.

"Ah!" Pinbrook said, raising his index finger as if he'd just scored a point. "All the doors in the hotel, apart from the front, are hooked to emergency alarms. If anyone goes in or out the staff would know. The front door is the only way in or out without raising an alarm."

Gwynn didn't look impressed. "Where are the recordings from your security cameras?"

The manager's little moment of victory was suddenly snatched away. He looked sheepishly at the Detective Inspector. "We have only one working camera – at the front desk."

"What about the others? I saw them in the halls."

"They're not actually working yet. That's Phase *Two* of our renovation."

"Do you record everything that happens at the front desk?" Father Gilbert asked.

Pinbrook looked at him as if he'd asked an absurd question. "Of course."

"May I see those recordings from nine to one last night?" Gwynn asked.

"I can arrange that."

"I'll wait," Gwynn said. To Father Gilbert, he added, "You don't have to."

"I'm meeting someone in the bar anyway," Father Gilbert said and moved to the door.

Gwynn stood up. "A quick word in the hall before you go."

They stepped out of the office, through the collection of outer offices, and into the hall.

Gwynn glanced around, and then said in a low voice, "I called London about Anong's fingerprints. Just to play fair, I went through the normal channels first. I got stonewalled. At first they said they didn't have anything. Then they said they could only confirm her death. I asked to see the files they used to confirm her death and they said they didn't have any. Just a line on the computer. Lost in the Immigration Department, they said. It was a bureaucratic runaround."

"I thought you had a friend there."

"Dan McCormick. I asked him to look into it personally. All he could find was a death certificate from nine years ago and a police report. She'd been killed in London after a hit-and-run. The police only knew her name because of the ID in her purse – some kind of card from Thailand. No response from Thailand's embassy after the death was reported to them. The driver of the vehicle has never been found. They're treating it as a cold case."

Father Gilbert shook his head. "So, how does a dead woman wind up being murdered nine years after her death?"

CHAPTER 7

Father Gilbert entered the hotel bar. It had the generic look of most seaside bars: the walls were covered with paintings of long-forgotten or imaginary beaches, ships with billowing sails, majestic sunsets spilling an orange glow on rippling waves. Faux golden sconces hung between the paintings, giving off a feeble yellow light. A man sat hunched over the bar at one end. Another man leaned against the bar at the other end, watching a match on the television above the bartender's head. Glasses and bottles glowed under a fluorescent light.

George Gilbert was sitting at a table, looking up helplessly at a heavy woman standing next to him.

"You're on that show, aren't you?" the woman was saying as Father Gilbert came close. "That television show about the retired cop who keeps getting dragged into cases. *Suspicious Times*, is it?"

"*Suspicious Minds*," George said.

"I've never watched it, but I hear it's good," she cooed.

"I'm glad someone thinks so."

"And you used to be in that show about the other cop who wasn't retired. You did it years and years and years ago."

"*The Rag and Bottle Detective*."

"No. The other one," she said.

"It's the only one I did."

"That can't be right. I'm sure it was you. It was that other show about the detective who came from a crime family."

"Not my show," George said, with a glance to Father Gilbert, then back to the woman. "Perhaps you're confusing me with someone else."

"Like who?" she asked.

"You want me to figure out who you're confusing me with?"

She chuckled. "You're the detective." She began to dig into her handbag. "Well, whoever you are, can I have your autograph?"

"Not a chance," George said. He directed his attention to Father Gilbert, standing up with his back to the woman. "Louis!"

The woman looked confused as they shook hands.

"Sit down. I'll order drinks," George said. Ignoring the woman, he walked over to the bar.

She watched him, stunned. Then she looked at Father Gilbert as if he should help her somehow.

"*I'll* give you my autograph if you want it," Father Gilbert said with a smile.

The woman eyed him. "Are you a famous actor?"

"No."

"Then why are you dressed as a priest?"

"Because I *am* a priest."

"Are you a priest like he's a detective?"

"No."

"Good. Because he isn't much of a detective." She looked over at George and said loudly, "I don't think we'll watch your show any more."

"I'm sure I'll miss you," George said.

The woman made a *harrumph* noise, turned her nose up, and walked away.

George returned with the drinks, placing them on the table.

Father Gilbert sat down, lifting his glass. "What is it?"

"A gin and tonic."

"I never liked gin and tonic," Father Gilbert said. "You know that."

"Do I? Oh. Then I'll drink it." He pulled the glass to his side of the table. "Tell the bartender what you want. Put it on my room."

There was a time when Father Gilbert would have been deeply irritated by George's casual inconsideration. But, apart from any of the other benefits of his sabbatical, he came to the realization that George would never change and it was a waste of emotion to try to change him, through either complaint or coercion.

"I'm all right," he said.

George took a long, luxuriant drink. His face was deeply creased, with the deepest lines around his forehead and eyes. His cheeks were sunken with red splotches. His nose had a scattering of tiny white hairs sticking out of the pores, with thin broken veins weaving like roads on a map across his skin. His lips, a faded pink, were bruised in one corner. But his eyes were a crystal blue and maintained a youthful alertness. It was George's eyes that often caught women's attention.

"How are you, Uncle George?"

George gazed at him. "I'm old. That's the sum of it. I'm old and I'm tired. I don't enjoy the things I once enjoyed."

"Is that age or maturity?"

A caustic smile and he took another drink. "I'd like to retire."

"I don't believe it. You – give up acting?"

"I'm serious this time," he said. "I want to retire."

"What's stopping you?" Father Gilbert asked.

"An ongoing lack of funds," George replied. He put the drink to his lips.

"Surely you've saved *something*," Father Gilbert said. "You couldn't have gambled it all away."

George gave him a guilty look.

"Honestly, Uncle George. Have you?"

"No comment." A waitress in a tight dress walked past. Without any discretion, George watched as she crossed to the bar. She must have sensed his eyes on her because she suddenly turned and looked at him. He smiled. She smiled back just before she disappeared through the door into the kitchen.

"Stop it," Father Gilbert said.

He lifted his glass again. "My eyes are the only things that work any more."

"I don't want to hear about it," Father Gilbert said. It was often his role to play the straight man to his uncle's antics.

George turned to face him. "What about you? What are you doing here?"

"I'm here for a church conference."

He rolled his eyes. "Maybe my life isn't so bad after all." He drained his glass.

There was an affectation about George's behaviour. The way he held his glass. The timing for his drinks. It seemed calculated, as if he were playing a role. Father Gilbert braced himself. Usually this kind of behaviour meant that George was leading up to something – a need for money or to deliver bad news.

"I did a tour in America, you know," George said casually.

"I didn't know."

"I was Polonius in an abridged version of *Hamlet*."

"Abridged? How does one abridge *Hamlet*?"

"Our writer did it with a rusty axe."

"How did it go? Were you well-reviewed?"

George nodded. "In Cincinnati. I wouldn't expect them to know any better." He rubbed the rim of his glass with his thumb. "We played Boston."

"I thought the city banned your troupe after that production you did of *1776*."

"It wasn't a ban," he said defensively. "They simply closed the production and asked us to leave. Who knew such a liberal city could be so closed-minded?"

"Uncle George, you played Benjamin Franklin as a *drag queen*. What did you expect?"

"Accolades, my boy. I always expect accolades."

They were silent for a moment. George started the second drink.

Father Gilbert decided not to let the charade carry on. "All right, out with it. What are you not telling me?"

George slowly turned the glass between his fingers. "I saw her," he said.

Father Gilbert almost asked *who?* – and then he knew. His daughter. The one he hadn't known he had. The one he'd learned about only because his mother had died and left clues for him to follow. "You saw Clare?"

"And her husband Robert. He works for some kind of technological company outside Boston."

Unsure of what to say next, he asked, "How is she?"

"Fortunately, she bears little resemblance to you," George said in an attempt to lighten the situation.

Father Gilbert thought about having that drink. It gnawed at him that his Uncle George could see his daughter while he couldn't. She didn't know he existed. She believed her father was a man named Kenneth Perry, a vicar from Berkshire. Katherine, her mother, wanted it that way. She didn't believe it would serve any purpose telling her daughter the truth now. *If not now, when?* he wondered. Maybe never.

"How does she know you?" he asked.

"I'm the husband of Grandma Clare, the old friend of her mother."

"She calls you *Grandpa* George?" Father Gilbert asked, resenting his estrangement.

"No. Funny enough, she calls me Uncle George. I'm not sure why."

"At least she calls you something." Father Gilbert knew he sounded petulant.

"What about Katherine? Do you ever see her?" George asked. "She lives in Southaven, doesn't she? That's near you."

"I haven't. I was away on sabbatical for a while, you know."

"Oh, yes. Your breakdown," George said.

Father Gilbert sat up straight. "It wasn't a *breakdown*."

"It certainly wasn't a *sabbatical*," George said, with a small smile at having goaded the priest.

Father Gilbert folded his arms and sat back again. He didn't want to talk about his personal feelings with George. That had never been the nature of their relationship, even when he had thought George was his father.

"Not that I blame you," George continued. "You had one shock after another."

Worse than being goaded was having George commiserate with him. "Thanks."

"I hope you're not angry with her," George said.

"With who? Katherine? Why should I be? I got her pregnant and abandoned her. She had every right to be angry with *me*."

"You didn't abandon her. You didn't know."

Father Gilbert glared at him. "Just like I didn't know that you weren't really my father. Or that, for years, my mother was playing grandmother to a daughter I didn't know I had. No, I'm not angry with anybody."

"Good. You're not angry," George said. "I'm glad I asked."

It took quite a few sessions with his spiritual director at the monastery for Father Gilbert to acknowledge that the real source of his anger was with his mother. She was the one who'd kept so many secrets from him. And though he understood why she had, it was a struggle to forgive her. And he believed he had. But the strength of his feelings now made him wonder.

George gave a long exhalation as his eyes scanned the room, probably in search of the waitress. "I'm sorry. I shouldn't have mentioned it."

"It's all right. I'd rather you told me," Father Gilbert said, meaning it. "I'm not angry with you, really. It's just an emotional sore spot."

George's eyes fixed on something behind Father Gilbert.

"Gilbert," Gwynn said.

Both the priest and the actor said, "Yes?"

Gwynn came up to the table and looked at them both. "Father and son?"

"Uncle," Father Gilbert clarified. "DI Morris Gwynn, meet George Gilbert, star of stage and screen."

George shook his hand with an expression of worry. Father Gilbert knew that any encounter with the police was anxiety-inducing for George.

"You're the Rag and Bottle Detective," Gwynn said, suddenly recognizing him. "I joined the police force because of you."

"That can't be true," George said.

"It is," Gwynn said. "I remember watching you and thinking, if *he* can do it, then so can I."

"It's kind of you to say so." George smiled at first, and then he raised an eyebrow as if the compliment might actually be a veiled insult.

"Have you finished with the manager?" Father Gilbert asked Gwynn.

"No one on the cleaning staff can remember in which room the necklace had been found."

"Are you working on a case?" George asked.

Gwynn put a hand on Father Gilbert's shoulder and patted him as a gesture of appreciation. "Your nephew is consulting."

George gave Father Gilbert a smirk and shook his head slowly. "You don't know how to stop, do you?"

Father Gilbert shrugged.

* * *

Before parting, George promised to leave tickets at the box office for the two men, if they wanted to see the play that night. Father Gilbert said he might try, though he still hadn't actually attended any of the meetings at the conference. Gwynn said it was unlikely he could go, considering his current workload. George went off to get ready for his evening performance. Father Gilbert and Gwynn walked back towards the police station.

"Are you planning to go to that conference?" Gwynn asked.

"I have to. My Bishop will never forgive me if I don't," Father Gilbert replied.

Gwynn smiled. "I thought Bishops were all about forgiveness."

"They should be," Father Gilbert said. "Did you look at the security footage?"

"It wasn't helpful. The camera is positioned to keep an eye on the employee and the cash drawer, not the customers."

"That isn't a surprise." Pinbrook struck Father Gilbert as the kind of person who'd be more suspicious of his own staff than of complete strangers.

"The only people you could see were those who stepped up to the desk directly. She wouldn't have done that if she came to meet a client. He'd have given her a room number."

Father Gilbert felt a few drops of rain hit his forehead. "Do you know anything about the Layton School of English?"

Gwynn gave him a sideways glance, and then said, "English is my first language. Though you wouldn't think so to hear me talk."

"There's one here in Englesea. Have you heard anything questionable about it?"

"Give me an example of 'questionable'."

"Could it be a front for kidnapping girls and putting them into the sex trade?"

Gwynn broke stride, slowing down to look at Father Gilbert. "Are you serious? Where did that idea come from?"

"Vadim. The Moldovan man who's looking for his daughter. He thinks she was kidnapped by a man who works at a branch in London."

"I'm aware of a lot of what's going on in this town," Gwynn said. "The Layton School of English hasn't been mentioned. More to the point, the woman who runs it is well-known in this town – highly respected."

"Have you ever been there?"

"I've seen it from the outside. It's in a terraced house on Campbell Street. Most of those houses have been converted into businesses."

"Is it far from here?"

"From where we are now, it's five minutes' walk."

Father Gilbert stopped.

Gwynn laughed. "You're going."

"Since I'm close."

"Try not to offend anyone," he said. "You don't want to upset Lorna Henry."

"Who is Lorna Henry?"

"She runs it."

"I'll be charming and diplomatic."

Gwynn started off again, leaving Father Gilbert. Then he turned around and asked, "Would you like me to put in a good word with your Bishop?"

"It won't help," Father Gilbert called back to him.

* * *

The Layton School of English was just as Gwynn had said: a terraced house converted into a business. It was built of grey stone, with gables that needed paint. Worn steps led up to a glass door that had replaced whatever traditional door had been there before. To the left was a large sign with "Layton School of English" printed in black letters on a white background. To the right of the door was a security pad and intercom button.

Father Gilbert stood on the pavement and could see through the large glass door to a reception area. A man sat at a desk, wearing the white shirt of a security guard. He looked like a weightlifter. Why, Father Gilbert wondered, would such a beefy guard be needed for a school of English?

He ascended the stairs and tugged at the door. It was locked. The security guard gestured towards the security pad and intercom button.

"What can I do for you?" the guard said in a low, melancholy voice through the intercom.

"I'm interested in the school," he said. Then realized he needed to push the button while he spoke. He did and repeated himself.

"Come in."

There was a loud click from the door and Father Gilbert went in.

The desk took up half of the hallway. Further ahead, Father Gilbert saw a couple of closed doors and what looked like the entrance to a larger meeting room. There was a staircase directly behind the guard.

The guard had a thick face, with large lips, a wide nose, and eyes that threatened to disappear into the lines between his heavy brow and large cheeks. He saw Father Gilbert's collar and the huge lips dropped naturally into a frown, as if their weight meant for them to be there all along. "What do you want to know about the school?"

"You can imagine that a man in my job often deals with immigrants who want to learn English. I'd like to be able to recommend a school."

The guard handed him a brochure. "Take this."

Father Gilbert looked at the staircase. "Is this a boarding school? Do students actually live here?"

"Arrangements can be made," the guard said.

"How?"

"You'd have to talk to Lorna Henry, the headmistress."

"Is she here?"

"Not now. Come back tomorrow."

He heard footfall on the stairs and a pair of shapely legs came into view, followed by a young woman wearing a tight dress and a jacket made of artificial fur. A small handbag hung by a thin strap from her shoulder. Still above eye level, she turned in Father Gilbert's direction, noticing his collar.

He recognized her immediately. It was Veronyka Dalca, Vadim's missing daughter.

Father Gilbert's mind raced with what to do. He wanted to announce himself, to tell her that he'd met her father. But his instinct said to hold back. If she was there against her will, then the guard might forcibly intervene. Father Gilbert would lose her and her captors would quickly move her to another location.

She lighted from the last step and looked at the guard. "I'll be back later," she said, her accent like her father's.

"Right," the guard said, more of a grunt than a word. "Do you want a taxi?"

"Is it raining?"

"Not now. But it might."

"I'll walk," she said. "It isn't far."

Veronyka looked at Father Gilbert. "Is something wrong?"

"You look familiar," Father Gilbert said. "You remind me of the daughter of a friend."

"Is that so?" Her voice sounded girlish, but her tone was heavy and jaded. "I hope your friend is a good parent to her." She turned and moved towards the glass door with a walk that made the most of her tight dress.

He wanted to follow her but still considered it risky. If he spoke to her on the street in front of the school, they'd be seen and explanations would have to be given. He'd wait.

Still, he watched as she disappeared down the steps and turned right at the bottom.

The guard rapped a knuckle against the top of the desk. "Put your eyes back in their sockets," he said.

Father Gilbert gave an expression meant to rebuke him. He took out one of his business cards and put it on the desk. "I'll come back tomorrow."

"You do that," said the guard.

Father Gilbert walked quickly down the steps with a half-hope that he might see Veronyka.

He spotted her at the next corner, waiting, and then crossing the street to head into town. He walked quickly, almost a run. The traffic light at the intersection changed against him. He had to stop for the heavy afternoon traffic. For the second time that day he found himself waiting and watching to keep from losing his quarry. She stayed within view, walking straight down the street towards town.

The traffic light changed. He ran across the road, just in time to see her turn to the right. He ran faster, his breath pounding in his ears. Reaching the turn, he slowed, stopped at the corner of a newsagent's, and discreetly peeked around. She was standing in a cobblestone street designated for pedestrians only. Her head was down as she worked her mobile phone. Was she texting? Confirming an address? Checking to find out at what club her friends had gathered? Then she resumed her journey, treading carefully on the uneven stones in her high heels.

He kept pace behind her. Far enough to keep from being noticed should she turn around, close enough not to lose her around the gently curved street. The street itself looked as if it had been transplanted from another time. The houses – pressed together and jutting out from one another like bad teeth – were a mix of styles; some brick, some with the plaster and cross-beams of the Tudor style, some hidden behind thick vines of ivy, roofs slanted at odd angles. If Sherlock Holmes had stepped out of one of the doorways, Father Gilbert wouldn't have been surprised.

She came to the end of the street and turned left onto a main road. Shops and restaurants lined each side. She didn't go far before she took another left and was out of his sight.

Father Gilbert rounded the corner and found himself facing an empty alley. High soot-covered brick walls lined the three sides. There were neither doors nor windows in the walls, and no skips or rubbish bins littering the alley itself. His eye went to the ground. It was dry; there were no puddles, no evidence of the wet day they'd had. Veronyka was nowhere to be seen. There was nowhere she could have gone.

He stepped into the alley and a darkness followed him in. He blinked, trying to focus his eyes. The walls and floor of the alley expanded and stretched as if he was seeing it through a distorted lens. The darkness gaped at him like a mouth screaming in silent terror. The bricks in the walls became translucent, with shadows pressing against them, as if trying to break through from the other side. An arm broke through and reached for him. Then another from the opposite wall. Two hands clawed through on the third wall. He staggered back towards the entrance, watching the shadows move and sway...

A cold breath touched his neck and he spun around quickly. *Nothing* was there. His heart pounded against his chest and into his throat and ears. He looked back into the alley, expecting the shadows to climb out of their black emptiness, but they had retreated again.

He heard the *clip-clop* of a horse's hooves on cobblestone. He turned to see a black horse, adorned with black blinders, come into view. It walked slowly, its head held low. It was harnessed to a black coach with large spoked wheels. The driver sat erect, high atop a bench. His face was thin, skeletal. His eyes were fixed directly ahead. He was dressed in black, with a black top hat and a long black whip that stood upright at his side. Two lamps hung from hooks on each side of him. They seemed to cast a darkness rather than light. The coach was a long rectangular box with a large opening in its side. Ragged red curtains were strategically draped to frame the plain wooden coffin inside.

Father Gilbert stepped to the edge of where the alley met the road. The entire street had changed from its modern self to something from another time. The newsagent directly across the road was now a haberdashery. The estate agent office on the corner to his right was an ironmongery shop. An electronic shop to the left had become a meat shop. A mangy dog sniffed at something below its window. The butcher, in a dark blue apron, stepped out and kicked, the dog scurrying off. A street vendor stood next to a covered cart with pots and pans hanging from hooks. Wooden signs and awnings, painted brick, and handwritten placards had replaced the neon lights and meticulously decorated window fronts.

The hearse continued on, drifting mournfully forward. A solitary woman dressed in a long coat followed it. Her head was covered with a black bonnet, obscuring her face. As she passed in front of Father Gilbert, she slowly turned her head in his direction. The right side of her face was streaked with vertical red and pink scars, as if someone had attacked it with a razor. Her grief-stricken eyes locked on his, then widened as if she was as surprised to see Father Gilbert as he was to see her. She pointed at him and screamed.

"Why are you following me?" a voice demanded. The question didn't come from the woman in front of him, but from behind him in the alley.

He swung around. Veronyka Dalca stood a dozen feet away.

The sounds of modern traffic on the road returned. The alley, which had been shadowed and empty, was now a mess of wet rubbish and rusted skips.

"Well?" Veronyka had a fierce look in her eye. Whoever or whatever she had become, there was no doubt that she would not be taken without a fight.

"I saw you at the school," he said.

"I know. And you followed me from there. What do you want? I don't do business on the street."

Business. Until she said the word, he had vainly hoped that she was dressed as she was for some other purpose: meeting up with friends, a special occasion. Not *business.*

"I'm not looking for business," he said. He knew she could see his collar. His being a priest clearly meant nothing to her. He felt a pang of sadness.

"Are you looking to convert me, then?" Her smile, which should have been beautiful, was marked with derision.

He was about to say "I met your father today" when a heavy hand fell on his shoulder.

"What's your game?" the guard from the school asked, more of a threat than a question. Father Gilbert understood now. Veronyka had texted her location to the guard so he could come and get rid of the pest.

Father Gilbert jerked his shoulder to get it out from under the thick paw. "I wanted to talk to the young lady."

"What about?" asked the guard.

A man stopped at the entrance to the alley. "Is everything all right here?"

"Beat it," the guard said with a bear-like growl.

The man didn't need to be told twice.

Father Gilbert faced the guard. He stood an inch or two above the priest, his face red and his nostrils flared. A small collection of spit collected in the corners of his mouth. "What's your name?" he asked.

The guard was perplexed by the question. "Derek."

"OK, *Derek*," he said in his *don't mess around with me* voice. "I wanted to ask this young lady about the school."

"What about the school?" Veronyka asked, moving close to the guard.

"I'm a priest and I deal with parishioners who don't speak English as a first language," he said, thinking of two members of St Mark's for whom that was true. At least it wasn't a complete lie. "I'd like to recommend the Layton School but want to know about it."

The guard huffed, "I told you to talk to—"

"I know what you told me," Father Gilbert interrupted. "But I would prefer to get an unvarnished view from someone who lives there, rather than the public relations version your headmistress will give me."

"I have nothing to say about the school," Veronyka said and walked away, disappearing behind the guard and then around the corner.

Derek positioned himself in front of Father Gilbert, just in case he might try to go after her.

"I don't know whether I should be offended or impressed," Father Gilbert said. "I suppose it's good that the school takes the security of its students so seriously. Those are points in your favour."

Derek locked his eyes on Father Gilbert, scrutinizing him. Then he took a couple of steps to the side to suggest that the priest could go. "Don't bother the students. Talk to Lorna Henry," he threatened.

Father Gilbert strode past the guard. Only after he was back on the main road did he let out a long exhalation. He felt queasy. When had he last eaten? The rain fell, quickly and hard. He turned into the door of the first pub he found.

* * *

He sat in the corner of the pub and shivered, his body quaking from head to toe. He wished he'd ordered a coffee rather than a fruit juice. He was tempted to have a pint, then thought of the smell on his breath once he returned to the conference.

Taking out his phone, he dialled Gwynn's number. The call went straight through to voicemail. He left a message for him to call.

He searched his pockets for Vadim's mobile number. Had Father Anthony written it down? He couldn't remember. He looked through the messenger bag with no success. He would look for Father Anthony at the conference centre.

Nibbling on a ploughman's sandwich, he surveyed the pub. It was classically dark-wooded and had been redone with multiple televisions and bright strip-lighting to look more like a sports bar. The result was something that was unlikely to appeal to customers looking for one or the other.

At the bar, a woman dressed in a bright pink top sat alone, her hands wrapped around a small drink. A man in a suit, seated several stools away, signalled the barman for two drinks and approached the woman.

A feeling of dread clung to Father Gilbert like damp air. His mind went back to the ominous alley. The deathly shadows had been real and threatening – not a manifestation of a human spectre, but something far more demonic, as if the inhabitants of Hell itself were about to burst through the walls. He thought, too, about the horse-drawn hearse and the disfigured woman. Clearly it was a scene from the nineteenth century. He thought of Cari Erim, describing ghosts from the past. While it wasn't the first time he had seen images like that, it was the first time he'd actually *engaged* with one. The scarred woman *saw* him and had reacted to his presence.

What was he to make of both experiences? Had he somehow crossed into their realities or had they crossed into his?

The man at the bar was now sitting down next to the woman. He faced her, his body language communicating openness. They talked and drank. He patted her arm lightly. She laughed at something he said and touched his knee. Familiarity and intimacy in the space of ten minutes, maybe fifteen.

Father Gilbert mused on Englesea and Brother Gregory's words came back to him. The town was corrupt. It was in its DNA, he'd said. "From its history of smuggling and thievery, bootlegging and piracy, to the drugs and sex trade."

Could a town be corrupt to its very core? Was it possible that, rather than a benign history shaping a town and its citizens circumstantially, a pervasive evil could infect the very place, like houses built on a toxic waste dumping site that was seeping its poison into the water and food supply, damaging the very bones and blood of those who lived there?

At a table to his right, a woman dressed in blouse and skirt as was stylish in the 1930s sat primly, looking straight ahead. Her hair was fixed in a tight bun. Her red lipstick was smeared across her mouth and onto her cheeks and chin. Her black mascara ran from the corners of her eyes. She sighed deeply and the smell of rotten flesh filled his nostrils. He gagged on his sandwich. She lifted her hands to check her hair, but chains on her wrists stopped them from reaching beyond her chest. She jerked at them a few times as if she didn't understand why she couldn't lift her hands any higher. Father Gilbert's eyes followed the chains down until they disappeared into a deep black pool that covered her feet, the bottom of the table, the legs of the chair, and the wooden floor of the pub.

Father Gilbert closed his eyes, and then opened them again. The woman was still there, but she was now slowly sinking into the black pool. She turned her face to him as all but her head were engulfed. She opened her mouth to scream and the black pool flooded over her lips, and then swallowed her nose and eyes. The top of her stylish bun was the last thing he saw.

The man and woman at the bar left together, his hand on the small of her back as they walked out.

CHAPTER 8

Bishop William Spalding was part of a panel discussion, perched on a stool on the platform of the largest meeting room at the conference. He shared the stage with two other men and a woman.

"At the heart of the issue is the wounded-ness of creation," the Bishop was saying, his voice resonant and smooth.

Father Gilbert saw that the chairs in the back row were all taken. Rather than draw attention to himself by trying to find a seat closer, he stepped over to the back wall.

"We have a distorted view of who we are as men and women," the Bishop continued.

Father Gilbert lost the thread of the Bishop's words almost immediately. Not because there was anything deficient in the Bishop's presentation – he was an excellent speaker – but because Father Gilbert couldn't concentrate on church issues while his mind was on murder, death, confessions, missing girls, a missing priest, and the mysterious dead that seemed to show up randomly regardless of time or place.

He saw the backs of the heads of the many clergy in the room. Suddenly, he envied them. Among their many problems, none were like *his* problems. He didn't feel self-pity about it. He simply yearned for a life less complicated – a life that allowed him to participate in a normal church conference, to talk to other clergy about mundane parish events, to drink too much coffee, to sit and be bored, to take notes or doodle on a page, to pray, to read, without dealing with death.

Reverend Planer stood up from his seat in the back row and moved towards the door, stretching his legs as if in pain. He spied Father Gilbert and sauntered over.

"Where have you been?" he whispered.

"Around," Father Gilbert said. "Have I missed anything?"

"Not much. Only this session on porn," Planer said.

He was surprised. "Is that what this is?"

"You don't think we'd have a crowd this size for anything else, do you?" Planer nodded to the stage. "And here comes the main attraction."

Reverend Andrew Berne had the microphone. He was a fiery evangelical who considered himself the heir apparent to John the Baptist. Given any opportunity to speak, he would denounce the sex-saturated, liquor-soaked, self-indulgent decadence of modern culture. No sin was too small nor pleasure too great to be repudiated.

"I've been waiting for this," Planer said with a grin.

"I'd like to know who decided upon *this* town for our conference," Berne said. He had a distinctive Northern Irish accent. "You can't swing a dead cat without hitting someone or something to do with sex in this town. The whole place is *tainted*. I was speaking with a hotel manager who said the use of porn on the in-room channels increases substantially during religious conferences. We should be *ashamed*."

A few mumbled acclamations came from the audience. Almost everyone shuffled uncomfortably.

"Have you read the history of Englesea?" he asked, his voice booming. "*Incessant* depravity, from the very beginning. Wesley preached here. Did you know that? He wrote later that the people were receptive to the gospel but were unlikely to give up their thievery and piracy to embrace it. It hasn't changed in 200 years."

Father Gilbert wasn't sure if he was arguing for a change of venue or encouraging the assembly to march out for an evening of street evangelism.

Berne reached into his jacket pocket and pulled out newspaper clippings. He held them up like a declaration. "Englesea is an entry-point for illegal aliens – *prostitutes*? They're brought in by boats to work in the sex slave trade."

"Whose boats?" Father Gilbert whispered to Planer. "Who is bringing them in?"

Planer shrugged. "I read that they caught the girls, but not the culprits."

"They're *victims*," the woman on the platform said emphatically. "One of those girls was murdered only last night!"

Father Gilbert thought of Brother Gregory's accusations earlier about Jack Doyle being involved in the local sex trade. Was Doyle bringing the girls in?

Berne seized the moment to launch into a sermon about the great shame of a compromised church that wouldn't face up to evil. "The evil of this town will *fight* because we're here. Be on your guard!"

Father Gilbert's mind drifted off, going again to the report about girls being brought in by boats to Englesea. How did that happen under the watchful eye of Detective Inspector Gwynn and his police force? Were Brother Gregory and Brother Sean right about the police? Were they in on it, too?

* * *

After the session, Father Gilbert moved quickly to catch Father Anthony before he left the room. The priest looked distressed to hear Father Gilbert's account about Veronyka.

"Vadim returned to London this afternoon," he said. "He had to go back to work. I have his phone number on my mobile phone, but left it in my room."

Father Gilbert gave him one of his business cards. "Take this. Give him my number. Meanwhile, I'll tell Detective Inspector Gwynn."

"Let's go to this so-called 'School of English' and get her out of there," Father Anthony said, his hands balling into fists. "Shall we?"

"I'd enjoy nothing more," Father Gilbert said. Unlike Anglican priests, Orthodox priests were prepared to use physical force to do the right thing if necessary. "But it's a bad idea. Not only would we have to fight our way in, but they would likely hide her or move her to another location."

"Shouldn't we take that chance?"

"That's for the police to do," Father Gilbert said, wishing it were that easy. "And I have to admit: there was no obvious coercion or restraint to keep the girl there."

"You know as well as I do that there are more ways to trap a girl like that than with physical restraints."

"Physical restraints?" Bishop Spalding asked as he came up to the two priests. "What on earth could you be talking about?"

Father Anthony caught Father Gilbert's expression and said, "Only that there are spiritual restraints that can bind us up and take us captive. Not all restraints are physical."

"Ah, yes," the Bishop said, as if making the connection. "Pornography."

"Do excuse me. I must go and find my mobile phone," Father Anthony said. He shook the Bishop's hand – and Father Gilbert's – and left them.

"I haven't seen you at all today," the Bishop said. His tone was light even while his eyes were filled with disapproval.

"I've been in and out," said Father Gilbert.

"In and out doing what?" Bishop Spalding asked.

"I bumped into an old friend."

"Here at the conference?"

"He's with the local police. I knew him at Scotland Yard."

The Bishop groaned. "And he wanted to reminisce. Or are you consulting on a case?"

Father Gilbert didn't reply.

"Father, I know how you get drawn into these things," the Bishop said, lowering his voice. "But I must remind you that you're here on *church* business."

"Yes, Bishop."

The Bishop eyed him. "Look, I have you in mind for a special commission. *Lambeth*. The Archbishop of Canterbury. It would be an important career boost. But I can't recommend you if you persistently allow yourself to be distracted."

Father Gilbert nodded. He didn't have strong feelings about career boosts or helping out with a commission at Lambeth Palace. However, he couldn't deny being distracted.

"I don't understand," the Bishop said. "By my estimation, you've now been a priest longer than you were a detective."

"That's true," Father Gilbert said.

"Then why are you compelled to go back to it again and again?"

"I don't *actively* go back to it," Father Gilbert said. How could he tell the Bishop about the appearance of the murdered girl, or anything else that had happened that day? Had he actively worked to be involved in any of it?

"I thought your spiritual retreat would have brought clarity. Honestly, I sometimes wonder if you've chosen the right vocation for yourself." Bishop Spalding didn't wait for a response to the statement. He turned his attention to another vicar standing nearby.

Father Gilbert felt like an unruly student who'd been rebuked by the headmaster. Feelings of inadequacy conflicted with feelings of defiance. The Bishop, who was meant to be his spiritual shepherd, had little understanding or regard for the world in which the priest had found himself. If he could let it go, he would. But it wouldn't let *him* go.

* * *

Father Gilbert mingled as the conference broke for dinner. *See and be seen* was the wisest course of action at the moment. He chatted with his fellow ministers about the weather and the difficulties of keeping youth engaged in church and which restaurants were the best in town and how to find money to repair aging church buildings. A group staying at the Masthead Inn agreed to meet in the dining room there. He didn't want to go, but thought again: *see and be seen.* It would make the Bishop happy.

On the way, he phoned Detective Inspector Gwynn and Brother Gregory, leaving messages for them both to call. He worried about Brother Sean and prayed for the young man's frame of mind and safety.

The rain had stopped again and a dim light resembling a late sun threatened to break through the clouds. The world shimmered around him. The air smelled of wet rope. He was watchful as he passed alleyways and shadowed entries, expecting to see people or scenes that would send chills down his spine and adrenalin through his entire being.

He went to his room at the Masthead Inn and it seemed smaller than it had that morning. Sitting down on the edge of the bed, he picked up the Book of Common Prayer – a pocket-sized leather version – and thumbed to a section he used for evening prayers.

Afterwards, he made his way to the hotel's restaurant. He hesitated as he entered, remembering that morning's encounter with the dead Anong. She didn't appear, though he noticed a spot on the carpet that looked wet and stained.

Planer was sitting with three other men at a table by the front window. "Come on over," he called out.

Father Gilbert knew two of the men – Mark Solegrove and Dan O'Shea, both vicars. The third man was dressed in a smart business suit, though his tie was pulled down and his crisp white shirt was unbuttoned at the collar.

"Nathan Rank," the man said, reaching out his hand.

Father Gilbert shook it and took in the man's demeanour: stylish dark hair, large brown eyes with almost feminine eyelashes, and a face that could have been sculpted as a Greek god – high cheekbones, an aquiline nose, and a decisive mouth.

Planer nudged a chair towards Father Gilbert. "Nathan is one of the organizers for the conference."

Father Gilbert sat down. He remembered the flies swarming out of the window and the Shadow Man on the street outside. He looked up and out, just to be sure they weren't going to give a repeat performance.

Mark Solegrove added in a conspiratorial whisper, "Be careful what you say. He works for an outside agency. *Non*-clergy. We wouldn't want to shock him."

"You can't shock me," Rank said with a smile made up of perfect teeth. "In the hospitality trade, there's little I haven't seen."

"For example?" O'Shea asked. He was thin and wiry, with a mortician-like pallor and sombre voice to match.

Rank gave a slight shrug. "I encounter people from all walks of life and professions. Imagine an entire conference on cement, with the attendees ranging from London CEOs to the owners of construction companies in rural areas. Just coming up with menus for meals was a nightmare. Bangers and mash to duck à l'orange. And dog shows where the people can't seem to understand why the hotels want the dogs kept in portable kennels. I spent four days in Ipswich comforting every breed of dog you can imagine. Dog breeders are worse than parents with babies."

"Ipswich? So you're not local?" O'Shea asked.

"No. I travel all over the country. It's my job to make sure the conferences run the way they should."

"Are you checking on us?" Planer asked. "Is this an informal customer service survey?"

"In a manner of speaking. I like to go around to the hotels and restaurants, just to eavesdrop, to make sure everyone's happy," Rank said.

"You're not staying here, then?" Solegrove asked. His round face and mop of salt-and-pepper hair reminded Father Gilbert of Friar Tuck.

"I'm at the Angel Sea," he said. "Though I'm hardly in my room."

"All right, then. Give us the inside scoop. What's the strangest conference you've had to manage?" Planer asked.

Rank stroked his chin, as if he had to think about it. Though Father Gilbert suspected he'd been asked the question before and already knew the answer. "Probably a fetishists' conference in London. We had three trips to casualty with that one. Don't ask why."

Father Gilbert noticed that the three men looked as if they wanted to.

"There was a conference in Bath for practitioners of black magic, Goths, New Age believers – that sort of thing. That was spooky. The locals locked up their cats for safety."

"Did anything happen?" Solegrove asked.

"One man was arrested for putting a curse on another."

"Surely you can't arrest a man for that."

"You can when the curse involves stabbing the man with a pagan spear."

The men laughed. Rank looked pleased.

"And there was the porn conference I handled in Swansea," Rank continued. "But that was strange only because the sessions were about the *business* of porn. They discussed their troubles in the same way that a conference on oil would talk about the price-per-barrel and refineries. Apart from the skimpy outfits, implants, and steroids, of course."

"I'm relieved," O'Shea said after another round of laughter had finished. "I was afraid you'd say religious conferences like this one are bad."

Rank shook his head. "No. I wouldn't put religious conferences in the top ten of strange experiences."

Solegrove turned to Planer. "He'll know whether it's true or not."

"If what's true?" Rank asked.

Planer leaned in, resting his arms on his knees. "We heard that there's an increase in the use of in-room televised porn at religious conferences."

"I've heard the same rumour," Rank said. "But only the hotel managers will know for sure. Or whatever techie keeps an eye on the website traffic on the hotel's Wi-Fi system."

"To listen to Berne, you'd think the hotels are overrun with prostitutes whenever the clergy come into town," O'Shea said.

"They wouldn't be that obvious, would they?" Rank asked. "Which one of you would want to be seen with a girl coming into your room? You'd sneak out for it, surely."

"Father Gilbert's been sneaking around most of the day," Planer said, a playful accusation. "He's a former policeman. I'll wager he knows where to go without getting caught."

Father Gilbert offered a small smile. "Thank you, Reverend. And as a former policeman, I also know how to find out what's hidden in the search history on your computer."

Planer laughed even as a slight blush rose to his cheeks.

"A policeman-turned-priest?" Rank said. He looked at Father Gilbert with a new appreciation. "I can add that to my list of unusual encounters."

"It's boring," Father Gilbert said.

A waitress walked up to the table. "Something from the bar or would you like to see the dinner menu?"

"Both, please," Planer said, confirming his answer with a quick read of the rest of them.

After she left, O'Shea said, "I can't imagine anyone coming to a conference like this and going off with a prostitute. It's too brazen."

"People get brazen when they travel. It's like they're in a fantasy land where their lives at home can't see them," Rank said. "I don't know why religious people would be any different."

"I would hope that people who profess faith – or claim to adhere to a moral code – don't abandon it just because they're on a business trip," Father Gilbert said, though he knew his hope didn't always match reality.

Rank gave the facial equivalent of a shrug. "I don't know how people are expected to be self-controlled or faithful these days. Sex is everywhere. It's in the very air we breathe. If you watch the telly at all, you'd get the impression that every encounter at the office or in a pub or on the street is an invitation."

"Has that been your experience?" Solegrove asked him.

"I'm not the sort of man to kiss and tell," he said with that sly smile. "I'm just saying that I wouldn't judge any of you if you travelled to a conference like this and took advantage of the local offerings."

Father Gilbert watched Rank as he spoke. There was a hint, ever so subtle, that he might help to facilitate taking advantage of the local offerings if anyone at the table wanted to take him up on it. Was that part of the hospitality services?

"There are consequences," Father Gilbert said.

They looked at him as if they'd forgotten he was there.

"One encounter, one night, one indulgence here doesn't *stay* here," he said. "It goes home with you. It goes back to your church with you. It marks your soul."

Rank chuckled. "If you're not careful, it'll mark you in other ways."

Father Gilbert's mobile phone rang. The screen announced it was Gwynn. He excused himself and moved from the table.

"This is Father Gilbert," he said.

Gwynn's voice was immediately drowned out by an announcement in the background of wherever he was. It could have been the train station, for all the noise. Gwynn stopped speaking, waited for the noise to subside, then started again. "Gilbert. One of your own has been found in an alley. He's only marginally alive."

"One of my own?"

"We couldn't find any ID on him. I hope you can identify him. Come to the medical centre. It's north, beyond the town centre. You won't be able to walk it. I'll send a car."

"I can take a cab. I'll be right there." Father Gilbert returned to the table. "I'm sorry. I have to go."

Rank made as if to stand up. "Is there something I can do?"

"No, thank you," Father Gilbert said, waving him back.

"All the same—"

"Don't worry."

Father Gilbert turned and headed for the front desk.

"He's meeting one of those women we were talking about," Planer said from behind him. The men laughed.

* * *

"It's Brother Sean from St Sebastian's," Father Gilbert said to Detective Inspector Gwynn. They stood at the foot of the hospital bed in a small, dim room. Brother Sean was lying with an oxygen mask obscuring most of his face. His eyes were closed with no movement behind them. There were four long scratches on the left side of his face, close to his ear. His hair was matted down. A white sheet covered his body up to the neck, with wires and tubes dangling from underneath and up to medical equipment on wheels around him.

"Last name?" Gwynn asked.

"I don't know." Father Gilbert took out his phone. "I'll call his superior – Brother Gregory."

The phone rang on the other end and went immediately to Brother Gregory's voicemail. Father Gilbert now suspected the priest was avoiding him. Maybe it was a stall while he tried to find Sean.

"It's Father Gilbert," he said after the tone. "Come to the Englesea Medical Centre. Brother Sean has been hurt. We're in the ward next to casualty." He hung up and turned to Gwynn. "Do you know what happened?"

Gwynn led Father Gilbert out of the room and into the hall; the pale green walls were covered with institutional posters proclaiming preventative programmes giving cautionary advice. Chairs lined the far wall for visitors.

Gwynn said, "We're trying to piece it together. He was found lying in an alley behind a shoe shop. An employee was taking out the rubbish and assumed he was a drunk. Then he saw the scratches and thought something worse had happened."

"They look too large to have been done by an animal," Father Gilbert said.

"They're human, I'm sure." The lines on Gwynn's face were deeper than earlier, suggesting he'd had a hard day or a bit to drink or both. The smell of breath mints was unmistakable.

"Why is he here?" Father Gilbert asked. "Surely he wasn't rendered unconscious by those scratches."

Gwynn looked down the hall towards the nurses' station as two nurses rounded a distant corner, then disappeared around another. "His vital signs were through the roof – blood pressure out of control, heart rate beyond belief. The doctor said he's also in a weakened condition, as if he hasn't eaten in days. That's why he's hooked up to all those machines. They're trying to get it all under control."

"Do they know what caused it?"

"The doctors believe your boy has taken an overdose of drugs," Gwynn replied. "They found an empty bottle of antidepressants in his pocket. So they pumped his stomach."

Father Gilbert thought of Brother Sean's confession. Was a suicide attempt the end-result of his guilt? But something didn't line up. "Do antidepressants accelerate a person's metabolism?"

"You wouldn't think so," Gwynn said. "But apparently they can."

"So we're to believe he got scratched somehow and, in a fit of depression, went into an alley behind a shoe shop to commit suicide?" Father Gilbert asked. Yet another piece that didn't line up. Suicides rarely happened that way.

Gwynn watched him as he said, "The alley behind the shoe shop is shared by the Lily Rose Massage Parlour."

The priest frowned. Was that where Brother Sean had gone after he'd left Father Gilbert? *If* he really had murdered Anong, why would he go there?

Gwynn folded his arms. "What are the chances that this monk

would go to die right behind the place where a murdered prostitute did business? Is there a connection?"

Father Gilbert knew this was the moment to say something, to tell the Detective Inspector what Brother Sean had said. He should have. Everything he once knew as a cop said he must. But his instinct told him to wait. Let it come from Brother Gregory. Or from Brother Sean himself. He bit his lower lip.

Gwynn didn't notice Father Gilbert's silence. "This gives me a good excuse to talk to Mamasan again. The more I find out about Anong, the more questions I have. I don't like having so many unanswered questions."

A nurse slipped past them and into Sean's room. She checked him and then the machines, making notes on a computer tablet. She slipped out again without speaking to either of them.

"Nigel finally got into Anong's mobile phone from the mattress," Gwynn suddenly said.

"Was there anything useful?"

"The photos were interesting: Anong in London with a young girl – she was probably seven or eight years old. They were playing tourists at Big Ben, the Eye, and Buckingham Palace. According to the data, they were taken only a month ago."

He reached into his jacket pocket and took out a small printout of Anong and the young girl. The London Eye rose up behind them in the background. There was no denying the resemblance between Anong and the girl.

"Who is she?"

"Maybe her daughter or a close relative," Gwynn said. "There was certainly a strong family resemblance."

Anong was a mother. The corpse found in a skip was becoming more and more like a human being rather than just a prostitute. She had a name and a life and possibly a daughter. The easy conclusions weren't so easy after all. But where was the girl? Did she know her mother was dead? Who knew to tell her? Mamasan? One of the other women at the Lily Rose?

"May I keep this?" Father Gilbert asked.

"Sure."

The priest pocketed the photo. "Were there any phone numbers in the contact list?"

"Numbers, yes. No names," Gwynn said. "We're checking on what's there. Most are individual calls, probably clients. I'm more interested in the numbers that appear regularly. Especially the ones from the night she was murdered."

Father Gilbert's mind worked through all the bits of information they'd collected. "What about the necklace and the soap?"

"The necklace from the hotel lost-and-found had traces of Anong's skin in the chain. That definitely places her at the hotel. And the soap confirms it."

"So the working theory is that Anong met a client at the hotel. There was violence, the necklace was yanked off her neck, and she was drowned in the bath, which is how the soap got under her fingernails."

"So far it's the only theory that fits," Gwynn said.

"Apart from Anong dying nine years ago in a hit-and-run," Father Gilbert added.

"Yes. There is that." Gwynn rubbed his eyes. "This is messy. I don't like messy."

"You have more mess than just this one," Father Gilbert said, suddenly remembering Vadim. "Veronyka – that missing girl from London – is at the Layton School of English. I saw her. I tried to talk to her."

Gwynn's bloodshot eyes narrowed. "Did she say she was kidnapped?"

"I didn't have time to ask," Father Gilbert said. "But you can be sure she isn't there to learn English."

"Was there evidence of restraint or coercion?"

"Nothing overt."

"So she could be a runaway who decided to make a few bob hustling."

"That's more than I'd assume," Father Gilbert said. He was afraid Gwynn would take the path of least resistance. Labelling Veronyka a runaway was the easy way out.

"It happens."

Father Gilbert weighed in his mind what he was about to say, thinking better of it but speaking anyway. "You said you know most of what goes on in this town and that Layton is a legitimate business."

"I thought it was."

"What about the boats? Did you know about them?"

"What boats?"

"The ones used to bring the girls in."

Gwynn suddenly stiffened. "What are you suggesting?"

"Only that you may not know as much as you think you do about this town."

Gwynn's expression soured. Beneath the statement was the hint of an accusation. "I'm going to talk to Mamasan."

Father Gilbert gestured to Sean. "What about him?"

"You're here, and so is she." Gwynn nodded to a uniformed constable walking towards them. It was a young woman, fresh-faced and bearing two cups of coffee.

She handed one to Gwynn, "Sir."

"Thanks."

To Father Gilbert, she said, "I'm sorry, Father. I'd have brought another if I'd known you were here."

"It's the thought that counts," he replied.

"I'll leave you in her capable hands," Gwynn said.

The phrase led Father Gilbert to think of Nathan Rank and the conversation back at the hotel. "I had a thought about the BackList Killer."

"Aren't we finished with that?" Gwynn asked.

"Do the investigators know what conferences were going on when the various victims were killed? Is it possible the BackList Killer is in the hospitality trade? I met someone earlier who does that for a living. He travels all over the place. Someone like that might have the means and the opportunity to meet and kill those women."

"It's an interesting idea," he said as if he actually thought so. "I'll ask."

They stepped aside while an orderly with an empty gurney rattled past.

Father Gilbert continued, "I wonder if there were any religious conferences happening in those areas at the times of the murders."

"You think the killer is a priest?"

"I'm only asking a question."

Gwynn looked amused. "Maybe I should check *your* alibis."

Father Gilbert gave a look to suggest that anything was possible.

"Arrest him," Gwynn said to the constable.

She was mid-gulp and nearly spat out her coffee.

* * *

Father Gilbert stood over the still form of Brother Sean and prayed for healing, peace, and serenity to work through the troubled mind of the young man. He gazed at the face and the scratches and wondered how his family would react when Brother Gregory phoned them. St Sebastian's was supposed to be a haven – a place to get sorted out, not entangled in murder and overdoses.

What's your connection to the Lily Rose and Anong? He wanted to ask it out loud, believing the stories that talking to someone in this state still penetrated to the far recesses of their thought.

A footfall sounded softly behind him and Brother Gregory stepped up. He gave a pained groan at the sight of the young monk. Father Gilbert nodded, then walked out to give him a moment alone.

Sitting down in one of the chairs in the hall, he looked around for the PC, whose name was R. Flack – "but not *the* Roberta Flack," she had made clear with a giggle. She was down the hall at a coffee vending machine.

She looked at Father Gilbert just as Brother Gregory came out of the room. She reacted with an anxious expression, clearly wondering whether she should run back to find out who the visitor was or stay until the coffee had finished pouring. Father Gilbert waved at her not to worry.

"I talked to the doctor," Brother Gregory said as he sat down next to Father Gilbert. "I never would have believed that Brother Sean would intentionally overdose."

"Isn't it possible because of his confession to me?" Father Gilbert asked.

"That wasn't a confession, it was an admission of guilt," Brother

Gregory said firmly. "Brother Sean was prone to that. He felt responsible for everything."

"Was he responsible?"

"I've told you—"

"He was on antidepressants," Father Gilbert said.

Brother Gregory rubbed his temples as if massaging away a headache. "That's true. But suicide? You know what the Catholic Church thinks about that."

"We have to consider his frame of mind when I last saw him."

"I'm not denying that he had his moods. He scared us once or twice. We watched him closely."

"Why didn't you get him to a counsellor?"

"I did. Just like his parents had for years before he came to us. But he said it didn't help anything." Brother Gregory looked into Sean's room. "I've been trying to help him ever since he arrived."

"How long has he been with you?"

"Almost a year." He dropped his hands onto his lap. His fingers began to rub together and Father Gilbert imagined a rosary moving between them. "I was never convinced that he belonged with us. But his family is fairly wealthy. They begged me to take him on. They thought it would do him good, even if he didn't stay."

"I hadn't thought that becoming a monk was supposed to be a form of therapy."

Brother Gregory looked at Father Gilbert. "I should talk to the Detective Inspector. Maybe he won't be so tough with me."

"I'm sorry," Father Gilbert said. "It's a mode I get into when I'm trying to find the truth."

"I made a mistake," Brother Gregory said, sounding defensive. "I should have sent him home a long time ago. He's been on an emotional roller coaster from the beginning. I had hoped for improvement, but he only spiritualized his problems."

"How did he spiritualize them?"

"By overdoing it with our disciplines."

"Fasting?"

"He did for very short periods. But I only just found out that he's been fasting for the past few days."

"Do you know why?"

Another shake of the monk's head. "No."

"Fasting is a form of repentance, you know," Father Gilbert said. "Sean was in agony over something that happened with Anong."

"Don't rush to judgment." Brother Gregory said as he turned sideways in the chair to face him. "Think it through, Father, since you're playing detective. What do they say about a suspect? Motive, means, and opportunity. Sean had none of those things."

"Are you absolutely sure of that?"

"When do they believe the girl was murdered?"

"Between 11:30 and 12:30."

"He was at St Sebastian's then. Brother Michael saw him brushing his teeth. There's no doubt about it."

"Then why is he lying here, hanging on for his life?" Father Gilbert asked.

Brother Gregory stood up. "I told you. This is a scheme by the local bosses to discredit us for trying to stop their sex trade."

"How does a suicidal monk help them?"

"I don't know yet. I'm not as cunning as they are. But I'm sure we're being set up." He paced a few steps back and forth. "The vandalism at the church. Now this. It's part of a conspiracy. You don't seem to understand how far these people will go to hold onto their business."

The machines in Brother Sean's room began to beep loudly. Down the hall at the nurses' station an alarm sounded.

CHAPTER 9

The doctor and two attending nurses did all they could. Brother Gregory administered last rites, though the young monk never recovered consciousness to know it. Brother Sean Damian, only twenty-four years old, was pronounced dead at 7:47 p.m.

Father Gilbert said his own prayer, hoping that Brother Sean would be welcomed by God's grace and find all the peace that had eluded him in life. He then said a prayer for himself, repenting for not telling Gwynn about Sean's confession and allowing the police to search for him. The young man might be alive if he had.

Police Constable Flack phoned to tell Gwynn the news. When Gwynn arrived a quarter of an hour later, he offered his condolences to Brother Gregory, then announced that he wanted both priests back at the police station to provide a statement with as much information about the deceased as they could muster.

"I will after I've called the other brothers – and his parents," Brother Gregory said. He walked away to find a room where he could make the calls privately. His shoulders were hunched and his head hung low as he shuffled down the hall. Father Gilbert guessed he would shift into organizational mode, to take care of the details and everyone else's grief – saving his own for later.

Gwynn gave PC Flack a nod to stay with the monk. "Bring him in as soon as he's done."

She nodded in return and followed Brother Gregory down the hall.

A nurse slowly unhooked the wires and tubes from the body. She moved slowly and carefully. Father Gilbert hoped it was out of respect. Too often nurses and orderlies treated the dead like training dummies, as if death had removed their shared humanity. In fact, death was the one sure thing that all humanity shared.

Gwynn waited until the nurse had gone, then said, "Mamasan gave me an earful about Brother Sean."

Father Gilbert glanced at the sheet-covered body in the room as if it might hear. "I'm not surprised."

Gwynn pulled car keys out of his pocket. "Let's go."

* * *

Father Gilbert stood in a small room, watching DI Gwynn on the other side of the glass with Mamasan, whose real name, stated by Gwynn for the sake of the recording, was Ushi Yan, the manager of the Lily Rose Massage Parlour.

"Spa!" she complained.

"Spa," Gwynn corrected himself and added that her voice, apart from his own, would be the only other voice on the recording. "Is that correct?" he asked her.

"Yes," she said. "I am Ushi Yan."

Gwynn had arranged to have Mamasan brought to the station while he and Father Gilbert returned from the hospital. She sat rigidly at the metal table, her hands clasped on top, her expression one of effrontery and indignation. "I do not know why you make me come here," she said.

"I need you to repeat what you told me before, for the record," Gwynn said.

"You pay me for lost work?"

"You're being a good citizen, remember?"

Mamasan pointed to the glass. "Who is watching me now?"

"Chairman Mao," Gwynn said. "Now let's go over what you told me about Brother Sean Damian."

She looked at the glass for another moment, then turned her attention to the Detective Inspector. "He came to my shop."

"Once? Twice? How often?"

"Once a week. Maybe more."

"Why?"

She frowned at him for asking the obvious. "For massage."

"Did he see any of the girls regularly or did he go with whoever was available?"

"Anong," she said. "He always wanted Anong."

"Anong Chuan."

"Yes."

"When I asked you earlier about Anong, you said she hardly ever worked at your *spa*."

"She was not a regular employee. That's what I meant." It was a lie, Father Gilbert knew. She was amending her story.

"Why did Sean see only her?"

She rolled her eyes. "He was a *nuisance*."

"Why?"

"Because some men see one girl and think there is lovey-dovey between them. He was like puppy dog. *Yip-yip-yip* around her. The girls call him her 'boyfriend'."

"Did Anong like him?" Gwynn asked.

"Anong liked *all* her paying customers." She gave a knowing smile.

"You knew he was a monk at St Sebastian's."

"I did not know. But I found out."

"How did you find out?"

"A woman has to know things to stay in business," she said. She upended her hand to look at her painted fingernails.

"You had him followed."

Her eyes stayed on her fingernails. She didn't respond.

Gwynn shifted impatiently. "Didn't you think it was unusual for a monk to come to your shop?"

"Monks have sore muscles same as other men. We work them out. We are very good."

"So Sean met only Anong."

"He was shy with the other girls. He only talked to Anong."

Gwynn paused for a moment and appeared to make an adjustment to a knob on the recorder. From Father Gilbert's position, the Detective Inspector didn't actually adjust anything. It was a ploy to disrupt the rhythm of the question-and-answer. "Did Brother Sean come to see Anong the night she was murdered?"

"Yes."

"What time?"

"Nine o'clock. Maybe nine-thirty."

"What happened?" Gwynn asked as he picked up a pen sitting by the edge of the table.

"*Big* fight," Mamasan said.

"Explain what you mean by 'big'."

"Anong gave him massage. Then he was very upset. He shouted. He made threats at her." Father Gilbert wouldn't have given her any awards for acting. Her entire demeanour was stiff, as if she had practised the words but didn't believe them herself.

"What kind of threats?"

"*Kill*," she said in a breathy whisper. "He told her he would *kill* her."

"Why would he want to kill her because of a massage?" Gwynn asked.

"No, not for massage. He wanted her to do *more* than a massage."

"'More' meaning services of a sexual nature?"

"Yes. But my girls do massage only. No hanky-panky. That is why he was angry."

"And then what happened?" Gwynn asked.

"We told him to go away. *Shoo! Shoo!*" she said and acted out the moment by flapping her hands.

"Did he go?"

"Yes."

"Did you see him again that night?"

"No. But Anong got phone call later. That is why she went out."

"What time did she go out?" Gwynn asked.

"Eleven o'clock," she replied. Then she tilted her head slightly as if deciding. "Maybe ten minutes before."

"Who did she go to see?"

"The monk."

"How do you know that?"

"Anong told one of the other girls."

"Which girl?"

She made a pretence of thinking about it. "Maybe it was May." Father Gilbert suspected that May was the most coachable one.

Gwynn wrote on a pad of paper. "I'll want to talk to her."

Mamasan shook her head. "She won't talk to you."

"Why not?"

"She doesn't speak English."

"We'll sort something out," Gwynn said. "Why would Anong go to meet a customer she'd just had a fight with?"

Another shrug from Mamasan. "Money. If he could pay, she would go. She knew she could make him behave."

"And then?"

She raised her arms in a *what is there to tell?* gesture. "She was wrong. The monk was still angry. He killed her." She sat back and folded her arms. *Case closed.*

"Why didn't you tell me all this before?"

She rearranged one of the several bracelets on her wrist. "I was afraid," she said in a small voice.

Gwynn chuckled. "You don't seem like the kind of woman who scares easily."

"The men in big church on the hill are powerful. They can hurt us."

"Why do you think that? Have you ever been threatened by them?"

"They threaten to close down business."

Gwynn tapped the pen on the pad of paper. "Tell me what happened with Sean this afternoon."

She suddenly brightened and sat up. It was telling to Father Gilbert, suggesting she could now answer questions she actually knew the real answers to. "He came to my shop. He acted like drunken crazy man. He shouted. *He grabbed me by the shoulders.*"

"Why did he grab you?"

"He wanted my necklace." She touched her neck and lifted the horse in the circle pendant.

"Why?"

"He said it was Anong's." Her tone of indignation returned. "It is *mine. She* bought one like *mine.*"

"Why did Sean want Anong's necklace?"

"Because he was lovey-dovey with her. He wanted..." She frowned. "I don't know the English word. Gift? Token?"

"He wanted something to remember her by?"

"I don't know. He was *crazy.*"

"What did you do when he grabbed you?"

She lifted her right hand and clawed at the air. "I scratched his face. He cried like big baby. Then customer told him to *go* or he call police."

"Did he leave then?"

"He was very angry. He went and didn't come back."

"The front door?"

She looked confused.

"Did he go out the *front* door or the *back* door?" he clarified.

"Front door. Back door sets off alarm."

"Thank you." Gwynn indicated to the recorder that he was terminating the interview and marked the time.

"Are we done?" She started to stand up.

He held up a hand. "Wait here for a minute."

She dropped back into her seat, annoyed. "How long? I have business."

"Just a tick."

Mamasan sneered at him as he got up and left the room. Father Gilbert saw it, Gwynn didn't. She continued to sit straight, like an eager schoolgirl. He wondered what had happened in her life to twist her morality so far out of shape. An abusive relative? Financial survival? Or had she freely chosen her vocation?

A few seconds later, Gwynn came into the viewing room. He positioned himself next to Father Gilbert, looking at Mamasan. She returned to her nail-watching.

"Well, she'd never last on the witness stand," Father Gilbert said. "She said one of the customers had to deal with Sean. Is it a credible witness?"

"A city councilman, if that counts for anything," Gwynn replied. "He threatened to physically throw Sean out if he didn't leave on his own." He turned to Father Gilbert. "I'm having a hard time with the idea that Sean went into the alley and took an overdose of pills. Put on your priest's thinking cap. Why would he do that?"

"*If* that's what happened…" Father Gilbert thought for a moment. "If he was truly in love with her, he might have been distraught over her death. It could have been a trigger."

"What if Sean killed her and experienced remorse for that?"

Father Gilbert struggled to keep an impassive expression. "That would be possible, too, except Brother Gregory said that Sean was at the monastery at the time Anong was murdered."

"He'll swear to that?"

"A brother saw Sean there around 11:30." Father Gilbert glanced at Mamasan again. She now tapped her fingernails impatiently against the tabletop. "Are there any witnesses to this alleged fight with Sean before Anong was murdered? Any customers?"

"Not that I know of," Gwynn said. "I'll bring in the other girl she mentioned. May."

"Mamasan will coach her."

"I'll get past that."

"Why is Mamasan talking now?" Father Gilbert asked. "I'm not buying the story that she was afraid."

"Someone put her up to it. Whatever happened with Brother Sean earlier today must have persuaded them that it's an opportunity of some kind." Gwynn dug into his coat pocket and unearthed a breath mint. He unwrapped it.

PC Flack peeked into the room. "I brought the monk, just like you asked."

"Take him into Interrogation Room 2."

"The big one?"

"Yes. We'll be there in a minute."

"You're going to interrogate Brother Gregory?"

He popped the mint into his mouth. "No. The three of us are going to have a chat."

"Hey!" Mamasan shouted at the glass. "Where is everybody?"

* * *

"It's a set-up to discredit us," Brother Gregory said after he heard the recording of Mamasan's interview. He paced the floor of the larger interrogation room.

"Your monk was well on his way to discrediting you without her help," Gwynn said. "What was he doing there? I thought you people took a vow of chastity."

"We do."

"*And* a vow of poverty."

"We do."

Gwynn snorted. "I can't afford to be a regular in a place like that. How could he?"

"You're assuming she's telling the truth," Brother Gregory said.

"I have at least one credible witness that places him there," Gwynn reminded him. "Did he have money you don't know about?"

"You mentioned before that he came from a wealthy family," Father Gilbert said to Brother Gregory.

Gwynn held a hand out as if to say *there's your answer*.

"We have rules," Brother Gregory retorted. "He's not allowed to access any private funds. He agreed to that. His *parents* agreed to that."

"Clearly he had access to *a lot* of things you didn't know about," Gwynn said. "Are monks allowed to have mobile phones?"

"Some are. As a novice, Brother Sean wasn't."

"That puts a question mark on Mamasan's account. She claimed Sean phoned Anong," Father Gilbert said.

Brother Gregory marched to the door. "There are more question marks than that. Is she still here? Let me talk to her."

"*Stop*. I let her go," Gwynn said. "Besides, you have no legal right to question her."

"Why did you release her?" Brother Gregory asked.

Gwynn glared at him. "She's not the one accused of murder. Your boy Sean is."

"My 'boy Sean' is dead, you'll remember," Brother Gregory snapped. "And you don't know why."

"I'll know when the tests from his autopsy come back," Gwynn said defiantly. "Right now it's a suicide as far as I'm concerned. He was stricken with guilt over murdering the girl he was 'lovey-dovey' with."

Brother Gregory prowled the room. "You don't know for certain that he had any feelings for her. That's Mamasan's version. But I know that he was at the monastery when the murder happened."

"Uh huh. Your brothers will swear to your story just like Mamasan's girls will swear to hers."

Brother Gregory seethed. "We wouldn't lie. Not even for another brother."

"Everybody has an agenda, an angle," Gwynn said, then shook his head. "I thought you priests were supposed to be meek as lambs or something like that. You're aggressive."

Brother Gregory harrumphed and turned away.

"It doesn't add up," Father Gilbert said, wanting to cut the tension between the two men. "Even if his alibi didn't hold up, think about the logistics. Where could Sean have committed the murder? At the hotel? Surely someone at the front desk would have noticed a *monk* walking through the lobby?"

"He might have been dressed in plain clothes."

"He would have had to check in, pay for the room," Father Gilbert reminded him. "Check the records. Show the receptionist a photo of him. And how did he transport her body from the hotel? He doesn't have a car. There's a level of planning – of premeditation – that flies in the face of everything Mamasan described."

Brother Gregory collapsed into a chair. "Sean didn't kill anyone."

"All the same, I'm going to have to search his room," Gwynn added.

Brother Gregory looked up. "Why?"

"To look for clues. A diary. Anything. As absurd as Mamasan's story is, he's undeniably connected somehow to the Lily Rose and Anong." Gwynn folded his arms. "As it is, no one has answered a basic question: why did he go there today?"

Brother Gregory was on his feet again. "How about this? The church had been vandalized. Brother Sean was deeply upset. He believed – as I do – that the people who run these flesh mills attacked us. He went to Mamasan because he thought she was in on it. He told her to stop or he'd go to the police. *That's* why he was there."

"And the scratches on his face?"

"She got angry and lashed out at him."

"What about the overdose?" Gwynn asked.

"They pumped him full of drugs to get rid of him once and for all."

"There's no sign of needles or any other means of getting drugs into his system."

"She had drugs under her fingernails and when she scratched him—"

"Now you're talking comic-book stuff," Gwynn said, waving him away.

"We need more information," Father Gilbert said. The banter between the two men was giving him a headache. "There's a growing list of people who need to be questioned. Did Sean say anything to the brothers about the massage parlour or Anong? Can you separate the women at the Lily Rose from Mamasan so you can question them properly?"

"All right, all right," Gwynn said.

"You have your work cut out for you, Detective Inspector," Brother Gregory said.

"You don't have to remind me," Gwynn growled.

* * *

Gwynn drove Brother Gregory back to St Sebastian's. Both men were emotionally ragged, for different reasons. Father Gilbert hoped they wouldn't get into an argument on the way. He wondered, too, if Brother Gregory would tell Gwynn about Sean's earlier admission of guilt. If so, Gwynn would have some harsh words for him tomorrow.

He chose to walk back to his hotel, taking the long way around towards the pier. A fog had rolled in, turning the lights into faint, colourful smudges. He realized he was retracing the steps he'd taken with Brother Sean earlier in the day. He felt a pang of regret for not being more astute about the monk's mental condition. He wished he'd been better prepared for the abrupt dash he'd made. A younger Gilbert wouldn't have lost him so easily.

He prayed for Sean – and Sean's family – and Brother Gregory and the rest of the brothers. The part that had been Sean Damian in their lives was now a black hole. Could such a space ever be filled again? And now that he knew Anong may have had a daughter, he ached for what the loss of her mother would mean to the girl.

Turning onto a street he quickly became alert, unsure if he'd entered another section of historic Englesea or if he'd been displaced in time again. The ramshackle buildings and leaded windows were there, along with uneven porches and large, foreboding doors. Where was he? Walking in the fog, he'd lost track. He heard what sounded like waves on the shore in the distance. Listening again, he thought the noise might actually be traffic. He came to an empty intersection with no street signs and turned left, his sense of direction telling him that it would take him to the vicinity of his hotel.

He looked at his watch, pushing the button to light its face. 12:14. He had had no idea it was so late. He saw a neon light flashing the word *Open* in a window ahead and hoped the shopkeeper would give him a clue of where he was. Reaching the door, he saw through the front show window the cases filled with Chinese herbs and medicines. He was at the Lily Rose Massage Parlour. How had he wound up here? He was sure he'd been walking in the opposite direction.

Thinking of Mamasan and all the questions he wanted to ask her, he decided to go in. A soft bell chimed. He looked at the door jamb and saw a small sensor. A tiny red light flickered. No one was at the front desk. A floorboard creaked under his feet. Everything else was eerily silent. He waited for a moment for someone to come. The place smelled of scented candles. Asian music played softly from a speaker overhead.

A door slammed down the hall and he walked towards it. Raised voices came from the office directly ahead. One was Mamasan's, the other was male – probably the white-coated bald man he'd seen at the front desk earlier. The door to the cellar – on the right – stood open. Gilbert was tempted to sneak downstairs, just to see if he could talk to the women there. He thought better of it. They might be busy with customers. Or they might scream at the sight of him. Either way, he doubted a visit would be productive.

He continued on to the office door and was about to knock when he heard Mamasan's raised voice, what sounded like a hard slap, and then the sobbing of another woman. To his right was a small, dark alcove with an open door. A burning candle flickered inside, giving him enough light to make out that it was a small room with a toilet.

The handle to the office door turned. He retreated into the shadow of the room, hoping he wouldn't be seen.

A woman came out of the office. She closed the door behind her and pressed a hand to her face. Then she wiped tears from her eyes. In the light from the hall, Father Gilbert remembered seeing her before. She had a similar look to Anong, with stylish black hair.

She suddenly looked up, as if she was aware that someone was watching her. He stepped back and a floorboard groaned. The woman squinted at the darkness, then her eyes fixed on him. He saw the blue make-up above her eyes. He came further into the dim light. She put a hand to her mouth to stifle a gasp and moved back against the wall behind her.

Father Gilbert raised a hand and opened his mouth to whisper an assurance, but the woman put a finger to her lips and shook her head. Her eyes darted to the office door then back to him. He signalled that he wanted to talk, but the office door handle turned again. The woman saw it and scampered down the hall.

Thinking quickly, he ducked into the loo again, closed the door, and flipped the light switch. He turned on the tap and washed his hands to give every impression that he'd shown up and needed to use the toilet.

Looking in the mirror, he was dismayed by the face looking back at him. Lines around his eyes, streaks of grey hair that he hadn't noticed before his arrival in Englesea. What was becoming of him? If he had to pick a word to describe that face, he'd say "melancholy".

He became aware of a particular scent and checked to see if it was coming from the candle. The candle was a battery-operated artifice, designed to flicker like the real thing. He lifted his soapy hands. The scent was coming from the soap. English Lavender. He was sure of it. He rinsed his hands, then dried them on a hand towel hanging from a ring on the wall. Using toilet tissue, he picked up the bar of soap with his forefinger and thumb. A worn symbol embossed in the soap was the same as the symbol he'd seen on the box of soap in the Angel Sea Hotel manager's office. He wrapped the soap up and tucked it in his jacket pocket.

He wiped his hands on the towel again and opened the door.

Mamasan stood in the hall, waiting for him. When she saw who it was, her mouth went taut. She held up a matronly finger and wagged it at him. "What are you doing here?"

"I came to visit," he said cordially.

"You want massage?"

"I'm afraid it's too late. But I would like to talk to you about Brother Sean."

"I told everything to the police." She pointed. "You go."

"Are you the owner of this business or just the manager?"

She held her position. "Go or I call the police."

"And do what?" he asked, annoyed. "Tell them I got angry and caused a scene? Maybe I grabbed you to get at your necklace?"

"Go."

"Was it your people who vandalized the church?"

"Go *now*."

He moved past her. "I like the brand of soap you use here."

Her expression shifted quickly, from stern to puzzled. "What?"

He continued down the hall to leave her wondering.

* * *

Father Gilbert had to use his room key to enter the front door of The Masthead Inn. A sign reminded the customers that the door would be locked from midnight to 6 a.m. All was quiet inside, apart from the sound of someone vacuuming the lobby. A woman in a hotel uniform saw him and stopped. He waved at her and said, "Goodnight." She waved back and continued vacuuming.

He went up to his room and was about to put the key card into the electronic lock when he saw that the door was ajar. On guard, he pushed the door wide open and stepped back into the hall. The room was dimly lit by an outside light through the window. He felt for the switch on the wall and pushed it. Lights came on. The room was tidy – having been cleaned by housekeeping at some point in the day. He wondered if they simply hadn't pulled the door fully closed when they left. He checked the bathroom, then slowly turned to see what, if anything, had changed in the room. Housekeeping had reset the room in the expected ways.

His messenger bag was open on a cushioned chair by the window. His tablet sat on the small desk next to it. He knew he hadn't opened the bag nor taken the tablet out when he was in the room earlier. He walked up to the tablet and pushed the button at the bottom to bring it to life. Rather than going to the login screen, the tablet displayed an image of Father Gilbert sitting in the café with DI Gwynn earlier in the day. The photo was taken from outside, with the two men seen sitting and talking through the window. He swiped his finger across the screen and the image changed. This time it was Father Gilbert walking out of the Layton School of English. Another image showed him sitting alone in a pub. Yet another saw him walking with Brother Sean. Another showed him with PC Flack in the hall at the hospital. And there was a photo of him talking to Father Anthony and Vadim at the conference café. The final image wasn't a photo but a message: "See You Sooner Than You'll See Me."

His feeling of being watched wasn't due only to the Shadow Man. Someone very human had been following him throughout the day. If the effect was meant to alarm him, it worked.

He picked up the tablet carefully, touching only the edges to avoid messing up any fingerprints. He realized that, though identical, it wasn't his tablet. There wasn't a protective cover on the back. Putting the tablet down again, he checked his messenger bag. His tablet sat inside where he'd left it. He walked over to the closet and took out the complimentary plastic laundry bag, using it to wrap up the tablet. Then he wrapped the soap in a smaller plastic bag he used as part of his shaving kit. He would take them to DI Gwynn in the morning.

Making sure the door was locked, he scoured the room and bathroom for any clues that might have been inadvertently left by the intruder. He also checked the lamps, clock, telephone, and smoke alarms to make sure cameras hadn't been installed. He didn't know who was watching him, but he had to assume they were clever enough to do that sort of thing.

He had a hot shower to help calm down, then kneeled next to the bed for prayer. Crawling under the covers, he knew he wouldn't sleep much, if at all.

CHAPTER 10

Father Gilbert was awakened by the sound of his mobile phone buzzing on the bedside table. It sounded like an electric razor, which explained why his waking thought was about shaving. He sat up, quickly registering the time as 7:00, then picked up his phone.

"Father Gilbert?"

"Good morning, Vadim."

"Father Anthony said you found her." He had the husky sound of a man who'd been smoking too much in the night.

"Yes. She's working at the Layton School of English here." He couldn't bring himself to say exactly *how* she was working there.

"I will go there. I will tear the place apart." Those were the only two sentences Father Gilbert could make out in a stream of Romanian.

"I understand how you feel, but you mustn't go there," Father Gilbert said. "If you go in and make a scene, you could be arrested. Let the police handle it."

Another stream of foreign words, then: "The police *won't* handle it."

"Please wait. I'll go by there this morning to see what more I can learn. They think I'm a priest interested in sending my foreign parishioners there. Do you understand?"

"You play *secret agent*."

"In a manner of speaking."

"Still, I will come down. I will call you when I arrive."

"Vadim—" Father Gilbert began, hoping he would wait longer. Vadim hung up.

Father Gilbert washed and dressed. He phoned DI Gwynn and left a message that he had something to bring to the police station in an hour or so. Grabbing his makeshift evidence bag, he shoved it into his messenger bag and went down to get something quick to eat.

In the lobby he saw the local newspaper with a headline about a local priest dying from a drug overdose. The article suggested that

127

Brother Sean Damian had committed suicide, without using the phrase outright. It also mentioned allegations from the manager of the Lily Rose Spa that Sean Damian was a regular customer there. Fortunately, it said nothing about suspicions that the victim had murdered Anong.

He entered the dining room, which was now packed again, many of the tables taken by conference attendees. Reverend Planer sat alone at the same table they'd dined at the morning before. He looked up at Father Gilbert and gestured to the empty chair. Father Gilbert wasn't in a talkative mood, but didn't want to be unsociable.

"I only have a minute," he said as he sat down.

"Busy day," Planer said. "I see you're participating in various panel discussions throughout the day."

"Am I?" He knew of one, but not "various" panels. Was the Bishop volunteering him for duty, just to make sure he came?

"They emailed the changes to the schedule this morning. Didn't you get one?"

"I haven't looked at emails."

"You're part of a discussion about church outreach at 10:00."

"Outreach?"

"Something to do with handling the needs of the community?"

Was the Bishop being ironic? Lately Gilbert's help to the community was often with police business.

A waitress appeared. "What will you be having, sir?"

"A tea and whatever pastry you have around," he said. He searched the room for Cari Erim, wondering if she had been sacked after what had happened yesterday. He looked down at the carpet. It had a dark stain where Anong had been.

"You should have stayed around last night," Planer said.

"What did I miss?"

"Nathan Rank regaled us with stories of the hospitality trade. Then he took us out for a night on the town."

"What kind of night can you have on this town?" Father Gilbert said with a hint of sarcasm.

"We started at an Indian restaurant a few streets from here. It had the best biryani I've had anywhere. Then he took us to the oldest pub in Englesea and told us all kinds of stories about the area. Did you know it's haunted? He said there are more reported sightings of ghosts here than almost anywhere else in England."

"What kinds of ghosts?"

"How many different kinds are there?"

"There are a lot of phenomena that people call 'ghosts'. Are they men and women?"

Planer gave it some thought. "Mostly women, come to think of it."

"Are they dressed in contemporary clothing or clothes from different times in history?"

"That's a very detailed question," Planer said, perturbed. "Why do you ask? Have you seen something?"

Father Gilbert forced a slight laugh. "I was curious, that's all."

The waitress brought Planer's breakfast. It was the same fry-up as he'd had the day before. He eyed it as he said, "Because this used to be a haven for pirates, there are all kinds of nooks and crannies that no one knows about. He told us about a few. There were little tunnels connecting a couple of the older buildings. The cellar of one of the hotels was used to store gunpowder and alcohol. It had a secret door to smuggle everything in and out."

"Which hotel?"

* * *

It was raining when Father Gilbert left the Masthead Inn. He couldn't shake the feeling of being watched. Should he smile for the camera? From which direction? He made as if he were going to the convention centre. Then he turned abruptly onto a cross street and walked quickly for the police station. He doubted it would make any difference. Whoever was following him wouldn't be easily tricked. But it amused him to play along for a moment.

"I was just about to ring you back," Gwynn said as he ushered Father Gilbert into the office area. Gwynn looked haggard, and it was possible he was wearing the same clothes as he'd worn the day before.

"Has anyone checked the Angel Sea Hotel for secret doors?" Father Gilbert asked.

"Secret doors?" Gwynn laughed. "What are you on about?"

They were standing in Gwynn's office now. Father Gilbert explained, "Apparently there are secret doors in a lot of the older buildings where the pirates sneaked in and out and stashed away the kinds of things pirates liked to stash away. If a door like that really exists, it may explain how Anong was taken out of the hotel without being seen."

"That suggests it was someone who knows about the door. Someone on staff?"

"Or someone who knows about the history of Englesea," Father Gilbert said. "A businessman or a tour guide or someone in the hospitality trade."

"You brought this up before. You're thinking of someone specific."

"Nathan Rank. He's staying at the Angel Sea. I don't have any other details. He took some of the clergy out on the town and told them about secret passages and doors. Apparently the Angel Sea Hotel has one."

Gwynn scribbled the name down on a piece of paper. "I'll talk to the BackList detectives again." He said on the edge of a groan, "Two more things to do."

Father Gilbert opened his messenger case and put the makeshift evidence bag on the desk. "Someone left this in my room last night while I was out."

"You had a break-in?"

"No sign of forced entry," he said.

Gwynn put on gloves and unwrapped it all. He lifted up the soap and sniffed at it. "Where did you get this?"

"The Lily Rose."

"Well, we knew the Angel Sea wasn't the only place to use this soap. What do you think it means?"

"What if Anong was killed at the Lily Rose? Is it worth checking their bath or talking to the girls again?"

"I intend to talk to the girls. But I'm unlikely to find any evidence or witnesses about Anong's murder." Gwynn re-bagged the soap and sat it on his desk. "It won't hold up in court."

"I only wanted you to know."

"Merely as a matter of curiosity, what were you doing at the Lily Rose?"

"I got lost in the fog."

Gwynn grunted, then unwrapped the tablet. "Is it yours?"

"No." He waved a finger at the device. "Push the button at the bottom."

Gwynn did. The screen lit up and he scrolled through the photos, concluding with the message. "Well. Those photos are a good definition of complete boredom."

"Had I known I was being watched, I might have tried to be more entertaining."

Gwynn suddenly swiped backwards through the photos and stopped at one with Father Gilbert and Brother Sean. "You saw him yesterday?"

Father Gilbert froze. If he'd swallowed, the entire office would have heard a loud gulp. "In the afternoon."

"You didn't mention it." An accusation.

"All things considered, it didn't seem relevant." The words rang hollow to his own ears. He could only imagine how they sounded to the Detective Inspector.

"It didn't seem *relevant?*" Gwynn said sharply.

"He wanted to talk, that's all," Father Gilbert said and he could hear the sound of a shovel as he dug himself deeper into a hole.

"About what? Who's playing at Wimbledon? Modern jazz? The latest debates in Parliament?"

Cornered now, Father Gilbert knew he had to come clean. He told the Detective Inspector the details of his encounter with Brother Sean the day before.

Gwynn listened while the muscles in his jaw worked overtime, clenching and unclenching his teeth. His face turned red. By the time Father Gilbert had finished, he looked as if he might punch the priest in the nose – or have a stroke – or both. His voice, however, was calm when he asked, "When were you going to tell me this little titbit of information?"

"I intended to tell you if Brother Sean didn't show up by the end of the day."

"Well, he *did* show up, didn't he? He showed up *dead*." Gwynn was seething now. "Has it occurred to you that your delay may have contributed to his death?"

"Yes," was all Father Gilbert could say. The sting of his culpability kept him from adding any more.

"Not to mention the significance of his confession to you," Gwynn shouted.

Heads appeared over the walls of the other cubicles.

"Back to work!" Gwynn shouted. The heads dropped down again. "You're a former copper! You should have told me. We would have rounded him up. But now…" Gwynn whispered a string of obscenities.

Father Gilbert waited it out.

Gwynn finally ran out of words. He glared at Father Gilbert.

"I'm sorry," Father Gilbert said. "It was bad judgment on my part."

"Too right it was," he said. "You're lucky I don't arrest you."

"Yes, I am."

"And don't play the contrition card with me. It doesn't work."

"Whatever you say."

The two men stood for a moment, the silence like a rock wall between them.

Gwynn finally gave a long, slow exhalation, as if releasing his anger into the atmosphere. He pointed to the tablet. "Any ideas why someone would follow you around all day? Is there something else you're not telling me? You're not with MI5 or MI6 or some covert operation, are you?"

Father Gilbert shook his head.

"I'll have Nigel go over it," Gwynn said. "Do you want a constable to stay with you today?"

"No."

"Maybe I'll assign one to you anyway. Just in case you get a visit from another suspect who decides to confess."

Father Gilbert gave a very small chuckle, hoping it was a joke.

"On the subject of Brother Sean Damian," Gwynn said. "When I took Brother Gregory back to St Sebastian's, I had a look around

Sean's room. There wasn't much there – those monks love their austerity – but I found a mobile phone tucked away in a drawer of socks. Brother Gregory was surprised, which seems to be his on-going reaction now. It was one of those pay-as-you-go models. Sean phoned Anong quite a few times, including the night she was murdered. The last call was 11:05."

"Mamasan said Anong was with him around that time. Why would he call her if she was with him?" Father Gilbert asked.

"Brother Michael saw Sean at the monastery at 11:30 brushing his teeth. I spoke to him about it last night. He's clear about seeing Sean, right down to the pyjamas he was wearing. They even had a quick discussion about some saint – Thomas Aquila or something like that."

"Aquinas."

"All the same, Brother Michael will swear to it in court."

"So that's Sean's alibi," Father Gilbert said, relieved. "Meaning that his admission to me was about something else."

Another cold look at the priest. "It's possible we'll never know now, will we?"

Father Gilbert accepted the barb silently.

"I don't think he murdered Anong," Gwynn said. "But I think Mamasan was telling the truth, in part. He may have been involved with her somehow, even if he was only a client to her."

"How could he afford her?"

"Brother Gregory said he'll try to access his bank records. As the head of their Order, he has the legal permission to do it, or something like that. It saves me going through the court."

"Any idea how he died?"

"Technically, he was killed by an overdose of his antidepressants, though there was another drug present in his system."

"What kind of drug?"

"It's called *ephedra*," Gwynn said. "It's used in various over-the-counter diet pills as an appetite suppressant. Bodybuilders use it. It's also used for asthma or bronchitis. In small doses, it's not bad. With higher doses, it can be trouble, especially if it's mixed with other drugs."

"Like antidepressants?"

Gwynn nodded. "It can cause dangerous elevations in blood pressure or heart rate."

"How much would he have had to take?"

"Anything over 100 milligrams. Sean was well over that."

"How many pills would that be?"

Gwynn shook his head.

"I can't imagine Brother Sean swallowing his pills *and* downing enough ephedra on purpose." His mind spun through the implication. "To do both says he intended to kill himself there. It wasn't a spontaneous decision. And why would he use that method? There are better ways to commit suicide. And why there?"

"You're asking questions we can't answer," Gwynn said. "The medical examiner can't find anything to suggest forced ingestion, so he must have taken it himself."

"In pill form? Wouldn't the toxicology report show that?"

"Yes it would and no the ME didn't check thoroughly." Gwynn rubbed his eyes. "You're digging deeper than the ME wants to. He's still thinking of it as a suicide, so he's not spending a lot of time on it."

Father Gilbert slowly shook his head. It didn't make sense. "What about Brother Sean's number on Anong's phone?"

"There were a lot of calls."

"What about the phone numbers of anyone else who called her?"

"Most were pay-as-you-go phones. We're checking the ones that weren't." Gwynn chuckled. "One poor idiot was in town a week ago on business and had a session with Anong. He was surprised to hear from us this morning. So was his wife."

"What about the night she was murdered?"

"There was a call at 10:29. Again, the number was to a pay-as-you-go phone. It lasted two minutes."

"Long enough to make an appointment," Father Gilbert observed. He then asked, "I've been out of the force a long time. Is there any way to track those kinds of phones?"

"It's possible to track back to a person *if* he bought the phone with a credit card from a legitimate mobile phone shop – anytime the user had to provide a name or personal information. We can also pinpoint from where the call was generated if it was made on a street or somewhere public. Though that's not admissible in court unless we get security camera footage coinciding with the same time the call was made. But that only gets us to a suspect. It's not enough for a conviction."

Gwynn's phone buzzed.

He looked at the screen then pocketed it. "I have to go."

"Have you had a chance to look into the Layton School of English and the girl – Veronyka – I told you about?"

"Since last night?" The question was tinged with incredulity. "Frankly, it's not a priority. But I did talk to a couple of veterans here. None of them know of rumours or accusations about the school being a front for prostitution."

"Meaning that it wasn't or your veterans didn't want to know about it."

Gwynn frowned. "It's possible that Veronyka is running her own show and using the school as a front."

"It's possible," Father Gilbert said. But until he had a chance to talk to her, how could he know for sure?

* * *

Father Gilbert walked back to the convention centre. The rain was an unconvincing drizzle again, adding to the greyness of his mood.

Along the way, he found himself speeding up and slowing down his pace, just to keep any watchful eyes from taking him for granted. Using an old ploy, he suddenly stopped in front of a shop window as if to eye exotic vacations in warmer and dryer parts of the world. He looked in the reflection at the movement behind him. Men and women passed by, along with the usual traffic. His eyes went to his own image for a second and he was dismayed to see again the deep lines that had spread around his face. His hair, matted by the rain, made him look wild and bedraggled. Reflections were cruel and unsympathetic, he decided.

He became aware of a change behind him. In the glass, he saw the traffic being obscured by a large crowd that slowly materialized from nothing. The crowd was made up mostly of women, but of different races and ages dressed in a variety of outfits from other times and places, all facing him. At first they stared at him as if perplexed. Then one woman, dressed in a tie-dye T-shirt, a short skirt, and high-heeled boots, made eye contact with him in the reflection. She came alive with a sudden panic, her arm reaching up and pointing. Suddenly the arms of the rest reached out and lunged for him.

Expecting to be mobbed from behind, he spun around with his arms up, in a defensive posture.

The crowd had disappeared. The street was as it had been. A woman pushing a pram frowned at him. He gave her an embarrassed smile. She looked away, passing from view.

In the alleyway directly opposite, the Shadow Man leaned against a brick wall. The head was tilted down, the face concealed by the brim of a black hat. But Father Gilbert knew the eyes were on him.

The priest took a deep breath to steady his nerves, then walked on.

* * *

Narrowly arriving at the conference hall in time for his panel discussion at 10:00, Father Gilbert walked up to the small stage in the small room and took a seat between two other panellists. One was an Anglican priest named Father Barry Crinklewedge – a name that made Father Gilbert immediately sympathetic to the nervous and demure man. The other was Reverend Shirley Tull, a Methodist minister known for her outspoken views on most social issues of the day. They greeted one another and the two dozen clerics sitting in the audience.

Father Gilbert opened his messenger bag and retrieved his tablet and a notepad and pen. He tapped the tablet and glanced quickly at the most recent schedule. Not only was he on for this 10:00 event, but for another at 2:00 and another at 4:00 and another at 8:00. The Bishop was not known for subtlety.

The panel discussion began with each panellist talking candidly about their local communities and the unique challenges they faced. Reverend Tull had a lot to say about the needs of gays, lesbians, bisexuals, and transgender people in her parish. Father Gilbert was surprised, never imagining that a village as small as Fordwich Green would have such cosmopolitan issues.

Father Gilbert, on the other hand, spoke about his very average parish of Stonebridge, with issues of boredom and indifference, especially among youth, leading the roster.

A hand shot up in the audience and a young priest said, "Your parish is hardly boring, considering the murders that took place there only a couple of months ago. You and your church were in the centre of it, if what I've heard is correct."

The press had done a fairly decent job of keeping Father Gilbert and St Mark's out of the news reports, but the "Stonebridge Killings" had been top-of-mind for the nation for a few days. Father Gilbert leaned into the pencil-thin microphone in front of him. "I think we're here to talk about normal issues, not the highly unusual ones."

"Father Gilbert is right," Reverend Tull said quickly. "And I believe the time to ask questions is *after* each panellist has spoken. Father Crinklewedge?"

Father Crinklewedge thanked her in a small voice and Father Gilbert thanked her with a small nod. Crinklewedge talked about Liverpool and the large Far Eastern community to which he ministered. One problem he faced was the integration of a particular brand of Chinese spirituality with orthodox Christianity. Feng shui, ancestral worship, Jian, Fan Tai Sui, as well as the use of Qi in therapy, acupuncture, and herbal medicine were often thrown into the mix of their Christian faith.

Reverend Tull immediately announced that there was no harm in allowing other religious beliefs to live side-by-side with Christian faith. This statement brought the audience to life with outcries, raised hands, arguments, and counterarguments.

Father Gilbert's mind wandered back to the Lily Rose. He tried to imagine the physical movements of Sean's last hour or so there – walking through the front door and arguing with Mamasan. Where did that happen: in the lobby? The office? In the cellar?

More questions. Had he already taken the pills before he arrived? If so, wouldn't that have been obvious to Mamasan and the witnesses? Surely he would have had a telltale reaction? Did he take the pills in their presence? If so, why would he do that? For dramatic effect? Wouldn't Mamasan and the others have seen him do it and reacted?

Finally, after he was told to leave, did Sean walk out the front door and around to the alley to take the pills?

None of it made sense, either as a planned act – or as a spontaneous one.

A few minutes before the end of the panel discussion – which had shifted topics a dozen times – Father Gilbert's phone buzzed. He looked at the screen, recognizing the number as Vadim's. He excused himself and stepped from the stage. He saw a door nearby and slipped through into a hall for the staff. "Hello?"

"Father Gilbert," Vadim said. "I am in front of School of English."

"Stay there. Don't go in," Father Gilbert said.

"I must find my daughter."

"Wait for me. If you go in – if they even see you – they may hide her away and you'll lose her again. I'll be there in ten minutes."

Father Gilbert returned to the stage. The meeting had officially ended and everyone had broken into small clusters to converse further. No one seemed particularly interested in talking to him about his very average parish. However, several people wanted to talk to him about the behind-the-scenes details of what had happened in Stonebridge a few months before.

He grabbed his things and made for the door.

As he crossed the lobby, the Bishop called out for him.

Father Gilbert spun around without stopping. "I'm late," he called back. "Sorry!" And spun around again before the Bishop could react.

* * *

Vadim was nowhere to be seen. Father Gilbert lingered for a moment before ascending the stairs to the front door.

He braced himself for the possibility that Vadim had rushed into the school.

The door opened without his having to be buzzed in. The chair where Derek-the-Guard had sat the night before was now occupied by a young man with short-cropped black hair, large round glasses, and pursed lips.

"May I help you?" the young man asked in an accent Father Gilbert couldn't identify.

"I'm here to see Lorna Henry."

"Is she expecting you?"

"I left my card last night and was told to come back today."

The young man stood up – tall, thin, and straight as a ruler – and strode down the hall.

Father Gilbert waited, wondering what had become of Vadim. From somewhere nearby, he heard a male voice giving phonetic instructions about the English language.

A matronly woman appeared at the end of the hall and paused to look at him. "Father Gilbert?"

"Yes," he said and moved towards her, his hand outstretched. "Lorna Henry, I assume."

Taking his hand, she grasped it more firmly than he expected. "You assume correctly."

She had a pleasant round face, with laughter-lines around her clear blue eyes. Her nose was petite, almost too small for the proportions of her face – possibly she'd had work done on it. She had full lips, shaded with a hint of pink. Her brown hair was cut in a short, easy-to-manage style. She was dressed in a smart-casual tan blouse and black skirt.

"I hope this is a convenient time," he said.

"It is. Come through to my office."

They walked down the hall and turned the corner to another hall. Her office was beyond an old wooden door – painted a nondescript blue – in one of the rooms on the left. The desk, the bookcases, the credenza, and the chairs were immaculately kept and strategically placed. Father Gilbert doubted it was actually the office she used. More likely its purpose was to impress potential students.

"What may I do for you?" she asked once she'd taken a seat behind the desk and he'd made himself comfortable in a guest chair.

"I wanted to find out more about the school and what it has to offer."

She smiled. "Well, as the sign says, it's a school that teaches English."

"To anyone from anywhere?"

"Yes. Our instructors are multilingual with internationally recognized teaching skills."

Father Gilbert nodded, then systematically went through a mental list of the kinds of questions he would be expected to ask. She gave all the right answers. If an illicit business were taking place in the school, he'd never know it from meeting her. She was the consummate professional, as smooth as marble and as personable as the best concierge in the best hotel.

Finally, he asked, "May I have a look around?"

"Of course," she said.

They stood up and she guided him back into the hall. The voice he'd heard earlier came from a large classroom a few doors down. Other doors led to smaller classrooms and several labs with isolated desks, headphones, and disc-players. It was all very impressive.

He gestured to a series of doors further down the hall. "What are those?"

"Private rooms."

"You take in lodgers?"

"What makes you think that?"

"The security guard at the desk last night said so."

"Derek told you that?" She frowned. "I'm surprised."

"It's not true?"

"It's not something we advertise. We have limited space for students with special needs."

"What kind of special needs?"

"Hardship cases. Girls who are struggling financially. Mr Layton, our founder, insisted that we keep that option available for the immigrants who need help. The point is to help them become productive and communicative citizens."

"Those rooms are upstairs?"

"They're spread out around the building."

"May I speak with one of the students who lives here?"

"I thought you did that last night." Lorna's eyes sharpened. It was the first hint Father Gilbert had of a toughness behind her public-relations veneer.

"We didn't have much of a chance to talk."

"I'll see who's available." She took him by the elbow and led him to a kitchen in a room beyond her office. "Help yourself to some coffee. I'll only be a moment."

The coffee-maker pot on the counter was full and hot. Father Gilbert found a mug hanging on a small rack and poured a small amount. He found sugar in a nearby bowl. The refrigerator had a large supply of milk and flavoured creamers. He doctored his coffee and sat down at the closest of three tables.

As he sipped his coffee – which was good, he thought – a young woman walked in. Her blonde hair had the tousled look found on someone who'd just crawled out of bed. This impression was reinforced by the fact that she wore an oversized pyjama shirt and little else. She banged around while making herself a cup of coffee. Then she turned to leave again, seeing him out of the corner of her eye.

"Hi," she said. She was a beautiful fresh-faced girl – tousled hair and all. No more than eighteen, Father Gilbert guessed. "Who are you?"

"Father Gilbert."

She smiled. "You're a real priest? Not just wearing a costume?"

"I'm a real priest."

She giggled and shook her head. "Fancy that."

Lorna Henry came in and stopped short at the sight of the blonde. "Brittany! *Please*."

Brittany looked at Lorna with a childish expression of contrition. She lowered her head and shuffled out of the kitchen. But right before she disappeared from view, she turned her head and gave Father Gilbert a wink.

"I'm so sorry about that," Lorna said. "The girls treat this place like home and sometimes forget themselves."

"I understand. That's a compliment to you, isn't it?" he said.

"I suppose so." Lorna turned, realized no one was behind her, and then stepped into the hall. "What are you waiting for?" she said impatiently.

A young woman came into the kitchen and stopped in front of Father Gilbert. She looked Indian, with dark skin and hair and deep brown eyes. A birthmark sat like a darker stain over the right side of her forehead and eye. She was plump, but not fat, and wore a school uniform. Father Gilbert couldn't imagine why. She was clearly in her early twenties.

Lorna didn't return, so Father Gilbert waved a hand at a chair by the table. "Can you sit for a moment?"

The young woman glanced at the door, then gave a slight curtsey and sat down. Father Gilbert sat opposite from her.

"You speak English?" he said.

She gazed at him, her expression impassive.

"Where are you from?"

She didn't respond.

Father Gilbert thought she didn't speak English after all. Why had Lorna Henry sent her in? "How long have you been a student here?"

She looked quickly towards the door again, then back at him, tilting her head slightly.

Father Gilbert spoke very slowly. "Do you speak English?"

The young woman looked puzzled.

"*En-glish*," he said again, and immediately felt like a tourist in a foreign country.

Lorna Henry returned with someone in the doorway behind her. "I'm sorry about that," she said.

Father Gilbert looked up and said, "I'm afraid we're having trouble communicating."

"Are we?" Lorna asked.

Father Gilbert lifted a hand towards the young Indian woman. "Your student doesn't—" He stopped and felt the blood rush from his face. The chair opposite was empty. He was sitting at the table alone.

"I don't understand," Lorna said, looking as if she'd missed a joke.

Father Gilbert was speechless.

Lorna, sensing something uncomfortable, pressed on. "This is Karolina," she said. "She'll be happy to answer any questions you may have." Stepping aside, a young, elfin girl came into view.

"You don't have any Indian girls here?" Father Gilbert asked, still unnerved by what had just happened.

"Why would you want to speak specifically with a girl from India?" Lorna asked.

"I don't. It's just that I—" He was at a loss for words again. What could he say? The Indian girl wasn't there. He gathered his wits and focused his attention on Karolina. She had a slender face, sandy-brown hair done in two braids, hazel eyes, and a deep dimple on her chin. She wore a white T-shirt and black jeans. "Can you sit for a moment?"

Karolina glanced at Lorna Henry, who nodded her permission. She sat down.

Lorna lingered by the door. Father Gilbert gazed at her. She took the hint and stepped out.

"Do you speak English?" he asked, feeling a sense of déjà vu with the question.

She held up her hand and wiggled it back and forth. "It's OK."

Father Gilbert's mouth had gone dry. He swallowed the rest of his coffee. "Where are you from?" he asked.

"Poland. My family is in Gdansk. I came here to study English and find a job."

"How long have you been a student here?"

"Three months."

"You live here?"

"I have a room, yes."

"They treat you well?"

"Yes." The answer came a little too quickly, almost before he'd finished the question.

"Do you feel safe here?"

"Safe?" Another glance at the door. "What do you mean?"

"You don't worry that anyone will hurt you?"

"No. I am not safe," she said, then corrected herself with a nervous laugh. "I *am* safe, I mean."

"Do the other girls here feel safe?"

"Yes."

"How many of you are there?"

Karolina looked puzzled.

Father Gilbert rephrased the question. "How many girls live here?"

She lifted her shoulders in an awkward shrug. "I don't know how many."

"You don't know how many girls live here with you?"

"I—" She looked at Father Gilbert helplessly. She had hit the limit of the questions she could answer. "Miss Henry," she called out.

Lorna Henry came back into the kitchen. She looked at him with matronly disapproval. "Is everything all right?"

"He wants to know number," the girl said.

"I asked how many girls live here," he explained. "To find out how many the school can accommodate."

"I thought you said you needed classes for your parishioners. Why are you asking so many questions about the rooms?"

"I'm in town for a conference with a large number of clergy from all around the country. They have parishioners with 'special needs', as you called it. I want to know what the options are."

"Thank you." Lorna signalled for Karolina to leave. The girl did so quickly, crouching as if wishing to disappear into a ball and roll out of the kitchen. "We have fifteen rooms."

"Are they all taken?"

"At the moment, yes," she replied. Lorna glanced at the gold watch on her wrist. "Is there anything else you would like to know? I really must get on with my work."

Clearly, the meter had run out on her public relations persona.

Father Gilbert stood up. "Thank you for your hospitality."

Lorna couldn't get him out of the front door quickly enough.

* * *

Back on the street, the sweat on his back turned cold. The Indian girl was an apparition, without a doubt. As with the others, he didn't know why they were appearing to him, or so frequently, or why they seemed to come from different times and places.

He was reminded of a radio scanner he used to have, picking up random frequencies from all over the world. On nights he couldn't sleep, he would sit and slowly change the tuner, picking up a Russian music show one minute, then a traffic report from Tulsa, Oklahoma, and a Spanish talk show the next. The experience led him to do a homily about how our spiritual sensitivities were like antennae: the Holy Spirit giving us the equipment to lock into God's signal so we could be completely tuned in to Him. Feeble as the analogy was, he still believed it. But he never expected it to receive broadcasts from the dead.

He slowly walked away from the school. Glancing around, he expected Vadim to step out from behind a car or a shop. Vadim didn't appear. He took out his mobile phone and dialled Vadim's number. The call went directly to voicemail with a feminine-sounding computer telling him to leave a message. He decided not to and hoped his phone number in the "missed calls" list would tell Vadim enough.

His mind was like a ball of string, one cord getting tangled with another. The complexities of Anong's murder and the bizarre report of her having "died" in London, Brother Sean's death by overdose, the missing Veronyka and how he might contact her – if that was even possible now, the mystery of Cari who also saw the apparitions... the evidence in each situation pulled tight, making the knots even harder to undo. He needed to focus.

But how? He had to put in another appearance at the conference.

Walking back to the convention centre, he prayed for clarity of mind and purity of heart in whatever he'd do next. Though he had no idea of what that might be.

A text from Detective Inspector Gwynn changed his direction yet again. "Room 201. Angel Sea Hotel."

CHAPTER 11

Room 201 of the Angel Sea Hotel was spacious and comfortable and had the sterile conformity to its furniture and arrangement that all corporate hotels seem to have. Detective Inspector Gwynn and a couple of forensics people were giving it the latex glove treatment.

Father Gilbert watched from the door, then stepped back into the hall when Gwynn saw him and came in his direction.

"It's Nathan Rank's room," the DI said.

Mark Pinbrook, the manager, paced down the hall, a mobile phone pressed to his ear. He had a pained expression on his face. It was probably someone from headquarters telling him to handle the PR spin.

"What led to this?" Father Gilbert asked, with a nod to the forensics team.

"One of the housecleaning staff found an open leather satchel with a collection of truncheons on the bed," Gwynn said.

"Truncheons?"

"Nicely laid out in the satchel like some people would do with fountain pens or expensive pipes," Gwynn said. "One was on the floor, with blood and matted hair on it. That's why they called."

"What kind of truncheons?" Father Gilbert asked.

"The small, thick, and heavy kind. All different sizes. And all very effective if you hit someone in the head with one."

That fit the BackList Killer's MO, Father Gilbert thought. Even down to the detail of the different sizes. "Where is Nathan Rank?" he asked.

"We don't know. I had Pinbrook try his mobile phone, but got a voice-message."

"You don't want to alert him. He'll run."

"Pinbrook left a message saying there was a problem with his room and to please call. No more than that. I sent a couple of my men down to the convention centre to see if he's working there."

"Pretty sloppy to leave evidence behind like that," Father Gilbert said. "I can't believe he forgot it was there. Suggesting that he left in a hurry."

"I've called the main detectives on the BackList Killer case to let them know," Gwynn said. "They said they'd done some checking. Nathan Rank was in all the cities on the dates the murders took place."

Father Gilbert thought back to the smooth, well-presented man he'd met the night before. It would be so easy for someone like Nathan Rank to lure women to a place where he could hurt them. But why prostitutes or women from BackList? Rank was a charmer. He could have picked up anyone without having to pay for it. His mind shot back to Anong and he said, "Anong wasn't bludgeoned."

"Not all of the victims were strangled, either. This guy may like variety in his work."

Father Gilbert peered into the room again. The forensics team was searching the drawers and under the bed. "Is this the room where they found the necklace?" he asked.

"The cleaning staff still can't remember which room the necklace came from."

"So it *could* have been this room."

"Or any one of the others."

Pinbrook approached them. "Well? Have you found anything?"

"I'll let you know when we do," Gwynn said.

Pinbrook frowned. "Do you know how disruptive this is?"

"I know," Gwynn replied. "Murder is a real nuisance."

"That's not what I meant," Pinbrook complained.

Father Gilbert asked, "Just out of curiosity: are there any secret passages going in or out of any part of the hotel?"

Pinbrook laughed. "Secret passages? You've been hearing the old legends."

"From Nathan Rank, actually," Father Gilbert said.

"They used to call them 'Pirate Passages'. The legends said that all the buildings in town had them. But this hotel was renovated in the sixties. Whatever was here before had been torn out. If you want a hotel with those kinds of passages, go to the Masthead Inn."

Pinbrook's mobile phone rang again. He put it to his ear and wandered away.

"So the murderer must've had another means to get Anong out," Father Gilbert said.

Gwynn nodded. "Let's talk to the receptionist at the front desk. According to Pinbrook, she was on duty around the time of Anong's death."

They headed for the lifts. Father Gilbert hooked a thumb back to the hallway. "Wouldn't Mr Pinbrook want to be present for the questioning?"

"He'll catch up if he can ever finish his phone calls," Gwynn said. "And I wanted to ask you about a vicar by the name of Mark Solegrove."

"What about him?"

"When we cross-checked attendees of religious conferences in the same towns when the BackList Killer struck, his name came up," Gwynn said. "He's staying at this hotel. And he was seen last night with Rank."

"I believe Solegrove was one of the vicars Rank took out on the town last night," said Father Gilbert. "It could be a coincidence about Solegrove and the timing of the conferences. You've got more than that on Rank right now. Isn't it better to concentrate on him?"

"We'll find Rank." The lift doors opened to the main floor. Gwynn held out his hand for Father Gilbert to go. "But I wanted you to know I've got Solegrove in my sights, too."

* * *

The receptionist was a petite young woman with hair dyed black with purple highlights. She had a small scar just above her left nostril where she'd had a piercing. Her eyes were dark brown, almost black, and were highlighted by black eyeliner. Corporations weren't as picky about staff appearance as they once were, Father Gilbert thought. The gold nametag on her white blouse said she was Mel Braddock. They were in the small security offices looking at what little they could see of the recordings from the night Anong was murdered.

She had looked at Father Gilbert, then Gwynn, for an explanation of why a priest was there. Gwynn didn't offer one.

"I know what you're after. I'm not sure I can help you," she said with a thick East End accent.

"Try anyway," Gwynn said. "You saw the young woman."

"I talked to Anna – I mean, *Anong* – once or twice," Mel said after the recordings didn't yield anything useful.

"You knew her name?"

"Sure."

"You knew what she did?"

"Massage Therapist," Mel replied.

The look in her eye told Father Gilbert she knew better. He suspected Mr Pinbrook wouldn't be happy to know that a known prostitute was working the hotel and a member of the staff did nothing about it.

Mel continued, "She came in that night, but I didn't see her come out again. That doesn't mean she *didn't* come out, only that I might have been in the back or away from the desk when she did."

"Who else did you see that night?" Gwynn asked.

"All kinds of people. With the actors staying here, lots of people come and go. I lose track."

"What about Nathan Rank?"

"The hospitality-organizer-guy? Yeah, he's in and out, usually carrying boxes and stuff."

"Was he here the night Anong was murdered?"

"Yeah. He was in his room for a while."

"What time?"

"I dunno. He may have come in around nine. I remember because he stopped to chat for a minute. He said he liked my style." She touched her hair self-consciously. "The purple is new. Used to be green."

"Did he leave again?"

"Yeah. Around midnight, I think. He had to take a few things back to the conference."

Gwynn leaned against a rack of monitoring equipment and folded his arms. "What kinds of things?"

"I don't know. He used one of those large grey containers with the clips on it. You know the kind, with its own wheels and a handle so you can move it like a dolly."

"How big was the container?" Father Gilbert asked.

She spread her arms out, then put a level hand in mid-air. "Maybe three feet wide and three feet tall?"

"Was it large enough to put someone your size in it?" Father Gilbert asked.

She looked surprised by the question. "Yeah, I s'pose I could fit in one of those. But why would I want to?"

"You wouldn't," Gwynn said, standing up straight. "And neither would Anong."

Mel's eyes grew wide. "You mean—"

"We don't mean anything," Gwynn said.

The door opened and Pinbrook came into the room. His face looked flushed. He was clearly agitated. "What have I missed?"

Gwynn ignored him. "Did Rank go in and out of the main entrance?"

"I can answer that," Pinbrook said quickly, drawing their attention back to him. "He often used the service entrance on the street level at the back."

"Show me," Gwynn said.

* * *

They took a service lift down one floor to an area that served as the mechanical heart of the hotel, with large units for heating and air conditioning, water pumps, thick pipes overhead, vents, and an all-pervasive hum of equipment doing what it should do. The service entrance was near a small bay where vehicles could load and unload goods. Even now, a linen lorry was backed up to the platform. A man, dressed in a white uniform, was moving large carts onto the back of the lorry.

Father Gilbert eyed the area. It would have been easy for Rank to bring Anong's body down in the large container and transport her away without anyone seeing.

"Is this the only service entrance?" Gwynn asked.

"Yes."

They stepped onto the loading platform. A drizzling rain sprayed beneath the rectangular roof overhead. Stairs led down to a wide alley that extended in two directions. A regular-sized door stood fifteen feet away with its own set of stairs.

"Is that the door Rank used?" Gwynn asked.

Pinbrook nodded. "Yes. It's easier for him to load and unload the materials he needs for the conferences. You know what traffic is like by the main entrance."

"He's a regular here?"

"He stays with us whenever he's in town."

"How often is that?"

"Two or three times a year."

Father Gilbert checked the corners of the back wall, above the platform and the pedestrian door. "No security cameras."

Pinbrook hung his head. "Another renovation phase, I'm afraid."

"Where does he keep his car?" Gwynn asked.

"I let him use the staff car park just around the corner."

"Do you know what he drives?"

"A white Vauxhall, I think," Pinbrook said, then added, "I need to know who owns what car so people can't park there illegally."

Gwynn said, "I need the details."

"They're up in the office."

"*Now* would be helpful," Gwynn said with a stern look.

With an anxious look to both men, Pinbrook hurried back into the hotel.

Father Gilbert walked with Gwynn around to the employee car park. It had room for only a dozen cars. A white Vauxhall Insignia sat near the end, bright from the sheen of the rain.

"Is it locked?" Father Gilbert asked.

Gwynn put on his latex gloves and tried the handle on the driver's side. The handle moved but the door didn't open. "Locked."

Father Gilbert looked through a side window. A white shirt and tie were draped over the back seat. A small open box of brochures sat on the back floor.

"I'll get forensics down here," Gwynn said.

* * *

Father Gilbert left the Angel Sea Hotel without knowing any more about Rank, his room, or his car. The officers Gwynn had sent to the convention centre had no success finding him. Father Gilbert feared that Rank knew his room had been discovered and had taken off.

Then there was this new question about Mark Solegrove. Was it possible the BackList Killer was a clergyman? Of course it was possible. Anything seemed possible now.

The two o'clock panel was a discussion about church finances and raising money for church restorations. Father Gilbert's parish church of St Mark's in Stonebridge had some experience with that. Midpoint in the discussion, the Bishop opened a door in the back, peeked in, saw Father Gilbert and nodded, then left again. Father Gilbert bristled at the thought that the Bishop was checking up on him.

He discreetly checked his phone for any messages from Vadim. Nothing. Where had he gone? Was it possible he had connected with his daughter somehow and left for London with her? But surely he'd let Father Gilbert know something that important. Or would he?

He thought about Brother Gregory and the rest of the monks. How were they coping with the death of Brother Sean? It gave him a pang of guilt that he'd been so busy that he hadn't thought of the obvious pastoral needs of the people involved. That was always a danger for him. The Bishop's admonition came back to him: what was his vocation?

As one of the panellists launched into a lengthy discourse on building codes and the difficulties of fixing a church that had been listed as "historical", his mind wandered to ways he could contact Veronyka directly. If he went back to the school itself, he'd be stonewalled. They would likely screen any calls for her, unless he was calling for her services. But how would he do that?

He remembered from his past experience as a detective that the cabbies often knew how to secure the services of a young woman like that. Would the Englesea drivers tell him if he asked?

The panel finished. Father Gilbert said very little. He gathered his things and headed out the door where he nearly bowled over his Uncle George.

"I'm sorry," Father Gilbert said. "What are you doing here?"

"I came to see you in your native environment," George said.

Father Gilbert guided George away from the crowd spilling through the doorway. "Isn't it late for you? Don't you have a show tonight?"

"It's only three o'clock."

Father Gilbert was surprised. "I've lost all track of time."

"How about a drink?" George asked.

"I probably shouldn't," said Father Gilbert. "But I'm happy to join you while you have one."

They walked around the corner to a pub. Father Gilbert ordered juice while George opted for a mixed drink that included three different types of alcohol. Father Gilbert watched him take the first drink.

"You think I drink too much," George said when he put the glass down after his first sip.

"I wouldn't know. Do *you* think you're drinking too much?"

"Not at all. I'm drinking too much when I can't remember my lines or marks."

"That's your guide?"

"Yes. It has served me well over the years." He lifted the glass and took another drink.

Father Gilbert watched him for a moment. "Is something wrong?"

"Not really," he said. He took a deep breath. "But I keep thinking about retiring. I wanted your advice about where to retire to."

"Do you still have that flat in London?"

"Yes. Should I live there?"

Father Gilbert settled back in his chair, glad to be having a normal conversation for once. "Why wouldn't you?"

George's eyes shifted away, his tone growing soft. "Would you visit me? It's quite a journey for you."

Father Gilbert was touched by the question. "Of course I would. It isn't *that* far."

"You know what I mean," he said and his gaze fell back to his drink. "I'm trying to understand our relationship now. Most of the time, I don't think you like me. Frankly, I'm not sure how I feel about you. We're very different. But a man gets older and he looks at family in a new way. Especially when you're the only family I have left."

"You have brothers and sisters. And there's Mum's side of the family, too."

"None of us get along."

Father Gilbert looked at the man seated across from him – the actor, the rogue, the gambler and drinker, the one who'd married his mother out of duty to his dead brother. He felt an affection he hadn't appreciated before. "Uncle George, it doesn't matter where you live. I'll visit you."

George said, "We could go to shows together in London."

"I'd enjoy that."

George looked relieved. "It's settled then."

"Is it?"

"I'll live in London. You'll visit me there. We'll go to the theatre."

Father Gilbert smiled. "Settled." They touched glasses as a toast to finish the deal.

As they relaxed into an unusually companionable silence, Father Gilbert had an idea. He asked, "Uncle George, how can I secure the services of a young prostitute?"

George choked on his drink. "What? Why on earth do you want to know that?"

"It's part of an investigation."

A sceptical look.

"Honestly, it is."

"What makes you think I'd know?"

"You're an actor."

"That doesn't mean I deal with prostitutes!" he said indignantly, then added with a touch of pride, "Besides, I don't need them. Women have been known to throw themselves at me. Not that I was ever unfaithful to your mother, mind you. I certainly had opportunities."

"Why didn't you take them?" Father Gilbert asked, only out of curiosity. "Your marriage to Mum was strictly for convenience."

"Not very convenient, as marriages go," George said. "But no one but the two of us knew what our marriage was. I never wanted her to feel the way some actors' wives feel when their husbands are on the road. I didn't want her to be hurt, so I stayed faithful."

Father Gilbert was impressed. "That's a streak of morality I didn't realize you had."

"You don't know me," George said. "If you really did, you wouldn't have asked me that question."

"But I still need an answer. You must know someone who does that sort of thing."

George gave it some thought. "Trevor Humphries."

"Wasn't he in that comedy back whenever?"

"*Every Mother's Hope*, yes. Clean, wholesome, and a bit of a perv privately. I stopped by his room the other night to retrieve a book I'd lent to him. I clearly interrupted him in flagrante. I think the girl – if it was a girl – had been shoved into the bathroom." He rolled his eyes. "To be honest, I think he stages those occasions so it looks like he's being a naughty boy."

"He was probably doing the crossword, or knitting."

George laughed, then looked at his watch. "I can arrange for us to have drinks before the show."

"I have another panel discussion from four to five. After that?"

"Go to the backstage door at the theatre. Give the porter your name. He'll send you back to my dressing room."

"Thank you."

George gave him a mischievous smile. "You're *sure* this is part of an investigation?"

"I'm helping a man find his daughter. She may be trapped in an operation running out of a school here in town. There has to be a way to arrange a time with her."

"So you're actually going to phone this place for a prostitute," he said in a pointed tone. "And she's going to come to your room at the hotel?"

"It's risky."

George shook his head. "The things the clergy get up to," he said. Father Gilbert chuckled.

"Does she know your name?" he asked.

"I think so."

George's brows pushed together in thought. He was working something out in his mind. He said, "You could meet her in *my* room at the Angel Sea. I'll be at the show. Less conspicuous."

Father Gilbert was impressed. George was thinking the plan through more than Father Gilbert had. "Do you mind?"

"Come to the theatre after five and we'll see what we can do."

* * *

With fifteen minutes to spare before his next panel discussion, this one about pensions, Father Gilbert sat at the conference café to have a cup of tea. He tried to collect his thoughts – not about pensions, but about the questionable, perhaps stupid, idea of arranging to have Veronyka meet him.

Just as he began to talk himself out of it, Father Anthony Reagan sat down across from him.

"I'm sorry to bother you," Father Anthony said. "Have you heard from Vadim?"

"No. But I've been wondering about him all day. He came to Englesea and then disappeared."

"I only just discovered a voice-message from him." He brought out his mobile as if it was evidence to back his story. "Vadim said *his* mobile phone had been stolen and he wasn't able to call you. He rang from a payphone. He was afraid someone was following him. And then the message cut off. I'm worried. Can you have your friend with the police check on him?"

"Detective Inspector Gwynn has been busy with other cases. A man looking for his daughter won't be a priority."

"What can we do?" Father Anthony asked. He stroked at his beard. "Vadim isn't in danger, is he?"

Father Gilbert hoped not. "If he made himself known to whoever is running the operation, they may not like him snooping around."

"Are you convinced it *is* an operation?"

"Something is wrong there."

Father Anthony closed his eyes and frowned. Father Gilbert suspected he was offering up a short prayer. "What happens next?" he asked, then opened his eyes again.

"I have an idea – and you just helped me decide whether I should do it or not."

"What's your idea?"

The question gave him pause. "It's better if I don't say. But I'll let you know what I find out."

* * *

His hopes weren't high as he joined the panel discussion about church pensions, and they plummeted quickly to mind-numbing boredom as talk went to church policies, standard of living increases, national averages, and pie charts. Father Gilbert didn't see the Bishop, nor did he wait around after the panel to be cornered by him. He went quickly to the theatre, following a painted sign on the corner of the building that pointed him down an alley to the backstage door. The porter – who looked more like a security guard – found Father Gilbert's name on a list and sent him down to dressing room "D".

The dressing rooms were part of a concrete labyrinth that reminded him of underground bunkers. He turned one corner, then another, realized he was lost, asked a woman wearing a communications headset where to go, and eventually found a dismal metal door with a "D" fastened into it. He knocked.

George opened the door. His hair was greased back to put on a wig he needed for his character. He had a bib to keep the make-up from getting on his shirt. He was already half made-up, with thick base on his forehead and cheeks. "Come in," he said.

Father Gilbert entered the modest dressing room. On one wall was a lighted mirror, a counter covered with make-up containers, toiletries, and bits of costume. A chair that reminded Father Gilbert of an old barbershop seat sat in front. Another wall was done up to look a little more cosy, with a sofa and an arrangement of framed covers from past programmes. A small table held a plate of vegetables and a bowl filled with ice. Bottled drinks sat next to it. There was a rack with hangers for clothes. An open door led to a small shower and toilet.

"It was the best my agent could negotiate," George said. "At least I'm not sharing this time."

"Did you talk to Trevor Humphries?"

"I invited him down for a drink – which he would never refuse – and told him that my nephew-priest wanted to meet up with a prostitute."

"You didn't."

"I did. Now watch this," George said. He opened a drawer and took out a bottle of whisky. "Trevor will magically appear as soon as he hears this." He set the bottle down on the counter with a heavy thud and did the same with three glasses.

There was an immediate knock at the door.

George smiled. "Go on."

Father Gilbert opened the door to face a tall man, elegantly dressed in a costume from the era of Oscar Wilde – a dark blue velvet jacket with a high-collared white shirt and frilly red bow-tie, an audacious plaid waistcoat, and pale trousers with red stripes. He wore a wig with dark, effeminate curls.

"Are you Wilde?" Father Gilbert asked.

"I can be for you, padre," the man said with a lecherous wink as he moved into the dressing room. "Are you pouring, darling?" he asked George.

George handed him the glass of whisky, nearly full.

Apart from the costume, Trevor Humphries was simply an older version of the actor Father Gilbert remembered. He conducted himself as if he were already on stage. His accent had a rich plumminess of wealth and stature that belied his childhood in the poverty of London's East End. It was a story Father Gilbert had read in the newspapers over the years.

"I must admit that this is one of the more unusual requests I've had," Humphries said. His words were slightly slurred. Had he already been drinking?

"The same for me," Father Gilbert said.

"I've never had to play pimp for a priest," he said loudly and then let out a roar of laughter. He sat – rather, he sprawled – on the sofa, leaving Father Gilbert to stand. George busied himself with his make-up.

Father Gilbert tried to explain: "I'm not actually going to—"

"It's all right, dear boy. It's not for me to judge." As he said it, Father Gilbert remembered Nathan Rank saying something similar.

George, facing the mirror, looked at Father Gilbert in the reflection. "I explained that you were trying to help a man find his daughter, but he thinks the idea of you meeting with a prostitute is far more interesting."

"It does my heart good to see the church move with the times," Humphries proclaimed.

Father Gilbert wanted to get on with the conversation and get away from the man. "How does it work?"

"Are you dealing with the woman directly?" he began, then quickly added, "It is a woman you want, right?"

"Yes."

"Then you would call or text her directly from your mobile phone."

"How do you get the numbers?"

"Oh, they post them in places like BackList or a few pornographic websites, or some of the newspapers or circulars. Back when we had phone boxes, they'd paste their pictures and numbers in those." He said it wistfully, as if he yearned for the good old days.

"What if the girls are being run through an establishment, like a school?"

There was a twinkle in his eye. "Lorna Henry's place."

"You know it?" Father Gilbert asked.

A warm smile. "It's the best in town. High-quality girls. So much better than the other establishments. As it happens, I have their phone number." He reached for a trouser pocket, then remembered he was in costume. He redirected his hand to the jacket pocket. "I must remember to put this back in my dressing room. It wouldn't do to have it ring during the show. I remember a production of *Julius Caesar* in Cardiff—"

"Father Gilbert is limited on time, Trevor," George said. "The phone number?"

"Oh, yes." Humphries found the phone number he wanted. He was about to show it to Father Gilbert when he suddenly stopped.

"You're only looking for the one girl, right? You don't intend to close down the school?"

"I can't promise what will happen once I meet with the girl," Father Gilbert said.

Humphries tipped his head back and forth as if considering the pros and cons. "Oh, never mind. I won't be back here anytime soon anyway." He gave Father Gilbert the number.

"I ring this – and then what?" he asked.

"Well. There's a *code* to getting what you want. The code, you see, is the language, what with it being a *language* school." He waved his drink around like a prop, flamboyantly, without spilling a drop. "You ring the number and tell them what *language* you want to know about. That tells them what kind of girl you want. Ask for Cambodian or Turkish or whatever you fancy and they'll know. Very clever, you see." He laughed, then asked, "Where is the girl from, by the way?"

"She's Moldovan."

"Right. So you'll say you want to learn to speak Moldovan and they'll know you want a Moldovan girl."

"What if you ask for a language and they don't have the girl?"

"Then they'll say they don't have classes available for that language and suggest you try something else."

"That's it?"

"Yes. Then you give them the time and the place and they'll say they will send a *representative* over to talk to you if one is available." He wiped his hands together as if the effort were entirely clean. "That's how easy it is. No more difficult than ordering pizza."

"Easy."

"They may take credit cards over the phone now. I can't remember."

"I'll stay with cash."

"Good idea," Trevor said. "Oh, and don't *ever* ask what the price will be."

"Why not?"

"That's how they know the caller is with the police. Or a novice, in which case they may be wary. If you're experienced, you know better than to ask how much the service costs or you could be nicked for solicitation."

"Is there anything else?"

"No. That'll get you your hour's pleasure."

Father Gilbert scrutinized the man for a moment as he took a large gulp of his drink. "I don't understand. A man with your looks and talent – why do you use prostitutes?"

"Dear boy, it's the only way," he said. "I've tried to have affairs but they always go wrong. The problem is that the women develop *expectations*. Expectations *kill* relationships for me."

Father Gilbert reached out to shake his hand. "Thank you. I think."

Humphries shook it without standing up. "Good luck, old chum. And please don't mention me to Lorna. I wouldn't want her to think I was being unfriendly."

George stood up and said to Humphries, "I'll see him out."

Humphries winked at him and put a thumb in the air, as he once had done in a movie about the Royal Air Force. *Wings Over the Rhine*, Father Gilbert thought it was called.

"Ghastly, I know," George said softly once they were in the labyrinth. "I can't stand the man."

"That's a lot of alcohol," Father Gilbert said. "How will he perform tonight?"

George shook his head. "It's uncanny. As soon as he walks onstage, he *becomes* the character he's playing. I have never heard him miss a line." He handed Father Gilbert a hotel key card. "Room 410."

"Thank you."

"Leave it as you found it, as they say."

"I will."

George pressed his arm. "I hope you aren't making a mistake."

"So do I."

Father Gilbert walked towards the stairs. From behind him, George called out in a Trevor Humphries style, "Tally-ho, old chap!"

* * *

When he reached the lobby of the Angel Sea Hotel, Father Gilbert was surprised to see Mark Solegrove standing near the front window. He was staring out at the street with a forlorn expression.

"Mark?" Father Gilbert said, wondering if Gwynn had talked to him yet.

Solegrove slowly turned, as if it took time for Father Gilbert's voice to penetrate his thoughts. "Father Gilbert." His face creased up as if he might cry. He fought it back.

"Are you all right?" Father Gilbert asked, stepping closer. "Do you need to talk?"

"Not here."

"Where?"

Solegrove looked quickly around, then spied an alcove with two chairs inside. He walked over to it, slumping into one of the chairs.

Father Gilbert followed and sat down next to him.

Solegrove's face was pale. He looked sick. "I wish I believed in confession."

"We have a form of it in the Church of England," Father Gilbert said. "What's wrong?"

"I heard that the police have been in Nathan Rank's room."

Father Gilbert didn't say anything.

"There are rumours that he's in serious trouble. They think he's that killer. The BackList one."

"You can't believe everything you hear," Father Gilbert said, knowing it was a feeble thing to say.

"It's not possible, is it?" Solegrove asked. "There's no solid evidence that it was him, is there?"

"I can't answer that," Father Gilbert said.

Solegrove's eyes darted nervously around the lobby. "The police will have checked the room for fingerprints," he said, as if to confirm his worries.

"More than likely, if they think he's a serious criminal."

Solegrove hunched over and put his face in his hands for a moment. Then he collected himself and sat up again. "They'll find mine."

"Why were you in his room?" Father Gilbert asked, remembering that Solegrove had been part of the group that had gone out with Rank the night before.

He struggled with his answer, his lips moving slightly, then pressing together again. Then he nodded as if he'd made up his mind about what to say next. "Nathan and I are..." He swallowed hard. "We've been involved."

"Involved," Father Gilbert repeated. "Just last night or longer?" he asked.

"Longer," Solegrove said with a frown.

"You were in an affair with him," Father Gilbert said, trying to work out exactly what Solegrove was trying to say.

Solegrove shook his head. "We weren't lovers, not in the sense that we were in love."

"Then what were you?"

"We were..." Solegrove began, then rubbed the back of his hand against his mouth. "There was no commitment. It was purely physical, whenever we happened to meet up."

"You met up often?"

"I go to a lot of conferences. Some of them coincided with his work."

That explained the connection between the religious conferences and the BackList murders and Solegrove and Rank.

Solegrove's face creased up. Tears squeezed out of his eyes. He hunched over again. "It sounds so tawdry. Clandestine sex rather than an act of love. At least love would be a reasonable excuse."

Father Gilbert took a second to offer a quick prayer, hoping for inspiration about how to respond. None of the words that came to mind made it as far as his voice. He put a hand on Solegrove's shoulder.

"I have to go to the police, don't I?"

"Yes. It's better for you to tell them rather than them coming to you."

He didn't speak for a moment. His face was an expression of pure anguish. "I'm married, you know. I have three kids."

Father Gilbert's heart broke. Everything in this man's life, family, and ministry might change now. "Do you want me to go to the police with you?" Father Gilbert asked.

"I want to be man enough to do this myself," Solegrove said. "And I wouldn't want them to think you're involved."

I'm already involved, he thought but didn't say. "They'll have a lot of questions for you about Nathan." Father Gilbert was already wondering if Solegrove might be an unintentional alibi for some of Rank's time.

"I'm sure they will. But I don't think I can tell them very much. I don't really *know* him personally," he said. Another look of pain crossed his face.

"Would you like to pray before you go?" Father Gilbert asked.

Solegrove collapsed into tears. "Yes please."

Father Gilbert closed his eyes and silently asked for God to give him the words to say in the prayer he was about to whisper to Mark Solegrove.

* * *

Room 410 looked identical to Nathan Rank's room. No wonder the cleaners couldn't remember in which room Anong's necklace had been found. Apart from a suitcase in a corner and toiletries in the bathroom, there was little evidence that his uncle was staying there.

Father Gilbert thought about all of the rooms like this George had made home over the years. Generic, impersonal, devoid of warmth. For a moment, he could understand how loneliness might drive men into the arms of strangers, even if it was for a short time.

Emotionally drained, Father Gilbert paced for a few minutes, praying again for Mark Solegrove, and then for any wisdom or guidance from God about what he intended to do. He picked up the telephone on the bedside table. He dialled to get an outside line, then punched in the number Humphries had given him.

As he waited for something to happen, he suddenly wished Humphries had given him a wrong number. It would give him an excuse not to go through with it. *Sorry, Vadim, I tried.*

There was a click and then the phone rang on the other end. After three rings, a man picked up and said, "Hello."

Father Gilbert's mouth went dry.

"Hello?"

He swallowed hard. "I'm interested in a language," he said.

"What language, in particular?"

"Moldovan."

The man paused. Was he checking something – a roster or schedule? "We have a representative to help you with that," he said.

"Good."

"Is this your first attempt to learn the language?"

Father Gilbert was thrown by the question. What did the man mean? Then he realized what was being asked: *is this your first time with one of our girls?* "Yes."

"Your name, please?"

He thought quickly. If he gave a fake name and Veronyka's handlers checked with the hotel's front desk to make sure he was a guest, they might stop her from coming if the name didn't match. He had to give the name of the room's occupant. "Gilbert."

"What time and location?" the man asked.

"Six o'clock at the Angel Sea Hotel, room 410."

"Our representative will see you then." The man hung up.

It *is* like ordering pizza, Father Gilbert thought as he placed the receiver back on the cradle. His hands were shaking.

***

Father Gilbert was no stranger to sexual temptation. Not since, at the age of eleven, he'd found a magazine filled with photos of nude women in a hedgerow. He'd smuggled it home under his shirt. Mostly he was curious about what he was looking at. The strange sensations came later.

Cousin Maeve was a precocious fifteen-year-old who thought thirteen-year-old boys were fascinating and that what she called their "awakening" was something she needed to be a party to. For her, lessons about anatomy and physiology ought to be experienced, if only through a kind of "show and tell" and strategic touching. Nothing more was allowed.

He was a virgin throughout his courtship with Katherine. Until the day he received his acceptance letter into the police-training programme. He went out to celebrate with his mates and then, later, went to her house a little tipsy. Her parents were at the cinema. Her brother and sister were spending the night at friends'. He thought what happened between them was a celebration of their future together. He didn't learn until years later that it was actually a last-ditch attempt by her to try to keep him in the relationship. Then, when she became pregnant, she realized she didn't want to be the wife of a policeman or to have her child raised by one. She let him drift away into his new life.

The years leading up to his marriage to Ellen were a wilderness sexually. He had no moral qualms about being active in that way, but he thought the games-playing and complications sex triggered were a distraction from his career. Then he took an injured suspect to casualty for treatment and met a young nurse named Ellen Greene. Within a few days, his resistance had gone completely. They married four months later.

After her death and his resignation from law enforcement, he retreated into a different kind of wilderness. Abstinence was essential to his newfound spiritual life. He had decided that sex was never a clarifier about the real issues of life. More often than not it only added confusion. It made more and more sense to him why God wanted sex to take place in the context of marriage.

That was his intellectual position on the subject. When it came to lust, he struggled as any man would. He fought it through willpower, distraction, and prayer. He sometimes tackled it as a subject to be dissected. He reminded himself again and again that lust was a liar that made promises it never intended to keep, it fed on a fantasy that ignored the realities of flesh-and-blood and the consequences of sex. For all that, he was no stronger than most men. Only a little more intentional, perhaps. But he became convinced that the majority of men never advanced beyond the age of fifteen when it came to their sexual thinking. Beneath the suit of maturity beat the heart of a boy who looked for any opportunity to be naughty.

Even now, the thought of being alone in a room with an attractive and available young woman brought back the kinds of feelings he'd had after finding that magazine in the hedgerow.

He prayed until the gentle knock came at the door at six o'clock.

* * *

As he went to answer the door, he imagined Veronyka as she walked through the lobby. Did she wave to Mel, the receptionist at the front desk? Did Mel know all of the prostitutes who visited the hotel? Did she get a gratuity for *not* reporting them to the police?

He put his eye to the spyhole.

Veronyka knew she was being looked at and stepped back so she could be clearly seen. She wore a tight white blouse under a black jacket that matched her short black skirt. She put a hand on her hip and looked in one direction, then another, like a model on a catwalk.

He slowly opened the door and moved aside so she could come in.

"Mr Gilbert," she said as she entered without looking at him. Getting out of the hall quickly was clearly a priority. She pulled a wheeled overnight case behind her as she went directly to the centre of the room. He looked into the hall, wondering if anyone had seen her. Several doors away, a clergyman – he couldn't remember the name – was trying to insert a key card into its lock. He glanced over at Father Gilbert, who ducked inside. He hoped he hadn't been seen. He closed the door.

Veronyka had put her case on the desk chair and said in her heavy Moldovan accent, "I think it is always best to get the business out of the way."

He was in clear view now when she turned to face him. They made eye contact.

Her practised smile fell as she recognized him.

"You," she said, and it was clear to Father Gilbert that the most obvious conclusion she could draw was that he *had* been soliciting the night before. He noted disappointment in her voice when she said, "One hundred pounds up front, please."

He reached for his wallet and thumbed through his cash.

"Most of the time they take off the collars," she said as she handed her the money.

"Do they?" he asked, pained to hear her admission.

"It stops embarrassment," she said. "You are not embarrassed."

"I'm not embarrassed because I don't want what you think I want."

"What do you want?"

"I want to *talk* to you. That's all."

"Talk?" She rolled her eyes. "You want therapy?"

"No."

"Are you going to preach to me? Try to convert me? I met with one of you before. He talked and preached and then he still did to me what I went there to do."

"I won't preach and I don't want anything else."

"It's no good if you think I'll convert." She took the case off of the desk chair and sat down. She crossed her legs and put her hands on her knee. "It's your money. Your time. What do you want to talk about?"

He looked at her and thought of the many other men who were in rooms like this with women like Veronyka. Sadly, he knew that whatever the men expected – whatever would happen between them in the hour they'd paid to have – it wouldn't fulfil the longing or emptiness they were trying to assuage. And the women would walk away with the money, their souls scarred yet again in ways they hardly realized.

"Your father is looking for you," he said.

Of all the things she had expected him to say, it was clear she hadn't expected that. Her face, which had been set in a look of defiance and cynical amusement, softened ever so slightly. "You've talked to my father," she said.

"Yes. I've been trying to find you for him."

"Is that so?" She fidgeted in the chair. "Then where is he? Hiding in the bathroom?"

"He came to Englesea this morning. But I haven't been able to reach him since. If I could, I would let him know that you're here."

"Why is he looking for me now?"

"He wants to save you from this."

She snorted. "It has taken him a long time."

"He didn't know where to find you. After you disappeared from the School of English in London, he didn't know what to do. He's been searching for you ever since."

She looked down and adjusted her skirt. "The School of English," she said in a way he couldn't interpret.

"Do you want to go back to London?" Father Gilbert asked, feeling a little confused.

"Is that what he wants? To take me back to *London*?" She looked up at him.

"Yes," he said.

She pressed her lips together, weighing her options. "I suppose London is better than this," she said.

Father Gilbert wasn't sure what to make of it. Rather than being relieved or grateful to be rescued, she treated it like he'd just given her a slightly better offer for a slightly better job opportunity.

"How will we go? They're watching."

"Who is?"

"My handlers."

Father Gilbert sat down on the edge of the bed. "It would help if you explain to me how the operation works. Let's start with what happened in London and how you were brought here."

She looked down at her hands and clasped her fingers together. She had decorative rings on three of her fingers. "Does it matter?"

"It does if we hope to stop other girls from falling into the same trap."

"Trap." She said the word like she wasn't sure of its meaning. "I went to the School of English and they led me to a back room. I thought it was the class. But it was a storage room with a door leading out. They put something over my head so I couldn't see. They dragged me out into an alley, put me in a car, and drove me away. I don't know where they took me. A house with a room. They locked me in. No windows. No way to get out. They took everything so I couldn't make a call. Then they put me to work and beat me if I didn't obey."

"Where were you then?"

"Somewhere in London, I think. I don't know where I was." She was impassive as she spoke. "I worked there for a month or so."

"Then they brought you to Englesea?"

"Yes."

"How long have you been here?"

"A month, maybe."

"You left the building on your own last night. I followed you. Why haven't you tried to escape?"

"I am always being watched. Someone follows me. Someone is waiting outside now."

"Is it the guard I saw last night?"

"Sometimes it's him. But they have others. I don't know them. I haven't seen them all. But I know they're there."

Father Gilbert thought about his own paranoia, the faceless Shadow Man, and whoever had left the message in his room. "Have you ever tried to escape?"

"Once I did a test," she said. "I walked down the wrong street. I went left instead of right. I wanted to see what would happen. But a man I never saw before came up to me. He said I went the wrong way and if I did it again or tried to escape they would kill me."

That's what Father Gilbert needed to hear. A clear example of coercion. "I'll take you to the police. They can protect you."

"The police can't help me," she said scornfully. "They are part of it. Some of the police are my customers."

Father Gilbert grimaced. "Then I'll take you somewhere else."

"Where?" she demanded. "Even if you could, what will happen next? *You* will take care of me?"

"If I have to," Father Gilbert said, his mind bringing up images of people in his parish who would be glad to help. "Then I'll work with your family. There are government agencies that do this all the time." Father Gilbert was desperate to believe what he was saying to her, even though he had seen from past experience the problems they'd encounter.

She laughed at him. "You make promises. But you can't even get me out of this hotel."

"I'll think of something." Father Gilbert thought of Anong again and the idea came to him. "There is a way out."

"Our time ends at seven o'clock," she said, glancing at the clock on the bedside table. "If I am not walking back to the school by ten minutes after that, they will come for me."

It was now 6:25. "We'll smuggle you out before they realize what's happening."

"And how will you do that?" she asked.

* * *

Father Gilbert made one call on his mobile phone. Then he picked up the hotel phone to reach Mel at the front desk. He considered inviting her into his plan, but didn't want to take the chance if she was in the pocket of whoever ran the operation. He asked to speak with Pinbrook, hoping he was still there.

Pinbrook picked up in his office and listened while Father Gilbert explained the situation. He didn't protest, as Father Gilbert had expected he would. He said, "I'll be there in a moment."

A few minutes later, Pinbrook knocked at the door. Father Gilbert opened it up, remaining in the doorway.

As he handed Father Gilbert a key, Pinbrook glanced past him into the room. He raised an eyebrow. "Bring it back to me when you're done." He walked away without any further comment.

"Come on," Father Gilbert said to Veronyka.

"What is your plan?" she asked.

He guided her down the hall to the service lift. Using the key, he summoned the lift. "Your chaperone will be watching out front, right?"

"Probably."

"We'll take you out the back."

The lift arrived and they got in. He used the key to send it to the lowest floor. They went to the rear door near the loading dock. He opened the door just as an old Range Rover drew up. He gestured for Veronyka to follow him to the car.

"Who is this?" she asked, trying to see the driver. "How do I know you're not kidnapping me?"

Father Gilbert opened the passenger door. Brother Gregory leaned over to look at him. His silver hair reflected in the streetlights.

"Veronyka Dalca, meet Brother Gregory," said Father Gilbert. "He's taking you to St Sebastian's until we can safely move you to somewhere better."

"I don't have to tell you how strange this is," Brother Gregory said.

Veronyka looked in at the priest, then back at Father Gilbert. "If this doesn't work, they will hurt me. Maybe you, too."

"It'll work," Father Gilbert said.

She threw her suitcase into the back and then climbed in.

"Nice to meet you," Brother Gregory said.

Father Gilbert closed the passenger door and the car pulled away.

* * *

He went back to George's room, made sure everything was as he'd found it, then went down to the front desk. Pinbrook was there.

"Thank you," he said, handing the manager the key and George's key card.

Pinbrook looked unhappy. He said from the corner of his mouth, "I don't like it. Prostitutes and murders. It's bad for our reputation. It's bad for business."

"You've just done one small thing to help stop it," Father Gilbert said. He walked out of the hotel and onto the front pavement. He paused to call Gwynn and to look around for anyone who might be watching – for him, or Veronyka. He smiled as he thought, *It's a wonder people aren't tripping over each other, what with so many people following other people around.*

He was about to push the button to dial Gwynn when a man stepped up next to him. Something that felt uncannily like a gun pressed into his side. *Just like in the movies,* he thought.

The man wore a suit jacket that looked like the seams might burst from his muscular frame. His face was a circle, his head clean-shaven. The only distinctive feature was a large moustache. "Get in the car."

"What car?"

The dark sedan that pulled up to the kerb.

Father Gilbert didn't move. "Where are we going?" he asked.

"Someone wants to talk to you," Mr Moustache said. His voice was surprisingly high for such a meaty person.

"I was taught never to accept rides from strangers."

"He's no stranger," Mr Moustache said, then nudged him with the gun.

At that moment, Father Gilbert wondered why people always seemed to cooperate at times like these. Yes, the man had a gun and, yes, it was assumed he would use it. But what if Father Gilbert suddenly jumped away and shouted for help from any of the passers-by on the street? That would be the unexpected move. The man with the gun would be seen. Someone would also spot the car and the registration number.

But, unfortunately, someone might also see Father Gilbert sprawled on the ground, the blood spilling onto the pavement from his gunshot wound.

Cooperating was the better option, even if it wasn't the better bet.

Father Gilbert walked to the rear passenger door. Mr Moustache opened the door for him. Father Gilbert climbed in and scooted over. Mr Moustache got in after him.

The driver wore a hoodie and was no more than a pair of eyes in the rear-view mirror.

The car pulled into traffic and drove away from the town.

CHAPTER 12

Father Gilbert was driven west along the coast to a small parking area next to an inlet, not far from the sea. The driver remained in the car while Mr Moustache led Father Gilbert down a stone path to a long wooden dock where a cruising yacht, close to forty feet long, white and sleek, was moored. There were two decks above the hull, each sheltered by roofs on top and dark Plexiglas wrapped around the sides.

They climbed on board and Father Gilbert couldn't help but admire the teak wooded decks and spacious lounge area with pristine tables and chairs. Whoever wanted to meet him had good taste.

The man with the moustache patted him down and took his mobile phone. He unfastened the back, took out the battery, and put the phone and the battery in his pocket. He gestured for the priest to go ahead of him, and they descended below the main deck. The cabins they passed boasted a slightly gaudy opulence. They reached a door at the front of the boat, where Mr Moustache tucked his gun away and knocked on the door. A muffled "Come in" came from the other side and Mr Moustache pushed open the door. They entered a vast stateroom fitted with teak and dark wood, curtained windows, a full bar, a day bed, and various fixed tables and chairs.

Jack Doyle stood next to a pool table, cue in hand, the balls moving from a shot he'd just taken. He turned to Father Gilbert, the cue held like a spear.

Father Gilbert had never met Jack Doyle in person, though he'd met Doyle's wife after the suicide of their son. He'd seen photos of Doyle in the newspaper. But the man in front of him was more formidable and intimidating than he expected. He stood tall and lean – lean the way a jaguar would look lean – with a slight curve to his shoulders that made him look like he might pounce at any minute. He had a pockmarked complexion, a thin cruel mouth, heavy-lidded eyes, and wiry metallic grey hair held in place by some kind of gel.

"Father Gilbert," he said, with a voice of rough stones scraping together. He put the cue onto a holding rack and gestured to a pair of chairs sitting on opposite sides of a small table. A bowl of crisps and a tray of drinks sat on top. "Take a seat."

Father Gilbert obeyed.

"Thank you for coming," Doyle said as he sat down.

"Did I have a choice?"

"Not really, no. But thank you anyway." Doyle poured bottled water into a glass, then held it up for Father Gilbert, who shook his head. Doyle shrugged off the rejection and took a long drink. "I thought about being a priest when I was a kid. Then I got interested in girls and that was the end of that."

"What can I do for you, Mr Doyle?" Father Gilbert asked. He had dealt with men like Doyle when he was a detective. A combination of respect and directness usually worked.

"I've been at a disadvantage for a while now," Doyle said. "You knew me – what with getting involved in my family life after Colin died – but I didn't know you."

"You could have invited me to dinner."

The corners of Doyle's lips moved to form what was nearly a smile. "I was interested in what I learned. Your father was a copper – your *real* father, I mean – not the actor you thought was your father."

Doyle was testing him, Father Gilbert knew. He didn't respond.

"Clare Gilbert, your mother, passed away not too long ago," Doyle said, then added a cursory, "My condolences."

"Thank you."

"Your wife Ellen Gilbert died of pancreatic cancer," he said. "That may have been why you left Scotland Yard. Or you may have left because of a case you mishandled. The Patricia Atkins suicide – though you claimed it was murder." He held up his forefinger. "More about that later." Then he resumed going as he had been. "The Atkins case and your wife's death pushed you over the edge, some colleagues said, causing you to reflect upon your life as a detective. You resigned, then surprised everyone by becoming religious. And not only religious, but a *priest*, of all things."

Father Gilbert remained passive, waiting for Doyle's performance to end.

"No children because your wife was incapable," Doyle continued. "But it turns out you had fathered a child by your first love Katherine Donovan, later Katherine Perry, a vicar's wife. Your daughter Clare, now Clare Thomas, wife of Robert, now lives in Boston—"

"Mr Doyle, I know you want to impress me with your research abilities. However, professional courtesy demands that you leave my wife or family or anything to do with my child out of this."

"Normally I would agree, but your appearance in my life was connected to *my* child's death. You came to *my* house. You spoke to *my* wife about *my* family. I think that puts us on rather intimate terms, don't you?"

"No," he replied. "I didn't ask to be drawn into your life."

"But you were," Doyle said. He paused and fixed his gaze on Father Gilbert. "Did you know that almost ninety per cent of marriages fail after the death of a child by suicide?"

"I've heard a variety of statistics."

"Do you know how my marriage has survived?"

"No."

"We don't believe our son killed himself," Doyle said. "Just like you don't believe Patricia Atkins committed suicide. It galvanizes you, doesn't it? It gives you something to fight for."

Or it helps ward off an extreme feeling of failure, Father Gilbert thought.

"The police have closed the case, as you know, but I haven't. Eventually I'll find out who murdered my son and made it look like suicide."

"If anyone has the resources to do it, you do," Father Gilbert said.

Doyle stood up and moved to the bar. "Don't patronize me."

"I'm in earnest."

Picking up a bowl of wrapped sweets, Doyle fingered through the selection, then put it down again without choosing anything. He turned to face Father Gilbert, leaning back with his elbows on the bar's rubber bumper. "Do you think my son killed himself?"

"The evidence says he did."

"You saw him on your church tower when he was supposed to be dead." His tone was sharp, angry.

"That's right," Father Gilbert said. *He was as real to me there as you are now*, he almost added. *But not because he was alive. At his home, miles away, he had hanged himself. But I wouldn't expect you to understand the spiritual realities I deal with, especially since I don't understand them myself.*

"Explain that to me."

"I can't."

"Why not? You're a *priest*."

"That doesn't give me a corner on the market when it comes to the dead."

A cool stare from Doyle. "You're not doing so well with the living either, are you?"

Father Gilbert met Doyle's gaze.

"Running around Englesea, stirring things up…" Doyle reached out and touched a bar stool, swivelling it back and forth. "It's been fun to watch."

"You should have your people follow me back home, too. That's even higher entertainment value." He rubbed the smooth wood of the armrests. "Thank you for leaving that message on the tablet in my room. Was there a point to that?"

Doyle spread his hands as a show of innocence. "It's an important lesson. You never know who's watching."

"God watches all the time."

"In *His* world," Doyle said. "Welcome to *my* world."

Father Gilbert thought of the arguments he could make. He decided against them. Better, this time, to play along. "I didn't realize Englesea was part of your world. I thought your world was back in Southaven."

"My world is *much* bigger than that. I'm connected to a lot of places. And, as you can guess, it's a lot of work."

"However do you cope?" Father Gilbert asked with unmistakable irony.

Doyle set the bar stool straight, then did the same with the other five as he talked. "I watch. I listen. I keep the upper hand by negotiating, persuading and, when necessary, use of effective force." He glanced over at Father Gilbert.

"Should I be intimidated?" Father Gilbert asked.

"I'm only giving you something to think about."

"All right."

"It's the way of the world you stumbled into."

"I'm listening."

Doyle continued, "Threaten me and I retaliate. If somebody hits me, I hit them back harder. If they take what's mine, I take back what was mine *and* something of theirs, so they won't take from me again. And if somebody *destroys* what's mine, then… well, you can guess the rest."

"Is this the summation of your business philosophy?"

"It's worked so far." He gave another smile-that-wasn't-really-a-smile.

"Based on what you've said, then, I could rightfully assume you had the church vandalized."

"I don't vandalize churches. It's amateurish and ineffective."

"But you *do* kidnap priests."

"This isn't a kidnapping. It's… a 'relocated conversation'." He laughed at his cleverness.

"Why am I here, Mr Doyle?"

"I wanted to say thank you."

"For what?"

"For bringing to light the things in Englesea I didn't know about. You've been a valuable resource. I'm grateful."

"I didn't realize I was being so helpful to you."

Doyle walked over to the pool table and picked up the cue again. "Father, the good intentions of guys like you *always* help guys like me."

Father Gilbert stood up. "Mr Doyle, worlds like yours always get sucked into a giant black hole and implode. You're better off in God's world, operating on His terms."

Doyle laughed.

Mr Moustache returned and stood by the door. *Here endeth the lesson.*

"Maybe we'll have that dinner in Southaven sometime," Doyle said as he lined up a shot.

"I'll look forward to that."

"It's time to go home to your little church, Father Gilbert. Do your eight o'clock panel and get out of here," Doyle said over his shoulder. He took the shot, the balls clacking loudly.

Father Gilbert followed Mr Moustache out of the stateroom and thought, *What does it profit a man to gain the whole world and lose his soul?*

* * *

As he was driven back to Englesea, Father Gilbert thought about the business lesson he'd received from Doyle. It was packed with messages, though the meanings weren't clear. *Retaliation, taking what's his, destroying those who destroy...* how did they apply to the circumstances of the past few days?

"Are you going back to the hotel or would you like us to drop you at the convention centre?" Mr Moustache asked. "You have plenty of time before your panel discussion."

Father Gilbert smiled at him. "You're quite the concierge."

"Four years at Brown's Hotel in Mayfair," he said.

"I wouldn't mind some spiritual direction after that meeting," Father Gilbert said, though he was actually thinking about Veronyka. "Would you mind taking me to St Sebastian's?"

"Not at all." Mr Moustache and the driver exchanged a look via the rear-view mirror. With little warning, the driver took a hard left.

Threaten me and I retaliate. If somebody hits me, I hit them back harder. If they take what's mine, I take back what was mine and something of theirs, so they won't take from me again. And if somebody destroys what's mine, then... well, you can guess the rest.

The words circled around in Father Gilbert's mind. He tried to take them one at a time.

Threaten me and I retaliate.

He thought about the vandalism at St Sebastian's. Is that what Doyle was talking about? Had Brother Gregory's outspoken attacks on the local sex industry provoked Doyle into counterattacking the church, in spite of his assertions to the contrary? Had Father Gilbert's investigation of the School of English been taken as a provocation?

The traffic came to a crawl. Father Gilbert looked out of the window. A constable with a flare was waving the cars past the road on the right. In the distance, flashing emergency lights sprayed blue and red on the houses and businesses. Black-and-yellow-jacketed personnel scrambled with hoses around a fire engine. Smoke billowed from somewhere beyond a large office building.

Father Gilbert craned his neck to see. He recognized the area and suddenly said, "Is the School of English on fire?"

"It looks like it," Mr Moustache said without looking.

Father Gilbert struggled to see until the scene passed from view.

It couldn't have been coincidence. Father Gilbert looked at Mr Moustache, who kept his gaze fixed straight ahead.

Slumping back into his seat, he realized he'd made a big mistake. When Doyle's name had been thrown around as the puppetmaster behind the sex industry in Englesea, Father Gilbert had assumed he had control of everything. That was wrong. Lorna Henry and her bosses were the *competition*.

Threaten me and I retaliate. If somebody hits me, I hit them back harder.

Father Gilbert's heart lurched. If Doyle had committed arson against the School, what else had he done?

The car pulled up to St Sebastian's and the electric locks clicked to announce his release. Father Gilbert opened the door and stepped out.

"Don't forget your phone," Mr Moustache said as he handed over the two pieces.

"Thank you for your consideration," Father Gilbert said.

Mr Moustache pulled the door closed. The car moved slowly away and disappeared around a turning.

Father Gilbert looked towards the town. From this vantage point he could see the flames licking at the roof of the school and the arc of water from the fire engine's water pumps.

He put the battery back into his mobile phone and turned it on. It cycled through its start-up routine and then buzzed in his hand for an incoming call. Father Gilbert pushed the button.

"It's about time," Gwynn said against a lot of background noise.

"Did you know the school is on fire?" Father Gilbert asked.

"Yes. Where are you?"

"I'm at St Sebastian's. I can see the fire from here. Is anyone hurt?"

"No, but apparently there were several young women running around in very little clothing. I'm sorry to have missed that."

"Where are you?" He walked quickly towards the church. Lights were on inside. He hoped the door was open, otherwise he'd have to walk around to the living quarters and find a way in.

"I got a court order to tow Nathan Rank's car from the back of the hotel to a garage where we can check it over for evidence."

"Did you talk to Mark Solegrove?" He pulled at the door of the church. It wouldn't budge. He headed for the side entrance.

"Yeah. Though he was a blubbering mess. He thought he might be Rank's alibi. It turned out to be the opposite. He filled in a few missing pieces about where Rank stayed and what he did around the days of the other murders. That helped me get the court order."

"I hope you didn't rake Solegrove over the coals. This could destroy his life."

"He should have thought of that before he started playing for the other team."

"Not funny."

"We're doing our best to keep him out of the news. But the BackList detectives will want sworn statements. Word may get out."

Father Gilbert had reached the side door. "I have to go," he said as he stepped into the small vestibule. "We need to talk about Veronyka, that missing girl from London."

"Listen to me, Gilbert," Gwynn cut in. "Veronyka Dalca is no runaway. I've seen her record. She was on the game in London."

Father Gilbert lowered his voice in case someone was within earshot. "They forced her into it after they kidnapped her from the school."

"I don't know where you got your information, but I had one of my men go through her record. She was arrested twice for soliciting in the street, the first time almost a year ago. The second was six months ago."

Father Gilbert felt like someone had hit him in the solar plexus.

Gwynn was saying, "You can look at the file for yourself. She came into the country with her father. The detectives believe she quickly became part of a national network of call girls and streetwalkers. Part of it is run by your pal from Southaven – Jack Doyle."

If they take what's mine, I take back what was mine and something of theirs, so they won't take from me again. Doyle was talking about Veronyka. Father Gilbert opened the interior door to the nave and peeked in. No one was there.

"Hello?" Gwynn asked.

"Is there any information on her father?"

"You can visit his grave in Shepherd's Bush. He died within a month after getting here. A heart attack."

"His named wasn't Vadim, I assume."

"No, it was Andrei." Gwynn grunted. "I know you invested a lot of yourself into this, but I think you were conned."

Father Gilbert didn't reply. *Conned and manipulated.* Just two of the ways he'd helped Doyle without realizing it.

"I have to go," Father Gilbert said and disconnected the call.

The lights inside had been strategically placed to highlight the altar, a few of the statues, and the overall beauty of the chancel – marred now by the tarpaulin and tapestries covering the worst of the vandalism.

His mind ticked through the evidence again. The graffiti on the church walls had been written by vandals that probably didn't speak English as a first language. That could have been someone from the School of English or the Lily Rose. The acts were profane, directed against sacred objects by someone who *knew* they were sacred. That suggested Europeans rather than Asians.

A door slammed, shattering the silence. Brother Gregory walked in at a fast pace. He saw Father Gilbert and slowed down, a look of relief on his face. "I'm glad it's you," he said. "Brother Michael saw someone on the security monitor, so I came to investigate."

"Security monitor?"

"They're new, because of that," he said and gestured to the vandalism. "I didn't expect you until after your panel discussion."

"I thought I'd see how Veronyka is doing."

"Didn't you get my message?"

"I was indisposed."

"She's gone. Her father came to get her," Brother Gregory said. "Vadim – the one you told me about."

"Dark hair and thick moustache?"

"That's him."

If they take what's mine, I take back what was mine…

Father Gilbert sat down on the front pew, feeling drained. "How did he know she was here?"

"Didn't you call him?"

"I couldn't reach him. I'd been told his mobile phone was stolen."

"Maybe *she* phoned *him*."

Father Gilbert's head began to ache. "Did she actually *say* he was her father?"

Brother Gregory frowned. "I don't think so. Why would she? He arrived, identified himself, and she left with him. She didn't *deny* he was her father. Why?"

Father Gilbert shook his head. Brother Gregory had already dealt with enough since Brother Sean's death. Telling him about the meeting with Doyle and the truth about Veronyka would be overkill.

"You're a wreck," Brother Gregory said to him. "Have you eaten? We have food in the kitchen."

"I have to get back for that panel discussion." Which was the very last thing he wanted to do now.

"I'll drive you."

* * *

In a car again, Father Gilbert fumed and sulked, repented of each, then fumed and sulked again. He recognized that Doyle had hurt his pride – no one wanted to be a gullible idiot. He could live with that. What bothered him more was that he'd inadvertently helped Doyle. Veronyka would be taken back to London and put back on the streets.

If there was an upside, it was that the School of English was shut down, if only for a while.

As they descended into the central part of town, Father Gilbert looked at Englesea as if seeing it for the very first time. The rustic seaside facade slipped aside and he saw a foul and depraved cancer that had latched onto a living organism and was eating its life away. Maybe what Doyle said was true. He was in Doyle's world now – a world of corrupt power and influence-peddling, of men who got involved with prostitutes or clandestine relationships with other men, of women used for twisted sexual pleasure, of fallen morality and distorted motivations. No one could be trusted.

Brother Gregory kept eyeing him surreptitiously.

"How are Sean's parents handling his death?" Father Gilbert asked, hoping to redirect his sour feelings to something more humane.

"They're stunned, of course. They came to identify the body, which was difficult. I was with them for that." He sighed. "When the medical examiner said he had post-mortem work to do, they went home again to sort out funeral arrangements and to deal with the rest of the family."

"Did he have brothers and sisters?"

"An older sister and a younger brother, one a mum and the other at Uni."

What parents ever expect to outlive their children? he thought. He had a brief moment of sympathy for Jack Doyle, who'd also lost his son. But it was only brief.

"He'll be buried near their home," Brother Gregory said. "Once the body is released."

"Did you talk to them about Anong?"

"Yes. They didn't seem surprised."

Father Gilbert turned to him. "He's had trouble with this before?"

"They would only say that he sometimes wandered off to the seedier parts of the city. They assumed, at first, that he was a young man being curious. Later they thought it was part of his depression."

"He frequented prostitutes?"

"They didn't say that," Brother Gregory replied quickly. "They got the impression that it was like window-shopping. He wanted to see what that world was like, but didn't want to join it."

Father Gilbert knew the type, having met them in places like Soho. There was an undue attraction to the darker realities of life.

An anonymous walk through the shadows. The Internet was rife with sites that allowed viewers to watch depraved sexual acts and violence while denying anyone was harmed by it. What few of them realized was how deeply it affected them. He wondered what had caused Brother Sean to cross the line from being an observer to a participant.

"And how are the brothers doing?" Father Gilbert asked.

"The same. Stunned, grieved. Even more so because of Sean's secret life. And there's the scandal that's bound to hit."

Father Gilbert thought about how the local media would sensationalize it as much as possible. The national media, if they deemed it worthy, would make it worse. He didn't envy Brother Gregory's position at all.

Brother Gregory took a quick right to avoid the traffic-laden one-way system. "Fortunately, we've been having ongoing discussions about what we can learn from this experience."

"What have you learned?" Father Gilbert asked. He thought it was early to take on such a discussion. One could hardly be expected to think so clearly while in the midst of shock and grief.

"We want to renew the precautions we can take against our temptations. It's easy to become lax. In the midst of it, we've agreed to increase our accountability to one another. We also want to make better use of our times for spiritual direction and confession."

"That sounds very *efficient*," Father Gilbert said. "But how are they feeling? Apart from the grief, what kinds of emotions are stirring up?"

Brother Gregory didn't speak at first. His expression was set as the lights from the cars and neon shop signs passed over his face. "Guilt is the prevailing emotion."

"Guilt about what?"

"The guilt we feel for failing Sean. We didn't notice that he was in trouble. We certainly didn't recognize the signs of infidelity to his vows nor that he might kill himself. We thought the vandalism at the church set him off. I thought he was angry on our behalf."

"Does that mean you now believe he committed suicide?"

"I don't want to believe it, but I have to accept the possibility." He drove in silence, acceptance looking more like resignation. "There's also the guilt that comes with relief."

"Relief?"

Brother Gregory's hands knotted around the steering wheel. His brow furrowed to reflect a deep tension. "Sean was hard work, Father. He demanded a lot from us emotionally and spiritually. As I've said, I was wrong to let him stay as long as I did. He wore us down. Some of us distanced ourselves from him. I'm sure he felt that. It's possible he turned to Anong for intimacy. I don't mean sex alone, but to have someone he felt he could connect with."

"You can't take that on your shoulders," Father Gilbert said, knowing it was a meaningless statement. Brother Gregory would bear the burden for what had happened to Sean. Just as Father Gilbert would always feel responsible for not acting more prudently after Sean had confessed to him.

They rode on in silence, the multicoloured lights highlighting the leftover drops of rain on the windscreen.

The mystery of Sean's behaviour and why he died, of what had truly happened with Anong, nudged Father Gilbert back towards an undercurrent of irritation. For all he knew, Sean's death was just another cog in Doyle's machinery – chewing them all up and spitting them out again. If so, he wanted to put a stop to it somehow.

CHAPTER 13

Father Gilbert walked into the convention centre wishing he could be anywhere else. The desire to go back to his room, pack his things, and catch the next train home was as great as any he'd ever felt. The only thing that stopped him was the stubborn refusal to let Doyle have yet another victory. Although, as he looked at the information screen, he wasn't sure how attending a panel discussion about "The Compassionate Church" was going to thwart someone like Doyle.

"Father Gilbert," a woman's voice said softly.

Startled, he turned. Cari Erim looked up at him with her sad, dark eyes.

"I've been looking for you, to talk," she said.

He weighed his options about missing the panel and knew that he shouldn't. "I have to appear at this meeting."

She looked disappointed.

"Can we talk afterwards?" he asked.

She nodded.

"Good," he said and moved in the direction of the designated room. "You can come and watch if you want, if you want to feel a new kind of boredom."

She gave him a small smile.

* * *

The panel discussion was the last event of the evening and the final session of the conference. The next morning would see a concluding breakfast and speech from the Archbishop of Canterbury.

The meeting room was full. Bishop Spalding stood at the main microphone introducing the other four panellists. He saw Father Gilbert arrive at the back and motioned in his direction. "And here is Stonebridge's own Father Louis Gilbert, making a dramatic entrance as always."

187

With a forced smile, Father Gilbert strode past the audience and their polite applause and took his seat at the end of the table on the stage. He sat down and realized he hadn't brought his messenger bag or any materials for a discussion about a compassionate Church. He hoped he wouldn't be asked to give anything more than a few quick thoughts on the subject.

The other panellists represented a cross-section of denominations and views, all espousing the virtues of compassion. The consensus seemed to be that Christians should put aside the "petty doctrines" that divided them and come together in love. Father Gilbert only half-listened, annoyed because he didn't consider the essential doctrines of the Christian faith to be petty at all, nor should they be put aside for an artificial show of togetherness or for a "love" that was mere sentimentality.

As he sat, struggling to stay engaged in the proceedings, he saw a black woman standing in the back of the room. She wore a blousy top and tight red miniskirt, the look of it reminiscent of something from the 1960s. She was incongruous in the room filled with clergy.

He became aware then of a Vietnamese woman standing in the far back corner of the room. He was sure she hadn't been there a few seconds ago. Her clothes, contemporary in style, were shredded, exposing parts of her body underneath as if she'd been mauled by something or someone.

A young white man, little more than a teen, dressed in tight leather trousers and a white shirt undone to his navel, appeared off to the right. Another woman, looking as if she'd arrived from 1800, sat at the far end of the back row, her face white with powder and her lips a gash of red.

He realized what he was seeing now: spirits were arriving as if summoned to this very meeting. Why, he didn't know. They weren't looking at him. They weren't looking at anything. They simply stared straight ahead with the vacant eyes of the dead. They seemed unaware of anything around them.

They kept fading into view, from a myriad of times and places, and he wondered if these were the many victims of the slave trade who were now being coughed up by Englesea, as if it were gagging on its own guilt. Then Father Gilbert saw Cari Erim at a side door, her eyes darting around the room. Her eyes were wide. Once again, she was seeing what he was seeing. She looked at him with an expression of confusion and fear.

"Father Gilbert?"

The Bishop's voice penetrated through the white noise in his brain. He looked over, now aware that he'd been asked a question.

"I'm sorry?" he said.

"You've been strangely quiet. What do you think?" the Bishop asked, his tone hardly masking his impatience. "Surely you have at least *one* thought on the subject."

Father Gilbert wasn't in a frame of mind to accept the Bishop's condescending tone. He asked, "Which subject—"

"Into the microphone, please," someone said.

He leaned forward towards the microphone on the table. "Which subject?" he asked. "Compassion or ecumenicalism?"

"Wouldn't you agree that we should unite in order to show compassion?" the Bishop asked.

"I agree," he said. "But only if our unity and compassion are true."

"What else could they be?" the Bishop asked.

"There's a false unity that tells us to compromise our doctrinal differences as if they aren't important. True ecumenicalism, on the other hand, isn't a denial of our differences but respect for them. Then, and only then, can we unite around the causes we hold in common. Then we can show true compassion – a compassion grounded in the truth. Otherwise, it's all self-indulgent twaddle."

There was scattered applause.

A scholarly looking white-haired man on the panel had turned to him. "I had no idea you were such a progressive."

"If anything, I'm a *regressive*," Father Gilbert said. "If you want true ecumenicalism then we have to go back to the 'faith once delivered', the Orthodox faith of the Ancient Church. Apostolic in its governance, biblical in its theology, Christ-centred in its execution. Honestly, I don't see anything progressive about the lightweight sentimentality of where we are now." His voice sounded loud to his own ears, and he realized that he was trying to talk above a din of noise in his head, loud moans from the dead in the room that filled his ears. "What we call compassion is mostly mindless affirmation."

A *harrumph* from a panellist with a strategically styled beard. "What's wrong with affirmation?" he asked.

Father Gilbert tilted his head toward him. "Nothing, unless we're affirming the wrong things. Jesus didn't meet people where they were to leave them in that state. He didn't *affirm* who they were, He affirmed who they *could become* if they would trust Him. There's nothing compassionate about affirming people in their conditions." He looked over the audience again. "Don't you see? We're like lifeguards with rescue apparatus who are affirming people while they drown, or emancipators dangling the keys to freedom while we affirm slaves in their chains, or doctors with a cure who affirm sick patients in their disease. Show me where Jesus ever did that. On the contrary, He exposed their true conditions, their slavery and sickness, to bring them to the truth. He suffered the tortures of the Cross to *save them* from all the things we now affirm – and to save us now. If you want to talk about unity and compassion, then let's talk about *that* and then do something that truly helps people."

The audience applauded. A few stood to their feet. But Father Gilbert's eyes were on the spectres, which now began to move, swaying slowly, and then to twitch and thrash. The moaning he heard in his head grew louder. Then came the screams as a violence took hold. Their faces began to melt; eyes burst in explosions of red; arms and limbs flailed. Some fell to the ground and writhed until they melted into pools, draining into the fabric of the carpet. Others turned black, as if burning from the inside out, smouldering and then disappearing into clouds of smoke.

Father Gilbert fought to keep his expression from reflecting the horror he was seeing. A hand patted him on the back as he realized the panellist next to him was also standing and applauding. The Bishop was speaking, but he couldn't make out the words.

Then it stopped. The phantoms were gone. The screams became a distant echo, and then silence.

Cari Erim was pressed against a back wall, as if she'd been pinned there by the phantom crowd. Then she relaxed and looked at him with an expression of calm – a serenity, he thought – and walked out of the room.

Father Gilbert stood up, wanting to call after her, but the Bishop was next to him saying, "I had no idea."

The crowd settled down. The Bishop made a few concluding remarks. Father Gilbert sat, numb. All he could think about was how to get out of there.

After a final prayer, the meeting broke up. There was no escaping the hands thrust at him to shake and the comments about what he'd said – mostly favourable, though a few people wanted to "talk further" to air their disagreements. He cordially pushed through. Then a hand grasped his arm and Father Anthony was guiding him away, saying loudly to everyone that he had an urgent meeting with Father Gilbert and to please excuse them for a few minutes. Escape came via a door into a service hall, empty except for a waiter sampling food from a tray of leftovers.

"What happened in there?" Father Anthony asked.

Father Gilbert offered a weak shrug. "Irritated by all the talk, I guess."

"I'm not talking about that." Father Anthony positioned himself in front of Father Gilbert and looked at his face, like a doctor about to make a diagnosis. "You *sounded* angry but there was something about your eyes…" he said. "You looked as if you were in pain. *Spiritual* pain. And it happened just as I felt something in the room – something terrible. *What happened?*"

Father Gilbert didn't know how to answer him. There wasn't time. He wanted to find Cari. She might be waiting for him.

"I'll tell you once we're away from *this*," Father Gilbert said.

"I'll take that as a promise," Father Anthony said. "Is it connected to Veronyka?"

"Veronyka is gone. Vadim took her back to London."

"That's good, isn't it?" he asked, his tone unsure.

"Vadim wasn't her father. The whole thing was a ruse to get her back from the School and into the hands of her London bosses."

"You mean, to prostitute herself in London?" Father Anthony asked, incredulous.

Father Gilbert nodded. "She went willingly, Father. That's the hard thing to understand. I'd given her a way out – I hid her at St Sebastian's, but Vadim came and—"

Father Anthony scowled. "I'm not prepared to let it go," he said. "The Orthodox community is well connected to people in all kinds of work around London. I will find her."

"And if you do…"

"I will let you know."

***

The service hall led back to the main lobby. Father Gilbert looked for Cari while trying to avoid the mingling clerics.

His phone vibrated. The screen indicated that he had a voicemail message. He put the phone to his ear while scanning the room again. There was no sign of Cari. He wondered if he would see her again.

Gwynn's voice cut through the surrounding noise. "Guess what we found in Rank's car? Rank himself. It's his blood and hair on that truncheon. Someone killed him and stuffed him in the boot."

And if somebody destroys what's mine, then… well, you can guess the rest.

Doyle again. He was scoring big today.

"The evidence is beginning to pile up against Rank as the BackList Killer. Though we have the same problem with Rank as we did with Anong. How did he get from his room to the boot of the car?"

"The service door," Father Gilbert said. And suddenly it struck him how Vadim knew to pick up Veronyka at St Sebastian's – and who had played informant about Nathan Rank as a suspect. Not Mel at the front desk. It was Pinbrook, the manager. He had to be on Doyle's payroll.

Gwynn said, "By the way, be on the lookout—"

"Father Louis Gilbert?" The voice came from a man in a black suit – could he be anything other than a detective? He had jet-black hair and the sharp look of a bird of prey.

"—friends from London—" Gwynn was saying as Father Gilbert disconnected and pocketed the phone.

"Yes."

"A word, please?"

"Who are you?"

The man turned his back to the room and showed Father Gilbert his identification. At least he was being discreet. "I'm Dave Brinkman with the National Crime Agency, Organized Crime Command. Would you come with me, please?"

Father Gilbert assumed that "No" wasn't an option.

* * *

"Is Detective Inspector Gwynn here?" Father Gilbert asked when he'd sat down in the main interview room at the police station.

"He's a little busy at the moment," Brinkman said. "Wait here, please."

Brinkman left the room, leaving the door slightly ajar.

A moment later, a woman entered carrying two mugs. "Tea," she said. She put one mug in front of him. "Milk and sugar, I heard," she added.

"Thank you."

"I'm Rebecca Hathaway, with the National Crime Agency," she said and shook his hand in a cautious grip. She wore a black jacket and matching skirt. The blouse beneath was white and collarless. She sat down across from him and hooked her blonde shoulder-length hair behind her ears. Her slender face emphasized her large green eyes, thin nose, and full lips. She had the fresh, make-up free complexion of a country girl. He guessed she was in her mid-to-late 30s, but she certainly looked younger. He wondered how someone this beautiful could survive in law enforcement. Her looks put her in danger of being stereotyped, or made into a token. Beneath that beauty, she had to be hard as steel.

"What can I do for you, Agent Hathaway?" he asked, breaking the unofficial protocol of allowing her to lead the discussion.

"Rebecca, please."

"Maybe after I find out why I'm here," he said. He wasn't going to play the *we're just pals* tactic the police often tried.

She cupped the mug in her hands and faced him. "Let's start with your meeting a couple of hours ago."

"Which one? I've had several."

She smiled and a dimple appeared to the right of her mouth. "Yes, you've been *very* busy, apparently. I'm thinking specifically about your meeting with Jack Doyle on his yacht."

Ah. Organized Crime Command. Of course. "I wouldn't call it a meeting so much as an abduction-with-conversation."

"Do you want to file a complaint?"

"Would it make a difference if I did?"

"No." She lifted the mug to her lips. "Why did he want to meet with you?"

"To do a little sabre-rattling and to let me know how annoying I am to him as a human being."

"We'll wrap this up sooner if you answer directly and specifically." She put the mug down again without drinking.

"All right." Father Gilbert smiled at her. Her green eyes were on him and he felt the way they were reading him. "*Specifically*, Agent Hathaway, Jack Doyle let me know that he's in a battle with Lorna Henry and her 'School', which is a front for call girls. I assume he owns the Lily Rose, so they're in competition for the town's sex business. Worse, the Layton School stole one of his girls from London. He has stolen her back, with my unintentional help, and you can be sure he torched the school. He likely had Nathan Rank murdered because he thought Rank had killed one of his girls. And I wouldn't be surprised to learn that he had the monk killed and made it look like a suicide."

"He told you all that?" she asked.

"Not directly. He's too clever for that," Father Gilbert said.

"Why did he take *you* into his confidence?" she asked, the question ironic.

"To impress me? To make me feel like a fool? To persuade me to give up and go home? You'll have to ask him."

"Give us probable cause and we will."

"It'd only be my word against his," Father Gilbert said. He rested his hands on the table and threaded his fingers. "I haven't told you anything you don't already know – or have guessed. What is so important about this town that people like Doyle and Lorna Henry are fighting over it? Why have you come all the way from London to talk to me?"

"The town is important because, for years, it's been the entryway for human traffickers to bring their 'product' into England. The boats arrive unchecked."

"There was a newspaper article about it. I thought you put a stop to that."

"We put a stop to one of the routes," she said. Three vertical lines appeared just above her nose and between her eyes. "We don't know how many others there are."

"And the second question?" Father Gilbert asked.

"What brought me to Englesea was DI Gwynn's inquiries about the victim you're calling Anong Chuan. My office deals with human trafficking."

"I'm glad somebody's office does. I was beginning to wonder," he said. "What was Anong's real name?"

"Jun Anong Li," she replied. "I picked up on the name 'Anong' when her fingerprints were flagged."

"So how is it that a girl who was already killed in London could be later murdered here?"

Hathaway seemed to have anticipated the question and been cleared to give an answer. "Jun was picked up by the London police in a sting. In exchange for immunity and a new life, she turned on her pimps and her big boss from Thailand. They call him 'The Sensei', we don't have an actual name for him yet. What we do know is that Jack Doyle manages his operations in London and areas south."

"Jack Doyle has a boss?" Father Gilbert asked.

"Let's say that Jack Doyle is providing a service to a foreign client," she said. "Jun's information helped us bust up the London ring – at least, the Far East side of it – and we were able to convict a few of the bad guys."

"But not Jack Doyle."

"No." Hathaway took a sip of her tea. "To help ensure Jun's safety, we faked her death and changed her name. We set her up nicely with her daughter. We gave them a new life in the North and, for a while, all was well."

It was easy to guess what happened next. "The Sensei found her."

"One of our own was on the take," she said with a flicker of resentment in her eyes. "The Sensei's gang went after her. She escaped. That's when she disappeared completely."

"She didn't leave you a forwarding address?" Father Gilbert teased.

Hathaway ignored him. "Until Gwynn's inquiries and the fingerprint match came in, we thought she'd left the country. We were surprised to learn that she'd turned up here – back in the business, until she was murdered."

"Do you have any theories about why she came here?" Father Gilbert asked.

"She needed the money and went back to what she knew. It happens all the time with these girls."

"Risky, considering it was bound to put her back on the Sensei's radar."

"Hiding in plain sight is sometimes the smartest thing to do," she said. "Jun looks different than she did before. The autopsy showed some discreet facial work. Her hair is a different cut and colour. She must have thought Englesea was remote enough to keep her anonymous."

"Except that it's a major port for the trade and a turf war seems to have broken out. Did she get caught in the middle of it?"

"That depends on when it started. If it began when Doyle learned that Veronyka was here, then no. That happened after Anong's death. *You* helped with that."

"No good deed is left unpunished, as they say."

"In your defence, you couldn't have known what you were getting into. Vadim played the anxious father effectively." Hathaway's words in his defence still sounded like an accusation.

"Do you know where he is? Or where he's taken Veronyka?"

"Not yet. Vadim wasn't his real name either. Though 'Dalca' is *her* last name. It's possible he's an uncle."

"An uncle who would put her on the game?"

She nodded. "Money can make family ties even stronger – in a rather sick way."

It was the kind of statement that could have been a proverb, he thought. "Do you know who killed Anong – or Jun – or—?" He stammered, struggling with which name to use. "I think I'll call her 'Jun Anong' just to keep it straight."

Hathaway nodded.

"Did Nathan Rank kill her?"

"You know as much as we do," she said. "It's likely the Sensei found her again and had her killed."

Father Gilbert thought about it. "Strangled and drowned by hand? That doesn't seem like a professional hit."

"Not all hits are professional," she countered.

"What about the daughter? Where is she?"

"We're looking into that."

"And Brother Sean. How is he connected?"

"We're looking into that, too."

"You don't know or you're not going to tell me?" he asked.

She presented a smile without the dimple. "The conference ends tomorrow. There's no reason for you to stay, is there?"

"I can't help but feel invested in what's happened here."

"DI Gwynn shouldn't have pulled you into this."

"It wasn't entirely his fault."

She drank some of her tea. "I've been puzzling over that. You came to Gwynn to talk to him about Anong's death. What prompted that?"

"Good citizenship."

"What else?"

"Actually, I knew DI Gwynn from my days at Scotland Yard. I saw his name in the paper and thought I'd drop in to say hello."

"But he said you were interested in Jun Anong's murder."

"There was something about it initially that reminded me of the BackList Killer's work. I thought I'd draw his attention to it, for whatever that might be worth."

"I looked," Hathaway said. "There was nothing in the newspaper that could have linked Jun's death to the BackList Killer."

"Really? I'm sure I read—"

"You didn't, Father Gilbert."

He wondered, just for a moment, how she might react if he told her he'd seen a spectre of Jun Anong.

She waited, her eyes still on him.

"Look," he said, sounding slightly embarrassed. "I'm a former detective working as a priest in a small parish. I came for a conference that I was sure would be boring. Playing the sleuth spices things up for me."

Her eyes told him she didn't believe a word he was saying. But how was she going to argue? Unless she thought he was the killer, his explanation had to suffice.

"Father Gilbert, do you see ghosts?" she asked abruptly.

He started. "I'm sorry?"

"The death of Jack Doyle's son was of great interest to us. I read everything about the events in Stonebridge. Colin Doyle appeared to you there at the same time he died miles away."

"Are you asking because you believe it or because you want to tear it apart?" He met her gaze. "I'm only curious because I'm used to both positions on the subject."

"I'm an interested enquirer," she said.

He decided to call her bluff. "All right, then how about this: Jun Anong appeared to me after she died and I saw that her wrists were bound. It reminded me of the BackList Killer, so I went to DI Gwynn to tell him to check for a connection. That's what really happened."

She didn't speak for a moment. Then she stood up. "Go home, Father Gilbert," she said and picked up her mug of tea.

"Did you get the girls from the school?" Father Gilbert asked.

"The girls?"

"The girls at the school. Did you rescue them?"

"We're tracking them."

"*Tracking* them?" Father Gilbert was aghast. "You're letting them continue to prostitute themselves?"

"We have to maintain whatever leads we can in order to get to the major players. If we pull the girls out now, we lose that possibility."

"And what are the girls supposed to do in the meantime?" he asked.

"What they've been doing all along," she said. "Goodnight, Father." She walked out of the room.

Father Gilbert didn't move. The coldness of her answer stunned him. His eye caught his reflection in the two-way mirror and he knew someone was on the other side. He looked up and said, "Did you get all that, DI Gwynn?" Standing up, he added: "By the way, Mr Pinbrook is probably Doyle's informant. I'll wager he covered for Doyle's men when they took Rank's body out and put him in the car boot."

He walked out of the interview room and didn't stop until he was on the street again.

* * *

Was he finished? He thought about it as he walked back to his hotel. His dismissal by Rebecca Hathaway and Gwynn's disappearing act told him he was. The cases would be closed to him now. He couldn't be Gwynn's unofficial consultant any more, not that he ever had been. The rain had moved on, but the air still carried the weight of moisture. He thought about Jun Anong's death. Hathaway's story presented a compelling case that someone connected to the Sensei had killed her. But it raised a question: what had she been doing at one of Jack Doyle's establishments? Hiding in plain sight was one thing. Hiding right under the Sensei's nose was another.

An absurd idea came to him: *what if Jack Doyle himself had hidden her there?*

He dismissed it immediately. Why would Doyle risk betraying what must've been a lucrative business deal with the Sensei?

Arriving at the Masthead Inn, he realized he would be checking out in the morning. The conference would officially end by noon. He had to go home.

A voice called for him from the front desk. He walked over to a petite woman who looked as if she'd worked the night shift in a lot of different hotels over her many years. "There's someone waiting for you in the lounge," she said.

"Thank you." Father Gilbert turned in that direction and hoped it wasn't Planer or any of the others wanting to nab him for a conversation or take him out on the town.

Cari Erim sat alone at the table where he'd seen the apparition of Anong. She looked up as he entered and shifted slightly in the chair as if she might stand up. He gestured for her to stay seated and took the chair across from her, putting him exactly where he'd been when Anong had showed up.

"You left with the police," she said. "I was waiting for you. I saw it."

"They had a few questions, that's all. I'm glad you thought to come here."

Using the thumbnail of her right hand, she scratched at the nail polish on the index finger of her left. "I saw *them*. I saw the way they... they disappeared."

Father Gilbert said, "I don't know why they come and go as they do. Why were they at that meeting?"

Cari shook her head. "Perhaps they were looking for the truth or for justice? Or peace."

"I don't know of anyone who ever found those things at a religious conference," Father Gilbert said as a joke.

Cari didn't laugh. She kept scratching at her fingernails.

"Cari, how did you wind up in Englesea?"

"It's a very long story."

"I have time."

"I have a large and rather poor family. A friend told me there was work to be found in Malask."

"Where is Malask?"

"It is part of Istanbul – a wealthy part, with many businesses and offices. I found a job cleaning offices in the evenings." She spoke proudly, as if she'd accomplished something remarkable. "One night, a man approached me. A handsome man. Young and well-dressed. He talked about how beautiful I was and how I could do so much better than emptying other people's rubbish bins. I didn't understand why he was flirting with me. I thought he might be one of those wealthy men who assumes a poor girl like me will be easy to get into bed."

Father Gilbert nodded. Some things were the same in every country.

Cari looked towards the front window and sighed. "He asked me out on a date. I was suspicious. But he was a gentleman. He took me out on many dates. He spent money on me. He talked about how intelligent and gracious I was. He let me believe he loved me."

"Did he say so?"

"No," she said sadly. "Maybe I thought he said more than he did. I even believed he would ask me to marry him. Then, one day, he offered me a job as his assistant – to travel to places like Germany and France and England. I was confused. I expected him to ask me to marry him, not ask me to take a job. But I was desperate to hold onto him, so I said yes. The first job would be in London. He knew it was a place I'd always wanted to visit. We flew to Heathrow together. It was almost like a honeymoon."

Her eyes flooded with tears. Father Gilbert handed her a serviette.

"We arrived and a big car was waiting for us, a limousine," she said, sniffling. "I was so impressed. He held the door for me. I got in and there were two men and a woman sitting in there already. I thought they were business associates. Then my boyfriend suddenly stepped away from the car and closed the door, leaving me in the back with these strangers. I saw him walk away. I tried to get out. The woman told me to be calm. When I screamed for him, one of the men hit me with his fist. I was shocked. I cried. He hit me again and told me to shut up. I tried to get out, and he hit me over and over and then they held me down and made me drink something that tasted like medicine. It made me fall asleep."

Father Gilbert noticed she had returned to scratching at the paint on her fingernails.

Her voice went hard as she said, "I awoke on a mattress in a small room. They had taken my clothes off. I knew I had been raped. I was shivering because the room was cold. There was nothing to cover with. One of the men came in and I curled up to hide my body. He sat on the bed and told me to relax, he didn't want to hit me again. He said if I cooperated I would do very well in England. I told him I wanted to go home. He said I might go home one day, but I had work to do first – to pay them back for my ticket to London. He said it would cost money to get my passport back, too. And clothes were expensive.

And food. And all the other necessities I would need. I began to cry. He spoke in a soothing voice. He hugged me and I felt hope. But it was a trick and he raped me." She paused, the tears returning to her eyes. "That's how it was. He would leave me, then come back and rape me. That is what happened for several days. Then the other man from the car came and did the same thing. One after the other, day after day. They said they were training me. I don't know how many days I was there. The woman from the car brought me food and made sure I bathed. She acted like a nurse. She kept checking me. She told me not to fight. There was no escape. Why did I want to go home in shame when I could stay and make very good money? I should learn to like it because no one else would ever love me. Not even my family."

She looked at Father Gilbert. He wanted to take her hand, to do something to show how sad he felt for her. But his instincts said that reaching for her might alarm her. "They lied to you. Love is still possible."

Cari didn't respond. She continued with her account. "They moved me to another place, with a much nicer room. I heard other people in the building but wasn't allowed to see them. They brought men to me. I was told if I did what they wanted with a smile, they would let me go to other parts of the house. If I complained or refused, they would beat me and take me back to the terrible room I'd come from. After enough time, you learn to do what they say. I looked forward to getting out of the room to take a shower or to eat in the kitchen. I saw some of the other girls but at first we weren't permitted to talk."

"Were the girls from Turkey?"

She shook her head. "They came from all over the world."

Father Gilbert frowned. The thought of girls being wrenched from their homes, from their families, from their towns and cities and transported to distant countries for the pleasure of sick men and women seemed beyond belief. Even with all of his experience, he found it hard to fathom.

"They allowed us to talk later on. They wanted us to become friends. Then they would use our friendship against us."

"How?"

"If I complained or tried to escape, they would hurt one of the other girls. They would say, 'You try to leave and we'll hurt *her.* Do you understand? Not you. *She'll* pay for your disobedience.' That taught us to do as we were told. Once the police came to our house and asked me questions. I was so afraid that I told the police I was all right. They were my family, I said."

"How long did this go on?" he asked.

"Five years."

Father Gilbert winced. Cari was only in her late twenties.

She went back to scratching her nails again. "I became sick. I had a rash on my face and body. A doctor looked at me. He gave me ointments and treatments, but the rashes wouldn't go away. The men I worked for said I was disgusting. No one wanted to be with me. They argued about killing me. One of the men said they could hand me over to the immigration authorities to be deported. The other men said no, I would talk. And the man said no one would listen to me because he had friends there who would make sure I was locked up until I was deported. I begged them not to send me back. What could I do? I thought about one of the legal brothels back home, but someone said women like me are not wanted there because of the *natashas* – the European girls, blondes and redheads, who have been lured into prostitution to service Turkish men who like that kind. I didn't know what I would do."

"Why didn't you want to go home to your family?"

"I was dead to my family and wanted it to stay that way, because of my shame."

"But surely if you –"

"*No*, Father. I can not go back to my family," she said firmly. "So I was at an Immigration building. I was put in a cell and they said they would send me back to Turkey. And I kept waiting for the deportation hearing or whatever they were going to do. But one day a woman came. She had a terrible fight with the people in charge. She demanded that I be set free until my hearing. She made such a fuss that they agreed and let me go with her. The woman said she would help me. But I was afraid she was going to sell me. I had heard about such things. So I ran away from her."

"To where? Where could you go?"

"Another woman I knew from the house had become too old for the job. She told me before they let her go where to find her. I went to her. She took me in. She had contacts to find jobs for cheap workers. There was an office in Brighton. I cleaned offices there. My skin disease went away. Then I heard about jobs in Englesea and came here because I thought it would be quiet and safe. Now I'm not so sure."

Father Gilbert nodded. She spoke without any sense of irony at all.

"I began to see the ghosts not long after I got here. I thought I was going crazy. Then I saw you and I knew I wasn't alone."

"What will you do now?" Father Gilbert asked.

"I want to leave. But I have things to do first."

"Like what?"

She glanced around as if she were afraid the ghosts might hear. "I think I know what *they* are."

"The ghosts? What are they?"

"They are *me*," she said. "Trapped between worlds, wandering in a terrible wilderness. I must set them free. Like you said in the meeting. 'Set souls free.'"

"Cari, we don't have the spiritual power or authority to set any spirits free. Only God can do that."

"Are we not agents of God, like you said?"

"To show His love," Father Gilbert explained. "It's dangerous when we presume to do anything else."

She slowly nodded. "I see."

"It's for us to engage the living."

She looked up at him, a plaintive air about her. "Yes. I understand," was all she said.

He looked at her hands. The cuticles around her fingernails were bleeding.

* * *

Cari made a quick exit to get some sleep before her 5 a.m. job at a breakfast-only café where she cleaned tables. His heart broke for her anew as he watched her leave the hotel. He couldn't imagine how a girl, or any woman, could suffer through her ordeal and recover. God's grace alone was the only hope, he thought. And he prayed that upon her as she walked out the door.

"It's for us to engage the living," he'd said. So he would. In the morning, he would contact his parishioners about a job and lodgings for her. He prayed that her experience with ghosts in Englesea wouldn't follow her to Stonebridge. But, considering his own experiences, he couldn't assume anything.

Back in his room, he collapsed on the bed. He rested for a moment, then decided to have a bath to relax. Turning on the small television while he undressed, he caught a recap of the day's news. He was about to run the water for his bath when footage of the fire at the School appeared. A reporter on the scene explained that the cause was under investigation. Lorna Henry appeared on screen. "All of our students are safe. We're making arrangements now to continue our classes in a nearby public school. We will not be defeated by this. And if it was arson, we will hope the police will find the culprits and bring them to justice."

Father Gilbert doubted there would be any justice if Doyle was involved.

In the bath, he eased into the hot water and closed his eyes. Exhausted as he was physically, his mind continued in high gear. It began to sort through random details of his day, like pieces to multiple jigsaw puzzles all thrown into the same box. He thought of the burden Brother Gregory now had and the guilt he'd taken on because of Sean. He thought, too, of the guilt Brother Sean had expressed. Guilt for what, though? He hadn't killed Anong. Yet he felt responsible for her death somehow. Why?

Brother Gregory's prevailing assumption was that everything that had happened was connected to his campaign against the local sex trade. It made sense that the vandalism at St Sebastian's was an immediate consequence, likely perpetrated by Lorna Henry and the bosses behind the school. Father Gilbert couldn't disagree, especially since Doyle himself had disavowed any part in the crime. "I don't vandalize churches," he'd said. "It's amateurish and ineffective." Father Gilbert didn't think Doyle was lying this time.

Besides, Doyle didn't have to vandalize the church. He had Brother Sean as leverage because of the Lily Rose. What was more ideal than to have Sean's indiscretions as an ace up the sleeve, the card they could play against Brother Gregory whenever they wanted? What better way to buy Gregory's silence than to threaten him with a public exposure of Sean's secret? Sean was more valuable alive.

But Sean was dead – something that wouldn't benefit Doyle. So who benefited? Sean alone? Mentally distressed, did he kill himself as a reaction to Anong's murder? What about the unexplained presence of ephedra in Sean's system?

He thought again about Anong. What was she doing in Englesea and where was her daughter? Was her murder a simple case of a hook-up gone wrong with the client she'd been summoned to meet? Was it retaliation by the Sensei? If so, why would Doyle put up with it, considering the lecture he'd given to Father Gilbert earlier?

The questions kept circling the drain in his mind. He was convinced the answers were somewhere in what he already knew. But would he be around to learn the truth?

Am I leaving tomorrow or staying? he asked as a prayer. *What else can I do?*

He dozed off and woke up half an hour later in cold water.

CHAPTER 14

The next morning the newspaper was filled with lurid accounts of Brother Sean Damian's life and death, based on misquotes, innuendos, and one or two facts. The reporter characterized him as the troubled child of a wealthy family whose mischievous nature led him to sordid sexual encounters with a local prostitute. Questions were raised – never statements – that he may have murdered her in a sudden fit of rage. Grief-stricken over what he'd done, he then killed himself by taking an overdose of antidepressants. Though an anonymous source was quoted throughout, there was no doubting that Mamasan had provided the guts of the reporter's narrative.

There was no mention of the local sex slave trade, though Brother Gregory's recent comments against the "immorality of the town" were noted – making him seem more like a right-wing vigilante than a citizen concerned about the moral state of the town. The reporter couldn't resist a jab at a Catholic priest daring to take a moral stance about anything, considering the recent scandals in the Church and the implications surrounding Brother Gregory.

Father Gilbert wondered what would happen if he made an anonymous call to one of the reporters and stated all he knew about the little turf war and Doyle's business lessons. Would they dare print it or was the newspaper also under someone's thumb?

Father Gilbert sat down in his usual seat in the dining room for breakfast. Planer wasn't there. It was likely he'd gone home after the panel discussion – many of the conferees did once the more official events had concluded.

He felt a cold chill on his neck and looked around to see why. Father Gilbert felt every muscle in his body tense when he saw the Shadow Man standing on the opposite side of the room. Even with the morning light streaming through the front window, its face was obscured by darkness. It – whatever it was – had never come so close before.

A woman at a nearby table complained to her husband about feeling cold and asked him to say something to the staff about closing the windows or turning on the heat.

The Shadow Man stood perfectly still, facing Father Gilbert with an air of malevolent emptiness. Father Gilbert decided to stare it down, whispering the Lord's Prayer *and* the prayer to St Michael the Archangel. The Shadow Man turned to one side, looking at him askew, as if something was troubling it, but it didn't know what. Then it lowered its head and slowly faded into the wallpaper behind it, leaving a dark stain there.

A waitress stepped up, startling Father Gilbert anew. He ordered tea, water, and a full English breakfast – breaking the promise he'd made to himself on the first day. It took him several minutes to fight back the residual feeling of unease.

Detective Inspector Gwynn sat down just after Father Gilbert's meal had arrived. He helped himself to a piece of toast and flagged the waitress to bring coffee.

"Are you here to escort me to the train station, just to make sure I leave town?" Father Gilbert asked, thinking that both Doyle and Rebecca Hathaway had told him to go home. In a flash of cynicism, he wondered which one Gwynn worked for.

"You don't think I'm going to let a bunch of suits from London tell me what to do?" Gwynn said. "Even if one of them fills out her suit very nicely, thank you."

"I'm still a priest, remember," Father Gilbert said.

"You're an Anglican priest. You don't take vows of celibacy."

"But we do take vows of chastity and aspire to purity," he countered.

The waitress brought Gwynn's coffee. He nodded to her, then said to Father Gilbert, "You're not seriously thinking of leaving, are you?"

"Why wouldn't I?"

"The cases aren't wrapped up."

"*Your* cases, not mine."

Gwynn leaned onto the table, jostling the cups and plates. "You're my only ally. The gang from London are trying to take over Anong's murder case. And they want me to drop the investigation into Sean's death since it's been ruled as a suicide," Gwynn said.

"I'm a civilian."

"Your collar gives you some authority." Gwynn reached over to an empty table and grabbed a set of cutlery pre-wrapped in a serviette. He opened it, took out the fork, and lanced one of Father Gilbert's mushrooms.

"You can order a breakfast of your own, you know."

"My cardiologist would have a heart attack," he said.

Father Gilbert pushed the plate towards him. "Go on. I'm not hungry anyway."

Gwynn positioned his fork over the plate and looked like someone trying to harpoon a fish. "Brother Gregory has access to Sean's financial records. I'd have to get a court order to see them, which won't happen while my superiors are bending the knee to Hathaway. The two of you could go over them to find out how often Sean withdrew money to see Anong – I assume he always paid cash – and if there are any other unusual transactions that might explain his behaviour."

"Brother Gregory doesn't need me for that."

"You'll know what to look for. He won't."

Father Gilbert nodded. "We'll go to the bank first thing."

Gwynn grunted and attacked the black pudding.

Father Gilbert watched him and wondered, *Am I being a sucker? If I stay, am I still being played as a pawn in someone else's game?* He couldn't shake off Doyle's machinations. Now he had to consider Hathaway. And he wasn't sure which game Gwynn was playing.

Gwynn put down his cutlery and took folded papers from the inside pocket of his jacket. He handed them over to Father Gilbert.

"What is this?" Father Gilbert asked.

"We haven't been idle, you know. It's a couple of pages of transcript from an interview we did with Derek Kenton."

"Who is Derek Kenton?"

"The security guard at the School of English."

"Ah. I remember him fondly," Father Gilbert said, thinking of their encounter in the alley after he'd followed Veronyka.

"They caught him late last night poking around the fire."

"What do you mean they 'caught' him?"

"He sneaked into the building – which is not only a crime scene but off limits because of structural damage."

"What was he after?"

"He said he was after his favourite pair of shoes. He'd left them under the security desk."

"Do you believe him?"

"Yeah, I do." Gwynn chuckled. "Those shoes were his undoing. An officer nabbed him, thinking he was the arsonist come back to the scene of the crime. Derek tried to do a runner. The officer caught him and brought him to the nick. That's when we discovered he has a record going back quite a few years – petty stuff, mostly, but more recently running girls for prostitution. He's wanted in Birmingham for allegedly attempting to grab a young girl off the street and for roughing up another. Hathaway put the pressure on him."

"I can imagine that."

"He talked rather candidly about the 'turf war' between Lorna Henry and Jack Doyle."

Father Gilbert sat up.

"Derek said they believe Doyle set fire to the school to get back at Lorna because of 'the girl'."

"Veronyka Dalca?"

"Read the transcript."

Father Gilbert opened it up. Though it was computer-generated, it had the look of an old typewritten page.

RH: Be specific, Mr Kenton. You claim Jack Doyle's employees set fire to Layton's School of English as revenge for what?

DK: The girl. You know.

RH: I don't know. Are you talking about Veronyka Dalca?

DK: Veronyka? No. That Chinese girl who was murdered. The one from the Lily Rose.

RH: Anong Chuan.

DK: How should I know her name? She was a nobody. But Doyle thinks we had something to do with it and we didn't. He burned our place anyway.

RH: You're saying that no one associated with Lorna Henry killed Anong?

DK: Lorna Henry doesn't kill people. That's not how she does business.

RH: What about her bosses in London? Would they kill someone?

DK: Maybe they would. But I'd know if their boys were in town and I'm telling you they wouldn't come all this way to kill some Chinese chick. Why would anybody care if she died?

RH: If Doyle burned the school because of Anong's death, then she must have meant something to him.

DK: Nah. For guys like Doyle, it's the principle of the thing. You can't let anyone get away with murdering your people.

RH: (silence) So what are the names of Lorna Henry's bosses in London?

DK: (silence) I want my lawyer.

"I got it wrong," Father Gilbert admitted as he handed back the pages. "I thought the trigger was Veronyka. It was about Anong."

"That's what Lorna Henry thinks, too, apparently," Gwynn said.

"Why don't you bring her in and find out?"

"She's up to her eyeballs in legal protection right now."

"So it's possible, then, that Doyle got it wrong?"

"Doyle gets a lot of things wrong," Gwynn said. "But here's where I'm getting hung up. *If* Doyle hit the School of English because of Anong's murder and not the kidnapping of Veronyka, then that means Doyle knew Anong was here. Even if he retaliated out of 'principle', it draws attention to Anong's existence. If what Hathaway said is true about the Sensei, then Doyle is in trouble. He was hiding a known informant."

"Maybe he didn't know who Anong was or even that she was there."

"Which means somebody was keeping it from him – or lying to him," Gwynn said.

"Mamasan?" Father Gilbert asked.

Gwynn shook his head, then grunted, "I wish Doyle would kidnap *me* so we could have a little talk and get those answers."

"You're not special like I am," Father Gilbert replied.

They finished breakfast. Father Gilbert walked him out to the front lobby. "Have you talked to May – the one Mamasan said could corroborate her version of Sean's behaviour?"

"Today sometime, I hope. If Hathaway will let me." They reached the entrance. Gwynn gazed out at the street beyond. "Not that I'm admitting anything, but the ME got a new round of toxicological results. Now he'd like to know why Sean had so much of that ephedra drug in his body when he died and how it got there. It was concentrated, not taken in the over-the-counter pill form. There was no evidence of it in Sean's room, or on his person, or in the alley where he died."

Father Gilbert asked, "Does that means he's rethinking the suicide verdict?"

"I don't know what he's thinking," Gwynn said. "But we need an answer to that question before we draw any conclusions."

* * *

Father Gilbert phoned Brother Gregory about a trip to the bank. After ending the call, he thought again about the nagging questions surrounding Sean's death. He estimated that he had just enough time to go back to the Lily Rose.

The shop was closed, as he expected for that time of morning, but he walked to the front door anyway. He peered through the front window. The reception counter stood empty. The shelves behind it were still stocked with the herbal medicines, the containers uniformly set, the labels written in Chinese characters with smaller writing underneath. The effect was persuasive. It said that this was a legitimate place of healing. His eye went to a space in the line – one of the containers was missing, the gap standing out like a missing tooth. No doubt a customer had made a purchase. But of what? What kinds of herbs and medicines did they provide?

He walked to the right of the front door to the corner of the building and gazed at the alleyway. It sloped downward, at enough of a decline to put the cellar of the Lily Rose on the same level as the alley further along. Only now did he realize that the cellar wasn't a cellar at all. Where was the back door? Mamasan said one existed; Sean hadn't used it because it would have set off an alarm.

The alley ended in a large courtyard of walls and rear doors, presumably to the other shops. A solid grey metal door, with no outside handle, was in the corner, hardly noticeable in the mix of skips and other containers that crowded the alley. Presumably it was the fire exit, though he didn't remember seeing it from the inside. Not that he would have noticed, considering the chaos of his last visit.

He now tried to imagine Sean's actions leading up to his death. After the confrontation, Mamasan said he'd come out of the front door and – then what? Headed down the alley to swallow a handful of pills? Was he carrying a drink to take with them? Father Gilbert scanned the ground. Bits of rubbish collected against the walls; gum wrappers, cigarette butts, and the usual scraps that had blown there from somewhere. There were one or two plastic bottles and soft drink cans and juice cartons. Sean could have used any one of them. Or he could have binned his drink into one of the skips. Father Gilbert doubted the forensics team would have taken on the scrupulous work of checking the fingerprints on all that rubbish – not for a death that looked clearly like a suicide. They simply didn't have the resources, time or, perhaps, even the skill.

He ventured over to the skip nearest the back door to the Lily Rose. Lifting the lid, he looked inside, flinching first at the stink of old rubbish. There was nothing unusual – except one of the herbal medicine containers, possibly the one missing from the shelf. He reached in and carefully picked it up – his hand large enough to wrap around a lip just beneath the lid. Habit told him to minimize his fingerprints as much as possible, just in case.

Like the other containers, this had a white label with Chinese characters. Underneath was typed in English: *ma-huang*. He held it up, looking through the thick glass. The container was half-filled with a brown, straw-type plant.

He wondered why someone in the Lily Rose would throw out the container. It may have been past its sell-by date, but why bin the container itself? He decided to take it with him, aware that mysteries were often solved by seemingly random details.

Glancing at his watch, he had just enough time to drop the container off in his room and meet Brother Gregory.

* * *

Brother Gregory was waiting for Father Gilbert in the main office at the Aardmore Bank, an old stone building on the main thoroughfare. Like so many other buildings, it had once been something else, and something else before that, time out of mind.

The manager, a young man named Tom Fuller, with all the looks and manners of someone who hoped to rise through the financial world, was sympathetic to their cause. He'd read about Brother Sean in the newspaper and was sorry to hear of all their subsequent problems. Brother Gregory showed him the legal documents allowing access to Sean's accounts. They were given a small office normally used for confidential consultations. Recognizing that he was dealing with a couple of Luddites, the manager brought printouts of Sean Damian's accounts and spread them on the table.

Both priests sat down and got to work. Brother Gregory began to highlight the cash withdrawals with a yellow marker. Father Gilbert scanned the pages to get an overview of Sean's assets. He had three accounts – a current account, a savings account, and a high-interest account. The current account had a balance of £2,500, the savings account had £10,000 in it, and the high-yield account held steady at £35,000.

"Did you know he had this much money?" Father Gilbert asked.

"I knew his family was wealthy – and a trust was mentioned – but I never expected anything like this."

The deposits were transfers that came at regular intervals, usually on the first and fifteenth of each month.

Father Gilbert gestured to the yellow highlights. "What are you finding there?"

"He withdrew sometimes fifty, sometimes one hundred pounds."

"Massages at the Lily Rose start at fifty. Gratuity could double that, depending on the service provided."

"Diplomatically put." Brother Gregory spread the pages out further. "All from the same cash machine – it's on a corner near the Lily Rose."

"It looks like *a lot* of withdrawals," Father Gilbert said.

"Twice a week for the past two months – and withdrawn on his 'free' days."

"A 'free day' being what?"

"We give the brothers a day off each week to leave, run errands, or simply relax by the water."

"You said the cash withdrawals are *twice* a week."

"Brother Sean was our shopping expert. He knew where to get the best deals for our food and supplies." Brother Gregory's face settled into a melancholic expression. "We wouldn't normally give a novice that kind of free rein, but Sean was good at it. I never questioned how long he took."

"Did he see Anong consistently?"

Brother Gregory leaned in to look. "The times for the withdrawals aren't consistent."

"Likely her availability wasn't consistent, depending on her clients."

Shaking his head, Brother Gregory said, "He saw her a lot more than I would've guessed."

"You said that, contingent on coming into St Sebastian's, Sean and his parents agreed that he wouldn't use personal funds."

"That was the rule."

"Wouldn't his parents know about these accounts?"

"They didn't. I asked them about it this morning, just to make sure they were all right with my having access, and they were unaware of anything other than the trust account."

"What was the nature of the trust?"

"Sean's grandfather was a very wealthy banker who made quite a bit of money from property deals. He set up the trusts for his grandchildren before he died."

Father Gilbert glanced over the various pages. £500 was going out every other week to another account. "What is this standing order? A car payment?"

"He didn't own a car, as far as I know," Brother Gregory said. "With all his other secrets, though, he may have a car stashed away somewhere. I'd be the last to know."

Father Gilbert went out of the office and found the manager at a desk in the main lobby. They returned and checked the coding on the standing order transactions. Then Tom turned to a computer on a table behind them and tapped at the keys for a minute. Finally he said, "It's not a loan payment of any kind. It's a standing order to an account with Barclays in London. I can't access the details on this end. You'll have to talk to them." He found a phone number for the department they needed and left them alone again.

Brother Gregory made the call, getting transferred to three different people before he found someone who could help him. As he began that conversation, Father Gilbert's phone buzzed.

Stepping out of the office to take the call, he saw on the screen that it was Uncle George.

"Our production is finished," George said.

"The show is closing?"

"Here, yes. We're moving on to Norwich. I have a few days off in the meantime so I thought I'd rest at the flat in London. Any interest in coming up?"

"I'd like to do that. Though things are a little unsettled at the moment."

"I saw in the newspaper about that monk."

"It's a mess. Can I get organized and ring you back in a few minutes?"

"Sure."

He hung up and slipped back into the office.

Brother Gregory had also just finished his phone call. He looked troubled as he began to shuffle the papers together. "The short answer is that the bank needs to see all the legal paperwork granting me the authority to conduct business on Sean's behalf. That includes the death certificate."

"That would come from the Medical Examiner."

"I could send it all by mail or electronic means, but it would be faster if I brought them in personally. That means a trip to Canary Wharf."

"Mind if I join you?"

"I was hoping you would."

* * *

Father Gilbert returned to the Masthead Inn to pack his things. He looked at the container of *ma-huang* and wondered what to do with it. On a precautionary whim, he wrapped it in one of the hotel's plastic laundry bags and left it with the front desk with a scribbled note. "Detective Inspector Gwynn may come by to pick this up," he explained as he checked out. "Don't let anything happen to it."

The young woman looked at the bag with an expression of awe – *an item to be picked up by a detective* – and promised to take special care.

As he waited in the lobby, he had the presence of mind to call Mrs Mayhew, his secretary at St Mark's, to confirm that Father Augustine, a semi-retired vicar who often filled in for Father Gilbert, was handling all of the weekend church duties. He also left a voicemail for Detective Inspector Gwynn to let him know about his excursion to London and the container waiting for him at the front desk of the hotel.

Brother Gregory showed up a few minutes later with enough documents to impress the bureaucrats at Barclays Bank. Though the medical examiner couldn't provide a final death certificate while the investigation was pending, he'd filled out an interim form confirming that Sean Damian was most definitely dead.

George Gilbert arrived a few minutes later in a taxi and was surprised to find out that he was travelling with not one but two priests. They shared the taxi to the Englesea station and caught the next train to Victoria.

Father Gilbert was afraid the journey would be awkward for his uncle and an unfamiliar priest. But the two men discovered a mutual love of old musicals and spent the time chatting about Noël Coward's *Bitter Sweet*, Ivor Novello's *Careless Rapture*, and Vivian Ellis' *Mr Cinders*, launching into the song "Spread A Little Happiness" to the surprise of everyone else in the cab. Father Gilbert smiled and nodded, not knowing the song nor any of the musicals they talked about, but appreciating the respite from the events of the past few days.

Amidst the crowds at Victoria station, the two priests parted company with George, who graciously took Father Gilbert's suitcase by taxi to the flat. Father Gilbert held onto his messenger bag, slinging it over his shoulder. He and Brother Gregory took the Tube to Canary Wharf station.

They found two seats together at the front of a carriage, passing a woman with piercings and tattoos all over her neck and face. Her eyes had dark circles under them and Father Gilbert thought, sadly, that she looked no more alive than many of the spectres he'd seen in Englesea.

He looked around the carriage and wondered why he didn't see more spectres in a city like London.

What were the rules for their appearances to him? The more he experienced, the more he detected certain patterns to the spiritual world, though he had yet to assemble those patterns into a coherent order.

He turned to Brother Gregory. "Do you think a town like Englesea can be corrupt to its very core?"

Brother Gregory was taken aback. "Do you mean corruption in the civil authorities or something else?"

"Spiritually corrupt through and through," he said, trying to strike a balance between a tone of voice that could be heard above the noise of the train but not one so loud as to draw attention.

"Yes – I believe a place can become so saturated in evil that it affects all who live there." A sorrowful look shaded his expression. "I've been meditating on the idea that Brother Sean was infected by it."

Father Gilbert looked at the underground darkness racing past the train window. "What about the dead?"

Brother Gregory touched a finger to his lips, rubbing them softly as he considered the question. "The decisions people make in life will determine what becomes of them after they die. A life lived in pursuit of evil will have terrible consequences eternally."

"What about those spirits that seem stuck in-between?"

"Are you asking me if I believe in ghosts?"

"Ghosts, spectres, apparitions…"

He turned in his seat to face Father Gilbert. "Why do you ask?"

"Englesea is overrun with them."

Brother Gregory laughed, read Father Gilbert's expression, then grew serious again. "You've seen them?"

Father Gilbert nodded.

"The stories about you are true, then. You experience paranormal encounters."

Another nod from Father Gilbert.

Brother Gregory shook his head slowly. "We need to have this conversation somewhere else."

"Give me a quick overview," Father Gilbert said.

"Orthodox Christian teaching states that ghosts are actually demons masquerading as the departed spirits of humans," Brother Gregory said carefully. "Some theologians speculate that they're the spirits of depraved humans who are trapped in a kind of 'purgatory' of deception, being used by Satan in the afterlife as he'd used them in life – spirits in bondage. Others argue that they're the souls of the departed that are stuck between worlds for one reason or another."

Father Gilbert knew the theories – even a few more. "What do *you* think?"

"I think it's good that St Sebastian's sits on consecrated ground overlooking the town." Brother Gregory let out a slow exhalation. "I've often *felt* something was wrong there. I was never sure what it was exactly."

"What does that mean for the living?"

"We have free will. Satan may coax or persuade or entice us, but he can't force us. As corrupt as the town may be, everyone makes choices. We make our chains and prisons."

"Even Brother Sean?"

Brother Gregory frowned. "Even Brother Sean."

* * *

They emerged from the Underground to the dazzling high-rises in the relatively new banking district that had overtaken the old and abandoned West India Docks.

They found the Barclays building and eventually reached the correct department and a woman named Leslie Tanner. Sharp in appearance and efficiency, she took them to her office, which had a stunning view of another office building. She quickly looked over Brother Gregory's paperwork, consulted with a superior about the "abnormality" of the medical examiner's document, then returned to find on her computer the information they needed.

"Tennyson and Proude," she said.

"I'm glad to hear it," Father Gilbert joked.

She gave him a cursory glance, then continued. "Tennyson and Proude is the law firm handling the standing order."

"Does that mean the £500 is going to the law firm or somewhere else?" asked Brother Gregory.

"You'll have to ask them about it," she said. She poked at a button on the keyboard. Within seconds, the printer behind her whirred into life and spat out a page. She handed it to Brother Gregory. It gave the address, phone numbers, and contact name for the firm. In total, the transaction took fifteen minutes.

"Why did we have to come all this way for that?" Brother Gregory asked when they were outside again.

Father Gilbert smiled. "If they make it too easy, then we'll wonder what all those fees and charges are on our accounts."

* * *

The offices of Tennyson and Proude were tucked away between a fine art shop and a bistro on Chancery Lane. The front was painted grey, with a glass door that led into a narrow reception area. A woman with a thick East End accent welcomed them and asked them to have a seat while she fetched Mr Englebert – Steven Englebert, as the printout indicated.

After sitting down on thick cushioned chairs, Brother Gregory leaned towards Father Gilbert and said, "One wouldn't be surprised to learn they once represented the Kray brothers."

Father Gilbert understood. The receptionist's accent didn't do the firm any favours, unless they liked catering to the London underworld. He expected Steven Englebert to look like Bob Hoskins from *The Long Good Friday*.

Steven Englebert looked nothing like Bob Hoskins – nor any other popular actor who'd made a career playing mobsters. He was tall and elegant, wearing a tailored suit and matching tie and handkerchief. His salt and pepper hair colour suggested that he was in his fifties, though his face had few lines and his blue eyes were sharp and energetic. He shook their hands, offered them coffee, and then guided them deep into the expensively carpeted and panelled halls to his office, which seemed far too large for the building.

"It's like the TARDIS," Father Gilbert said.

Brother Gregory laughed at the Doctor Who reference.

Steven Englebert looked thoughtful for a moment, then said, "My wife says David Tennant was the best of the new lot."

The office was an interior decorator's dream: the dark wood of the panelling, the complementary paintings, thick shelves with leather editions of law books, and high Georgian-styled windows gave a sense of cosy wealth. Four leather wingback chairs sat around a conference table apart from the desk – as if to suggest that meeting with clients should never be confused with dreary paperwork. They sat down and Brother Gregory explained to Mr Englebert that Sean Damian was dead, probably by suicide.

Englebert looked genuinely upset. "That unfortunate young man," he said. "What a tragedy."

An assistant appeared with a gold tray of coffee. The cups and saucers were made of fine china, along with the jug for cream and the sugar bowl.

"I almost feel as if we should have a drink," Englebert said while the assistant made the coffee to their liking. He glanced at his watch. It was nearly one o'clock. He looked tempted.

After a pause, Brother Gregory said, "We're trying to find out about a mysterious standing order that Sean set up. The bank told us it is being managed by you."

Englebert held his cup of coffee over the saucer while he drank. "It's a fairly straightforward transaction, though the instructions on our end were slightly more involved."

"How so?"

"The money goes to a privately run school in Twickenham called the Tianzhu Academy to cover all the needs of a student there. An eight-year-old girl. An adorable child. Her name is Jasmine Li."

Father Gilbert and Brother Gregory exchanged looks.

"You know her," said Englebert.

"We know a little about her," Father Gilbert said.

"Will you explain her to me? I honestly haven't the slightest idea why Sean decided to fund this girl."

"She's not his, is she?" Brother Gregory asked. "His daughter, I mean."

Englebert shook his head. "I asked him directly about that, since it would have legal ramifications if she were his daughter. He assured me she wasn't. But he wouldn't say any more about her. He wanted her taken care of, that's all."

"Even after his death?" Brother Gregory asked.

"Yes. It's one of the provisions of his will. She stands to receive a substantial sum of money from his trust, distributed over time. The rest goes to you, Brother Gregory."

"Me?"

"Well, to your Order, I should say."

Brother Gregory looked astonished.

"I was rather surprised, too," Englebert said. Father Gilbert couldn't imagine what such a calm face would look like surprised. "Everything changed within the last two months. He changed the beneficiary of his will and set up the standing order for the girl."

"Was he anticipating his death?"

"I never knew what he was thinking. He always had a kind of melancholy about him."

"We saw the balances in his accounts," Brother Gregory said. "We don't know the value of the trust."

"Since you're inheriting it, so to speak, I can tell you." His eye went from Brother Gregory to Father Gilbert.

"I could cup my hands over my ears, if you want," Father Gilbert said.

"It's all right," said Brother Gregory.

"The trust was valued at 10 million pounds when we redid the will."

Brother Gregory's mouth fell open. Father Gilbert tried to stay poker-faced.

"Jasmine stands to receive a million of that."

"She's a young girl," Father Gilbert said. "Who serves as her guardian?"

"Her mother, whose name is..." For the first time Englebert consulted a pad of notes on a side table. "Jun Anong Li."

"And if the mother is dead?"

"What about the father?"

"Unknown."

Englebert rubbed his smooth chin. "I'll have to dig deeper. I believe it would be the next of kin."

"What if the next of kin can't be found?"

"Then you would be her guardian," he said to Brother Gregory.

Once again Brother Gregory looked shocked.

"Does your Order have provisions for the care of orphans?" Father Gilbert asked him.

Brother Gregory nodded. "Our sister Order does."

"You can care for her however you think is best," Englebert said. "It doesn't have to be within your Order. But that's only the case if we can't find her next of kin."

"So, Sean set this up only two months ago," Father Gilbert said. "We think he met Jun Anong only two months ago. Was he prone to what looks like rash decision-making?"

"Yes. I joked that he was like a man who would come in with lost puppies and ask us to take care of them on his behalf. We advised and cautioned him, of course. Sometimes we persuaded him to think twice about his decisions. But in this case, he was adamant." He pressed his fingers together to form a spire. It was hard not to notice his perfectly manicured nails. "So you're saying he was romantically involved with Jasmine's mother?"

"It would seem so," Brother Gregory said.

Englebert looked puzzled. "You are a *Catholic* Order, aren't you?"

Brother Gregory sighed. "Brother Sean broke the rules."

"That's not a surprise either," Englebert said. "He never struck me as a rule-follower. He always seemed to be on his own, doing things the way he wanted. I was a bit flummoxed by his decision to join your Order. Frankly, I was concerned that he was heading into a cult. But I investigated you thoroughly and was satisfied with what I'd learned. Though I put a qualifier in the will to readdress your participation in the trust should you fall into scandal or disrepute."

"What if Sean is the cause of the scandal?" Brother Gregory asked.

"His parents are the default trustees. We'll have to consult with them." Englebert frowned. "This woman, though. Had I been more astute, I would have checked into her background to find out whether or not she was a confidence artist. Was she?"

"We don't know. We're trying to solve that mystery."

"There's more to Sean's death than you've told me." Englebert glanced at his watch again. "If you have the time, it would be prudent for you to tell me everything you know."

* * *

It hadn't been Father Gilbert's plan when he awoke that morning to bounce back and forth around London. But once again, he and Brother Gregory were on a train, heading west on the last leg of a journey towards Twickenham. The loud clack and clatter of the train kept the two priests from talking, leaving Father Gilbert to sit on the worn bench, clutching his messenger bag like a life preserver, lost in the new questions that sprung up every time one was answered.

Had Anong known that Brother Sean was wealthy? If so, had she been playing with his affections to get to his money? Was this tied into her murder – or his, if he had indeed been murdered? If so, how? Who benefited the most from his death?

Father Gilbert brought out his phone, checked the signal, and dialled Detective Inspector Gwynn. He went into the voicemail system and left a brief message about Sean, the trust, and Anong's daughter. A moment after hanging up, a text arrived from Gwynn: "Couldn't pick up. In meetings with Hathaway. Picked up container at hotel. What is it??? More later. Keep up the good work."

Father Gilbert showed Gwynn's message to Brother Gregory. "Keep up the good work," Brother Gregory said loudly. "He means, 'keep up doing *his* good work'."

The train slid into Twickenham station and they stepped onto the platform. They used the map application on Father Gilbert's phone to find the Tianzhu Academy, which was in a large Victorian house situated on a suburban street filled with other houses like it. A modest sign on the fence along the front garden stated its name in English and Chinese. From somewhere behind the house, children were laughing and shouting. They went to the main door and rang the bell.

A minute later, it was pulled open and a Korean man with his sleeves rolled up and what looked like flour on his forearms invited them in. "I'm sorry," he said. "Come into the kitchen. I'm making snacks."

They followed him down the hall to a large kitchen with a dining table that had places for at least a dozen people. Just beyond the kitchen were French doors leading to a conservatory and, beyond that, a large garden where children in school uniforms were playing on swings, climbing frames, and slides. Two women strolled the perimeter, watching the children. Another woman was crouching down, talking in earnest with a young girl about a flower she held up.

The Korean man put on mitts and took a baking pan from the oven. He set it onto the tiled counter. "We're a mess, I'm afraid. I'm Pastor Rick Nee." He waved a gloved hand.

"We're sorry to show up unannounced," Brother Gregory said.

"I'm Brother Gregory with the Order of St Sebastian. This is Father Gilbert, from Stonebridge."

"Then you're not the priests from the diocese?" Pastor Rick asked.

"No, we aren't."

"Ah. That's quite a coincidence, then. The diocese wants to talk to me about our work here and said someone was coming this afternoon."

"What *is* your work, Pastor Rick?" asked Father Gilbert.

As he spoke, Pastor Rick took a lump of dough from a bowl and began to form it into animal shapes on another baking pan. "The Academy was founded over fifty years ago to serve the Far Eastern community in this part of London. Over the past twenty years, we've focused on helping the children of Asians who come to this country and work in fields that aren't conducive to family life, or children who have been orphaned." He tipped his head towards the playground. "The boy on the swing – his father is on an oil rig up north. The little girl talking to the teacher is an orphan. Her parents died in a car accident only a year ago. Her family in China didn't want her."

"So you're a boarding school and an orphanage?" Father Gilbert asked.

"Of sorts."

"The children live here around the clock, then."

"Yes, though we have a couple of students who are dropped off in the mornings by their parents."

Brother Gregory turned to watch the children at play. "How many do you have here?"

"Twelve right now. We've had up to fifteen, at most eighteen. But not everyone can afford us."

"Are you expensive?"

"Not compared to other schools. But many of the parents hold itinerant jobs. Or jobs that don't pay well. We're subsidized mostly by donations from area churches. All kinds. The Academy was founded as a non-denominational ministry."

"How long have you worked here?" asked Brother Gregory.

"Thirteen years. I keep forgetting," he said. "I'm an ordained Baptist minister, originally from Korea." The next baking pan went into the oven. He leaned back against the counter. "If you're not from the diocese – why are you here?"

"We need to talk to you about Jasmine Li."

"Oh?" Pastor Rick held up his flour-covered arms as if he wasn't sure what to do with them. "Why?"

"Do you hear from her mother very often?"

"I have to ask again: why do you want to know?"

A girl appearing at the French doors interrupted them. Father Gilbert recognized her from the photograph. It was Jasmine.

She peeked in and puffed breathlessly as she tried to talk.

"Take your time, Jasmine," Pastor Rick said.

She bowed and then asked, "May I come in? I would like to practise my piano."

"Yes. Come in."

The girl looked at the two priests, her eyes bright and excited. Father Gilbert saw the resemblance to her mother, clearer than it was in the photograph.

"Show these gentlemen how well you play," Pastor Rick said.

She nodded enthusiastically and took three steps into the kitchen, then suddenly remembered to take off her shoes. She ran past them to the hall. In less than a minute, they heard her playing a tune on the piano. Bach, Father Gilbert thought. She played confidently and well.

"That's Anong's daughter, isn't it?" Brother Gregory asked.

"Anong?"

"Jun," Father Gilbert clarified. "Anong is a middle name."

"Again, I have to ask why you're asking all these questions," Pastor Rick said.

Father Gilbert and Brother Gregory looked at one another to decide who would break the news. Brother Gregory nodded. Father Gilbert drifted to the doorway to make sure Jasmine couldn't hear them. He thought of the poor girl and how her life was about to change.

Pastor Rick moved closer to Brother Gregory. He spoke low. "What is going on?"

Brother Gregory said, "Jasmine's mother is dead."

Pastor Rick put his hand to his mouth, the flour leaving a white smudge on his cheek. "No," he whispered. "What happened?"

Brother Gregory gave a cursory version, leaving out the worst details.

Pastor Rick listened in stunned silence, then asked, "Was it a client?"

"What do you mean, 'client'?" Father Gilbert asked.

"Jun wrote letters that I read to Jasmine. She never said what her job was specifically, but I've been doing this kind of work long enough to read between the lines."

"We don't know who killed her," Brother Gregory said.

"When did you last see or talk to Jun?" Father Gilbert asked.

"She talks to Jasmine every Monday and Thursday evening on the computer – one of those online video chat services. She doesn't get to visit in person very often."

"When did she last make contact?" Father Gilbert asked.

"Last Monday evening," Pastor Rick replied. "She missed the Thursday call, which was sad. Normally she lets me know when she can't do it, but didn't this time. Jasmine was disappointed."

Father Gilbert kept an eye on the hall. Jasmine continued to play. "Where did Jun usually call from?" he asked.

Pastor Rick gave it some thought. "From the look of the background, I'd say it's an Internet café. She said the Wi-Fi was terrible where she lived."

"What else did you pick up from the letters – or any conversations you had with her?" Father Gilbert asked.

"I got the impression she was in serious trouble before she came here. She behaved like a woman on the run. I wondered if she was escaping an abusive husband, maybe Jasmine's father. She didn't say outright to keep Jasmine a secret, but things weren't normal."

"Definitely not normal," Brother Gregory said.

Pastor Rick looked at Father Gilbert, then beyond him to the hall. "What will become of her?"

"Do you know Sean Damian?"

Pastor Rick brightened. "Oh yes. He's been here a few times. He sponsors Jasmine."

"Sponsors?" Brother Gregory asked.

"He's a benefactor," Pastor Rick explained. "A couple of the kids get money from church members or others who want to help. Why?"

Brother Gregory looked to Father Gilbert again, then said, "I'm afraid I have bad news about him."

The piano playing from the other room stopped. Father Gilbert moved towards the silence as Brother Gregory began to deliver the next blow.

The parlour was a room just beyond a staircase to the left. It had the look of a typical front room, with a small fireplace, painted plaster walls, and a light overhead. But there were chairs, small easels with pads and crayons, low shelves of books, and a games table with puzzles on it. The piano faced the front window.

Jasmine sat at the piano, turning the pages of a music book. She saw Father Gilbert as he came in. "I want to find another song," she said. Her English was precise, though she still had the hint of a Chinese accent.

"What kind of music do you like best?" Father Gilbert asked, crouching down next to the piano bench.

"I like to *listen* to the Beatles," she said. "But I like to play classical music."

"Who is your favourite composer?"

"I like Handel," she said.

"Oh – that was Handel you were playing? I thought it was Bach."

"They sound alike," she said, as if to comfort him in his ignorance.

"Do you like Vivaldi, too?"

"Yes. I want to learn the violin so I can play 'The Four Seasons'."

"That's ambitious."

She tilted her head, not understanding the word.

"'Ambitious' means that you want to do great things."

"Oh."

Her look told him she was trying to decide whether she really wanted to do great things or not. He said a small prayer asking God to ease the pain she was about to feel – and to do great things with her life in spite of it.

"Why do you look sad?" she asked him.

The question caught him off guard. His eyes burned. "Do I look sad?"

"Yes."

"That's all wrong, isn't it?" he said, standing up again. "One shouldn't come to this lovely place and look sad. Especially when such a beautiful girl is playing such beautiful music."

She giggled.

He took a few steps to the doorway. "Are you happy here?" he asked.

"Yes. Very much, thank you."

"How long have you lived here?"

She pursed her lips and looked at the ceiling to think. "Two years."

"Where did you live before that?"

"Far away. In a village." Her gaze fell to his collar. "Are you a priest?"

"Yes."

"Are you like Pastor Rick?"

"We do similar jobs."

"Do you have a school?"

"No. But if I did, I would hope to have a girl like you come there."

"You have to ask my mum about that," she said.

Father Gilbert felt his heart drop and a knot tightened in the pit of his stomach.

There were footsteps down the hall and then Brother Gregory came to the door. Pastor Rick – his arms now dough-free – came up behind him. Both men looked shaken, as if they'd had a contest of delivering bad news and ended in a tie.

"It was nice to meet you," Brother Gregory said to Jasmine.

Father Gilbert understood the signal. "Me, too," he said softly to her.

"Me, *three*," Jasmine said, laughing.

"I'll walk you out," Pastor Rick said. He turned to Jasmine. "Keep playing. They want to hear your lovely music while they leave."

Jasmine nodded and began to play a song Father Gilbert knew was by Bach. He suspected she was playing it for him and was deeply touched.

At the front gate, Pastor Rick said, "I won't tell her yet. I want to know exactly what will happen to her first."

"You'll hear from me or Mr Englebert," Brother Gregory said.

"And the relative we talked about?" Pastor Rick asked.

"We'll see about that."

"Thank you." He shook their hands and, with a mournful look, turned and walked back to the house. When he opened the front door, the sounds of Jasmine's playing wafted out to them.

Father Gilbert felt an ache somewhere in his heart, maybe his soul. *Life shouldn't be like this*, he thought. *But it is.*

* * *

As they walked back to the Tube station, Brother Gregory explained that Anong's letters to Jasmine gave Pastor Rick every impression that Sean wasn't merely a client. He was in love with Anong – and Anong felt the same for him.

"How could he know that?"

"The way she wrote about him," Brother Gregory replied. "She kept calling him her 'special friend' and used words and phrases that convinced Pastor Rick there was true affection on her part. He remembered the day Anong took Jasmine sightseeing. He didn't realize they went with Sean – they must have met somewhere – but both mother and daughter were aglow when they came home."

"Aglow?"

Brother Gregory nodded. "He remembered it vividly. He'd never seen her so happy."

"That doesn't sound manipulative or cynical," Father Gilbert said.

"It was serious enough that Anong revised her instructions should anything happen to Jasmine and Pastor Rick couldn't get through on her mobile. She said he was to call Sean – and the number looked like the one he'd been using – or, failing that, he was to use Steve Englebert's number at the law office, giving Sean Damian's name."

Father Gilbert wished he'd seen whatever Pastor Rick had in writing about that. "What instructions did he have before that change?" Father Gilbert asked. "Does he know of any other next of kin?"

"Anong's mother."

"Her *mother?*" Father Gilbert asked. "Where does she live?"

"Englesea."

The news caught him off guard. "How is it that no one knows about her mother? What's her name?"

Brother Gregory struggled to say the name correctly. "Ushi Yan."

Father Gilbert felt a wash of fire burn through his veins. He stopped on the pavement and turned to Brother Gregory. "Are you sure that was the name?"

"I couldn't have made it up. Why?"

"Ushi Yan is Mamasan."

* * *

Father Gilbert paced the Tube station platform as he talked to Detective Inspector Gwynn on his mobile phone.

"She's Anong's *mother*," he said, his voice shaking. "Why didn't we know that?"

"We don't get full family histories with these people. They're on and off the radar," Gwynn said irritably. "They use names and we have no way of knowing if they're real or not. How in the world are we expected to connect Ushi Yan with Anong Chuan or Jun Li? And it may not be true."

"Rebecca Hathaway would know."

"Maybe," Gwynn said. "But the department she works for is relatively new. The database of information is still localized and fragmented."

"Well, we know that Mamasan has been lying to us from the start."

"The problem is that we don't know *what* she's lying about."

"If Mamasan *is* Anong's mother, then she's in line to be the guardian for Jasmine, which means she'll have control of a lot of money."

"Do you think Mamasan knows that?"

"It would give her a motive to kill Sean."

"Explain that to me."

"Mamasan knew that Anong and Sean were in love. After Anong

was murdered, Mamasan realized Sean would take his money and leave. So she killed Sean before he could make any changes to his instructions – to get control of the money."

"That's *if* she knew all the details of Sean's financial arrangements. How could she know? She wouldn't have had access to his will. Sean certainly wouldn't have told her."

"Maybe Anong told her."

"You're assuming a lot."

"Maybe so," Father Gilbert said. But his instincts told him he was on the right track. "I can't cope with the thought that Mamasan will benefit from these murders. And what will become of Jasmine?" He could imagine Mamasan bringing her to a place like the Lily Rose to live. "There must be something we can do to protect that girl from a woman as heartless as Mamasan."

"There is. We have to prove your theories. Any one of them." Gwynn jostled the phone for some reason. "Are you coming back to Englesea?"

"I'm staying with my uncle in London, unless you have a specific reason for me to come back."

"No. Stay there. Take a break from this. Your brain is no good to me all tied up in knots."

They hung up.

The train pulled in, crowded with the rush-hour commuters. Brother Gregory and Father Gilbert got on. Everyone pressed in close together.

Brother Gregory was inches away from Father Gilbert's ear and said, "I'm going back to St Sebastian's. I don't want to be away overnight. Do you want to come with me?"

Father Gilbert shook his head. "I'm staying with my uncle. I ought to spend some time with him. My suitcase is there anyway."

They changed trains at Richmond station and took the District Line back to Victoria. Brother Gregory went off to find the next train to Englesea while Father Gilbert navigated the crowds to the taxi stand. As he waited in the queue for the next available cab, he watched the traffic move at a crawl around the station. His eye fell on a light blue compact car. In the rear passenger seat he saw Veronyka

Dalca. She looked out the window with the dull expression of jaded indifference. Then, as if sensing his eyes on her, she looked over at him. Her expression didn't change – she didn't register surprise nor even recognition. She simply stared at him. Until the traffic began to move again. Then she gave him a small smile and a wink.

* * *

George's two-bedroom flat was one of several in a renovated house on Litchfield Street. By "renovated", that meant it was done sometime after the Second World War. It was directly across from The Ivy restaurant, within view of the St Martin's Theatre where *The Mousetrap* was celebrating its second millennium – or so it seemed to Father Gilbert. George had bought the flat sometime in the 1960s, during his first wave of modest fame. Father Gilbert wasn't sure how much he'd paid for it then, but he knew it was well worth 2 or 3 million pounds now. Each room was spacious and though it needed paint and updating, George had kept it in good condition. He'd decorated it with antique furniture – of no consistent era – and had turned it into a shrine to the world of theatre – mostly *his* world of theatre, with photos of him with actors, directors, and producers, framed posters of plays he'd been in or enjoyed, and a painting of George himself posing as Hamlet and poor Yorick's skull.

"It was a joke," George explained. "If you look closely at the skull, it was done to look like Laurence Olivier."

Father Gilbert looked closely and, true enough, it was the great actor himself.

"Sir Laurence came here for a party one night. He thought it was delightful. He wouldn't shut up about it."

"I knew it was a joke before you told me," Father Gilbert said.

"How?"

"Your legs never looked that good in a pair of tights."

The obvious choice for dinner was The Ivy itself. The maître d' welcomed George like an old friend and gave him his "usual" table in the centre of the room.

"Is this so people can see you when they come in?" Father Gilbert asked.

"Of course," George said, then returned a wave to Kenneth Branagh and another to Derek Jacobi.

Father Gilbert saw a handful of other actors he recognized from various television programmes. He couldn't place any of their names.

They drank and ate and laughed over stories of theatre past and present. After the meal, they returned to the flat. Father Gilbert enjoyed a long soak in a bath one could drown a small village in. When he came out, George was sitting at the dining table working on a large scrapbook.

"What is this?" Father Gilbert asked, working part of a towel in his ear to get it dry.

"I keep scrapbooks of my work," George said. "This one has programmes, flyers, and press clippings from the recent tour."

Father Gilbert was impressed. "You've done this for all of your productions?"

"I've tried to," he said. "With less success when I was especially busy. But now, there's more time." He taped a press clipping from the Englesea newspaper onto a page. "Besides, if I don't keep track of my career, who will?"

"Are you afraid you won't be remembered?"

"I know I won't be remembered," he said. "Do you know Robert Coote?"

"I'm afraid not."

"You'd know him if you saw a photo. He was in films like *Gunga Din* and *The Three Musketeers* and *The Ghost and Mrs Muir* and *Othello* and *The Prisoner of Zenda*. He played Colonel Pickering in the Broadway premiere of *My Fair Lady* and Pellinore in *Camelot*." He picked up a small flyer and held it for a moment. "No one knows him now. No one."

"Uncle George, you'll always be remembered. The question is: by whom and for what?"

"If you're going to get deeply theological, we can stop now."

"You brought it up," Father Gilbert retorted. He wandered into the kitchen and made them a pot of tea. He dropped into an easy chair and picked up one of George's scrapbooks.

"That's part one of this production," George said without looking up.

Father Gilbert began to flip through the pages. "It's nicely laid out," he said as he scanned the various clippings and photos. Some of the pictures were taken candidly backstage. George posed with an actress in one labelled "Blackpool". There was another from "Bournemouth" with Trevor Humphries. They performed in all the major cities and towns: Edinburgh, Reading, Cardiff, Liverpool... the list went on.

The list of cities struck a chord with Father Gilbert and he stopped to figure out why. His eye went back to Trevor Humphries again. The "old perv" was camping it up in the photo, smiling with leering delight at an attractive backstage worker.

"Do you have a list of all the cities and dates for this production?" Father Gilbert asked his uncle.

"It's in the front of the book," George replied.

Father Gilbert found the list and scanned it. He found his messenger bag back in the guest room and brought out his laptop.

"What are you doing?" George asked.

"Just checking..." He went to the Internet, after picking up the free Wi-Fi from a restaurant nearby, and searched for a concise list of the BackList murders, including the dates and locations. He cross-referenced it with the production. They lined up.

Father Gilbert's adrenalin surged. He sat up and double-checked each date and each location. Was it possible? He looked at George, who was now looking at him with a quizzical expression on his face.

"What?" George asked.

Father Gilbert took the list and the laptop to the dining table and put them in front of his uncle. George looked back and forth at the lists.

"You're not saying..."

"I'm not saying anything."

"You think someone in our company is this Blacklist Killer?" George asked.

"BackList," Father Gilbert corrected him. "I don't know. But they line up. And the dates correspond with the times the killer wasn't active. You weren't touring."

"Does that mean *I'm* a suspect?"

"Were you in all of these towns at these times?" he asked, pointing to the killer list.

"Yes. So were a handful of our company." George paused and looked again. "No, actually, Trevor Humphries and I were the only two who did that entire tour. We lost some of the cast for various reasons. Even the crew changed."

"Then you could be a suspect."

"This is ridiculous. I thought they caught the killer," he said.

"They *think* it was him, but there's room for doubt – little things that don't quite fit."

George gnawed at his lower lip, then pressed a finger against it to stop.

"What's wrong?" Father Gilbert asked.

"I was thinking about Trevor Humphries."

"What about him?"

"If you told me you suspected Trevor Humphries of being the killer, I'd say you were crazy. However, if sometime later I read that the police had arrested him for being the killer, I'd probably shrug and say, 'it makes sense'."

"Why would it make sense?"

"There's a kind of depravity about him."

"He's an *actor*."

George shook his head at the jab, then his eyes widened and his face went pale.

"What now?" Father Gilbert asked.

"I told you how, the other night, I went to Humphries' room to get a book I'd lent him."

"I remember."

"He was out of sorts, uncharacteristically dishevelled. He seemed shaken up. The room was a mess. The bathroom door was closed and I thought he had someone in there."

"He invited you in to see that?"

"Well, I knocked and walked in. The door was slightly ajar."

Father Gilbert felt confused. "He had someone in the room and left the door open?"

"It didn't make sense to me either, once I saw the mess," George said.

"Put that aside. What else did you see?"

"I don't remember anything."

"You do. The brain stores all kinds of things we don't think we remember. What else was unusual?"

George closed his eyes. "Women's undies. They were on the floor. Then Trevor distracted me with the book and when I looked again, they were gone. He must've kicked them aside."

"And?"

"That's all," he said.

"What time was all this?"

"Eleven-thirty-*ish*."

Father Gilbert brought out his mobile phone.

"Do you really think it means something?" George asked. He stood with his hands clasped in front of him like a worried child.

"What night was this?"

"Wednesday night."

"That's when Anong was murdered," Father Gilbert said. He hit the auto-dial for Gwynn.

It was late, but Gwynn picked up on the first ring. The noise behind him suggested a busy pub. "Isn't it past your bedtime?" he asked in lieu of "hello".

"Do the BackList detectives think they've closed their case?"

"Not yet. They're arguing over some of the inconsistencies in the methods. Why?"

Father Gilbert told him about Trevor Humphries.

By the time he'd finished, the ambiance behind Gwynn had changed. He'd moved from the pub to the outside. Gwynn's breathing suggested he was walking. "Where is Humphries now?"

Father Gilbert put the question to Uncle George.

"He was staying behind in Englesea for the weekend," George said. "I assume he's still at the Angel Sea Hotel."

"Thanks. I'll get back to you," Gwynn said and hung up.

Father Gilbert looked at George. "Well," was all he could manage to say.

"I think I'm going to be sick," George replied.

CHAPTER 15

Father Gilbert awoke to the sounds of London: the high-pitched squeals of taxi brakes, the snorts and puffs of buses, and the horns of irate drivers. Nearby Charing Cross Road was in the full throes of a busy day and it was only eight on a Saturday morning.

He sat up in bed and rubbed at his face, as if cobwebs had fallen on it in the middle of the night. He thought about Anong and Sean and Mamasan, their actions and motives all tangled up in his mind. He wondered about Trevor Humphries and what Gwynn had done with the information he'd passed on. Nathan Rank was curled up somewhere in his memory, like the body in the boot.

He dressed and went into the kitchen. Uncle George stood next to a small window near a breakfast-for-one table. He stared at nothing, his mug held frozen in mid-air.

"Uncle George?"

George turned his head only slightly. "They arrested him in the middle of the night."

"Trevor Humphries?"

"I've had three calls this morning from people who'd heard about it."

"How did they hear?"

"We're actors. These things get around very quickly. They say we're like bees – if you kill one, the rest of the swarm senses it."

Father Gilbert checked the kettle. It was still hot. He began to make a small pot of tea. "What happened?"

"They were so *indiscreet*," he said. "They went to his room at the Angel Sea Hotel and demanded that he come with them right then. They hardly gave him time to dress. They didn't even allow him to put on his toupee."

"He might be a cold-blooded killer, Uncle George."

"Still, there are civilized ways to do these things. We're not Soviet Russia."

Father Gilbert wasn't sure how to deal with this moment of pique. "Are you having regrets?"

"Of course I am," George said, turning around. "The whole thing could be a mistake, and it's all my fault."

"Or it could be that you were right and you helped the police catch a monster."

"I don't know how I feel either way." He sat down at the table as if the moment had been choreographed for the stage. "He's not a young man."

"Are you saying he was too fragile to commit murder?"

"Heavens no. The man is as strong as a bull. I've seen him lift things that a young man in peak condition couldn't lift. I'm afraid of what they'll do to him in prison." George upended what was left of his mug into his mouth.

"I'm going back to Englesea, Uncle George," Father Gilbert said, his own cup in hand. "Do you want me to check on him?"

"Let me know what you find out."

"I will."

George stood up and put his mug in the sink. He looked at Father Gilbert with haunted eyes. "Should I apologize to him?"

"Not until you know whether he's a killer or not."

He shook his head. "I don't know what I was thinking."

"Perhaps you're developing a moral compass," said Father Gilbert.

George groaned. "That won't help my career *at all*."

* * *

On the train from Victoria station, Father Gilbert phoned Detective Inspector Gwynn again.

"Humphries admitted having Anong in his room," Gwynn said. "He claims that he was not happy with the 'service' she was providing. He got a little rough and she complained. He told her to leave. She did. That was the last he saw of her."

"Rough?"

"I won't go into detail."

"Just as well," Father Gilbert said. "How does that scenario fit with the timing of her murder?" He glanced around, realizing that others in the carriage might hear him. He turned to the window and cupped his hand over the phone's microphone.

"He said she left around 11:30, so that might let him off the hook."

"You're releasing him?" asked Father Gilbert.

"No. Hathaway doesn't believe him. We did a cursory search of his room and found a pair of undies under the bed, like your uncle said."

"It's a good thing the hotel's housekeeping isn't very thorough."

"More than you realize. First thing this morning a cleaner admitted she found the necklace."

"Why didn't she come forward before?"

"She's not a properly employed cleaner," Gwynn said. "She filled in for her sister who actually works there. No one usually cares and Pinbrook claims he didn't know. She showed up this morning and, when he saw her, he had a fit. Fortunately, he had the presence of mind to ask her about the necklace."

"That's conscientious of him."

"He wants to get back on my good side. I threatened to arrest him as an accessory to murder because of his side-work for Doyle."

"He *is* an accessory, isn't he?" Father Gilbert asked.

"Not in a way that would hold up in court. He said he lost his key to the service lift and door. He had it replaced and the only person he lent that one to was you."

"That's convenient." Father Gilbert watched as the train slowed for the Wandsworth Common station.

Gwynn continued, "The cleaner said she found the necklace outside the door to Trevor's room, not in the room itself."

"Outside? Anong dropped it?"

"Yes. According to Humphries, he'd *accidentally* pulled it off her neck when he started getting a little 'rough' with her. He wasn't sure what happened to it."

"That still puts it in proximity," Father Gilbert said. "Can you check the necklace again for his fingerprints?"

"Done. We've got partials of her fingerprints."

"Surely there are tests you can do to find out if the undies were hers." A woman across the aisle gave him a disapproving look. He turned to the window again.

"The ME has them," Gwynn said. "Rebecca Hathaway is frothing at the mouth about this. She's gone to London to get a court order to search Humphries' flat there."

"Where is his flat?"

"Westminster, I think."

Doors on the train began to open and close with loud clicks and bangs. Father Gilbert watched as a man on the platform struggled with his bicycle. The wheels had been folded in to fit on the train but didn't want to unfold again. "Doesn't this case belong to the BackList detectives?"

"Not according to Hathaway," Gwynn replied. "The connection between Humphries and Anong makes it a human trafficking case as far as she's concerned. She's more ambitious than I realized."

"If Humphries is lying about Anong's leaving – and Pinbrook *isn't* lying about the key to the service lift and door – how was Anong's body removed?" Father Gilbert asked. The man with the bicycle began to swear and jerk the bicycle around.

"Humphries owns a rather large steamer-type trunk. He said it's because he's on tour for weeks on end. He lives out of it."

The train pulled away from the station. The man with the bicycle was kicking at the uncooperative wheel as the scene disappeared from Father Gilbert's view. "Did anyone see him leave with the trunk?"

"The girl at the front desk did. She claims he left with the trunk for an hour or so and then came back. And we actually can see a glimpse of it in the security recording."

"And Humphries said?"

"He left to do laundry. There's a twenty-four-hour launderette several streets away."

"He did laundry at one in the morning?"

"He said he couldn't sleep and going in the middle of the night ensures his privacy. Apparently his fans mob him otherwise." Gwynn's tone was derisive.

Father Gilbert tried to imagine his fan base being the kinds of people who frequented launderettes. "Are you doing forensics on the trunk?"

"Yes. There is evidence of it being used to carry something wet."

"A girl murdered in the bath?"

"Or laundry that hadn't been dried properly," Gwynn said. "They're going through the trunk with tweezers and microscopes."

The train picked up speed. Father Gilbert watched as the hard edges of the city gave way to the softer lines of the suburbs and countryside. "If Rebecca Hathaway can't find any evidence in Humphries' flat, will you have to let him go? Surely you don't have enough evidence to convict him for murdering Anong – not based on a pair of undies and that necklace. He already admitted she was in the room."

"I'll leave that with Hathaway."

"Meaning that you'll let her take the fall if it goes pear-shaped."

"Exactly." Gwynn's smile nearly came through the phone.

"Meanwhile, what will you do?"

"Take advantage of Agent Hathaway's absence and raid the Lily Rose."

Father Gilbert was surprised. "On what grounds?"

"I finally took a look at that container you found – the *ma-huang*. Nigel looked it up online. It's *ephedra*."

"Good heavens," Father Gilbert said.

"The ME is running new tests to see if the ephedra in Sean's system is the *ma-huang* from the Lily Rose. Unlike the over-the-counter version, this stuff could have triggered the reaction that killed Sean."

"How is it taken?" Father Gilbert asked.

"Tea would have done the trick," Gwynn replied. "The question is: did he drink the tea himself or was he poisoned by someone else?"

"Does that mean you're willing to consider murder rather than suicide?"

"It's enough to allow me to bring people in for questioning, to 'help with our inquiries in an ongoing murder investigation' as the newspapers like to say. That's why I'm raiding the Lily Rose."

"I should be there within a couple of hours."

"You can watch the fun."

* * *

Father Gilbert spent the rest of the train journey thinking through the various scenarios for what had happened to both Anong and Sean.

One scenario saw Trevor Humphries strangling Anong in the hotel bath and sneaking her out in his steamer trunk. In the end, her death had nothing to do with Sean.

Another scenario saw Trevor Humphries letting Anong go, as he claimed, and she left his room – only to be murdered by someone else somewhere else, putting them back where they had started.

As for Sean, one scenario saw him go to the Lily Rose for some unknown reason, *willingly* drink tea laced with *ma-huang*, stumble back into the alley as his body reacted, and then die from what looked like an overdose.

Another scenario saw Sean return to the Lily Rose, still for some unknown reason, *unknowingly* drink tea – or be *forced* to drink tea – with *ma-huang*, wind up in the alley, and then die later.

Motives were still a mystery. For all of their frenzied activity to learn the truth, a motive still hadn't been forthcoming.

The endgame for each scenario meant a young girl in London had lost her mother and her benefactor's money would wind up with a grandmother he knew to be corrupt. Whichever scenario was the right one, the inevitable ending pushed him to uncharitable and completely unchristian thoughts.

* * *

A delay with the train from Brighton meant that Father Gilbert arrived in Englesea nearly an hour after he was supposed to. He caught a taxi from the train station to the police station. He left his bags behind the front desk. PC Flack led him back to the interrogation rooms. He heard the noise before he reached the hall: half a dozen Chinese girls were seated along the wall complaining loudly in as many dialects. As he passed them, they addressed themselves to him as if he not only understood but were able to do something for them. He raised his hands and apologized.

One woman – he remembered seeing her during his first visit to the Lily Rose – put her leg out and caught his. She smiled at him.

"Now, now, behave yourself," he said.

PC Flack escorted him into the viewing area for the larger interrogation room.

"He let her sit for quite a while," PC Flack said. "He's only just gone in."

Mamasan sat with her arms folded, seething. Her jaw was set and her eyes were shooting fire at the Detective Inspector.

He moved with intentional slowness as he sat down and adjusted a pad and pen on the desk. He indicated for the recorder the time, date, place, and those present. He stated her name – Ushi Yan – rather than "Mamasan".

"I'm not here to accuse you of anything," Gwynn said sympathetically. "I don't think you've done anything wrong. I'm sure we can clear up any misunderstandings."

"Good," she said.

"I think you're the keeper of the truth. You're the only one who knows what's *really* going on."

She smiled proudly and folded her arms. She nodded as if to concur with his assessment.

Gwynn then poised his pen over the pad of paper as if about to write and said casually, "Tell me about Jack Doyle."

She didn't react. "Who's he?" she asked.

"Your boss."

"I am the boss," she said.

He wrote it down on the pad. "Ushi Yan is the boss," he said softly. She watched him, her expression reflecting concern until he looked up at her again. She returned to a posture of stubborn defiance.

"Tell me about the Sensei, then."

"What is a Sensei?"

"It means 'master'. You know. The master back home that really runs things. We British are too weak to be masters, which is why Jack Doyle is a servant to him here."

Mamasan smiled. "Weak, yes. Servants, yes. But I don't know Jack Doyle. I don't know a Sensei."

Gwynn said aloud as he wrote down, "Ushi Yan does not recognize Sensei as the master."

She flinched and pointed to the pad. "That is not what I said."

Gwynn ignored her. He sat up as if he had written all he wanted to.

"Who usually serves the tea at your spa?" he asked.

The abruptness of the question stopped her. Father Gilbert could tell her mind was working through the reason for the sudden change. "Chan."

"Always?"

"It's one of his duties."

Gwynn nodded, then said: "We may have found the man who killed Anong."

Her expression reflected her confusion over the disjointed question. "You found him already. It was Sean."

"You know Sean didn't do it. We have witnesses that prove Sean couldn't have killed Anong. Why do you keep insisting he did it?"

"Because he was crazy about her." She spun a finger around her temple. "Do you know 'crazy'? And if he did not kill her, he made her go out and be killed by someone else."

"How did he make her?"

"He scared her when he got so angry. So she went out."

"She went out to meet a client, Ushi Yan. You liked her to meet clients. She made more money for you that way."

"Why should I care about her money?"

"Where is it all, by the way? Did she put it in a bank?" he asked.

"I don't know what she did with her money."

"Maybe one of the other girls stole it. When Anong was murdered, she took the money and hid it somewhere. Or it could have been your bald companion. Chan."

She tossed the suggestion away. "Maybe."

"Or maybe Anong sent her money away to someone? Is there anyone she's taking care of? In London, perhaps?"

Father Gilbert recognized what Gwynn was doing – testing her response to see if she knew anything about Anong's daughter.

There was nothing in her reaction to suggest she did. "No."

"Maybe she sends it back to family in China."

"Maybe she does."

He paused, a slight sideways turn in his chair. "Does she have any family in England?" he asked.

Her eyes went up to him. "How should I know?"

Gwynn made notes on the pad of paper. Then he asked, "Ushi Yan, why didn't you tell us that Anong was your daughter?"

If he wanted shock-value, he succeeded. Mamasan reeled back in her chair as if Gwynn had struck her. She was speechless.

"Well?" Gwynn said.

Mamasan composed herself and gave him a cold look. "My family is none of your business," she said.

"It is when one of them is murdered," Gwynn said. "You've lied to us about Anong over and over again. That makes us suspicious. It makes us think you're guilty of something."

"Of what?" she asked, returning to her tone of confidence. "Do you have evidence of my guilt?"

"We have recordings of your lies," he said.

"I did not tell you everything about Anong because she is my family. That is not lying, it is protection." She waved a recriminating finger at him. "If she was not my daughter you would still have to find her murderer."

He held a warm and understanding tone. "I'm sure it must be difficult for you. But it seems cold-hearted that you never mentioned it. Why not?"

"I just said. To protect her."

"That didn't work out very well, did it?" he said. "Where is her father?"

"In China. Dead. Bad sickness."

"How long ago did he die?"

"Fourteen years."

Gwynn jotted another note. "You came to Britain before or after your husband died?"

"After. No work for me in China. Good work here."

Father Gilbert frowned as he thought about the kind of good work she had found.

"You've been here a long time, Ushi. Did Anong come with you?"

"She came later."

"She lived with you after she got here?"

"No."

"Why not?"

"She was a teenager then," she said. "Rebellious. She went her own way. Did her own work."

"You've been in Englesea..." He hesitated as if to think about it. "Five years?"

"Five years, yes."

"I want you to give me a list of where you've been since you arrived in the country – and how long you were there."

"I don't remember them all."

"You want to be a good citizen, don't you?" He pushed the pad and pen in her direction and indicated for the recording that he was ceasing the interview. She looked confused by his sudden departure. He closed the door. She sat staring at the pad. She didn't pick up the pen.

* * *

Gwynn came into the viewing area. "You're here," he said.

Father Gilbert nodded. "You didn't mention Anong's daughter."

"One surprise at a time," he said. "This is a warm-up."

Father Gilbert glanced at Mamasan. She was still staring at the pad without a pen in hand. "She won't write anything down."

"Probably not. It's a stall tactic. I want to keep her busy for now."

She picked up the pen and began to scratch out what Gwynn had written.

He laughed. "She doesn't want any evidence that she denied the Sensei was master."

"Are you ever going to find out who this Sensei is?"

"That's Hathaway's job." Gwynn looked at his watch. "I have to keep moving. Her lawyer should be here any time."

"She called him?"

Gwynn smiled. "She was in the middle of calling him when we raided the place. Chan – her man up front – must have signalled her when we came in."

Gwynn opened the door. The chatter of the Chinese women echoed into the room.

"What are you going to do with the girls in the hall?" Father Gilbert asked.

"Wait for an interpreter. We found one in Eastbourne. He's on his way."

"You're not really going to interview all of them, are you?"

"Only as a smokescreen. Then I'll single out May. She's the one Mamasan said could corroborate her stories about Anong and Sean."

"She's also the one I think was grieving over Anong's death," Father Gilbert said. "She covered for me in the hall at the Lily Rose. I don't think she cares for Mamasan very much."

"If that's the case, then I'll get the truth out of her." Gwynn stepped into the hall. "I have Chan in the next room. Let's see how he does."

* * *

Father Gilbert followed Gwynn down the hall to the second interrogation room. It was smaller than the first and also had an even smaller viewing room.

Chan – Chan Zhang – had even less to say than Mamasan. Unlike her, he wouldn't engage, not even to confirm his name for the recording. His only response was: "If you say so."

That's how it went through all of Gwynn's questions until Gwynn asked, "Do you like tea?"

The sudden change baffled him. "Yes."

"You serve tea at the Lily Rose, don't you? It's courtesy for your customers."

Chan looked suspicious about where this questioning was going. "Yes," he said warily.

"Did Brother Sean like tea?"

"Everyone likes tea."

"Did he have tea the last time he was at the Lily Rose?"

Chan opened his mouth to answer, then suddenly thought better of it. "If you say so."

"It's not what I say, it's what Mamasan says. You serve the tea," Gwynn said. Father Gilbert recognized the bluff – positioning Chan against Mamasan. "If you usually serve the tea, then you served Brother Sean tea. You're not calling her a liar, are you?"

"If Mamasan says that I gave Brother Sean tea, then I did."

"With *ma-huang* in it."

"What is *ma-huang*?" he asked.

"You sell it," Gwynn said. "It's on the shelf behind the counter."

"I don't know those herbs."

"Then who does? Mamasan?"

"If you say so."

"Mamasan knows everything, doesn't she?"

"If you say so."

Gwynn leaned close. "I know something Mamasan doesn't know."

Chan didn't respond. He waited.

"If I tell you, then you'll be a big man. It'll give you power. Mamasan doesn't let you have a lot of power, does she?"

Chan held his expression.

"It must be very hard for you," Gwynn said. "Look at you. Strong, virile. But there you are, serving Mamasan hand-and-foot. You're not her husband, so what are you? Her manservant?"

"If you say so," Chan said. But his tone had weakened.

"Just between you and me, mate, I don't know how you do it – surrounded by young girls who are so much more attractive than she is. You must be tempted to sample the merchandise, if you know what I mean."

Father Gilbert cringed. He knew what Gwynn was doing and why, but didn't like it.

Chan's face changed ever so slightly, a tightening in the muscles underneath the already tight skin of his shaved head.

"Of course you do," Gwynn said, oozing with empathy. "So that's something you know that she doesn't. Or does she?"

Chan's jaw was working, his teeth grinding.

Gwynn moved in closer. "It doesn't matter. I know something that will make Mamasan sit up and take notice. Are you ready?"

Chan didn't answer.

Gwynn looked around as if making sure he couldn't be heard. "Anong has a *daughter*."

Chan's rigid expression melted away into disbelief.

"That would make Mamasan a *grandmother*," Gwynn said happily. "What joy!"

"If you say so," Chan stammered.

"There," Gwynn said, jabbing his finger onto the table as if sealing their friendship. "Now you know something she doesn't."

"If you say so," Chan said, trying to regain his self-composure.

"I say so." Gwynn abruptly stood up and left the room. Father Gilbert noticed that he left the recorder running.

Gwynn poked his head into the viewing room and said to Father Gilbert, "Stay here. I'm putting them in together." He went out again.

A minute later, he ushered Mamasan in with Chan. "I'll be back in a tick," he said and closed the door behind him.

Chan stood up and offered her the chair.

Gwynn came back into the viewing room.

Chan began talking to Mamasan in Chinese. Mamasan shook her head. Chan persisted. She snapped at him and pointed to the mirror, shouting.

Chan lowered his head. Mamasan paced back and forth a few steps.

"It's gnawing at him," Gwynn said. "He has to tell her. He's afraid that if he doesn't, I will – and I'll say that he *knew*."

Chan moved close to her. He whispered.

"Will the recorder pick up what they're saying?" Father Gilbert asked.

"Yes."

Chan must have delivered the news because Mamasan retreated from him, her face a mix of emotions. First came the surprise. Then came the disbelief. Then the anger. She put a fist to her mouth. She responded to him in an urgent tone.

He said something in return.

Then Mamasan suddenly remembered that they were being watched. She slapped Chan hard across the face and rebuked him.

He moved to the corner of the room and cowered there.

She looked at the mirror, her eyes unable to fix on anything. Then she turned to the recording device. She saw the green light was on to indicate it had recorded what they'd said. She screeched, shouted at Chan, and pounded the button with the palm of her hand. Then she began to claw at it, as if she could open it up somehow and remove what had been recorded.

Gwynn laughed. "She thinks it's an old cassette player."

"Where's your interpreter?" Father Gilbert asked.

"He's in the other room now with PC Flack and one of the girls."

The desk sergeant peered in. "The lawyer for Ushi Yan is here."

"Bring him here."

* * *

The lawyer's name was Eli Cummings and the only way Father Gilbert could think to describe him was that he looked like a bowling ball in a suit. His perfect roundness belonged in a nineteenth-century cartoon, complete with a waistcoat that looked ready to burst at the buttons. His face was a smaller bowling ball poised on top, with wisps of hair matted against an oily head. His eyes sat behind narrow folds of flesh. His nose was a petite protrusion that sat unconvincingly above round lips. His voice was thick and sounded as if it came from somewhere deep within him rather than just his throat.

He glanced at Father Gilbert, grunted, and then turned to Gwynn.

"Well," he said with a laboured breath. "What are the charges?"

"No charges," Gwynn said. "They're helping us with our inquiries into the deaths of Mamasan's daughter and a customer from their massage parlour."

"*Spa*," Cummings corrected him. "And now that I'm here, there won't be any further interrogations."

"*Interviews*," Gwynn corrected him.

"You're going to release them now. All of them."

"You're representing the whole lot?" Gwynn asked. "That's quite a retainer from Jack Doyle."

Cummings ignored the reference.

"By rights I can hold them all for twenty-four hours."

Cummings snorted. "All of these girls in close quarters with your officers? Do you really want to face accusations of sexual harassment?"

"Is that what you'll instruct the girls to do?"

Cummings shrugged. "You're creating an environment for it to happen."

"Do you speak Chinese, Mr Cummings?" Gwynn asked.

"Enough to order intelligently when I'm having a meal." He laughed at his own joke.

"I have a murder and a suicide to deal with," Gwynn said.

"Let's be practical. Release them and I'll be happy to oblige your interviews one at a time, with me present." He took a deep breath as if the effort to speak a long sentence was taxing.

"How do I know they won't run?"

"Why would they run? They haven't done anything wrong," he said. "Unless you're going to admit that you believe they're suspects for something criminal. Are you?"

"They're connected to the case, but not prime suspects," Gwynn said.

"Good. Then Ushi and Chan will be glad to come tomorrow morning to answer your questions."

"If you guarantee their return."

"Of course."

The two men nodded at each other, satisfied to have had such an amiable negotiation.

"Oh," Gwynn said as an afterthought. "May Pan stays."

Cummings' brows lifted, showing a tiny glimpse of his eyes beneath. "Why?"

"I have what I need from everyone else, except May. Mamasan – I mean, Ushi – has said she can corroborate her account of events. I'd like to hear what she has to say."

"I'll be present for that."

* * *

Father Gilbert watched from Gwynn's cubicle as the staff of the Lily Rose were ushered out of the station. Mamasan watched them, too. *Counting her chicks*, he thought.

"Where is May?" Mamasan asked.

"A few questions and then I'll bring her home," Cummings assured her.

Mamasan frowned. "I'll wait."

"No," Cummings said. "You want to go *now*. Otherwise, Detective Inspector Gwynn might change his mind and keep you for twenty-four hours. You wouldn't want to undo my hard work on your behalf, would you?"

Mamasan looked doubtful. Chan spoke to her in Chinese. She barked at him and left.

Gwynn rounded the corner with two polystyrene cups in his hands. He handed one to Father Gilbert.

"Thanks," Father Gilbert said, taking the cup. "Why did you let them go? You have twenty-four hours no matter what Cummings says."

"Let them go back to the Lily Rose and deal with the turmoil from the news about Anong's daughter," he replied. "It messes up the pack mentality. Mamasan is out of sorts – she has no control or knowledge to act on. It knocks her down a few pegs. Chan may question his loyalties. The girls may think twice about their security."

"What about May?"

"I didn't expect Cummings to threaten me with the harassment allegations."

"There are ways to keep that from happening."

"It doesn't have to happen. It only has to be *suggested*. Imagine the headlines."

Father Gilbert did as he sipped the coffee. It was a difficult situation. "Have you heard from Agent Hathaway?"

"Not a peep."

"Trevor Humphries?"

"He's in the tank, regaling anyone who'll listen with stories about his life in the theatre."

"He's calm?"

"I didn't say that. He's hoping to charm everyone, make friends, assure everyone that he's not really a bad person."

Father Gilbert took another sip of the coffee and gave up. He binned it. "Does Humphries fit the profile of a serial killer?"

"He's an actor. They're *all* potential serial killers as far as I'm concerned." He made a face and threw his coffee into the rubbish bin as well. "Let's talk to May."

* * *

Ron Rutter, the interpreter, was not Chinese but a British-born professor who had lived in Hong Kong for years teaching English. He looked as if he'd been dragged out of bed, though Father Gilbert suspected he always looked that way. He had wild grey hair in the Einstein style and wore large, round glasses that looked as if someone had drawn black circles on his pale skin. He sat in the interrogation room next to May, who cradled her arms and rocked ever so slightly in her chair. He said something softly to May, who gave him an appreciative nod. They brought in another chair for Cummings, who squeezed in behind her. Gwynn sat across the desk from them all.

Father Gilbert took a position in the viewing room where he could see May's face. He thought of her at the Lily Rose – the only one who had seemed upset about Anong's death, standing at the front door looking as if she wanted to say something to him. He still had a nagging feeling that he'd seen her somewhere else, but couldn't imagine where.

Gwynn began the recording by stating the place, time, and names of everyone present, asking each, in turn, to speak so listeners could later identify their voices. He then asked, "How close were you to Anong Chuan?"

The interpreter relayed the question and then the answer. "She was closer to me than the others. But she didn't tell me everything."

"Did she talk about her clients?" Gwynn asked.

"Sometimes, if they were funny or strange."

"Did she talk about Sean Damian?"

There was some confusion until she clarified that Gwynn was talking about "Brother Sean".

"That's what we called him," she said.

"Why? Did he wear his monk's habit when he came in?"

"No. Never. But Mamasan had Chan follow him after he kept coming in. She wanted to know what he did for a living."

"Did Mamasan do that with the rest of your customers?"

"Brother Sean wasn't like the rest of our customers. He was a regular and she wanted to know if he was up to something."

"Up to something?"

"Spying on us."

"For who?"

"Other businesses. Then she found out he was a monk. We thought it was very funny." There was nothing to suggest she thought anything was funny now. Her face was solemn.

"Why?"

"Because we didn't think monks were allowed to have massages."

Gwynn cleared his throat. "You mean, spend money on massages with 'extras'."

"Don't answer that," Cummings said to May. He waved a fat finger. "Detective Inspector Gwynn, my client is graciously answering your questions about the victim. If you're going to turn this into something else, say the word and we'll stop now."

Gwynn conceded to Cummings. "All right, Brother Sean came in regularly and saw only Anong?"

"Yes."

"Would you say he liked her?"

"Yes."

"Did she like him?"

"Yes."

Gwynn held up a small evidence bag with Anong's necklace in it. "Did Brother Sean give her this necklace?"

The sight of the necklace brought tears to May's eyes. "Yes."

"So Brother Sean felt strongly enough about Anong to buy her a present. It wasn't just a professional relationship."

Rutter struggled to explain the question to her. After a moment of going back and forth, she said, "It was more than a professional relationship."

Gwynn turned the evidence back and forth. "I'm curious about the design. The horse and the circle. Why did he buy that design?"

"It's Anong's family symbol," she replied.

Father Gilbert moved towards the glass. *A family symbol.* There was now no doubt in Father Gilbert's mind that Mamasan was Anong's mother.

"Was there an argument between Brother Sean and Anong the night she was killed?"

May paused for a moment. "There was an argument, yes."

"Did he threaten her?"

Another pause. "There were threats, yes."

Father Gilbert wondered if Gwynn had caught the nuance of her answers. An argument and threats, yes, but she didn't specify who was arguing or who did the threatening.

"After Anong was murdered, Brother Sean was upset and came back to the Lily Rose. Is that correct?"

"Yes."

"Did he threaten Mamasan?"

"He grabbed her by the shoulders."

"Why?"

"He was sad because Anong was murdered. Maybe he wanted to take it out on someone. Maybe he thought Mamasan was responsible." Then she added quickly, "But she wasn't."

"Did Brother Sean act as if he was on drugs?"

The interpreter had to work through the translation again. Eventually she said, "It's hard to tell when someone is on drugs when they're emotionally upset, too."

"Did Mamasan do anything to help him calm down?"

"Yes, she talked to him. She made him sit down to relax."

"Did she do anything else?"

May shook her head.

"Did she give him anything to drink? Tea, maybe?"

May lit up with the memory. "Yes. She told Chan to make him special tea."

"What kind of special tea?"

"I don't know. Tea to help him calm down."

Cummings leaned forward again. "What's all this about tea? What are you after, Detective Inspector?"

"We've been trying to identify what drugs were in Sean's system, that's all. Herbal teas have properties that can affect or confuse the results."

Cummings frowned. "That's all?"

"That's all," Gwynn said. And Father Gilbert knew that, if challenged, Gwynn's statement wasn't technically a lie.

"Go on."

"Did Brother Sean act sick while he was there?"

"He was calm and then he was upset again. He was out of control. We had to make him leave."

"Mamasan keeps saying that Sean killed Anong. Do you think that's true?"

May shook her head. "No. Brother Sean loved her. He wouldn't do anything intentional to hurt her."

"Mamasan told me that he did something that led to her death. Do you think that's true?"

She gave it some thought. Father Gilbert saw something that looked like anguish work its way into her expression. She fought it back and said, "Yes. He wanted her to leave her work. She wasn't ready to do that. It caused conflict."

"Did you know that Anong was Mamasan's daughter?"

May's head snapped quickly to the interpreter, as if he'd asked the question. Her eyes were wide. The tears formed in her eyes again. She roughly wiped them away. "Yes."

"Mamasan didn't seem very upset that her daughter was murdered."

"Mamasan is very private. She doesn't show her emotions."

"Except anger."

May didn't respond.

"What can you tell me about the Sensei?" Gwynn asked.

May gasped, then shook her head.

"What's wrong?" Gwynn asked.

"My client is tired," Cummings announced. "Do you have what you're after?"

"Let's take a break," Gwynn said. "I have only a few more questions."

* * *

Cummings asked for coffee and went off with PC Flack to find some. May didn't want anything, except to be left alone in the interrogation room. Rutter came into the viewing room and sat down at the table in the back. "I miss the days when you could smoke in places like this," he said. He took out his mobile phone and began to punch the keys. Father Gilbert assumed he was sending texts.

Gwynn came in with his hands in his pockets. He looked unhappy. "It throws me off having to go through an interpreter," he said, then acknowledged Rutter in the back. "Not your interpretation. I'm having a hard time reading her expressions and tone."

Father Gilbert was about to mention the ambiguity of May's answers when the door was thrown open. Rebecca Hathaway stood in the frame, her fists clenched. She shot a glance at Father Gilbert and Rutter, then said, "A *word*, Detective Inspector Gwynn?"

"Sure," he said, standing up to his full height. "Go ahead."

"*Privately?*"

"I'd rather have witnesses," he said. "Just in case you complain later that I got a little rough with you."

She seethed as she stepped in and slammed the door. Father Gilbert moved back towards the desk. Rutter stayed focused on his mobile phone.

"You acted without me. This is *my* case."

"You were the latecomer," Gwynn replied. "It's *my* case and I brought suspects in for questioning. Standard procedure. I would have included you, but you were in London taking over someone else's case. Like you have with mine."

"The Superintendent will have something to say about that."

"I'm sure he will."

Father Gilbert looked at May in the interrogation room. She sat quietly with her hands folded on the table. She was lost in her own thoughts and clearly couldn't hear any of the voices on this side of the glass.

Gwynn relaxed. "Did you find anything in Humphries' flat?"

Hathaway didn't relax. "Yes, we're charging him."

"With what?"

"Just count the number of victims. He's the BackList Killer."

* * *

Father Gilbert watched Rebecca Hathaway work her interview technique on Trevor Humphries. It was like watching someone take a sledgehammer to a sparrow. Humphries sat, a diminutive version of himself, age spots brown through the few strands of hair he had left on his scalp, his tall and formidable body now hunched over and saggy. He was slowly deflating with each statement from the agent.

"We found your trophy room," she said. "The one behind the bookcase in your library."

Father Gilbert knew she wasn't talking about acting awards. His trophies were the items he took from his victims.

"Shall I go into detail?"

"No," he said softly.

"What?"

A little louder. "No."

"There's no escaping from this, Trevor. This isn't a film where the music will cover your exit. The curtain won't fall. The scene won't fade to closing credits. This is your life. And your life meant the deaths of those women."

"What do you want from me?" he asked.

"Tell me that you killed those girls. Tell me the truth. Are you the BackList Killer?"

"Yes," he said with a practised tone of despondence. "I confess."

If Humphries expected relief, it wasn't forthcoming. Not from Hathaway. She now wanted details – how it started, who his first victim was – and Father Gilbert didn't stay to hear it. He'd heard it all before from others like Humphries: how it had started as a bit of role-playing with the girls, but then one time it went wrong and he'd accidentally killed her. He got a thrill out of it. He began to repeat the experience in the different towns, using BackList as his means of finding the victims. He'd kept souvenirs from all the girls he'd killed to remember and relive the excitement…

Stepping into the hall, he thought about Nathan Rank. That murder would be a new case for Detective Inspector Gwynn. How many more would there be? When would this spiral end?

* * *

Father Gilbert returned to the viewing room for May. She hadn't moved from the table. There was none of the agitation or boredom that many others in her position displayed.

The interpreter was still at the desk, thumbing his mobile phone. "Am I finished or not? Can I go home now?"

"That's not for me to say. They want to talk to May again."

Rutter yawned and stretched.

"There's one thing you can do for me while we're waiting," Father Gilbert said. "Will you translate a recording from earlier? They all go digitally into the computer system, right?"

"Sure. It's easy," Rutter said and swivelled to a computer behind him.

"Don't you need a password or something like that?"

"I'm a registered translator. I need to be able to access the system to create transcripts when they need them."

"I don't know how it would be labelled. Ushi and Chan, maybe."

"Here it is, with the case number." Rutter turned a speaker around so they could both hear the playback.

The scene between Mamasan and Chan began with Gwynn saying, "I'll be back in a tick."

The interpreter closed his eyes and repeated in English what he heard on the recording.

"It's Mandarin," he said quickly, then translated from Chan. "'What are we doing here? Where is our lawyer? He asked me about the *tea* and the *ma-huang* and that monk.'"

"Ushi: 'Shut up, you moron. Don't talk. There are people listening on the other side of that glass.'"

There was open air – the slight shuffle of clothes and body movement – and Father Gilbert remembered that Chan was regrouping. Then he leaned in to whisper to her. His whispering on the recording was as clear as his regular voice.

"Chan: 'The detective said that Jun has a daughter,'" the interpreter said. "'Did you know that? Does she have a daughter?'"

There was a tiny hiss of a noise from Ushi as she reacted, then, "Ushi: 'No! He's lying to you. I would know if she has a daughter. May would have told me. She knows everything.'"

"Chan: 'Not everything. Jun didn't tell May everything.'"

"Ushi: 'What does that mean? You stupid man. You made me talk and they're watching.'"

"Chan: 'What will we do about——?'"

"Ushi: 'The recorder is on! They're recording us! How do I stop this thing? Where is the——?'"

There was a loud bang and the sound cut off.

"That's it," Rutter said.

Father Gilbert looked at May through the glass. "She knows everything."

"I've met women like her. Still waters run deep."

Father Gilbert moved to the centre of the room to look at May directly. "I've seen her before," he said.

"Go on. I dare you to say they all look alike." Rutter chuckled.

Father Gilbert shook his head. "It's been nagging me from the beginning," he said, taking in her features. Was he confusing her with Anong? "Before this all started. I saw her somewhere." He mentally retraced his steps after arriving in Englesea. That first breakfast. The apparition of Anong. The Shadow Man. The rain...

It came to him. "Boots. I went in to buy an umbrella. I saw her in Boots. She was talking to the assistant – *in English.*"

With that realization, Father Gilbert strode out of the viewing room and into the interrogation room. May looked up at him, startled. She spoke to him in Chinese.

"I'm Father Gilbert," he said. He sat down across from her. "You are May Pan."

She gazed at him. He could tell from her eyes that she recognized him.

He spoke with deliberate calmness. "I know you speak English, May. I saw you in Boots the other morning. You spoke to the clerk. You handled the conversation well."

She feigned her struggle to comprehend.

"You do it for protection, don't you? If someone says something in English that you don't like or you can't answer, you can pretend you don't speak the language."

May shook her head, as if to say she didn't understand.

"Listen to me. Mamasan has been lying to us. We found the man Anong met at the hotel. Or should I call her Jun?"

May blinked at the mention of Jun.

"Did you know her as Jun? Did you know her before she came to Englesea?"

May said something in Chinese.

He held up his hand. "If you want to play that game, fine. But I'm going to call her 'Jun Anong' and continue. The man she met – her client – told us what happened. He wanted to do things she wouldn't do. She sneaked out. But she left a couple of things behind."

May began to wring her hands. She spoke again in Chinese.

"*Stop*," Father Gilbert said. "You know I don't understand you, but you understand me." He wanted to turn to the mirror and signal Rutter to come in. But that would defeat the purpose of getting her to speak in English. She could keep hiding behind the language barrier.

"We know that Sean was poisoned with the *ma-huang* from the Lily Rose. The question is: who put the poison in the tea? Mamasan? Chan? Or you?"

She spread her arms and gestured as if she didn't know what he was saying.

"I don't believe you," he said. "Talk to me."

She shook her head. No comprehension.

He dropped his elbows on the table. It rattled. "Tell me, May: who are you more afraid of? The police – Mamasan – or the *Sensei*?"

She winced.

"Here's what *I'm* afraid of." From his jacket pocket he brought out the photo of Anong and Jasmine, taken in London, and slapped it down in front of her. "Do you know who this is?"

May looked at the photo, then at Father Gilbert.

"Her name is Jasmine. She's the *daughter* of Jun Anong Li."

May's eyes widened. She looked at the photo again.

"Mamasan said that you know everything. But you didn't know about her, did you?"

May's face turned red. She reached up and grabbed her hair in a fist.

Father Gilbert continued, "Mamasan didn't know about her either."

The slight rocking May had done before now started again.

"I've met her," Father Gilbert said as he reached over and tapped the photo with the tip of his forefinger. "She's a sweet, sweet girl. Wonderfully innocent."

He could see May was fighting hard to keep her emotions in check.

"How did Jun Anong keep it a secret from you? She talked to this girl on her computer every Monday and Thursday." Father Gilbert levelled his gaze at her. "Here's what I think. I think she slipped away from the Lily Rose and led Mamasan to believe she was looking for clients. She sneaked off to one of those Internet cafés and talked to her daughter. Tell me if you think I'm lying. Mondays and Thursdays. Think about it, May."

May lowered her head and began to sob.

"So, here's my biggest fear, May. I'm afraid that if we don't get to the truth, Mamasan will get Jasmine. You know what that means. Mamasan will take over her life. She'll control her. You know the kind of woman Mamasan is. If you cared anything for Jun you won't let Mamasan have this girl."

Tears fell from her face to the table, hitting in large splashes.

Father Gilbert wanted to comfort her, but knew he mustn't let up. "You understand what I'm saying. Mamasan will take her and raise her. What will become of that poor girl? Who will she become?"

May lifted her face and said in clear English, "She will become like me." There was a hitch in her voice as the emotion took her breath. "She will become what Mamasan raised me to be."

"Mamasan raised you?" Father Gilbert asked her.

"She is my mother," she said and saw the look on his face. She put a hand to her neck and lifted out a necklace from under her blouse. It had the horse and circle design. "Jun Anong Li was my sister."

With that admission, she dropped her head onto the table and began to cry in a loud wail.

* * *

"Chinese," she said. "I can't say in English."

Father Gilbert turned to the mirror. He hoped Rutter was still there and watching. He waved for him to come in.

Rutter appeared at the door a minute later, his lips pressed together, his expression grim.

"Are you all right?" Father Gilbert asked.

He put up a hand as if to say it was better not to ask and sat down next to May. He spoke softly to her in Chinese. She said something back. He handed her tissues he'd brought from the other room.

"She's ready," he said.

"Why didn't you know about Jasmine?" Father Gilbert asked.

She looked at Father Gilbert as she answered to Rutter. Her entire demeanour had changed. She seemed older and her voice was low and drained of energy. Rutter translated: "When we came to England, we were separated. Jun was seventeen years old and they wanted her in London."

"Why London?"

"Better work for her there. She was—" Rutter and May wrestled with the phrasing and then he said, "—in high demand. Mamasan was very angry. She was jealous. She thought *she* should make the big money in London and that Jun stole it from her."

"What happened to you?" he asked.

"I was only twelve. They didn't work girls my age in London because the police watch closely. They sent me to places where the police don't look."

"To work? You were working at the age of *twelve?*" Father Gilbert asked, his throat tightening. He swallowed hard and tasted a bitter rage.

"I had a high price at ten, to lose my—"

Rutter stopped his translation. He looked anguished to repeat it.

"—my virginity – in China." May looked at the photo of Jasmine. "Eight-year-old girls cost even more."

"I don't know that I can do this," Rutter said.

"You have to." Father Gilbert felt a visceral anger that shook him. He took his hands off the table so she couldn't see his fists. He turned to May and spoke as calmly as he could. "Where was your father then? Why didn't he stop it?"

"My father was very sick. We needed the money," she explained through Rutter. "We could not pay the doctors." She shrugged. "He died anyway. That's why we came to England."

Father Gilbert tried to pick up the thread of narrative. "So Jun stayed in London and you went to—"

"Bristol first, I think. Mamasan knows. She took me everywhere she went. She was stuck with me."

"Stuck?"

"She hated me," May said. "She thought her children were a punishment for something she'd done wrong. Mamasan wanted to be a singer or an actress. But my father made her pregnant before they got married. That baby was Jun and ruined her plans. Five years later I was born. More plans ruined. My father got sick right after that. Mamasan blamed me. Children are a curse, she said. She made me work hard to earn my keep."

Father Gilbert had a hard time believing what he was hearing. What kind of mother could say and do such things?

"I was in different parts of England and no one would tell me where Jun was. I don't think Mamasan knew. For nine years, we didn't see or hear from her. Sometimes I sneaked onto the computer and looked at websites."

"Like BackList?"

"Others, too, for live-cam girls. I thought I might find her. I never did." She stopped to rub her cheeks as if the drying tears irritated them. Rutter slumped as if the work were exhausting him. She continued, "When we were sent to Englesea, Mamasan was very angry. She didn't understand why she was being banished."

"Banished?"

"She thought she was smarter than her bosses. She thought she should be a powerful woman for them. She thought she should be the boss in London. Then they told her that Englesea was very important. It was the way in for new girls."

"How was it a way in?"

"Boats. The boats could come and the police wouldn't know," she said. "Mamasan would train them at the Lily Rose and the other massage spas along the coast. It was a great position of power for her. But one day Jun came. She said she was in big trouble. She said that men were trying to kill her. She needed her mother and sister to help her."

"What did Mamasan do?"

"Mamasan promised to help. But she said Jun must earn her keep. She must be *Anong* and do whatever Mamasan said. Mamasan hated her more now because she was so beautiful. Mamasan thought that Jun would take power from her and become boss. So she made her work all the time and take on bad customers who would hurt her. I think Mamasan hoped Jun would be killed."

"She got her wish then," Father Gilbert said.

Rutter took a deep breath.

"Did you and your mother know what happened to Jun Anong in London?" Father Gilbert asked her.

"Mamasan learned the story about a girl who betrayed the Sensei in London and was hidden by the police. She knew it was my sister. When Jun came here, Mamasan blackmailed her. She said she would give her to the Sensei if she didn't make her a lot of money and behave. Mamasan demanded more and more of her. Jun didn't complain. She didn't make trouble." May touched the photo of Jasmine. "Now I understand."

"Tell me about Brother Sean."

"Brother Sean came one day for a massage. He looked lost and confused. He went in to the room with Jun. She told me after that she gave him a regular massage."

Father Gilbert looked at Rutter. "By 'regular massage', she means—"

"No extras," he said.

May continued. "Jun didn't offer because he seemed like such a lost person. They talked while she gave him the massage. That was all. He gave her more money than he should have. That made Mamasan think he was a good customer. Then he came back two days later. And he kept coming back. And every time he and Jun talked during the massage."

Father Gilbert thought about the lurid accounts the newspaper had suggested. How disappointed they would be to find out that nothing happened.

"When Mamasan found out Sean was a monk, she was filled with—" Rutter stopped again while they consulted on the correct word. Then he resumed for her: "—*scorn*. She made fun of him when he came in. She taunted Jun. She thought Sean was falling in love with Jun and that made her worse. She told Jun to make him think she loved him so he would give her more money."

"Is that what Jun did? Did she pretend to love him?"

"No. She truly fell in love with him. But it was good because Mamasan thought she was obeying her. One day Sean took her to London to see Big Ben and the famous places. He didn't know she had worked there for a long time. He didn't know anything about her old life."

Father Gilbert said, "I think Sean met Jasmine that day. Jun Anong introduced him to her daughter. There were pictures on her mobile phone."

"It was good because Mamasan said Sean would help us. When the other monk talked about closing our shop, Mamasan said Sean would make him stop."

"Did Sean ever say he would?"

"Sean was going to save us. First he would save Jun. Then he would take the rest of us away." She closed her eyes and said, "Then came that horrible, terrible night."

Father Gilbert noticed that she was shredding the tissue in her hand.

"What happened?"

"Mamasan got angry because she thought I was—" There was another break while May and Rutter decided on a word. He continued, "Mamasan thought I was *intimate* with Chan."

"Were you?"

"Chan tried to make me, but I refused him. I was nice to him. I didn't make fun of him like the other girls did. He would talk to me like he wouldn't with anyone else. Chan wanted her to believe we were intimate because he saw how it made her jealous. Mamasan didn't believe me. She screamed at me and called me names and told me how stupid I was. I was so angry that I told her *she* was the stupid one because she didn't know… she didn't know about…"

May collapsed into tears again. Rutter waited for her, then looked helplessly at Father Gilbert.

"You told her the truth about Jun and Sean," Father Gilbert said.

May nodded and responded through Rutter: "It was all my fault. I didn't know she would do what she did."

"What did she do?"

She replied. Rutter looked stricken. He asked her again to be sure of what she said. May repeated herself and Rutter turned to Father Gilbert. "Mamasan killed Jun."

* * *

May let out a long, slow, mournful breath, as if she were releasing a foul spirit that had been trapped inside of her.

"Tell me what happened."

She dropped the shredded tissue on the table and swept it away with the side of her hand. "Jun came back from a client and Mamasan screamed at her and said she knew the truth about Sean and their plans to run away together."

Father Gilbert held up a hand. "Wait. Did they plan to do that?"

"Maybe one day. Not that night. Mamasan believed they would and hated it. She hated us to have what she couldn't have. She hated us to be happy. She said she would kill Jun if she left. Or she would tell the Sensei and Jun would be killed by them. Jun was upset. She phoned Sean. He came to the Lily Rose. Mamasan called him a liar and a thief. She told Jun that Sean was using her to ruin our business. Sean said they loved each other and would go away. Mamasan told him to leave or she would tell everyone that a priest was coming to the massage parlour and using *all* the girls for his pleasure. Jun begged Sean to leave so Mamasan would calm down."

Father Gilbert watched her. Her eyes moved around the room as if she were seeing the events unfold again.

"That's when the phone call came for the client – the actor at the hotel. He told her to bring her kinky stuff. So Jun took her 'bag of tricks', including—"

Rutter stopped his translation. Another consultancy about what she was saying. He frowned and paraphrased, "She was describing handcuffs that looked real but were made to unsnap if she pulled hard enough on them, so she couldn't be trapped or hurt by the client."

Father Gilbert asked, "So they looked and worked like normal handcuffs, but without a key?"

Rutter put the question to her. She nodded, then continued, "Jun said later that the man was scary. There was something about him that she didn't like. He wanted to use leather straps but she said they had to use her handcuffs. He tied her to the bedposts. He thought they were on tight. He began to do things to her. He grabbed her hair and neck. It hurt. She told him to stop."

"Did the man break her necklace?" Father Gilbert asked.

"Yes," May said. "She was angry because the man made it snap. She thought she had put it back on her neck. But it had fallen off somewhere."

"Then what happened?"

"The man apologized to her and said he would behave. He then went into the bathroom. Something made her nervous. She realized there was plastic under the bed sheets. Why would he need plastic? She thought about it. What if it was to stop blood from getting into the mattress? She jerked at the handcuffs. They wouldn't break loose at first and hurt her wrists. Then they came apart. She grabbed her clothes and escaped before the man came out of the bathroom."

Father Gilbert thought about how Trevor Humphries had left out anything about the plastic cover. He wondered if the police had found one anywhere in the room or in the steamer trunk.

"Mamasan went to her office," May went on. "I had run a bath for myself in the big bath downstairs. Business was slow. Then Jun came back and told me what had happened with the client. She laughed because she had rushed out without her underwear. She showed me the special handcuffs and said they saved her life. But her wrists were red and bruised. She was scared. She didn't want to do this work any more. She wanted to leave with Sean right away. I told her to get in my bath and relax. Then Mamasan came down. She heard what Jun said about leaving with Sean. She thought the bath was for Jun to clean herself up for Sean so she could run away with him. She was filled with rage."

May suddenly stood up and began to act out what she described.

"She went into the bathroom. There was shouting. I heard Jun scream and there was a loud splash. I ran in. Mamasan was holding Jun under the water by the throat, drowning her."

Her voice was shrill as she reached out her arms, her hands like claws. "I pulled at Mamasan to get her away. We both fell back on the floor. Jun was gasping and coughing. Mamasan got up and kicked me in the stomach. I still have the bruise. Before Jun could get out of the water, Mamasan grabbed her by the ankles and pulled her legs far up above the water. Her head went under. Mamasan was strong. I tried to scream but couldn't get air. Jun thrashed, then was still. Chan ran in to see what the commotion was. It was too late."

Sitting down again, May put a hand to her throat. Her breathing was hard and shallow. She closed her eyes and her fingers found the slender chain of her necklace. She rubbed it gently.

The scene she'd described was exactly what Father Gilbert had imagined from the beginning, except it was a bath in the Lily Rose rather than the hotel. Even the soap under Anong's fingernails made sense with his discovery of the same brand in the main floor bathroom.

Rutter looked pale. Father Gilbert held up a hand to him not to say or do anything.

May sat up and tipped her head back. She took a deep breath. "Mamasan saw what she did and panicked. What to do now? She asked it over and over. She made Chan get Jun out of the bath. He wrapped her up in towels and they laid her on the floor. I cried. I begged. They took her out through the back door. Chan told me later what they did – how they couldn't decide what to do with the body. They put her in the boot of the car and drove to the pier. They were going to throw her off but thought they would get caught. They went to a corner of the car park next to the pier and carried her down the path to the place under the pier. They took her into the water, but the waves kept washing her ashore."

Father Gilbert shivered as he thought about the body being thrown against the sand and pilings.

"Mamasan got angry," May said, her words broken by her struggle to hold back her tears. "She said Jun was tormenting her and wanted them to get caught. So they threw Jun in the rubbish skip behind that restaurant."

May had to steel herself against another breakdown of tears.

Father Gilbert blocked his imagination from envisioning the scene. He had to stay with the facts. If he thought beyond them, he wasn't sure what he would do. He looked at Rutter. "Are you all right to continue?"

"I want to get it over with," he said.

Father Gilbert asked May, "Tell me about Sean. What happened to him?"

"After Jun was killed, he came to the Lily Rose. He was angry, like Mamasan told you. Sean said Mamasan had killed Jun. That's why he tried to snatch the necklace from her neck. He said she wasn't worthy to wear the family symbol. He said he would go to the police."

"How did Mamasan react?"

"She was very polite and reasonable. She said she didn't kill Jun. She said the Sensei came that night and killed her. He didn't know what she was talking about. Mamasan told Sean about Jun's life in London and how she had become an informant for the police and testified. She said she would never kill Jun because she was sacrificing everything to protect her from the Sensei. Then she said that it was Sean's fault the Sensei found her. The fuss the priest called Gregory made about the business had drawn their attention to Englesea and they learned Jun was there."

Father Gilbert wondered how Mamasan had become so malevolent that she would put the murder she'd committed onto Sean and Brother Gregory.

"Sean didn't want to believe her. But Mamasan was so calm and reasonable. She got him to sit down and have some tea so they could talk. He didn't know they had put *ma-huang* in it."

Rutter stopped again and looked at Father Gilbert. "*Ma-huang?*"

"Ephedra."

Rutter nodded.

"I did not know," May said in English, then gestured to Rutter for them to continue. "They gave him a cup and kept talking and gave him another cup. Mamasan knew what she was doing. She knew he took other drugs because she had seen them once when Sean had come in. Once, when he came in, she searched his pockets and found a bottle for the drug he was taking. She was clever about drugs and Chinese herbs. She gave him the *ma-huang* and he reacted. He staggered around and shouted at her that he needed help. That's when he grabbed her and she scratched him. Then a customer told him to leave or he'd throw him out. Sean was confused. He felt sick. Chan took him to the rear door and pushed him into the alley. He fell on the ground and begged for help. Mamasan saw it but she wouldn't let any of us do anything. Then Sean was unconscious. She wanted to get rid of him, but she heard someone coming. She closed the door and left him there."

"And the employee from the other shop found him," Father Gilbert concluded.

They sat in silence for a moment. Father Gilbert tried to think of anything he'd missed.

"Is that it?" Rutter said.

"That's it." Father Gilbert said to May, "You have to stop her. You can't let her have Jasmine. She will ruin her life."

"How can I stop her?" May asked in English.

"You have to testify in court. You have to tell everyone what you told us."

"I can't," she said. "I can't. She is my *mama*."

Just then the door opened and Hathaway came into the room. She looked coldly at Father Gilbert and Rutter and said, "Out. Now."

The two men left May and went into the viewing room. Gwynn was there, leaning on the desk and eating crisps from a bag. He shook his head slowly.

Hathaway followed them in. She swore in ways that would have caused a seasoned sailor to blush, let alone a priest and an interpreter.

"What was that?"

"She told us everything," Father Gilbert said. "Did you see any of it?"

"Only the part where you said she had to testify." Hathaway stepped between Father Gilbert and the glass, blocking his view of May. "So you cleverly got her to talk and no one in authority was present. No rights. No legal representation. No proof, beyond your word, of what she said or that she even said what she said."

Rutter raised his hand. "Actually, I—"

"No," she said to him with the raising of her hand. "This was completely out of line. You should know better."

"I'm sure you can work your magic on her again," Gwynn said.

She gave him a withering glance, then said to Father Gilbert, "How dare you presume to come into this building – into that room – and interview a witness?"

Father Gilbert reminded himself of his priestly vows – of the acts and attitudes of charity he had promised to practise. "I shouldn't have," he said softly.

"Agent Hathaway—" Rutter said.

"*What?*" she snapped.

"It's all recorded," he said.

"What?"

"When Father Gilbert went in, I turned on the recorder through the computer. The whole thing should be there, just like any interview."

Gwynn circled around the table and checked the computer. He looked up at Rutter and Father Gilbert and smiled.

* * *

Agent Hathaway wasn't about to show her relief. May's lawyer of record – Mr Cummings – was not present for the recording, nor had she been advised to bring him in. Leaving the greater issue of getting May to agree to testify. Father Gilbert cautioned her against using threats. "This is a girl who has been bullied and threatened by worse people than you," he said.

"We'll see about that," she said and signalled Rutter to return to the interview room with her.

Gwynn wiped his hands of the salt and oil from the crisps. "She's a charmer, you have to admit."

Father Gilbert faced the interview room. May looked anxiously at Hathaway as she sat down. Rutter took his seat next to her and chatted in Chinese, gesturing to the agent. Whatever he said didn't comfort May.

"We recorded what you told Father Gilbert," Hathaway said. "However, we need you to testify in court."

May looked at the mirror. She was searching for him, he knew. He wanted to go in.

"Best not," Gwynn said.

May shook her head and said through Rutter, "I can't testify against Mamasan. She's my mother. She will arrange to have me killed." She didn't seem to grasp the incongruity of what she said.

"We can protect you," Hathaway said.

"Like you did my sister?" May countered.

"We learn from our mistakes."

May shook her head again. "No."

Hathaway put her hands lightly on the table. "It's all right. I understand," she said in a tone that surprised the two men in the viewing room.

Gwynn moved towards the glass to watch. "What's she up to?"

Hathaway stood up. "Thank you, May."

May looked confused, as did Rutter.

"She can go?" Rutter asked.

"Yes. She's free to go."

There was a moment of indecision, as if neither May nor Rutter believed it was true.

As they were about to stand up, Hathaway made a soft noise in her throat, as if she had bad news to deliver.

"Here it comes," Gwynn said.

"You realize that if you leave, we can't protect you." Hathaway ran a finger along the top of the table.

"Why do I need protection?" May asked.

"The recording of what you said." She gestured to the recording device on the table. "It goes into our computer system and a lot of people have access to it. I can't promise that it won't fall into the hands of Mamasan or Jack Doyle or even the Sensei."

Gwynn shook his head.

Father Gilbert turned away from the scene and walked back to the table. He slammed his fist against the top, making the computer jump.

"You would give it to them?" May asked.

"I wouldn't *give* it to them, but it could slip out. And then where will you be?" She walked to the door. "How long will you last?"

May and Rutter exchanged looks.

Hathaway walked out. Father Gilbert braced himself for her arrival in the viewing room. She didn't disappoint him.

"I give her two minutes at the most," she said and watched May in the other room as she slumped back, a look of despair on her face.

Rutter stood up, then lingered awkwardly, glancing at the mirror and back at May.

Father Gilbert took two steps towards Hathaway. Gwynn moved in between them.

"It's all right," Father Gilbert said. "I was only going to ask one question."

"Go on," Hathaway said.

"How could you do that to her?"

"Are you saying you wouldn't if you were me?"

"I don't think I could ever be that heartless. Not with someone who's been through—"

"This isn't about *her*, Father Gilbert," Hathaway said, turning to him. "It's about Mamasan and the two murders she committed. It's about the information Mamasan can give us about Jack Doyle and the Sensei when we offer her a deal. It's about stopping all the other abusers out there – and the many ways we can save more of those girls. It's about making the hard choices."

Father Gilbert met her cold stare. "Hard choices I understand, but I don't understand how you can be so hard-hearted about it. You're about to throw May to the wolves and you don't care. She's one of *those girls*, remember."

"Father," Hathaway replied. "*I* was one of those girls. I lived it, day in and day out for six years, doing what they're doing now. That was most of my teenage life. So, question my methods if you want, but don't *ever* question my motives."

Stunned, Father Gilbert watched her walk out again.

"Excuse me," Rutter said from the interview room. He and May were looking at the mirror. Rutter said, "She wants to talk to Father Gilbert."

* * *

May looked at him with a doleful expression. "What should I do?"

Father Gilbert leaned with his back against the door, his arms folded. "I can't give you legal advice," he said. "Though the first thing you must do is fire Mr Cummings. He works for Jack Doyle. We'll find another attorney for you."

"This will change my life."

"Without question," he said. "But isn't it time for your life to change? Do you want to spend the rest of your days at Mamasan's beck and call, doing what she has you doing now?"

May's eyes drifted to the mirror. She beheld herself there for a moment.

"You believe helping the police may kill you, but it's more likely to save you."

"What about the Sensei and Mr Doyle?"

"Though they may think of themselves as gods, people like Jack Doyle, and whoever this Sensei is, are mere mortals. They're not as all-powerful as they believe."

The door at his back moved. He stepped aside as Rebecca Hathaway marched in. "Time's up. What's it going to be?"

Father Gilbert looked to May as she said quietly, "You are looking at a dead person. I am a ghost. I will testify."

CHAPTER 16

With the certainty of the case against Mamasan and Chan, Hathaway gave Detective Inspector Gwynn the OK to arrest them both.

"I hope they haven't bolted," Father Gilbert said. They strode to the area behind the station where the police vehicles were kept.

"You don't think I left them on their own, do you?" Gwynn said. "I've got eyes on the Lily Rose. If Mamasan or Chan make a move, I'll know it. Let's go."

"I'm going?"

"I assume you want to see the end of these cases. The policeman in you demands it."

Father Gilbert nodded his appreciation and followed along.

The strike team was ready within five minutes. Gwynn announced that he wanted "everything done calmly and efficiently. We're not jackbooted Nazis. No tearing the place apart. We're making a clean arrest of these two." He held up a photograph of Mamasan and one of Chan, each lifted from some official document somewhere. "In and out," he concluded, then quickly added: "And no messing with the girls."

There were seven of them, plus Father Gilbert. They drove in two separate cars and a police van. The lateness of the hour meant they wouldn't have to fight through traffic.

When they pulled up to the front of the Lily Rose – the "Open" sign was on – Father Gilbert climbed out of the car and moved away down the pavement where he had a clear view of the front of the shop and the alleyway to the right. Gwynn led three officers through the front door, which swung open and didn't close. A fourth officer ran down the alley. The last two officers stayed with the vehicles.

The entry by the police began quietly enough, but was soon followed by shouts from inside. Hard and heavy footsteps pounded the wooden floors. There was a loud crash. From deeper inside, the girls screamed and shouted. Things quieted down for a moment, then doors slammed and there were more sounds of running. The sound of a crash drew Father Gilbert's attention to the alley. It was steeped in darkness apart from the light of a single street lamp that illuminated part of the entrance. Father Gilbert saw a figure lurch from the back of the alley towards the street. As it came into the light, Father Gilbert recognized it as Mamasan. Her walk was laboured and she turned her head in one direction, then another, as if she wasn't sure where she was going.

Father Gilbert looked frantically around for one of the PCs. The one from the alley was nowhere to be seen. The two at the vehicles must have run inside. He prepared himself to stop her and wondered what he would do if she refused.

The street light shone on her. She looked directly at him, but showed no recognition that he was there. She stumbled slightly and lifted her hand to her stomach. Her dress – light-coloured with a floral pattern – grew dark with blood. She was down on the pavement now. He took another step, this time to help her, then stopped again as everything in his instincts said it wasn't really her. This was an apparition.

She turned away from the Lily Rose and headed down the street, her gait tilted to one side, her pace as steady as a funeral march. He watched her as she disappeared into a shadow between the pools of street light, then emerged again into view on the other side.

Another figure appeared ahead of her. It was the Shadow Man. She continued towards him and he spread out his arms in a friendly welcome. When she was just within reach he put his arm around her shoulder. The shadows around them came alive – the faces contorted in silent screams and hands reaching out. The Shadow Man ushered her forward, like a kindly doorman helping a lady across a threshold. Later, when Father Gilbert could think about it clearly, he realized the only way to describe what happened next was that the Shadow Man *fed* her to them.

His blood turned cold and he felt a burning like a fever behind his eyes. The Shadow Man turned to him and stood still, watching him.

An agonizing scream echoed from the alley, followed by a painful

"Help!" Without thinking, Father Gilbert turned from the vision and raced towards it. The alley ended in a cul-de-sac of back doors to various shops. Under a small light over one of the shop doors, Father Gilbert saw Chan on his knees, bending over the sprawled-out body of Mamasan. She wore a light-coloured dress with a floral pattern and blood spread rapidly across her stomach, and down her side.

Chan's face was twisted up as he wept. He muttered incoherently in Chinese, then saw Father Gilbert and said, "Stabbed! She was stabbed by the shadows!" He ran forward just as the back door was pushed open. Gwynn appeared, with the PC whom Gilbert had seen go down the alley. Gwynn took in the scene in front of him and then turned to someone inside and shouted, "Get a light back here! We need an ambulance!"

"She's dead," Chan cried, his voice a low lament. "Killed by the shadows." He pulled her close to his chest, her blood quickly staining his white shirt.

Gwynn came close and said, "I know first aid."

Chan arched himself over her protectively. "Go away!" he said.

"What happened?" Gwynn asked him, kneeling at a safe distance.

"The shadows," he said again. "Stabbed."

Father Gilbert moved back to survey the area. Had the shadows reached out and hurt Mamasan? Were they capable of stabbing a living being?

While Gwynn attended to Chan and the woman in his arms, a PC dashed down the alley with a torch – the light flashing back and forth as he ran. Father Gilbert saw a shadow move in a corner to his right. The hair stood up on the back of his neck. He didn't know what to expect.

"Here!" he said sharply to the PC. The young man – one of the drivers – came over. Father Gilbert took the torch and directed it to the spot.

The light caught the knife first with a flash of reflection that made it glow; the rest of it was covered with blood that dripped onto the fingers wrapped around the handle. Its owner, Cari Erim, stood frozen, as if she thought that by standing still no one would see her.

"Put down the knife, Cari," Father Gilbert said as he ventured closer to her.

"It's the only way to free them," she said.

***

Lorna Henry had disappeared and the assumption was that she'd fled to safer parts after the arson. Her body was found in the back garden of her house a day later. She had been covered by a plastic tarpaulin and the decomposition of her body indicated she had been dead for two days. She had been stabbed to death. In the newspaper article, Detective Inspector Gwynn was fairly confident that the assailant was the same woman who had stabbed Ushi Yan, the manager of the Lily Rose, a local spa. Rumours were spreading that a vigilante group, spawned by the "hate-filled rhetoric" of Gregory Stearns, head of the Order of St Sebastian's, was taking action against the "innocent owners" of adult-themed establishments.

***

"Hate-filled rhetoric," Father Gilbert said to Brother Gregory. They were sitting on the bench near the front of St Sebastian's. Englesea spread out before them, angular roofs and gables, industrial air conditioner units, and the occasional line of washing swaying like flags in the breeze from the sea. It was a beautiful sunny day. At this moment, only a week after the terrible events that had shaken the town, it seemed as if nothing bad could ever happen here – or should.

Brother Gregory swatted at a fly that had alighted on his knee. "They never printed a retraction, or even a correction, about Brother Sean."

"The newspaper industry isn't known for its apologies."

"The Trevor Humphries case pushed our story to the back pages."

"Just as well." A gull careened overhead and shouted for no known reason. Father Gilbert asked, "Are you sorted with Mr Englebert?"

He nodded. "For the moment. With Mamasan dead and May being placed in witness protection, I'm responsible for Jasmine. We moved her from the Academy. Agent Hathaway wanted her where she could be protected."

"How did Jasmine take that?"

"It was hard, especially following so close after the news about her mother. She seemed to understand that her mother's death meant she needed to move again. It's almost like she expected it."

"She probably remembers doing it before." Father Gilbert sighed. "No eight-year-old should have these kinds of experiences."

"Pastor Rick cried more than she did," Brother Gregory said. "The facilities and children at the new place are excellent. The sisters there are very caring. They know enough about Jasmine's situation to be extra sensitive."

Father Gilbert didn't ask where Jasmine had been moved. It was better for him not to know. "Have you spoken to Sean's parents?" he asked.

"Daily. The news that Sean's behaviour had more to do with love and sacrifice than mere lust has been a consolation." Brother Gregory stretched his legs out and shoved his hands into his pockets. "His funeral is next week. You're welcome to come. They'd love to meet you."

Father Gilbert anticipated that the meeting would be intense and difficult. He would dread going right up until he arrived for it. "Send me the information." He leaned forward, resting his elbows on his knees. He turned towards Brother Gregory, who had his head back and eyes closed.

"How are you and the rest of the brothers doing?" he asked.

"Healing. Slowly."

He tipped his head towards the church. "And the clean-up?"

"The money from Sean will take care of the restorations, with plenty left over. We'll dedicate an area to him."

Light glinted off boats in the distant water. Father Gilbert thought of the girls who'd been smuggled into Englesea. By the hundreds, the police estimated. Probably more. Chan had accepted a plea bargain and given up all he knew about the operations. Without Mamasan to bully him, he proved to be a compliant witness. Without Mamasan to serve, he didn't care whether he lived or died.

Father Gilbert stood up and stretched. Brother Gregory looked up as if he'd forgotten Father Gilbert was there.

"You're going?" he asked.

"I have a few more errands to run before I go back to Stonebridge."

Brother Gregory stood up and shook Father Gilbert's hand. Then he suddenly pulled him close for a hug. "Thank you."

Father Gilbert thought of all the things he wanted to say but didn't. They'd stay in touch. There'd be other times for conversations.

* * *

It was Cari Erim's last day in the Englesea jail. She was being relocated to a secure mental health facility in Eastbourne. "For observation," Detective Inspector Gwynn explained. "Meaning that she needs to be watched so she doesn't kill herself and to evaluate her competency to stand trial."

"Do you think she's insane?" Father Gilbert asked. They were walking from Gwynn's office to a holding cell in the back of the station. Gwynn assured him they could talk there without too much interruption.

"She keeps going on about seeing ghosts," he said with his eyes on Father Gilbert. "That's a pretty good indicator."

Father Gilbert nodded. *It goes without saying that anyone who claims to see ghosts must be insane.*

The holding cell was the first one in as he came through the door. A hall led to other cells behind it. Trevor Humphries had enjoyed the hospitality of one of the cells until a few days after his confession. He was moved to a prison in Lewes until the arguing stopped over where he should be tried.

Cari was dressed in a black long-sleeved T-shirt, dark blue sweatpants, and white laceless trainers. She sat on a bench and looked up at Father Gilbert as he entered. Gwynn closed the cell door behind him.

"Hello, Cari," he said. He sat on a bench facing her.

"Hello, Father." She had a remarkable look of peace in her eyes. The lines of anxiety he'd seen before were gone.

"How are you?"

She looked around. "It's not that much different from working in the hotels," she said and smiled. "Except I don't have to work here."

"They're treating you well, then."

"The guards are friendly. I don't see the other inmates."

It reminded Father Gilbert of what she'd said about her life in a brothel. Apart from that, he hoped her overall experience was vastly different.

"They say you confessed to killing Mamasan and Lorna Henry."

"Oh yes. There was no point denying it."

"Why did you kill them?"

"You know."

"Tell me anyway."

"Mamasan was evil. Her eyes, even when she smiled, told me that her entire being was filled with hate. Her soul was poison. It was poison to everyone around her. I saw it in the bald man. He was poisoned by her." She spoke with simple directness, without the nervous energy he often saw in the mentally ill.

"When did you see them?" Father Gilbert asked.

"I went to the Lily Rose parlour because of the death of the girl and the monk. I said I wanted a job. They told me to leave. But I saw them. I could *feel* what they were and what the place was. So I followed her. I saw her go to the police station. I saw her go back to the massage place. I watched and waited. When the police came, I ran down the alley to hide. She and the bald man sneaked out of the back. I thought she was going to escape. So I stopped her."

"What about Lorna Henry?"

"I went to her home after we spoke. It was easy to find out where she lived. I found a way to get over the garden wall. I was only going to watch her for a while. But then she went into her back garden to smoke a cigarette. She was alone. The opportunity was too good to be missed."

"You were carrying the knife with you?"

"I've carried a knife ever since I was released from my former life." She tapped her side to show where she had kept the knife. "I always thought someone might grab me to take me back. I wouldn't go without a fight."

"Did you kill anyone else?"

"I didn't get a chance."

"You were planning to?"

"There are others in Englesea who are doing very bad things to girls and women. I told the police about them." She shrugged. "The police won't do anything, though. They think I'm crazy."

He gazed at her, musing on how she had gone from fear to aggression so quickly.

"There was no other way to stop them, you know." She looked thoughtful, as if she'd considered all of the alternatives and had to settle on the most effective one. "There was no other way to set the spirits free."

"Are they free?" he asked.

"I don't see them now. Do you?"

He gave her a reassuring smile, keeping his eyes away from a woman dressed in a jumpsuit from the 1970s, sitting at the end of the bench by the wall. He'd seen her when he'd first entered the cell. Her head was shaved and an angry scar circled from her temple around her ear to her neck. She stared straight ahead as if waiting for something to happen.

"Will you visit me, wherever they send me?"

"I'll do my best," he said. And he would.

* * *

"She's crackers," Gwynn said as he walked Father Gilbert out of the station. "Besides, doesn't she realize that there's another Mamasan for every one that gets arrested, deported, or killed?"

"She knows," Father Gilbert said, thinking of the life she'd led before coming to Englesea. Did Gwynn know? Had she told them? "Are you investigating the Nathan Rank murder?"

"We're working on it."

Father Gilbert gave him a doubtful look. "Are you?"

"We've followed up on the few leads we had. Dead end."

"Killed in his room, stuffed in his boot and you can't make *anything* out of it?"

Gwynn shook his head. "Rank had no family and no one is asking since we caught Trevor Humphries. My boss has given me explicit instructions to make other cases a priority. Hey, it saves your friend Solegrove a lot of trouble."

"So what's the explanation for it?"

"A one-night stand gone wrong," he offered. "After Solegrove, Rank cruised again and met up with the wrong sort of people. What do you expect with a man who collects S&M gear like truncheons?"

"What?"

"We found a receipt for the truncheons from an antique shop in Englesea. Rank was a collector of 'exotic weapons'. Though, considering the accessories they found in his home flat in Norwich, we don't think he used them for personal safety."

Father Gilbert spent only a second to think about the implications of what Gwynn was saying – and gave up. He didn't want to know.

"He also had gambling debts, so it might have been payback for money owed," Gwynn said. "With someone like Rank, it could have been anything."

"People in the hospitality industry apparently make a lot of enemies," Father Gilbert said, ironic.

"That's right." Gwynn opened the door to reception. They stepped through. "I don't expect to see you soon."

"Not unless they make me testify somewhere."

"Rebecca might insist. As an excuse to see you." He winked at the priest. "I think she fancies you."

Father Gilbert laughed.

The duty officer behind the security glass called out to Gwynn, "Phone call for you."

"All right." He turned to Father Gilbert. "Listen, Gilbert, for all your help…" He looked down and shuffled his feet like a shy schoolboy. "We'll send you a thank you card and a couple of quid."

"It's more than I deserve," Father Gilbert said.

"Too right," Gwynn said.

"It's the *Chief*," the duty officer said.

"*All right*," Gwynn shouted and, with a quick wave, went back to his office.

* * *

Father Anthony rang him that afternoon. Father Gilbert had just walked into the vicarage and was about to make a pot of tea.

"I found her," Father Anthony said.

"Veronyka?"

"Well, Vadim first, then Veronyka."

"How did you do that?" He poured water in the kettle and turned it on.

"I knew someone who knew someone else who knew another person."

"Do you want to give me the address?" he asked. He felt as though he had a promise to keep.

"Don't bother," he said. "I've been there."

"And?"

"Vadim was contrite and tried to deny doing anything wrong. He's a distant relative who was only doing a favour for a cousin who was worried about Veronyka."

"It makes perfect sense." Father Gilbert pulled a mug from the dishwasher and glanced inside to make sure it was clean. "Who wouldn't lie, deceive the police and a couple of priests for the cousin of a distant relative?"

"He's not her pimp," Father Anthony said, and the word seemed jolting coming from him.

"You talked to her?" He thought of seeing her in the car outside Victoria station.

"Vadim gave me her address. A flat near Goldhawk Road. I stopped by to check on her. She's a feisty girl."

"I got that impression, too." The kettle began to growl at him.

Father Anthony sighed. "I did all I could to talk her into giving it up. I said I would help her. I said there were plenty of organizations that would get her away. I said she deserved a better life. I asked her to think of her future – her soul. She wasn't interested."

Father Gilbert's mind went to all of the opportunities she had to escape – yet she hadn't. "Why won't she leave it?"

"She said she likes her job. It's something she's good at. It makes her a lot of money. The only thing she doesn't like is people telling her what to do."

"That's strange, considering what she does."

"I said so, too. She said she meant the bosses. The pimps. She said she's a 'self-manager' now."

"I wonder how long that'll last." He checked the bowl for sugar.

"In London? Not long."

"It's sad," Father Gilbert said, stopping to think about the victims, and the many victims who didn't realize they were victims.

"People make their choices." Father Anthony asked, "What can we do?"

The kettle clicked; the low growl of the boiling water subsided. "We stand by to help them pick up the pieces when it all goes wrong."

* * *

Father Gilbert received an invitation for dinner with Jack Doyle the following week. Mr Moustache delivered the message personally to the church. Mrs Mayhew didn't know what to make of him or it.

"Jack Doyle wants to meet with you?" she asked, concerned.

"Don't worry. We've become fast friends," he said.

They met at 7:00 on a Thursday at the Jade House Chinese restaurant in Stonebridge. Sitting at the far end of the high street, "The Jade", as Doyle called it, offered the best Chinese in the area. Doyle had insisted on Chinese food. Father Gilbert assumed it was his idea of a joke.

"You did pretty well for yourself," Doyle said in the middle of his course of chow mein. He used chopsticks with impressive dexterity.

"Did I?" Father Gilbert used a fork and toyed with a plate of chicken fried rice. It was incredibly tasty, but he was too uneasy to enjoy it.

"The way everything played out in Englesea, I'd say 'score one for Father Gilbert'. You put a dent in things there for some of us."

"I'm sure you'll find a way to cope," Father Gilbert said.

"I'm a survivor," he replied through a mouth full of noodles. "It was a learning experience."

"Do you still have those? I thought you had everything figured out."

"I still make mistakes."

"Like what?"

"Trusting Mamasan, for one. I took action based on what she told me, and it was wrong."

"And Nathan Rank?"

"An honest case of mistaken identity. One the police made, too." He smiled. He shrugged. "Oh well. There are always innocent casualties. Part of the price of doing business."

"But he didn't know he was paying it."

Doyle shrugged. "Then there were all the things Mamasan *didn't* tell me. And now I have to deal with both the Sensei and Lorna Henry's people. They're not happy. It's going to cost me."

"Not what it cost Rank, I'm sure."

"You really have to let that go," Doyle said.

Father Gilbert made a show of getting some chicken fried rice onto his fork.

"I have an idea," Doyle said, wiping the napkin across his mouth. "I could make a peace offering. That would settle everything."

"What kind of peace offering?"

"The sister. May. If I gave her up, the Sensei would be grateful."

Father Gilbert couldn't look him in the eye. He hoped it was a bad joke.

"There's also that girl you think you've hidden away. Jasmine – is that her name? I could offer her."

"As jokes go, I wouldn't call that a funny one."

"It's not a joke," Doyle said. "The Chinese love family vendettas where a brother in one family is killed because a sister in another family was murdered. It's like an Oriental opera, all that bloodshed. Handing over the granddaughter of the woman who bungled her job so badly *and* the daughter of the woman who grassed on them, *plus* the sister who's grassing on us all now? That would be a triple win."

Father Gilbert put his fork and knife down. He was tired of listening to Doyle, of being near him.

"It's business, you know. Nothing personal," Doyle said and drained the small cup of Chinese tea.

"Talking about an eight-year-old girl like that is *entirely* personal," Father Gilbert said.

"And you'll do what about it, exactly?" he asked, amused.

Father Gilbert levelled his gaze at Doyle. Mr Moustache, who stood near the door, watched him. "I won't have to do anything. Men like you are usually devoured by other men like you."

Doyle laughed. "Maybe in your world. It won't happen in mine."

Father Gilbert pushed away from the table. "Thanks for a lovely evening, Mr Doyle. The yacht – and now this – our times together keep getting better and better."

Doyle gave a subtle wave with his hand. Mr Moustache came up behind Doyle and pulled his chair out. The two men stood up.

"I like you more than I thought I would," Doyle said. "Priests are usually... I don't know. Sycophantic. Weedy."

They reached the front door and Doyle waved to the manager. Father Gilbert noted the look of relief on the man's face as Doyle exited the small restaurant.

The sun was lost somewhere behind the rooftops, giving the buildings, the cars, even the street and nearby roundabout a vibrancy of colour that Father Gilbert relished. He would walk home to enjoy it longer, and to get rid of the sour feelings Doyle gave him.

Doyle produced a toothpick from somewhere and jabbed at his teeth. "You want a ride somewhere?"

"No thanks. I'll walk."

He nodded. "See you around, Father."

"Goodbye, Mr Doyle." Father Gilbert didn't move from where he stood. He watched him walk away. Father Gilbert cupped his hand next to his mouth and shouted, "Give some thought to repenting. God's world is so much bigger than yours. And you'll have a better future in it."

Doyle turned and lifted his hand with a double-digit expression. "God's gonna cut *you* down," he called back over his shoulder. He laughed as he walked on. Mr Moustache kept a few paces ahead of his boss.

They'd parked the car further down in an isolated spot along the kerb, presumably to keep anyone from sandwiching it in. Mr Moustache opened the door for Doyle, who slid into the back. He closed it, then scurried around to the driver's door. As he opened that, Father Gilbert gave a little wave.

To Father Gilbert's surprise, Mr Moustache waved back. Then he climbed inside.

Out of the corner of his eye, Father Gilbert saw a figure move beneath the awning of a closed shop across the road. He barely noticed it as he turned and walked in the opposite direction from Doyle's car. He began to think about how to keep Jasmine and May safe from someone like Doyle. He'd call Brother Gregory and Rebecca Hathaway to tell them about Doyle's threat.

Behind him, Mr Moustache turned the ignition and the motor roared with power.

Something about the figure under the awning registered in Father Gilbert's conscious. He turned back around. The Shadow Man stood in the shade of the awning. He wasn't facing Father Gilbert. He was looking in Doyle's direction.

The car exploded in a giant fireball, blowing Father Gilbert off his feet and to the pavement. The glass windows of the shops shattered in all directions. Even with the high-pitched ringing in his ears, he could hear car and shop alarms going off. A woman was screaming; a baby cried. The smell of tar filled the air.

Dazed, Father Gilbert slowly got to his feet. Something sharp stabbed at the side of his neck. He reached up and pulled out a small piece of glass. What was left of Doyle's car was in flames, black smoke billowing into the pale blue sky. He ran towards the screams.

Organizations Created To
Stop Human Trafficking

This is a small sampling. Please inquire into the organizations in your area for help and information.

Agape International Missions (agapewebsite.org)

COATNET (caritas.org)

Faith Alliance Against Slavery and Trafficking (faastinternational.org)

Hope for Justice (hopeforjustice.org)

International Justice Mission (ijm.org)

National Human Trafficking Resource Center (US; traffickingresourcecenter.org)

Oasis (oasisuk.org)

Polaris Project (polarisproject.org)

Slavery No More (slaverynomore.org)

Stop The Traffik (stopthetraffik.org)

UK Human Trafficking Center (nationalcrimeagency.gov.uk)

Death in the Shadows is the second book in the

FATHER GILBERT MYSTERY
series

Don't miss the first in the series…

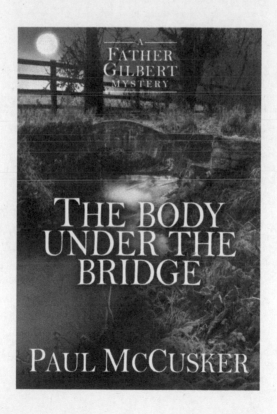

THE BODY
UNDER THE
BRIDGE

CHAPTER 1

The feeling had come upon Father Louis Gilbert suddenly. Cold slimy fingers caressed the back of his neck. His eyes burned and a taste like old nicotine filled his mouth and the back of his throat. An acrid smell of ammonia assailed his nostrils.

He sat perfectly still at his desk. The pen in his hand held steady two inches above the notepaper. He waited for the feeling to pass. It didn't. He carefully lowered the pen and took off his round, gold-rimmed reading glasses. His eyes turned to the closed door.

Something had changed just outside of his office. Mrs Mayhew, the secretary for St Mark's since time began, had stopped typing on her computer keyboard. Her chair scraped across the hardwood floor as she pushed back from her desk. In his mind's eye, Father Gilbert saw her stand up, responding to the rapidly approaching footsteps.

He braced himself. The feeling meant his adversary was nearby – one he'd known as a Scotland Yard detective. It had often sneered at him from the shadows and taunted him out of the corner of his eye. It was Death.

Father Gilbert rose to greet it.

Mr Urquhart, the church sexton, burst in. His face was red, his bald head dripping with sweat. "Father," he spoke in a deep Scottish accent. "Come quickly. There's a man on the tower. He says he's going to jump."

* * *

"Please phone the police, Mrs Mayhew," Father Gilbert said as he rushed past her desk.

"Of course, Father."

Father Gilbert hurried after Mr Urquhart down the hall leading to the nave of St Mark's. "How did he get up to the tower?" The door was usually locked.

"I was cleaning the vestibule," Mr Urquhart called over his shoulder. His voice came in gasps. "I had moved some hymnals into the closet just inside the staircase. He must have slipped in when my back was turned."

Reaching the nave, the two men broke into a run – a straight race between the neat rows of polished pews. They reached the vestibule where the door to the church tower stood open.

"I saw him just as he rounded the first turn in the stairs," Mr Urquhart said. "I chased him up to the belfry. He told me to stay away or he'd jump."

At the bottom stair, Father Gilbert paused, remembering what a long climb it would be. "Please wait here for the police."

"Yes, Father."

A large man, barrel-chested and broad-shouldered, Father Gilbert reached out and grabbed at the railing – a rope, actually, that had been threaded through strategically placed eyelets. He propelled himself upwards.

The stairs circled up and up, winding like a coiled spring inside a square box. He couldn't remember the measurements – how many stairs, how tall the Normanesque tower was. What he *did* remember was that he hadn't been to the gym in weeks.

He could feel the sweat on his scalp under his thick and dishevelled hair. Damp formed at the back of his grey clerical shirt. His stiff white dog collar was cutting into his throat.

Reaching the door to the belfry, he hesitated. The air was thick and musty, relieved only by a ribbon of fresh air coming from the open hatch above. The formidable iron bell hung still and alone, the ropes dangling down all the way to the bottom of the tower. He followed the planking along the wall to the opposite side where an iron ladder stretched up. Grabbing the ladder, he climbed upwards towards the square patch of blue sky above. The ladder shivered under his weight.

He reached the top rung and grabbed the two handles that allowed him to heave his body onto the sun-baked tar. The cool breeze of a beautiful late spring day chilled the hot moisture on his face. Fumbling to his feet, he squinted against the bright sun.

The church tower was square and framed on all four sides by waist-high parapets. Directly opposite from the hatch, a man stood with his back to the priest. Shaggy sun-bleached hair felt onto broad shoulders, the top of a Y-shaped torso – a lean and muscular body shown off by a tight T-shirt. The man wore faded denims, the back pockets torn. His well-worn boots were splattered with mud, cement, and plaster. Presumably he was a builder.

The man reached over and placed a hand on one of the parapets. He seemed to be admiring the view of the town of Stonebridge below.

Father Gilbert took a step forward. His shoe scuffed the gravel. The man spun around to face him.

Father Gilbert held up his hands in a gesture of submission. "This is my church. I'm Father Gilbert."

The man's face was prematurely aged from too much time in the sun. There were deep lines on his forehead and around his eyes, blond stubble on his cheeks and chin. He might have been in his thirties but looked older. Rivulets of tears had smeared the dust on the man's cheeks. Father Gilbert saw something dark in his eyes, a terrible despair. This man would not come quietly down the stairs.

Somewhere behind the normal sounds of Stonebridge's traffic, a police siren wailed.

The man's eyes darted in the direction of the sound. He looked at the priest in accusation.

"It's standard procedure when a man threatens to jump from my tower." Father Gilbert attempted a casual step forward.

The man took a step back, pressing himself against the parapet. With a grace that matched his body, he pulled himself upwards onto one of the embrasures.

"Don't!" Father Gilbert said sharply. He raised his hand, as if he could pull the man back with sheer force of will.

"There's nothing you can do," the man said.

"Then you have nothing to lose by telling me who you are and why you're up here."

The man shook his head.

"Don't I have a right to know why you want to throw yourself off of my tower?" Father Gilbert kept his hand outstretched.

The sirens were below them now. Father Gilbert wished the police had shown better sense. Then came the slamming car doors and urgent shouts. The man glanced over the side. Wiping the back of his hand across his eyes, he let out a small whimper.

"What's your name?" Father Gilbert asked. "I've told you mine. It's common courtesy to give me yours." And it was police procedure to establish a rapport as soon as possible. Something as simple as an exchange of names sometimes brought a would-be suicide back to humanity.

"It's all in my wallet. The police will find it when they collect my body." His voice was a painful rasp.

"Then tell me why you're here."

With a sudden sob, the man lowered his head. "I don't have a choice."

"Of course you do."

He shook his head. "It's the only way to stop them."

"Them?"

"Before they make me do things." His tears fell freely. "It's not fair." He faltered, his words lost in his sobs. He muttered to himself. Father Gilbert couldn't make out what he was saying.

"Look at me," Father Gilbert said. "Keep your eyes on mine. Whatever you're thinking and feeling right now will pass. But, go over that wall and your situation will become permanent."

The man tilted his head as if listening to something. Then he said, "It shouldn't have been found."

"What?"

He reached into his pocket and pulled out a gold chain. He held it up. A large medallion, the size of a drinks coaster, dangled in the light.

"What is it?" Father Gilbert wanted to get the man's focus on something other than dying.

"A curse."

"What does that mean?" Father Gilbert moved a step closer.

"Are you a holy man? Maybe if I leave it with you…"

Voices and footfalls echoed up from the hatch to the belfry.

The man's eyes darted towards the sound. "Before this is over, there are a few people who'll wish they did what I'm doing now."

"Whatever the trouble is—" Father Gilbert began to say.

The man cut him off. "Staying alive is too painful." He spoke with a voice choked by a deep anguish.

"Tell me what you mean," Father Gilbert said. "We'll talk it through."

The man shook his head. His face contorted as he fought back more tears. "I don't want to be an angel."

"An angel? What kind of angel?" Father Gilbert hoped the questions might keep the man engaged.

The capped head of a police officer appeared at the hatchway.

The man looked at the medallion, still dangling from his hand. "I'll leave this with you."

Father Gilbert took another step forward. "Listen to me, you don't—"

"*Take it*," the man snapped and tossed the medallion at the priest, the disc spinning and the chain spiralling in the air.

Father Gilbert instinctively reached out to catch the medallion and knew he'd been duped. The man brought up his free arm. In his hand was a Stanley knife. The blade was out.

"Stop!" Father Gilbert shouted and threw himself at the man.

With a firm stroke, the man slashed the blade right across his throat. Blood pumped out of the gash, a warm spray in the wind that hit Father Gilbert's face.

Like a diver pushing off from the side of a boat, the man thrust himself backwards and disappeared over the edge of the tower.

Father Gilbert cried out as he rushed to the parapet.

He leaned over the edge, harbouring the unlikely hope that the man was clinging to the side of the tower. The man was not there.

Nor was he lying on the bed of flowers that bloomed directly below.

Mr Urquhart stood next to a wheelbarrow filled with pulled weeds. He looked up at the priest, shielding his eyes with a dirty hand. "Father? What are you doing up there?"

"Where did he go?" Father Gilbert shouted. His voice was a strangled croak. "Did you see him?"

The old Scot looked around, then up again. "See who?"

"The man! He was up here in the tower and..." Father Gilbert's voice trailed off. There were no police cars in the car park, nor any sirens. He glanced over at the hatch to the belfry. No one was there. Everything was perfectly normal.

He felt sick.

"I'm sorry, Father, but I don't know what you are talking about!" Mr Urquhart shouted up.

"Never mind." Father Gilbert stepped back. Leaning heavily against the stone, he gazed at the roof and replayed the scene in his mind. It was as vivid as anything he'd ever experienced.

He looked down at his shaking hands. He was clutching the gold medallion.